I0822795

The Rings of King Solomon
Book One

Written by

E.S. Bennett

First Edition   Printed in U.S.A.
Cover design by E.S. Bennett
ISBN: 979-8-218-99969-8

Library of Congress number:

2025910932

For more information, visit.

www.TheMegaverseCity.com

Table of Contents

Prologue

The Seal of Solomon, or Ring of Solomon, is a legendary signet attributed to the Israelite king Solomon, a figure whose wisdom, wealth, and influence left an indelible mark across centuries and cultures. Rooted in Jewish, Islamic, and Western mystical traditions, the seal is often depicted as a pentagram or hexagram. In Jewish lore, it was said to grant Solomon dominion over the supernatural: commanding shedim (serpent or demon spirits), binding djinn (genies), and even communicating with animals. Seen as an amulet of immense power, it became a central symbol in medieval magic, Renaissance occultism, and alchemical writings. Crafted from brass and iron, its dual nature allowed Solomon to seal commands to both good and evil spirits. In one tale either the demon **Asmodeus** or **Sakhr**, obtained possession of the seal and ruled in Solomon's place for 40 days. The demon eventually threw the seal into the ocean where it was swallowed by a fish caught by a kindhearted fisherman, who unknowingly fed it to the displaced **Solomon** therefore restoring him to power.

Chapter 1

Present day.

Three suited men from an unnamed entity shows up at the **Megaversity of Southern California**, where they find Professor **Lorrisa A. Santos**, a Latino American who teaches and studies theology. Standing approximately five feet 5 inch tall in three inch heels, with shoulder length dark brown hair, big green eyes hidden behind glasses and a svelte hour glass figure, she commands the classroom of students' attention; The young ladies for her striking fashion sense, gorgeous hair and beautiful skin, the young men are kept mesmerized by the three-inch heels which accentuates her shapely legs and her gorgeous figure. She notices the three suited men who enter her classroom and stays to the back of the room but pays them no immediate attention while the class is in session. When the university buzzer sounds, Lorrisa gathers her papers and turns toward the trio. "Gentlemen, may I help you?" she asks, calm but alert.

The first man speaks, “We were hoping you would.” The third cuts in smoothly, “We represent a party interested in information you’re well-versed in.”

Curious, Lorrisa tilts her head. “And that would be?”

“Your research on mystic Jewish lore,” the first man answers. “According to your book, you spent years studying legends spanning Jewish, Islamic, and Western mysticism.”

“Oh that”, she starts coyly, “I wrote that book when I was young and impressionable by others”. Lorrisa starts gathering papers and a thoughtful smile appeared on her face. The Second man clears his throat then speaks up, “Are you referring to your husband, **Jesus Rodriguez**?” She stops what she is doing and turns to the man to quickly correct him, “Ex-husband”. “My apologies, ma’am”, replies the Second man, “I meant no disrespect”. “None taken...so who are you?” she asks “I’m Williams. These are my colleagues, Smith and Johnson,” the first man introduces, his tone even. “We represent a party that values your work.”

“And which party is that?” Lorrisa asks.

Smith offers a tight smile. “We’re not at liberty to say. But rest assured, your time will be well compensated.”

Lorrisa sizes them up, reading posture, eyes, the subtle tension in their shoulders. “I have another class, but after that, we can talk.”

“Excellent,” Johnson says flatly. “Shall we return here or—”

“We’ll meet at EEZ Oasis, off campus,” Lorrisa interjects. “Look it up. Let’s say three hours. I’d like to freshen up.”

The men look at each other to affirm the time and place. All three force a gratuitous smile and shake her hand. The men leave and she packs up her books and notes from the class. As she exits her classroom, she bumps into one of her colleagues, **Bashir Uneve**, a professor of psychiatry and behavioral sciences. “Good day **Rissa**, how was your class today?’ “**Bass**! it was more of the same mundane routine until the end”. “Why, what was different about this time?” he asks. “Three unidentified men came in my classroom and want to meet me in a few hours to discuss things from my book on Jewish Lore”. “You mean the one about mysticism and such? You hate that thing!” he states surprisingly. “I did and still do", she starts, "It was a pet project for my insane ex-husband. I only wrote it to pacify him and at the time I needed a topic for my doctorate". "So why after all these years would someone have a sudden interest in it?" asks Bashir. She shrugs her shoulders. "Well, I'll find out when I meet them at the café later", she replies. "Do you want some company? ...They being strangers and all. One cannot take chances these days. Especially when one is petite and as attractive as yourself", Bashir notes out of concern. She flashes Bashir a girlish smile. "I should be fine on my own. Thank you though, it'll be in a public place and as such, high visibility. Plus, I carry my pocket mace if needed", she answers. "Well do be careful, I've grown accustomed to seeing you on campus", he says lovingly. He smiles gently and touches her arm softly. She smiles at him and says, "Don't worry, if **Gee** couldn't take me away, then no one can".

—

Later that day Lorrisa meets with Mr. Williams and Mr. Smith at the café. Both men are currently seated in a booth as Lorrisa walks into the establishment.

The men stand to greet her as she approaches. “Ms. Rodriguez we are glad you could make it”, starts Smith. “I’m usually good with keeping appointments and it’s Santos not Rodriguez”, she quickly points out as she takes a seat, “I used Rodriguez in the book because I was married at the time, but since the divorce I went back to Santos”. “Our apologies once again”, says Smith. She looks around the café quickly and asks, “What happened to Mr. Johnson? and just what is your interest in my book?” A waitperson comes to deliver menus and water to the table. All three individuals stay silent until the waitperson leaves the area. “Mr. Johnson could not be here as he needed to attend another matter. Our interest in your book is genuine”, Mr. Smith starts, “We wanted to get information about a specific section in your book, the chapter regarding King Solomon’s ring”. Lorrisa leans back in her seat and smiles slightly. She looks at both men surprised, “The Seal of Solomon was just a legend. I wrote about it to fill some of the pages in the book. I didn’t take the text I found on it seriously. Why would you be interested in that?” Mr. Williams side eyes Mr. Smith and says, “Let’s just say that we have reason to believe that the legend has a basis in fact. That the actual ring did exist”. “Really”, she says sarcastically, “and what brought on that conclusion? A conversation with my ex-husband?" Almost dismissive Lorrisa raises her eyebrows and tells them, " You may have heard he's the one you should really be talking to about this". "Well, we are here with you now. Please tell us what you know about it", asks Williams. She looks at both men. Their faces are stern but not threatening. She signals to the café waiter as she begins," The earliest reference to Solomon's seal comes from Jewish traditions. It was first mentioned by Josephus, the first century historian". The waiter comes and takes her order of a latte, and she continues, "A first century Greek manual of Judeo-Christian magic known as the Testament of Solomon also makes reference to the Seal. Later on The Seal made its' way into Islamic Arab sources. But that is all based on conjecture". Williams looks at Smith briefly before speaking, "Our researchers have proof that the Ring did exist". Lorrisa giggles slightly and says, "Gentlemen you understand that the 'Ring' wasn't an actual ring, The Seal was circular and on a tablet. The legend of the of the Seal of Solomon was developed primarily by medieval Middle Eastern writers, who related that the Seal was engraved by God and was given to the king directly from heaven. When the stories started is hard to date back to. If such a tablet existed, there would be numerous depictions of it in scrolls and in writings. If the legends were true, then whoever had such a tablet would be the possessor of great powers”. The men nervously chuckle. Lorrisa’s eyes float from one man to the other. The waiter brings her drink, and she takes a sip slowly while still eyeing the men. She sets her drink on the table and asks, “What do YOU know about the tablet of Solomon?” Williams clears his throat and speaks like a person who knows the topic intimately, “During the last days of **WWI**, fearing the act of desperate men, the original tablet, with the crest, was cut into many pieces and made into actual rings”. Williams pauses a moment then continues, “Each ring was given to a trusted protector. Each protector of the ring was not told who held the other pieces, nor did any one person know how many rings there were to make up the entire ancient tablet. It is believed that when all of the original rings were pieced together, the tablet seal will enable the supernatural properties to be restored”. As Williams concludes, Smith takes out a check book, “Ms. Santos, we are prepared to write you a check, right now, if you agree to supply all of your notes regarding the seal and be on a team that is in search of these rings”. Lorrisa with a surprised look on her face, “You must be kidding. Is this an episode of **Impractical Jokers**? Am I on tape?" Her head looks around feigning surprise, "Where's the camera?" "Smith reaches out aggressively and grabs Lorrisa's wrist firmly while looking her straight in the eyes. Her fingers tingled from the strength of his grip, his passive demeanor became very aggressive and threatening. He tells her in an unknown accent, "This is no joke, and you are not on television", he scowls, "and we are very serious". Lorrisa snatches her hand away quickly and leans back in her chair. She rubs her wrist that was clenched by Smith. Her face hardens as she gathers her possessions, "Gentlemen, I must say that this has been an amusing time for me, but I respectfully decline your offer to chase ghosts and myths and as far as my notes on the topic, I believe I threw those out years ago with the husband". As she stands to leave, Williams throws Smith a cross look before he turns to Lorrisa, "Please forgive my associate Ms. Santos, As you can see, he is very passionate about this project. Please do not let my associate's action deter you from assisting us. We hope you will take some time and reconsider our offer further". Smith sheepishly looks downward to avoid any eye contact with Lorrisa. Before she steps away from the men she says, "I met you because I was curious about why you and your unnamed benefactor would have any interest in a book,

I wrote 15 years ago. Now that I heard the story, I have no desire to associate with you and the ridiculous fairy tale you just spun".   As she proceeds to the café exist, she stops by the cashier and pays for the latte she ordered. The cashier rings her up and asks, "How was everything?" As she hands the money to the cashier she replies, "The latte was fine, the company was creepy". Then she exits the café.

Then she exits the café. Outside the café, Lorrisa walks about a block before hailing a taxi. "William, Smith, Johnson, how inconspicuous can you get?" she says sarcastically mumbling to herself.

The taxi ride to Lorrisa's apartment was short and quiet. As the cab pulled up to the curb, she gathered her briefcase and papers, handing the driver a few bills. "Keep the change," she quipped with a wry smile, "I've already got a purse full of coins." The driver gave a silent nod, his eyes leering a moment too long in the rearview mirror before she stepped out.

Outside, the cool evening air brushed against her skin. Lorrisa fumbles through her purse searching for her keys while juggling her briefcase and classroom papers she needs to grade. Finally finding her keys she enters her apartment to find it in disarray. Her clothes are thrown about, books from her shelves are knocked down and random pages are found torn. She speaks out loudly, “Oh no, not my plants too!” She eyes the apartment looking for additional damage. Setting her belongings on a nearby table, she removes her shoes and silently stalks the apartment for the responsible party. She opens each room door slowly, taking deliberate small steps. Her eyes squint carefully looking at each detail in each room until she hears something coming from the kitchen. She walks into the kitchen and exclaims, “You! There you are you little gremlin”. She walks over and picks up her pet Capuchin-monkey, *Kong*. “You have been a mischievous little thing today “, she says lovingly, “haven’t you? Look at this mess you made”. The monkey puts its’ hands over its’ face as if to show embarrassment. She picks up the simian and cuddles it a bit then opens the refrigerator to grab a piece of fruit. Not waiting for it to be offered, the monkey grabs the fruit from her and jumps to the nearby counter to begin eating. She looks at the monkey adoringly and says, “You know you’re going to help me clean all this mess up. There was no reason to be upset because I was a little late to get home to feed you”. She looks around the apartment to survey the cleaning task set before her and sighs.

Lorrisa enters one of two bedrooms in the apartment and begins to change clothes. Kong walks in behind her looking for either attention or food. Lorrisa slides off her dress slowly as her mind drifts to the events earlier in the day. She puts on a pair of jeans and a sweatshirt. Slipping her feet into flip-flops she tells Kong, “Before you get anything else from me, you had better make sure your room is clean”. The monkey pauses a moment as if to let that statement sink in, then it runs off to the other bedroom. She smiles as she follows Kong into his room. It’s the smaller bedroom of the two and it is equipped with everything Lorrisa needs to take care of her pet and everything Kong wants to enjoy. She looks around the room as if she is inspecting it. Kong was anxiously at the doorway for her to make her way back to the kitchen. His little body sways back and forth in anticipation. Lorrisa slyly eyes the monkey and lets out a slight giggle, “Okay, it looks good to me. Let’s get you some food”. With that, the monkey scampers off to the

kitchen. As Lorrisa hands Kong another piece of fruit, the doorbell rings. She walks over to the intercom-camera and sees that it's her best friend, *Xenia Silva Ayala*. She presses the speaker button and tells her," Come on in Xenia". Xenia walks in and looks at the surrounding chaos in the apartment, "Dios Mio! Kong was at it again, wasn't he". Lorrisa was a bit exhausted after still picking up nods the affirmative. Xenia continues, "I have four kids and one slob of a husband and yet your place always looks like a tornado hit it". Xenia bends down and starts helping Lorrisa clean up as Lorrisa reminds her, "You know how temperamental Kong can get". Just as the monkey enters the room with the two women, Xenia looks at him and answers, "No, I just know how mental he can get". The two women laugh briefly then Lorrisa says, "You know I had a pretty strange day today". "Oh yea, what happened?" "These three men came to my job and wanted to talk about my book". "You mean the one with all that creepy stuff", Xenia asks while performing a holy cross gesture over her body. "Yea", answers Lorrisa, "there was something weird about them. Their demeanor was too aggressive for something that was seemingly fictional. It almost made me think that what they were talking about or looking for existed". "The world is full of nuts, mi pequenita". "Maybe so, but these guys were willing to pay me whatever I wanted to help them". "Nah uh, that sounds like they were only after one thing alright, but it wasn't in no book. Nina, you better be lucky they didn't take you over to one of them countries where they trade women like horses, 'cause you'd get a good price the way you look and I would probably too, but I ain't into that kind of kink and..." "Hold on Xenia", chuckles Lorrisa, "I'm fine. I'm here with you and Kong. They didn't seem like those type of men". "Mmm-hm, every man is one of those type of men", responds Xenia. They laugh. At that time the monkey walks up to Xenia and holds her arm. She looks down at Kong and says playfully, "Yea, we be talking about you too". Lorrisa seems to drift off, gazing toward the window until she feels a hand touch her shoulder. Xenia asks, "Hey, are you okay? You seem distracted?" "Yea, I'm fine. I was just wondering what if the Ring of Solomon is true?" "What ring, I don't know what you mean?" "Hold on Xenia, let me see if I have a copy of my book around here". Lorrisa looks around the apartment quickly. She drops to her knees and shuffles among the fallen books on the floor. Xenia looks on patiently. Kong begins to imitate Lorrisa's actions and begins to move the books about. Lorrisa sees something out of the corner of her

eye, “Aha, this is it!” Xenia walks over to her and peers over her shoulder, “So what is this ring, do you have a picture?’ “No, not a picture, but an artist rendition based on centuries of descriptions”, replies Lorrisa as she flips through the pages, “Here, here it is”. “Looks like a flat rock to me”, Xenia says almost bored. Lorrisa studies the tablet picture then starts to speak, “See, the actual tablet was supposed to be made of brass and iron. That would be difficult to break. However, if it did exist and it was as powerful as told, then I can see where it may have been cut up into many pieces to create rings”. Lorrisa grabs her glasses and a large book that was still on the shelf. She flips through the pages searching paragraphs for some unseen information. Xenia grabs hold of Kong, and she begins to play with him. Kong performs small tricks for Xenia’s amusement until Lorrisa exclaims. “Here it is!” Xenia stops what she is doing with Kong, and responds, “Here is what?’ Lorrisa answers, “A picture of a variant form of the Seal”. “Oh pequenita, are you still on that subject?’ Lorrisa looks up from the book and pauses a bit before answering.

"Well, yes. I guess so. I mean it woke up something in me and now I can't get it out of my head". "Santo Cielo!" bemoans Xenia, throwing her hands up in the air, "What will it take for you to forget about this fantasy with rings?" Lorrisa sits back and shrugs her shoulders, "I don't know. Up until a few hours ago I really didn't think of it or cared…but now I feel so compelled to find out what's going on with this tablet, those men and why it has become a subject of interest at this time". Xenia rolls her eyes and sighs heavily, "I'm worried that you may get into something over your head and then become too difficult for you to get out of". Lorrisa pauses to think for a moment then talks softly, as if unsure of her words, "I'll just make a few calls and inquiries. I mean what's the worse that can happen?" Xenia presses the palm of her hand against Lorrisa's forehead and states, "Ultimas palabras famosas".

The following morning Lorrisa had just finished caring for Kong when her cell-phone rings. She looks at the number being displayed. Not familiar with either the area code or the number, she allows the call to go to voice mail. She waits several minutes before calling her voice service to retrieve any message left by the caller. She anxiously dials. She hears the computerized voice, "You have one phone message from phone number two zero two three two four three zero zero zero. 'Good morning, this is Special Agent *Carlos Conchata* of the F.B.I. and I am hoping to speak to you sometime soon regarding an important matter. Please call the main number of the Bureau and they will connect you to me'. Lorrisa saves the message and ends the call. She immediately goes into a deep thought of what is transpiring before her. What was going on really? Up until yesterday she was not the attention of anyone, save her ex-husband and a few friends. Now less than twenty-four hours she has strange men asking questions and now F.B.I. agents calling. Surely the F.B.I. has better things to do than to investigate religious myths and legends. Giving herself a moment to get her thoughts together, Lorrisa prepares to go to the gym before proceeding to work. She showers and dries herself off. She puts on form fitting exercise pants which displays her curves nicely. Her sports top matches the pants, and she slips her feet into cross training shoes to complete the outfit. Her thoughts replay the meeting with the three men and then the two.

The image of Smith's face is burned into her thoughts, and she gets a bit angry that she let him get away with that action. She'll have a lot of pent-up aggression to let loose on the heavy bag today. She calls for a ride-share to the gym. The ride was slow and quiet, allowing her to think things out further. She decided she would call the F.B.I. after leaving the gym. Upon arriving, she is met just outside the building by Mr. Williams and Johnson. The men approach her causally and cautiously, "Good morning, Ms. Santos. May we have a word with you?" Her eyes roll and then scans the area for any hint of Smith being in the vicinity. The two men await a response from her. "The interested party that you supposed to represent...are you from the F.B.I.?" she asks. The two men look quickly at each other, then Williams speaks up, "Yes, yes we are". "So how did you know that I would be here at this time. Am I being monitored or watch for something?" she asks them. The men hesitate to answer immediately when a light blue cargo van screeches around the corner attracting attention to itself and pulls up in front of the three people. The side van doors slide open quickly. Williams quickly pulls out his side arm and seemingly aims at the van. With that, Johnson grabs Lorrisa around the waist tightly and jumps into the van with Lorrisa followed by Williams, who is covering their escape. In an instant, the van doors slammed shut, the engine roared, and the vehicle peeled away from the curb, leaving a trail of shocked pedestrians and an empty stretch of pavement where Lorrisa had stood just moments before.

Taghazout, Morocco.

Jesus Christopher 'Gee' Rodriguez is strolling through the crowded marketplace carefully eyeing ever little

piece of jewelry shown to him by the local vendors. The overhang of the tents and shops offers little relief from the heat of the day. Some of the pieces he looks at are polished well and shine nicely in the overhead midday sun, other pieces are adorned with hand etched carvings of symbols and characters. He inspects them all carefully. His baggy clothes, overgrown beard and dirty fedora make it seem as if he cannot afford anything in this market, however the wedding ring he still wears on his finger tells his true worth and value. He continues to look until he is approached by a thin man with a worn face. His clothing is a bit dirty, but he tries to wear it with dignity. The man is a local inhabitant and knows many of the people in the village. He walks up to Rodriguez, "Mr. Gee, Mr. Gee. I have news that you may find important". Rodriguez stops what he is doing and responds, "What is it, *Samir*?" Samir's head waves around a bit, his body language stiffens up a little and his skinny arms slithers out like a desert snake when he says, "Such information must be of worth to you. I would hate to insult your integrity by offering it for anything less than twenty dirhams". Rodriguez's eyes roll first then he digs into his pockets to pull out 20 dirhams. He hands it to Samir who quickly hides it among his tattered clothing. Rodriguez looks at Samir patiently waiting for the information just paid for. Samir looks around the marketplace as if someone would be listening in on their conversation. Then he starts to speak softly, "There are more outsiders in Taghazout, that are looking for the same things you seek. Then there are the ones who seek you as well". Rodriguez eyes the area and asks, "How many?" Samir scratches his head, feigning memory loss. Rodriguez digs back into his pocket once more and pulls out another 20 dirham and hands it to Samir. Samir quickly speaks up, "From what I was told, there are twenty men. Eight seeks the same ring chip you are after, and the rest are looking for you". Rodriguez looks at Samir with suspicious eye and asks, "You didn't happen to let them know where to find me?" "Oh no!" reassured Samir, "I told them nothing". Rodriguez relaxes a little and says, "Good". "However," Samir starts with a matter of fact tone, "My brother, *Akbar*, may have been trying to buy food for his children". "Oh great", snarls Rodriguez. His eyes widen and he looks around frantically. Samir taps him on the shoulder and asks, "Why do these men seek you out?" Rodriguez, while still looking around responds, "They believe I have taken something from them". "Such as?" Rodriguez looks at Samir and flashes him a quick smile, "Is this how you obtain your market ware?" Samir shrugs his shoulders and smiles a crooked smile. His teeth, decaying and brown, are shown when he says, "I find knowledge in this part of the world is more valuable than water". With that said, Samir turns and leaves. Within moments he had disappeared into the marketplace crowd. Rodriguez tilts his hat downward to cover much of his bearded face as he continues through the crowd. Now that he has been given a warning of caution from Samir, every face is suspect and every tourist a potential problem. He touches the wedding ring on his finger and looks at it lovingly, then his hands slide into his pocket and touches another ring. Its' texture is rough metal. Its' edges are uneven and a bit jagged. He reassures himself of this ring's importance by clenching it tightly before releasing it back to the bottom of his pocket. He makes his way through the streets, one by one, still searching, but now highly cautious and aware of his surroundings. Upon passing one of the any shops on the street, an old woman, who is sitting in the doorway, calls out to him, "Hey (mister)!" The vernacular is uncommon in this part of the world, so it grabs Rodriguez's attention. Rodriguez carefully approaches the woman, "Yes, may I help you?" he asks cautiously. "No", starts the old woman in a raspy voice, "It is I who will help you". She motions for him to enter the small shop. They slowly step inside, and she closes the door behind them. The heat inside is more unbearable than the heat outside. The shop is filled with pottery and clothes. There is an attached room that enlarges the size of the shop than what is seen from the outside. The lighting is dim so that it doesn't increase the temperature inside. The rotting wood floor buckles, creeks and gives a little under Rodriguez 170 lb. weight. Rodriguez removes his hat and wipes the sweat from his forehead with his forearm. He sets his hat on the counter that separates the woman and him. The woman passes him a small towel that was cooled by some ice. He nods to her gratefully then says, “You said that you can help me, how? What do you know about me?” The old woman pulls up a chair and sits. Her eyes seem to go into a trance-like state when she responds to him, “You are looking for a piece of the tablet of Solomon are you not?” Suspiciously Rodriguez respond to her, “What tablet and who says I’m looking for it?” “The desert has eyes and ears. A secret as holy as the one you seek begets many guardians”. Rodriguez quickly leans towards the woman and asks, “What do you know of the tablet?” The woman looks at him intently. Scouring his face and features, “I can see the good in you. Your heart is troubled but pure. You can be trusted”. Rodriguez smiles slightly and nods to acknowledge the woman’s assessment of him. She continues, “The tablet has been divided into many pieces for protection. These pieces have been fashioned into rings”. Rodriguez nods in affirmation but anxiously says, “Of that much I know, but how many rings are there?” The woman leans back in her chair and answers," No one is certain as to how many rings exist. However, I will provide you with this one". The woman rises from her seat and walks a few feet behind the counter, She kneels down and reaches for a floorboard and lifts it up revealing an ordinary looking box. Within the box is a cloth wrapped around what appears to be an old ring. Very similar to the one Rodriguez has in his pocket. Excitedly Rodriguez takes out his glasses and looks through the lens to examine the ring produced by the old woman. He mumbles out loud, "The metal is similar, the marking is of the same tool", He reaches into his pocket for the ring in his possession and sets both rings side by side. The woman's eyes widened, surprised at the appearance of the second ring. Rodriguez continues his analysis of both pieces and concludes, "They are from the same source". "Praise be to Allah", the woman silently whispers. The woman stands and grabs Rodriguez's hands and tells him, "Take the ring and protect it. It has been in my family for generation after generation. Be safe as you continue your search". Rodriguez asks solemnly, "Why would you just hand it over to me, a person you do not know?" The woman smiles back at him and says, "I DO KNOW YOU". Puzzled, Rodriguez envelopes both rings together in one cloth. He places the rings in his pocket and carries the box. “Go now”, the old woman starts, “There are those who will kill you for what you possess…as they have my own son”. Rodriguez nods to her and places his hat back on his head. He opens the door to the shop, pauses a moment but does not look back, then leaves. The old woman watches as he too disappears into the crowd. Silently she offers a prayer and a tear. Rodriguez makes his way through the crowded area unsure of what just happened with the old woman and who could be following him. His mind races with thoughts as he turns abruptly and walks back to the shop of the old woman. There were many questions he should have asked her; however, he was so enamored by the second ring he lost his train of thought. He reaches the old woman’s shop and proceeds to enter. This time the small shop is in disarray. Rodriguez looks for the woman, not knowing who to call out for or if he should call out at all. He slowly makes his way behind the counter to where the woman pulled up the floorboard and to his dismay, there she lay. Dead from an apparent gun shot wound to the head. He bends down to look closer at the body when he hears a sharp click. His reflexes carry his body forward as his ears detect the whistling of a bullet where he was. Several more gunshots shatter items

surrounding Rodriguez, but no loud noise is heard. A silencer is being used he concludes to himself, so no one outside will hear the commotion or investigate. Frantically Rodriguez looks around for something he can use as a weapon or defense. He can't see his attacker, but he can feel their steps they take on the raggedy floor. For a moment there is silence within the shop. Rodriguez can only hear the bustling of the outside marketplace. His attacker then breaks the silence with an English accent, "Mr. Rodriguez, I believe you have something that belongs to a client of ours. Our employer would like his item returned to him". Rodriguez does not respond. His eyes continue to search for something when he feels the vibration of the floor again. His attacker is moving. The man speaks again, "Had you not have us chase you all over this horrendous country I may have let you simply return the item and live. But now that all this time, money and resources were utilized to find you...well, you understand. We must keep a neat and proper balance sheet". The floor begins to buckle more and more as the gun man gets closer to Rodriguez's position. Not able to find anything in which to distract the gun man, Rodriguez calls out, "Okay, I'll give you the item". He put his hands up and slowly rises to his feet in front of the gun man. Rodriguez speaks to the gun man softly, "Are you going to kill me here *Sebastian*?" "That depends Rodriguez", Sebastian starts, "Where is the item?" "Well as you may have guessed, I don't have it here, but I can take you to it", Rodriguez answers. "Oh well", Sebastain sighs, "I guess I'll just have to shoot you here and hope we can find it on our own. Goodbye Rodriguez". Sebastian squeezes the trigger of the gun just as the shop door begins to open startling him, causing his aim to be off enough for the bullet to miss Rodriguez's head. The person entering the shop is surprised by what they had walked in on and pays a definitive price for his interference as Sebastian turns and shoots him out of frustration. The innocent bystander staggers back with his wound. These precious seconds is time enough for Rodriguez to lunge at Sebastian and grapple with him over the gun. Both men struggle to control the firearm in play. Sebastian is a tall man measuring six feet and three inch. His build is average. His clothes give away the story pf his lavish lifestyle and his personal grooming displays his unspoken entitlement. Rodriguez, who stands at five feet ten inches tall, has spent his professional years digging in the earth for fossils and climbing rocks. His clothes demonstrate a man who does not fear getting rough and tumble for his work. The men's struggle continues until Rodriguez knees Sebastain in the lower ribs, buckling him for a moment, but long enough for Rodriguez to wrestle the gun from his hand. Rodriguez steps back with the gun and points it at a surprised, but arrogant Sebastian. "Why did you kill the old woman?" Rodriguez demands. Sebastian grins an evil grin and merely states. "She was of no use to me". Shocked at the answer Rodriguez motions for Sebastian to step clear of the doorway to the outside. Sebastian composes himself and neatens his appearance while slowly stepping clear of the exit. Rodriguez slowly picks up his hat and walks to the door keeping the gun aimed at Sebastian who stands with calm demeanor looking at Rodriguez. Sebastian carefully reaches into his top shirt pocket causing Rodriguez to motion the gun more aggressively, when Sebastain produces a pack of cigarettes. Rodriguez is only slightly surprised at Sebastians demeanor says, "You were always a pompous asshole". Sebastian smiles slightly and says, "I must keep up appearances you understand". He lights his cigarette with a match to which he throws the lit match on the dead woman's body. Suddenly flames take hold of the body and begin to consume the shop as well. Rodriguez grabs for the doorknob while still keeping his eyes and the gun trained on Sebastian. Before Rodriguez leaves Sebastian tells him, "We will find you again Rodriguez, and you will return our item to us, or you will never see your wife again". Rodriguez pauses a moment, his eyes squinting as he looks angrily at Sebastian. His finger sliding along the trigger slowly. Rodriguez then stuffs the gun in his pocket before leaving the shop, which has started to fill up with smoke. He turns to tell Sebastian, "You think my wife is helpless, I feel sorry for your men who have her". With that said Rodriguez leaves the shop just in time as the police and fire department arrives.

Southern California

At a warehouse near Carlsbad, California, Lorrisa sat upright in a battered metal chair, her hands resting calmly on her lap despite the tension crackling in the air. Across from her, Smith paced like a caged animal, the gun in his hand a dark extension of his mood. The cavernous space echoed each footstep, the faint hum of distant traffic filtering in through cracked windows high on the walls.

Neither of them spoke.

Their eyes were locked, a silent battle playing out between predator and prey—though it was still unclear which was which. Lorrisa's soft green eyes tracked his every movement, calculating, calm on the surface but burning with the fire of survival underneath. Smith, by contrast, was restless, his sharp features tight with impatience, his polished shoes clicking sharply against the concrete.

The room smelled of old oil and dust, the overhead bulb casting a pale cone of light that barely reached the rust-streaked walls. Lorrisa's heart thudded in her chest, but outwardly she appeared composed.

Finally, Smith stopped. His hand tightened on the gun, lips curling into a humorless smirk. "You're surprisingly calm, Professor," he murmured, voice smooth but edged with menace.

Lorrisa's lips twitched upward into a small, defiant smile. "You don't know me very well."

With that, the standoff deepened—each waiting for the other to make the first mistake.

Lorrisa's eyes followed him carefully. She sized him up the way Bashir had taught her years ago when they took self-defense classes together. Wide stance, favors right hand, loose with the weapon. Cocky. Overconfident. Perfect.

As Smith turned his back for half a second to check his phone, Lorrisa sprang from the chair, grabbed Smith's gun wrist with both hands, and twisted sharply while pivoting her hips. Using his own momentum against him, she threw him over her shoulder in a classic judo move. Smith hit the concrete with a heavy thud, the gun skittering across the floor.

Before he could react, Lorrisa snatched the gun, kicked him once in the ribs for good measure, and bolted for the exit.

She didn't bother looking back. She raced across the open floor of the warehouse and shoved the heavy side door open. Bright California sunlight poured in, blinding her for a second, but she didn't stop. She ran barefoot across the gravel and broken asphalt, the sharp edges biting into her feet, until she spotted a busy main road up ahead.

She flagged down the first car she saw—a rusted old pickup truck driven by an elderly woman with a purse bigger than she was. Lorrisa yanked the door open and climbed inside without asking. “¡Maneja! Drive!” she shouted.

The woman gaped at her for a second, then hit the gas, launching them down the road as Lorrisa dropped the gun onto the seat between them.

Twenty minutes later, after explaining herself, the police arrived at the warehouse.

Lorrisa filed a report, but the officers didn’t seem overly interested in chasing down a kidnapping with no official IDs, no real names, no traceable license plates, no camera footage. Lorrisa didn’t expect much more—but at least her butt was covered.

Exhausted and sore, she finally made her way back to her apartment.

The door was open.

Her heart stopped.

She rushed inside. Books were scattered, couch cushions shredded, the small kitchen a wreck. But this time, something far worse was missing.

“Kong?!” she screamed.

She darted from room to room. No tiny monkey leapt into her arms. No mischievous face peeked from under the bed. The apartment felt hollow without him.

Fighting back tears, she yanked out her phone and called the only person who might understand what the hell was happening.

Gee.

The line rang… and rang…

Finally, he picked up. “Lorrisa?” His voice was tense.

“Gee… it’s happening. Those men you warned me about. They took Kong!”

A heavy sigh from the other end. She could almost picture him rubbing his forehead the way he always did when stressed.

“Listen carefully,” he said. “You have to stay safe. Avoid them at all costs. Don’t be a hero. Don’t try to fight them alone.”

“Gee, where are you?”

He hesitated. “I’m in Morocco. Taghazout.”

“Morocco?!” she nearly shouted. “Why the hell are you there?”

“I’m… looking for something.”

“You found a ring, didn’t you?”

Silence.

“I knew it!” she hissed. “Cabron/a, idiota!, you’re neck-deep in this and didn’t tell me? Estas loco?”

“I was trying to keep you out of it,” he growled. “And you’re doing a bang-up job staying out, huh?”

She slammed her hand on the kitchen counter. “I’m coming to you.”

“No! Lorrisa, it’s too dangerous.”

“I’m not asking, Gee.”

Before he could argue, she hung up.

Lorrisa immediately fired up her laptop. After a few frantic searches, she found the fastest and *only* flight out of LAX and booked it. One ticket. First class. Screw it.

She sat back, heart racing, her thoughts a tornado of anger, fear, and adrenaline. She wasn't just going to Morocco for Kong.
She was going to end this thing once and for all.

Meanwhile,

halfway across the world, Gee sat in a dimly lit hotel room overlooking the Atlantic, the call with Lorrisa still echoing in his ear. His jaw clenched as he stared out over the rooftops of Taghazout, the ocean shimmering under the moonlight. He tried calling Lorrisa back but her phone must have been off at this time. He frantically called the airport to check for flights out of the United States. One. There was only going to be one. His fingers fidgeted with the two jagged rings in his pocket, their metal cool against his skin. For a brief moment, he panicked and tried to determine his next move. Sweat traced a path down his temple as he checked the room's lock for the third time. He knew the men hunting him were close—he could feel it in the way locals avoided his gaze and the way shadows lingered a little too long outside his window. His phone buzzed again, anxiously he looked at it, but this time it wasn't Lorrisa. It was a text, untraceable, just four words: "We have your wife." Gee's stomach twisted. He shoved the phone into his pocket, took a slow breath, and began assembling the pieces of a plan he wasn't sure he'd survive. Outside, the narrow streets of Taghazout were alive with the sounds of night—vendors calling out their last sales, fishermen mending their nets by lantern light, children's laughter echoing faintly down the alleys. But

Gee's mind was a storm. He moved to the small table by the window, spreading out a worn map and a stack of crumpled notes he had gathered over weeks of chasing whispers and relics. His fingers trembled slightly as he traced the markings he had drawn himself: locations, names, and question marks where leads had gone cold. He could hear footsteps outside—measured, deliberate. Not locals. His heart pounded as he switched off the lamp and pressed his back to the wall. The weight of the rings in his pocket was suddenly heavier, as if they knew what was coming. Gee's breath steadied as he slipped the rings into a hidden pouch beneath his shirt. Footsteps drew closer, voices low and sharp in a language he half-recognized. Without a sound, Gee eased open the window and swung himself onto the narrow balcony. Below, the maze of alleyways beckoned—tight turns, weathered stone, and shadows deep enough to vanish into. He took one last look inside, then dropped to the street.

Behind him, the door burst open, the men's curses echoing through the room. Gee bolted down the alley, weaving between crates and laundry lines, his breath ragged but his mind sharp. He ducked through a side street, narrowly avoiding a black SUV that turned onto the main road, headlights slicing through the dark.

At the edge of the market square, he spotted a battered taxi idling by the curb. Gee threw open the door and slid inside, gasping, “Aéroport, vite!—Fast, please!” The driver, an older man with a cigarette dangling from his lips, gave him a puzzled look but nodded and slammed the car into gear.

As the taxi roared toward the airport, Gee pressed his forehead to the clouded window, heart pounding. He had to reach Lorrisa before they did. Before any more pieces were lost—or anyone else paid the price. Forty-five minutes later Gee burst through the airport's sliding doors, heart hammering as he scanned the arrival boards. His breath hitched when he saw the bitter truth: Lorrisa's flight had been rerouted to an airport nearly a hundred miles away. Arriving at 6:30pm local time. He quickly calculated, with the vehicle he's been in and the rate of speed it could travel, it would take him over four hours to get to her. He looked at his watch and saw that it was 2:10pm. His stomach dropped, but there was no time to curse his luck. A flicker of movement caught his eye near the baggage claim—three men, familiar faces from his pursuers, spreading out like wolves on a scent.

2:14pm

Gee backed toward the nearest pillar, slipping into its shadow. But one henchman caught his movement, a sharp whistle slicing through the terminal noise. Two of them lunged, shoving through travelers. Gee's survival instincts snapped into focus. He sidestepped the first, driving his elbow into the man's ribs, then pivoted sharply to kick the second in the knee, sending him sprawling. But the third was faster.

With no time to think, Gee dove onto the luggage belt, sliding across the rubber conveyor as startled tourists yelped. The belt jolted, pulling him toward the yawning mouth of the luggage chute. Without hesitation, Gee wriggled into the narrow opening, the cold draft rushing past him as he tumbled into the darkness beyond, leaving his would-be captors shouting at the jammed belt...2:31pm.

Meanwhile, 6:25pm local time at the farther airport, Lorrisa stepped off the plane like a runway model disguised as a professor. Her dark brown hair caught the sun as she removed her sunglasses, scanning the bustling terminal with a sharp, practiced eye. Rolling her suitcase behind her with effortless grace, she waved down a taxi. The driver, eager to help, loaded her bags and began to pull away just as an old, battered truck rattled into the terminal loop—Gee behind the wheel, dust-streaked and wide-eyed. His heart lurched as he caught sight of Lorrisa through the rear window of the taxi. He slammed the truck door and sprinted after them, yelling, "¡Espera! Stop!"

By a stroke of luck—or fate—the taxi was snarled in airport traffic. Gee pounded on the window, and Lorrisa, startled, climbed out in a whirl of annoyance and relief. "¡Dios mío, Gee! ¿En qué estabas pensando? ¡Mira cómo estás! ¡Pareces un desastre!" She planted her hands on her hips, firing off rapid Spanish reprimands as Gee caught his breath, grinning despite himself.

As Gee went to hug Lorrisa, she pushed him away with a wrinkle of her nose. "¡Ay, no, no! You're sweaty, and you smell awful!" she scolded, swatting at his shoulder. A small puff of dust flew off his jacket, making her wave her hands dramatically near her face to clear the air. Gee just looked at her, shrugged with exaggerated innocence, and flashed a sheepish smile. "Hi, honey. I said you didn't have to come." Lorrisa gave him a long, unimpressed stink-eye, crossing her arms as she shook her head.

Chapter 2

The sun hung low over the Moroccan coastline, casting gold and rose hues across the rippling waves as Lorrisa and Gee pulled up to the *Riad Amira*, a charming resort perched above the beach. The scent of sea salt mixed with jasmine drifted through the air as they stepped inside.

Lorrisa glided through the entrance like she belonged there, head held high, sunglasses pushed up into her sun-streaked hair. Gee, on the other hand, trudged in behind her—dusty, sweat-streaked, and clutching a battered duffel bag like it was the only thing holding his life together.

The lobby was a cool oasis of polished tile floors, low-hanging lanterns, and cushioned benches arranged in little clusters. Guests in flowing linen and wide-brimmed hats sipped cocktails by the fountain. Gee wiped his brow on his sleeve, earning a disapproving glance from the concierge.

At the front desk, Lorrisa breezed through the check-in with enviable efficiency, tapping her card, confirming the room, and accepting a cool towel with a gracious smile. Gee, meanwhile, hovered awkwardly beside her.

"So..." Gee cleared his throat, shifting his weight from one foot to the other. "About tonight. I was thinking maybe—since, you know, funds are tight on my end and there's that whole *people-trying-to-kill-me* situation—you wouldn't mind if I..." He motioned vaguely, "crashed in your room?"

Lorrisa arched a perfectly shaped brow, her lips curving in amusement. "Gee, you've slept in tents on archaeological digs, under trucks in the Sahara, and once, if I recall correctly, in a canoe."

"Technically, *on* the canoe," Gee corrected. "It was upside-down, and it rained."

She laughed softly, handing him a keycard with a wink. "Here's one for the lobby bathroom. Maybe you can sweet-talk a couch out of the concierge."

"Ah, the cold heart of academia," Gee muttered, grinning as she sauntered off toward the elevators, her suitcase gliding effortlessly behind her.

Hours later, after a failed attempt to charm the night manager into a cot, Gee resigned himself to the wide lobby couch. He sank onto it with a groan, pulling his hat low over his eyes. Guests murmured around him, the soft clink of glassware and low music blending into a lullaby. But peace was short-lived.

Through half-lidded eyes, Gee saw movement at the front desk. His body stiffened as he caught sight of Sebastian—pristine as ever, his suit crisp, hair immaculate, a smirk lurking at the corner of his mouth.

Gee slid lower into the couch, heart thudding. Sebastian leaned in to speak with the receptionist, gesturing with a polished hand.

Of all the hotels in Morocco...

Carefully, Sliding lower on the couch, Gee made himself small, but Sebastian's bodyguard types had already begun scanning the lobby. Gee's heart thudded in his chest.

Careful as a cat, he slipped off the couch, ducked behind a potted palm, and began inching toward the elevators, sending a silent prayer to whoever was listening.

Halfway there, his luck ran out.

"Gee?" Lorrisa's voice drifted from above. She was leaning over the railing on the mezzanine, wearing a hotel robe, her hair loose, a glass of wine in hand. "Are you... are you *crawling* through the lobby?" He froze.

Lorrisa leaned over the mezzanine railing brows furrowed in utter confusion.

Gee waved both hands in a frantic *shush* motion.

She blinked. “What the hell are you doing?” she whispered.

He pointed toward the lobby, then jabbed his thumb toward the elevators, mouthing: *trouble.*

Lorrisa frowned, watching the men at the desk. “Is that... someone we know?”

Gee shook his head sharply, eyes wide. *Bad guys,* he mouthed.

Lorrisa set her wineglass on the ledge, sighed, and rubbed her forehead.

“Fine. Room 204. You’re on the floor.”

Gee flashed a grin, gave a thumbs-up, and darted toward the stairwell just as one of Sebastian’s men turned his head.

As Lorrisa disappeared into her room, she muttered under her breath, “God help me, I should’ve booked a place without Wi-Fi.” Gee slipped into Room 204 with the softest click of the door latch he could manage, his breath still coming hard from sprinting up two flights of stairs. He leaned back against the door, hat in hand, sweat-damp hair clinging to his forehead.

Across the room, Lorrisa stood by the open balcony, her silhouette framed against the moonlit ocean. She'd swapped her robe for a soft t-shirt and yoga pants, her bare feet sunk into the thick rug. Her long hair, usually pinned back, fell loose over her shoulders.

Gee gave a sheepish smile. "Nice view."

Without turning, Lorrisa replied coolly, "And it was even nicer before a sweaty fugitive came crashing in."

Gee edged toward the corner by the sofa, lowering his duffel to the floor with exaggerated care. "For the record, I didn't *crash*. It was more of a... tactical infiltration."

Lorrisa turned, arms crossed, arching an eyebrow. "Oh, is *that* what we're calling it now?"

He gave a playful shrug. "You're welcome for the dramatic entrance."

She moved to the mini-fridge, plucking out a small bottle of water and tossing it to him. "Here. Hydrate. You look like you fell into a campfire."

Gee caught it with both hands, cracking it open gratefully. "You're a saint, you know that?"

"I know," she deadpanned.

He flopped down on the floor at the foot of the bed, pulling a pillow from the couch and tucking it behind his head. His eyes roamed the ceiling, then drifted to her as she perched on the edge of the bed, scrolling on her phone. Her shapely legs hung seductively to the carpet.

"So..." Gee started, voice light, "no room on the bed? You sure? It's a big bed. Queen size, maybe even king..."

Lorrisa's head snapped up, her eyes narrowing to thin slits.

"Gee," she said with mock sweetness, "if your foot so much as *touches* this bed, I will launch you off that balcony, and you can bunk with the seagulls."

He lifted his hands in surrender, grinning. "Message received, cariño."

For a few minutes, they sat in companionable silence—Lorrisa tapping at her screen, Gee sipping his water, eyes half-closed as the adrenaline finally ebbed.

Then, softly, Lorrisa spoke without looking up. "Gee... who *was* that man downstairs?"

Gee let out a long breath, rubbing his face. "His name's Sebastian Voss. He works for the people after the rings."

She paused, eyes flicking up to meet his. “And now he’s here. In this hotel.”

“Yeah.”

“Wonderful,” Lorrisa muttered, sinking back onto the pillows. “Because what’s a vacation without a homicidal treasure hunter lurking in the lobby?”

Gee stretched out on the floor, folding his hands behind his head. “You gotta admit,” he murmured with a crooked smile, “life’s never boring with me.”

Lorrisa sighed dramatically, tugging the blanket over herself. “One of these days, Gee, I’m going to choose boring.”

A beat passed.

From the floor, Gee’s voice floated up, drowsy but amused. “But not tonight?”

Lorrisa rolled her eyes, turned off the light, and muttered into the dark, “Go to sleep, Gee.”

And for the first time in weeks, despite the chaos swirling outside their door, they both did. The morning sun crept through the sheer curtains, casting soft golden patterns across the floor of Room 204. Outside, the sea whispered against the shore, gulls calling in the distance.

Gee stirred slightly, half-waking at the sound of running water—then drifting back into a light, dream-laced doze.

That is, until something cold and wet smacked him square in the face.

He sputtered awake, squinting against the sunlight—and found himself staring up into Lorrisa's face, framed by damp raven-black hair still dripping from her shower. She loomed over him, poking at his shoulder with the extended tip of her index finger like he was a suspicious package left unattended at the airport.

"Ugh," Lorrisa muttered under her breath, lips twitching in half-disgust, half-amusement. "You're still alive. Impressive."

Gee blinked up at her, water droplets sliding off his cheek. A slow, goofy grin spread across his face. "Morning, gorgeous."

Lorrisa rolled her eyes and, without ceremony, shoved a disposable razor and a bar of soap into his chest.

"Fix your face," she ordered, deadpan. "You look like a homeless pirate."

Gee stretched languidly on the floor, scratching at his stubbled jaw. “You wound me, querida. I was going for ‘rugged explorer.’”

She crossed her arms and tapped one bare foot impatiently on the rug. “Rugged smells a little less like a gym sock left in the sun.”

He sat up with a chuckle, running a hand through his unruly hair. “You know, you’re adorable when you’re bossy.”

“And you’re insufferable even when you’re unconscious,” Lorrisa shot back, turning to the small dresser where she’d laid out her things.

Gee stood, stretching his arms over his head with a satisfying pop of his shoulders. As he shuffled toward the bathroom, he called over his shoulder, “Want me to serenade you in the shower next, or are you saving that pleasure for tonight?”

From across the room came the unmistakable *thwap* of a hotel pillow bouncing off the back of his head.

“Shut Up, Gee.”

Grinning to himself, Gee slipped into the bathroom, the soap and razor in hand. As the door clicked shut, Lorrisa shook her head with a small smirk, muttering under her breath, "How do I always get myself into this?"

Outside, the city was already waking up—and so was the trouble waiting for them. Gee emerged from the bathroom, a light cloud of steam curling out behind him, the scent of hotel soap and fresh skin replacing the musk of last night's chase.

He was shaved now, his jawline sharp and clean, his dark hair towel-dried into messy waves that somehow made him look effortlessly magnetic. His towel wrapped around his waist in a way that reminded Lorrisa—just for a flicker of a moment—why she'd once been so hopelessly tangled in this man.

Her heart gave a tiny, involuntary flutter.

Shaking her head and blinking her eyes as if she awoke from a dream, she stamped it down immediately.

"Don't just stand there smirking, Gee. Get dressed," she snapped, tossing a clean shirt, she dug out of his duffle bag, in his general direction without looking up from buckling her heels.

Gee caught it one-handed, a cocky grin spreading across his face as his gaze swept over her. She had dressed while he was in the shower—of course.

Perfectly tailored linen pants, a soft silk blouse in pale sea-glass green, a delicate gold pendant at her throat. She looked like she belonged on the cover of an international fashion magazine. Lovely, shapely, confident.

“Aw, querida,” Gee drawled, pulling the shirt over his head, “you dressed without me? You always knew how much I loved watching that part of the morning. Total crime, you know.”

Lorrisa shot him a look so sharp it could’ve cut stone. “Please. The only thing you loved was stalling so you wouldn’t have to do the breakfast dishes.”

Gee pressed a hand to his chest with mock offense. “Wounded again. You’re cruel before coffee, you know that?”

She crossed her arms, the corner of her mouth twitching despite herself. “Enough flirting, Casanova. Sit. Explain. Everything.”

Gee’s face sobered immediately. He sat on the edge of the bed, elbows on his knees, fingers rubbing at his temples as though trying to sort the mess into words.

“It’s Simean Mogull,” he began quietly. “He’s the one behind this. Simean’s been after the pieces of the tablet for years—longer, maybe. He hired me as an advisor for his excavating team. I didn't know how dangerous he was. He's got money, connections, and a crew of hundreds of people willing to tear the world apart to get what he wants."

Lorrisa's brow furrowed, arms tightening across her chest.

"Sebastian," Gee continued, "he's Mogull's right hand. Ex-military, ex-mercenary, and completely loyal. Charming as a snake and twice as deadly. He's leading the search. And he's not here to negotiate, Rissa. He's here to clean up loose ends—people, places, anything that gets in his way."

Lorrisa's stomach turned cold. She sat down beside Gee, their shoulders nearly brushing.

"So," she murmured, her voice tight, "we're the loose ends."

Gee gave her a half-smile, rueful and tired. "Looks like."

For a long moment, they sat in silence, the weight of it all settling between them. Then Lorrisa straightened, clearing her throat.

"Well," she said briskly, "at least one of us smells good today. Let's figure out our next move."

Lorrisa paced the length of the room, her heels clicked on the cool tile floor, fingers tapping against her chin as Gee leaned casually against the window, arms folded. Outside, the hazy light of morning crept across the resort's terracotta rooftops, casting soft golden stripes across the room.

"Alright," Lorrisa said sharply, spinning on her heel. "First, we change your appearance, then we get you clothes."

Gee raised an eyebrow, amused. "What, this isn't working for you?" He stretched his arms lazily, his clean T-shirt pulling across his chest.

Lorrisa shot him a dry look. "You're one beat-up pair of sneakers away from looking like a backpacker who wandered into the wrong continent. We need you polished, invisible. No one is going to be hunting for a man who looks like a model in a GQ spread."

Gee gave a crooked grin. "So, basically... you want to fix me up like one of your research assistants?"

Lorrisa smirked, walking to the closet and pulling out the hotel's shopping guide. "No, I want you to look like someone who belongs in this resort, not like a man who just dodged a hit squad and slept in the lobby."

"Fair enough," Gee admitted, raking a hand through his damp hair. "And you think Sebastian's men won't recognize me?"

"They've never seen me," Lorrisa said, flipping through the hotel guide. "And you, freshly showered and shaved, could pass as a whole new man. We get you into a crisp shirt, decent shoes, haircut, maybe a hat—and we'll be able to walk right past them."

Gee whistled low. "You've done this before."

"I read," she said sweetly, flashing him a smug little grin. "Now, after we handle that, we focus on Kong. I need to find him before we even think about leaving this country."

Gee softened, the cocky tilt of his mouth fading. "We'll get him back, Rissa. You know I'm with you on this."

She let out a long breath, the tight line of her shoulders easing just a fraction. "Good. Because I can't do this alone."

Gee pushed off the window, coming to stand close, a spark of that old, magnetic energy flickering between them. "When have you ever been alone?"

Lorrisa's gaze flicked up to meet his, steady and just a little exasperated. "I was alone on the plane, thanks to you."

He chuckled. "You were first class, mi amor. You had champagne and legroom. That's practically a honeymoon."

Lorrisa gave his chest a firm poke. "Focus, Romeo. Clothes. Monkey. Escape."

"Got it." Gee raised his hands in surrender, still smiling. "Lead the way, boss."

With a quick glance out the window to check the hallway below, Lorrisa tucked her bag under her arm and motioned to the door. "Alright. Let's turn you into someone they'd never suspect—and then we find Kong."

"Adventure date it is," Gee murmured as they slipped out of the room, his grin widening as she rolled her eyes—but didn't disagree. The boutique they found just off the hotel lobby was a small but luxurious haven of European labels, linen suits, and beach-chic accessories. Lorrisa swept in with purpose, her wet raven hair now pinned up, sunglasses perched on her head, and a look on her face that suggested she was about to invade and conquer the men's section.

Gee trailed behind her, hands in his pockets, wearing a half-smirk, half-grimace.

"Do we really need to do this now?" he muttered, eyeing the price tags with a wince. "I mean, can't we just grab a pair of shades and a baseball cap and call it good?"

Lorrisa shot him a sideways look as she rifled through a rack of pale linen shirts. "Sure, if you want to look like you're in hiding. But we want the opposite, remember? We need you to look like you belong here—someone who drinks overpriced cocktails by the pool, not someone who sleeps under it."

Gee leaned casually against a mannequin, tilting his head. "So basically, you're dressing me like your type."

She arched an eyebrow, not missing a beat. "If I were dressing you as my type, you'd be in a lab coat and glasses, debating theology over red wine. Trust me, this is purely survival."

He gave a soft chuckle. “Ouch. Okay, what’s the uniform, then?”

She held up a pale blue button-down, crisp and just the right amount of casual, then eyed a pair of tailored khaki trousers. “This, with... hmm...” Her eyes flicked to his battered sneakers, and she wrinkled her nose. “We’re burning those.”

Gee laughed, holding up a pair of sleek leather loafers with exaggerated horror. “These? You want me to wear these? I’ll break an ankle, Rissa.”

“Somehow, I doubt that,” she quipped, thrusting the loafers into his hands. “You climbed cliff faces in Peru barefoot.”

“That’s different! That was survival. This is...” He looked down at the polished shoes with theatrical despair. “...fashion homicide.”

“Gee.” She crossed her arms, amused but firm. “We are on the run from armed men who are probably already looking for us in the lobby. Humor me.”

With a defeated groan, Gee took the clothes and disappeared into the dressing room.

Minutes later, when he stepped out, Lorrisa paused, lips parting slightly before she masked it with a playful eye roll. The linen shirt fit him a little too perfectly, the khakis rested easy on his frame, and the loafers—well, even Gee looked sheepish as he caught his reflection.

He spread his arms. “Not bad, huh?”

Lorrisa tossed him a light straw fedora. “Perfect. Now you just need to stop smiling like you’re proud of yourself.”

“Come on,” he grinned, placing the fedora on his head at a rakish angle, “admit it. You’re thinking about Peru right now.”

She snorted, grabbing her purse. “I’m thinking about how I should’ve left you in Peru. Let’s go, Mr. GQ. We have the other monkey to find.”

As they exited the boutique, Gee fell into step beside her, still grinning. “Hey, if we survive this, you owe me a drink by the pool. I think I’ve earned it.”

Lorrisa shook her head, unable to hide the ghost of a smile tugging at her lips. “We’ll survive. Just stay close—and try not to trip over your new shoes.”

“Deal,” he murmured, casting a quick glance behind them.

They slipped out of the boutique with practiced casualness, Lorrisa linking her arm through Gee’s as if they were just another well-heeled couple on vacation.

Outside, the midday sun blazed down on the waterfront promenade, casting rippling gold reflections off the sea. The air smelled of salt and hibiscus, the faint chatter of tourists blending with the rhythmic slap of waves against the dock.

Gee adjusted his new fedora, grumbling under his breath, “I feel like a yacht salesman.”

“You look like one, too,” Lorrisa murmured, scanning the street. “Relax. You’re blending in.”

They moved through the crowd, stopping now and then to glance in shop windows or linger at a café terrace—just long enough to keep from looking rushed. Gee's eyes, though, flicked constantly toward alleyways and doorways, tension thrumming under his new polished exterior.

"So," Lorrisa said as they rounded a corner, "we track Kong. Any brilliant ideas, Mr. World Explorer?"

Gee rubbed his chin. "Well, we know one thing: those men wouldn't have taken him far. A capuchin isn't exactly low maintenance, and he's trained to come back to you."

"Trained to come back when he's not drugged or caged, you mean," Lorrisa said dryly.

"Fair point," Gee allowed. "But if they're smart, they're holding him somewhere close to the action. Somewhere they can keep watch for us."

He pulled a folded map from his pocket—already creased and marked with a few hasty notes. "I say we start with the marina. A lot of private boats, easy to move cargo or, in this case, a monkey."

Lorrisa frowned. "We can't just waltz onto a dock."

"No," Gee agreed, "but we can bribe the right dockhand. Got any money?"

They wove their way down to the waterfront, where boats bobbed at anchor and crew members hauled nets, supplies, and crates. Gee peeled away briefly to chat with a wiry local leaning against a stack of barrels. Money changed hands discreetly.

He returned to Lorrisa with a faint grin. "Good news. There's been... unusual cargo taken onto one of the larger yachts—cages, lots of noise, and a man fitting Sebastian's description overseeing it."

Lorrisa's jaw tightened. "So they're planning to sail."

"Soon," Gee confirmed. "We need to move fast."

They crossed the marina, slipping between shadowed alleys until the sleek white yacht came into view. Two guards loitered near the gangplank, laughing over cigarettes.

Lorrisa exhaled, steadying herself. "Alright, Gee. What's the play?"

He flashed a mischievous grin. "Follow my lead."

She grabbed his arm, yanking him back. "No, no, no. That grin is how we almost got arrested in Istanbul."

“It worked, didn’t it?” he shot back, winking.

“Barely!” she hissed.

They ducked into the shadows, close enough to hear the guards, close enough for the first crackle of adrenaline to hit. Lorrisa’s fingers brushed Gee’s arm briefly—not in affection, but as a silent anchor.

“Ready?” Gee whispered.

Lorrisa gave a sharp nod. “Let’s bring my monkey home.”

They crouched in the shadows, watching the guards laugh and smoke by the yacht’s gangplank.

“Alright,” Gee murmured, “two guys, one dockhand loading crates... we need a distraction.”

Lorrisa peeked around the corner, calculating angles like a chess master. “If I take the dockhand, can you handle the two gorillas?”

Gee gave her a sideways look. “Since when are you the muscle?”

She smirked. “Since you started dressing like a Bond villain.”

He chuckled softly. “Fair. Alright, you peel the dockhand away. I’ll improvise.”

Lorrisa moved first, graceful as ever. She strolled up to the dockhand, her heels clicking softly on the planks. "Excuse me," she called in accented English, flashing her brightest smile. "I seem to be lost, and you look like a man who knows this marina well."

The dockhand straightened, puffing out his chest. "Of course, señora, where are you trying to go?"

As they fell into conversation, Gee slipped from the shadows, rolling his shoulders. He approached the two guards like an old friend, tipping his fedora.

"¡Amigos! Beautiful day for a sail, huh?"

The men turned, puzzled, their cigarettes hanging from their lips. One squinted suspiciously. "Who are you?"

Gee gave them a wide, easy grin. "Don't you remember? We met at the harbor bar last night. Fantastic drinks, awful music."

They blinked, exchanging a glance.

"Ah, no matter," Gee continued breezily, "just came by to tell you: your boss is looking for you on the other side of the marina. Something about... paperwork."

The taller guard frowned. "What paperwork?"

Gee shrugged. “Man, I just pass the message.” He started to turn away.

“Wait,” the second guard barked, stepping forward. “Who sent you?”

In a flash, Gee swung his elbow, catching the taller one square in the jaw. The man crumpled like a folding chair. The second lunged, but Gee sidestepped neatly, grabbed the man’s wrist, and twisted it behind his back, shoving him hard against the railing.

Meanwhile, Lorrisa finished her distraction with a gentle hand on the dockhand’s shoulder. As soon as the guards went down, she whispered, “Thank you for your help,” and shoved the man backward into a pile of fishing nets.

She darted to Gee’s side. “Subtle.”

“You love me for it,” Gee shot back, panting slightly.

Rolling her eyes, Lorrisa climbed the gangplank, Gee at her heels. The deck was silent save for the creak of ropes and the slap of waves. Somewhere below, Kong’s familiar chatter echoed faintly.

Lorrisa’s heart tightened. “That’s him.”

Gee squeezed her arm gently. “Let’s get your monkey and go.”

They slipped below deck, the narrow hallway dim and smelling faintly of diesel.

From somewhere ahead, voices drifted—Sebastian’s unmistakable English drawl, low and commanding.

Lorrisa drew a sharp breath. Gee placed a finger to his lips.

“Ready?” he whispered.

Lorrisa balled up her hand making a fist. She gave a fierce little nod.

Below deck, the air was thick and musty, filled with the sour smell of old diesel, salt, and damp ropes. Gee crouched low, guiding Lorrisa along the narrow corridor with one hand behind him, the other pressed to the wall for balance. Kong’s faint, agitated chittering floated from a nearby cabin door, each high-pitched sound like a needle to Lorrisa’s heart.

“There,” she whispered urgently, pointing to a half-open hatch where the sounds came from.

But Gee’s hand shot out to halt her.

Footsteps. Voices.

Sebastian's unmistakable English drawl rolled down the corridor like cold smoke. "—I want the perimeter of the city checked again. I don't care how thorough you think you were." A sharp pause. "She will come for the monkey and he will come for her. And if that damn animal's gone, I'll have your hides hanging from my stern rail."

Lorrisa's breath caught, but Gee gently nudged her behind a stack of crates. He crouched, pulling her down with him, slipping the edge of his jacket over her brilliant hair as if it might muffle the gleam.

Sebastian's footsteps approached, heels clicking against the metal floor. A flicker of polished boots, a dark silhouette brushing past—and then, mercifully, moving on.

Lorrisa buried her face in Gee's shoulder, exhaling a long, shaking breath. "I owe you for this," she mouthed, and he smirked without sound.

Once Sebastian and his men vanished down the corridor, Gee eased the hatch open with the quietest motion he could manage. Inside, Kong was perched on a crate, his tiny face a tense mask of panic and fury. The moment he saw Lorrisa, he let out a high-pitched squeal and launched himself into her arms, nearly knocking her backward.

"Oh, mi amorcito," she cooed, wrapping her arms around the trembling monkey. "You're safe now."

"Touching," Gee murmured. "Now can we move before they realize the guest list just got shorter?"

They slipped back up the narrow stairs, Lorrisa cradling Kong under her coat, Gee leading the way with a readiness that surprised even him. They emerged onto the deck just as a confused pair of henchmen stumbled into view at the dock, rubbing their heads.

Gee jerked his chin toward the opposite side of the yacht. "There."

They scrambled over the railing, dropping softly onto the dock and slipping into the shadowed side alleys of the marina just as the first shouts of alarm rang out.

By the time Sebastian's men regained their feet and staggered up the gangplank, the yacht was empty of intruders. One guard gestured wildly as Sebastian stormed up, sharp-eyed and furious.

"We were hit—local thieves, we think. Damn street rats saw the monkey and figured they'd make money off it."

Sebastian's mouth twisted. "Idiots." He turned a slow circle on the deck, eyes narrowing at the dark alleys beyond. "Find them. I don't care if you have to search every alley, every market stall. I want that animal back—and the rings. Now."

Meanwhile, deeper into the city, Lorrisa and Gee hurried down a narrow stone alley, the buzz of the night market growing ahead.

"We can't walk around with Kong like this," Lorrisa hissed, adjusting the lump under her coat. "We'll have every street kid and pickpocket on us in five minutes."

"Got an idea," Gee said, grabbing a ratty old blanket from a laundry line. He wrapped Kong snugly, turning the monkey into what looked like a bundle of clothes.

"Congratulations," Lorrisa deadpanned. "You're a proud father of laundry."

"Could've been diapers," Gee shot back with a wink.

Lorrisa rolled her eyes but bit back a laugh as they slipped into the bustling market.

"We lay low tonight," Gee murmured, scanning the crowds. "Tomorrow—we figure out how to stop Sebastian."

“Tomorrow,” Lorrisa agreed, her hand brushing his briefly as they melted into the noise and color of the city.

Back at the hotel, the room door barely clicked shut before Kong wriggled free of Lorrisa’s arms, launching himself across the room like a caffeinated tornado.

“Kong—¡no, no, no!” Lorrisa shrieked, dropping her coat and diving after him. But the little monkey was already bounding across the bed, overturning a lamp, scrambling onto the dresser, and batting at the curtains like an untamed child on a sugar rush.

Gee leaned against the doorframe, arms crossed, a smirk tugging at the corners of his mouth. “You sure you don’t want to check him into daycare before we save the world?”

Lorrisa huffed, grabbing at Kong’s tail only to be met with an acrobatic leap to the chandelier. “¡Ay, Dios mío! This is not the time for your monkey madness!”

Finally, Kong seemed to settle, perching triumphantly on the curtain rod, surveying the chaos he had unleashed with an innocent tilt of his head.

Lorrisa threw herself onto the edge of the bed, raking her fingers through her damp hair. “I’m done, Gee.

Finished. I just want a plane, a boat, a camel, hell—strap me to a submarine and get me out of here."

Gee's expression softened, but his voice stayed steady. "Riss... we can't just run."

She glared at him. "Oh, can't we? Watch me." She hopped up, pacing the room in tight, furious circles. "We find a flight, we go home, we tell the authorities, and we let the professionals handle this. No more treasure hunts, no more rings, no more shadowy British villains with fashionably murderous tendencies."

Gee pushed off the wall, reached into his pocket, and pulled out the two jagged rings he'd carried across continents. "You really think this is just a treasure hunt?"

Lorrisa stopped mid-pace, her arms folded across her chest, brows raised. "Oh, please."

"Look," Gee said calmly. He set one ring on the nightstand and slowly moved the other toward it.

Lorrisa sighed dramatically. "Gee, if this is some sleight-of-hand trick—"

But her voice cut off.

A soft hum, faint but unmistakable, filled the space between the rings. The second piece, still in Gee's hand, pulled forward—visibly, undeniably—drawn toward the first with a magnetic force that defied logic. Within a foot, it leapt from his fingers and clicked into place against the other with a pulse of faint, bluish light.

Lorrisa's jaw dropped.

"What the...?"

Kong let out an excited chatter from his perch, as if even he understood the moment's gravity.

Gee gave a crooked smile. "Yeah. That's why we can't just run."

Lorrisa stared at the fused pieces, a flicker of reluctant awe breaking through her skepticism. For a long beat, she said nothing. Then, quietly, she muttered, "I need a drink."

Gee chuckled. "That's my girl."

Chapter 3

Lorrisa sat cross-legged on the bed, her damp hair tied loosely at the nape of her neck, eyes fixed on the nightstand in front of her. She gave a little smirk, placing the two jagged rings exactly twelve inches apart.

"Alright, show me the magic," she murmured under her breath.

Sure enough, within seconds, the faint hum started. A whisper of vibration rippled through the air, and the top ring began to edge forward on its own, scraping slightly against the polished wood. Lorrisa leaned in, fascinated, as it crept toward its mate like a moth drawn to a flame.

Click. The faint glow pulsed as the two locked together again.

She let out a soft, almost disbelieving laugh and reached for her drink on the nightstand—half a glass of something sweet and strong from the minibar. She took a sip, savoring the warmth in her chest, then reset the rings.

“Twelve inches apart… and go,” she whispered, watching the dance play out all over again.

Across the room, Kong sat perched on the edge of the fruit bowl, stuffing a grape into his mouth with the elegance of a toddler at a birthday party. His tiny hands darted between the bananas and kiwi, occasionally pausing to eye Lorrisa’s glass as if weighing his odds.

Gee, meanwhile, sat cross-legged on the floor, his elbows propped on the coffee table, a battered old map spread out in front of him. His hair, now neatly trimmed, still fell boyishly across his brow, and the fresh shave did nothing to soften the intensity in his face.

“We need to get to Sidi Ifni,” Gee said aloud, tracing a line down the Moroccan coast with a pencil. “Local legends say a merchant there carried a piece of the tablet back from the Ottoman courts. If that’s true, it’s probably hidden in one of the old sea caves. They’re tricky, though—tidal patterns, collapsed tunnels—”

He glanced up toward the bed, fully expecting Lorrisa to be taking notes or shooting down his plan with one of her sharp-tongued quips. Instead, he found her resting her chin on one hand, watching the rings slide together with the dreamy focus of a child watching a lava lamp.

“Riss,” Gee said dryly, “you’re totally listening, right?”

“Mm-hm.” She didn’t look up.

“We’re probably going to have to climb through wet caves, possibly outrun some criminal treasure hunters, maybe bribe a corrupt port official or two.”

“Sounds delightful,” she murmured, resetting the rings yet again.

“And you’re completely on board.”

“Absolutely.” Sip. Watch. *Click.* Soft glow.

Gee sighed, running a hand through his hair. “Well, at least one of us is getting entertainment out of this.”

Kong let out a satisfied squeak as he jammed an entire slice of banana into his mouth, giving Gee a cheeky grin around the pulp.

Gee smirked. “Glad to know I’m the only one doing any planning here.”

Lorrisa finally tore her gaze from the rings, arching a brow at him. “Gee, the last time *you* planned something, we ended up crashing a wedding in Casablanca. Forgive me if I’m not leaping up to pack a backpack just yet.”

“Hey, that was one time—”

“And the time before that was a goat market.”

“Okay, okay,” Gee grinned, holding up his hands in surrender. “But this time, we’re going in smart.”

Lorrisa gave him a wry smile, stretched lazily, then slid off the bed. “Alright, Indiana Jones, let’s hear the genius plan. Just let me grab another drink first.”

Kong clapped his tiny hands as if in applause, and for the briefest moment, the tension in the room eased—just three souls, tangled in a chase none of them fully understood, standing on the edge of the next step into chaos.

Gee tapped his pencil against the map, eyes flicking between scribbled notes and the jagged coastline drawn in faded ink.

“All right, here’s how I see it,” he said, glancing up as Lorrisa padded back from the minibar, glass refreshed, her dark hair still damp and curling softly at the ends. She raised an eyebrow as if to say *go on, professor*.

"We head to Mogadishu," Gee continued. "It's about three hours or more south—long drive, but it keeps us off the radar. Once we're there, we split up at the port. I'll work the docks, ask the fishermen if they've heard anything about the sea caves. You—" he pointed the pencil at her, "—you work the locals. The markets, the guesthouses, the little cafés. Someone's always seen something."

Lorrisa flopped onto the armchair, crossing her legs gracefully. "And what makes you think they'll tell me anything?"

He gave her a crooked grin. "Riss, have you *seen* you?"

She smirked. "Flattery's cheap, Gee."

"Works every time."

Kong squeaked from the fruit bowl, as if seconding the vote.

Lorrisa waved a dismissive hand. "Fine. But when you end up charming a group of Moroccan sailors into an impromptu drinking contest, don't come crying to me."

"I'll have you know, I've been working on my discipline." Gee flashed his best innocent face.

Lorrisa snorted into her drink. "Right. That's why you nearly got pickpocketed *twice* at the market yesterday."

"Details, details," he muttered, tracing a finger along the map again. "Anyway. Once we have a lead, we regroup. But we need to be ready to move fast. Sebastian's not going to sit around waiting for us to get our act together."

The humor faded slightly from Lorrisa's face. She set her glass down with a soft clink. "Tell me more about him."

Gee's jaw tightened. "I told you. Sebastian's Mogull's right hand. He's ex-military. Efficient. No conscience. He doesn't care who gets hurt as long as the pieces end up in Mogull's hands. And Mogull—" Gee shook his head. "—Mogull wants the whole damn tablet. For power, money, I don't even think he knows what the tablet can do. He just wants it because no one else has it."

Lorrisa's lips pressed into a thin line. For a beat, neither of them spoke.

Then, softly, she asked, "And Kong?"

Gee's expression softened. "We'll get him home. I promise."

Lorrisa took a deep breath, stood, and smoothed her blouse. “All right. We finish this drink, we rest one hour, and then we move.”

Gee leaned back in his chair, watching her with a flicker of admiration. “See? That’s the woman I remember.”

She shot him a dry look, picking up her glass again. “Don’t get sentimental, Gee. I’m still billing you for my plane ticket, this room, the clothes,.. everything.”

He grinned. “Worth every penny.” Lorrisa leaned back in her chair, swirling the amber liquid in her glass as she stared at the rings. On the table before her, the two ancient bands sat inches apart—until, as if driven by an unseen force, they suddenly slid together with a faint *clink*.

She let out a low whistle. “Still freaks me out every time.”

Kong, seated beside her with a large fruit bowl, chirped contentedly, stuffing chunks of melon into his mouth without a care in the world.

Gee didn’t look up from the spread of maps and old manuscripts covering the bed. “You should be freaked out. This is real power we’re messing with.”

Lorrisa set down her drink and nudged the rings apart again, watching them creep back together as though magnetized.

"You really believe this next place will have another piece?" she asked, her voice half-skeptical, half-hopeful.

Gee finally turned to face her, eyes sharp. "I don't believe—I *know*. The coordinates cross-reference with the Phoenician trade routes, and there's a record of a relic going missing around 300 BC. I've been chasing this lead for years."

Lorrisa raised an eyebrow. "And now you've got me and a stolen monkey along for the ride."

Gee smirked, folding up the map. "Best team I've ever had."

Kong gave an indignant grunt at being called a monkey and lobbed a piece of pineapple at Gee, who ducked just in time.

"Alright, alright!" Gee laughed. "An *ape*—a brilliant, food-obsessed, pain-in-my-ass ape."

Lorrisa watched the rings pull together again and sighed. "Where is this next lead taking us?"

Gee's smile faded. "Mogadishu."

She blinked. "Somalia? You're kidding."

"Nope. There's a warlord down there sitting on something he doesn't even understand. We get in, we get the piece, and we get out. Clean."

Lorrisa shook her head slowly. "Nothing about that place is clean. Especially now."

Gee's eyes darkened. "That's why we move fast. And quiet."

There was a long silence between them, broken only by the sound of Kong noisily slurping fruit juice.

Finally, Lorrisa stood and stretched, gazing out the hotel window at the busy city nightscape below. "You know... we could just let this go. Walk away. Sell what we have and disappear."

Gee joined her at the window, eyes tracing the lights. "And let someone else put the pieces together? Someone who won't hesitate to unleash whatever Solomon locked away? You've seen what those rings do—and that's just *two* of them."

Lorrisa didn't respond, her fingers unconsciously toying with the pendant around her neck. Deep down, she knew Gee was right. But the weight of it all felt heavier by the minute.

"We leave tomorrow at dawn," Gee said quietly. "Get some rest."

She nodded, though rest felt a million miles away.

As Kong curled up on the carpet with a satisfied grunt, Lorrisa sat back down, absently separating the rings once more... and watching, mesmerized, as they slid together again, as if destiny itself refused to let them part. The morning haze over Marrakesh clung to the rooftops as Lorrisa leaned against the hotel balcony, staring down at the pulsing city streets. The last of her coffee had gone cold, but she barely noticed, lost in thought. Every instinct screamed at her to get on a plane, a boat—*anything* to get them out of Morocco and far from Sebastian's reach.

But that wasn't an option.

Inside the room, Gee was on his burner phone again, hushed but urgent, flipping through a battered notebook as he spoke. Kong sprawled lazily across the bed, arms and legs spread out, occasionally batting at the rings on the nightstand like they were toys.

Lorrisa stepped back inside. "Any luck?"

Gee shook his head, covering the receiver. "Not yet. The main roads are being watched. Airports, too. If we make one wrong move—Sebastian's guys will be on us within the hour."

She sighed, glancing at Kong. "And we can't just leave *him* here."

Gee's eyes flicked to the ape. "Even if we could, he's as much a part of this as we are now. We go together."

Lorrisa rubbed her temples. "So… what's the plan? We walk?"

"Close," Gee said, ending his call. "I've got a guy who can get us a clean vehicle—off the books. No plates, no questions."

She exhaled sharply. "Right. Just two fugitives and a freaking ape driving across North Africa. Real subtle."

Gee gave her a tight smile. "Hey, it's worked so far."

Her eyes dropped to the rings—*their* rings. One had been in Gee's possession for years, stolen from Sebastian's dig site in a reckless act that started all this. The second, smaller but no less powerful, had come from the frail hands of the old woman Sebastian murdered in cold blood. The tragedy of it still sat heavy between them, even if neither said it out loud.

And now, those two pieces hummed with a silent magnetism, as though waiting to be joined with a third.

Lorrisa crossed her arms. “You’re still sure this next lead is solid?”

Gee picked up a folded piece of paper, the ink faded and worn. “According to the elder woman’s notes, there’s another piece hidden inland. The original trade routes trace it to an old stronghold—somewhere in the mountains, near the Algerian border. Not exactly easy terrain, but it’s our best shot.”

She shook her head, almost laughing. “You know, I didn’t sign up to be some knockoff Indiana Jones.”

Gee’s eyes twinkled. “You’re starting to look the part.”

Lorrisa glanced down at herself—jeans and a simple blouse—and frowned. He wasn’t wrong. Already, her outfit was changing piece by piece: the flat boots she’d swapped in that morning were sturdier, and a utility belt she’d borrowed from Gee’s gear bag now circled her waist. She hadn’t even realized how much she was adapting—until now.

She gave a dry chuckle. “Guess I’d better finish the look.”

Later that afternoon

They slipped through the maze of market stalls to a discreet corner shop, the kind that sold everything from climbing gear to counterfeit passports. Inside, the air was thick with the smell of leather and oil.

Lorrisa fingered a rack of fitted cargo pants, pausing at a rack of moisture-wicking shirts and breathable jackets. She held up a lightweight field hat, eyeing it critically, before tossing it into the growing pile. A holster. A blade. A compact first-aid kit. Bit by bit, the "city girl" look fell away, replaced by something leaner, harder, more prepared.

Gee was haggling at the counter for a portable GPS and water purification tablets when he glanced over at her haul. "Look at you," he teased. "Full-on tomb raider now."

She gave him a smirk. "If I'm going to run for my life, I'd rather be comfortable."

Kong, ever the helper, waddled over clutching a bundle of rope and dropped it proudly at her feet.

"Nice touch," she said, giving him a scratch behind the ear. "We might need that." The shopkeeper, gruff and weathered, handed over a slip of paper with an address scrawled in Arabic. "Your truck," he said. "Tomorrow, sunrise. Don't be late."

Gee folded the note and tucked it into his jacket. “We won’t.”

Back at the hotel

Lorrisa stood in front of the mirror, adjusting the straps on her new tactical vest. She slipped the field hat low over her eyes and studied herself. She hardly recognized the woman staring back—someone hardened by necessity, eyes sharper, shoulders squared.

She didn’t know when the change had started. But now? There was no turning back.

Kong curled up in the corner, eyes already drooping, while Gee spread out their updated map, tracing the route they’d be driving.

“Seventy-two hours to the border,” he said quietly. “If we’re lucky.”

Lorrisa crossed the room, fingers brushing the two rings, which vibrated faintly under her touch. “Let’s not count on luck.”

She met Gee’s gaze—resolute now—and gave a curt nod. “We move at dawn.”

Chapter 4

The sun was just beginning to rise as Gee and Lorrisa navigated the narrow, dusty backroads on foot, heading toward the outskirts of Marrakesh. The streets were quiet at this hour, save for the occasional street vendor setting up shop or a stray cat darting across the alleys.

They'd left Kong behind at the hotel—too conspicuous, too risky. He'd protested with a loud series of grunts and sulked on the bed, but Lorrisa had promised him fruit when they got back.

"Are you sure this guy's reliable?" Lorrisa asked, her eyes scanning every doorway and rooftop.

Gee, walking briskly beside her, nodded. "Used him twice before. He moves vehicles that don't officially exist. Bulletproof, cash-only, no questions."

They turned a corner, arriving at a rusted-out garage wedged between two crumbling buildings. The steel door was half-open, and a battered neon sign flickered above:

"Moura Imports."

Gee paused, frowning slightly. “He said to meet here at sunrise.”

Lorrisa crossed her arms. “So where is he?”

Before Gee could answer, a sharp female voice called from inside. “*Gee?*”

Both turned as a figure stepped into the light—a tall, striking young woman, no more than twenty-two, with sun-kissed skin, glossy black hair tied up messily, and piercing hazel eyes that locked onto Gee like a hawk spotting prey.

“Marta,” Gee breathed, scratching the back of his neck awkwardly. “Didn’t expect... you.”

She strode toward him with a feline grace, wiping her hands on a ragged cloth. Her fitted tank top and low-slung utility pants did nothing to hide her athletic figure. She smiled, slow and a little dangerous.

“My father’s in Tangier. Family business. *I’m* handling things today.”

Her eyes lingered on Gee a beat too long, full of something both teasing and proprietary.

Lorrisa raised an eyebrow, her gaze flicking between them. “And you two... know each other?”

Gee coughed lightly, avoiding her eyes. "We've worked together before. She, uh, helps her father out sometimes."

Marta tilted her head, smile deepening. "*Helps*... sure."

Lorrisa's lips tightened, just a fraction. "Right."

Marta finally seemed to notice her. "And you are...?"

"Lorrisa," she said smoothly, stepping forward, hand out. "Gee's... partner."

Marta shook her hand, firm grip, eyes glittering. "Partner. Of course."

The air between the three of them hummed with something unspoken. Gee cleared his throat loudly. "We're here for the truck. You have it?"

Marta gave him a slow once-over. "For *you*, Gee? Always."

She sauntered back into the garage, waving them to follow. Inside, the space was surprisingly well-kept—racks of tools, spare tires, and in the center, a rugged, sand-colored Toyota Land Cruiser, modified for off-road travel. Reinforced bumpers, extra fuel canisters, steel mesh over the windows—this was a beast built for rough country.

Lorrisa let out a low whistle. “This’ll do.”

Marta leaned against the hood, folding her arms. “Fresh oil, full tank, new tires. She’ll get you anywhere you need to go.” Her eyes flicked to Gee, her voice dropping. “*Anywhere.*”

Gee looked distinctly uncomfortable, scratching at his jaw and mumbling, “Looks great. Really solid work.”

Marta’s smirk widened. “Want to check under the hood, or… you trust me?”

Lorrisa, watching this little dance, stepped in smoothly. “We trust you. How much?”

Marta’s eyes didn’t leave Gee as she said, “For *him*? Discount rate.”

Gee shot a look at Lorrisa, almost pleading, but she just smiled sweetly. “We appreciate that.”

There was a moment of silence as Gee handed over a thick wad of cash, and Marta tucked it into her waistband without breaking eye contact.

“You two be careful,” Marta purred, brushing a bit of invisible dust off Gee’s sleeve, lingering just a second too long. “The roads out there aren’t safe. But… you know that.”

Gee cleared his throat, stepping back quickly. “Yeah. Thanks, Marta.”

Lorrisa’s smile was tight. “We’ll take good care of your truck.”

Marta’s eyes sparkled. “You’d better. Because I love riding my truck”

They climbed into the Land Cruiser, the tension following them like a shadow. As Gee fired up the engine and pulled out onto the road, Lorrisa stared straight ahead, silent.

Finally, after a beat too long, she said lightly, “She seems… nice.”

Gee winced. “It’s not like that. It’s nothing”

“Didn’t *look* like nothing,” Lorrisa said, a touch too casual.

Gee kept his eyes on the road, gripping the wheel a little tighter. “We got the truck, didn’t we?”

Lorrisa smirked, leaning back in her seat, boots propped up on the dash. “Yeah. We got the truck.”

But neither of them said anything for the next few miles, each lost in their own thoughts as the city slowly gave way to the endless, empty roads of the desert. The Land Cruiser rumbled along the cracked, dusty highway as the morning sun rose higher, casting long shadows across the barren landscape. They’d doubled back briefly to the hotel, where Kong had practically *vaulted* into the back seat, clutching a bag of fruit Lorrisa had bribed him with. Now, he lounged across the rear bench, feet propped up, peeling a banana with lazy satisfaction.

Lorrisa adjusted her field hat and squinted ahead. “So remind me again—what’s the plan if we hit a checkpoint?”

Gee, eyes locked on the road, sighed. “We don’t hit a checkpoint. That’s the plan.”

“Real comforting,” she muttered.

Kong let out a loud belch from the back, prompting Lorrisa to glance over her shoulder. “Nice. Real classy.”

Gee smirked. “He’s got manners. He just chooses not to use them.”

Kong responded by tossing a banana peel forward, which slapped against the dashboard and slid down onto Gee's lap.

"Hey!" Gee barked, swerving slightly. "Come on, man!"

Lorrisa laughed, shaking her head. "He's fitting right in."

They drove in silence for a few minutes, the thrum of the tires on cracked pavement filling the air. The desert stretched endlessly on both sides—orange dunes, scrubby patches of thornbush, and the occasional lonely goat herder in the distance.

Finally, Lorrisa broke the quiet, fiddling with the strap of her holster. "So... Marta."

Gee's grip tightened slightly on the wheel. "We're really doing this?"

She shrugged, tone casual but eyes sharp. "Just making conversation."

"She's... resourceful," Gee said carefully. "And yeah, maybe she's... *interested*. But nothing happened."

Lorrisa tilted her head, a teasing smile playing at her lips. "You sure? Looked like you were about to melt back there."

Kong, sensing the change in mood, let out a low "ooooh" from the back, covering his mouth in mock scandal.

"Don't *encourage* her," Gee muttered, glaring at Kong in the rearview mirror.

Lorrisa laughed, genuinely this time, and for a moment the tension between them cracked open, lighter and easier. "Relax, Gee. You're allowed to have... history."

Gee blew out a breath. "It's not even history. More like... an awkward footnote."

"Well," Lorrisa said, leaning back in her seat, "at least she gave us a hell of a truck."

Gee grinned despite himself. "That's true."

Kong suddenly scrambled upright, pointing out the window and chattering excitedly.

"What is it now?" Gee asked, slowing down a bit.

Kong pressed his face against the glass, eyes wide as they passed a herd of camels, lounging lazily near a roadside watering hole. One particularly fat camel stared directly back at Kong, chewing methodically.

Lorrisa burst out laughing. "It's like he's seeing his long-lost cousins."

Kong puffed up indignantly and gave her a playful smack on the shoulder, making her laugh harder.

Gee smiled, shaking his head. “This is going to be a *long* trip.”

They drove on, the landscape shifting gradually—desert dunes giving way to rockier, more rugged hills. The air inside the truck grew thick with heat and the smell of dust, fruit, and worn leather.

Lorrisa pulled out the battered map Gee had marked up earlier and traced their route with a finger. “You really think this next piece is out there? In the middle of nowhere?”

Gee’s voice softened a bit. “It’s not just about thinking anymore. I *feel* it. Those two rings we have—they’ve been... humming stronger ever since we crossed into this region. It’s like they know we’re getting closer.”

Lorrisa glanced at the rings resting in the glove box, their quiet weight pressing on her chest in ways she couldn’t explain. “What happens if we find all the pieces?”

Gee’s eyes stayed on the road, but his jaw tightened. “We pray we’re smart enough not to wake something we can’t put back to sleep.”

For a moment, the weight of that settled over them like a heavy blanket.

Then Kong farted loudly in the back seat, flapping a hand and making a face.

Lorrisa burst out laughing, swatting at the air. “Ugh! Oh my god, *Kong!*”

Gee coughed, rolling down his window. “Okay, new rule—he rides *on the roof* next time.”

Kong cackled, clearly pleased with himself.

Lorrisa wiped tears of laughter from her eyes. “Best road trip ever.”

Gee just shook his head, grinning as they barreled down the empty highway—three unlikely fugitives bound together by fate, ancient relics, and the kind of trouble you don’t walk away from unchanged. The sun dipped below the jagged horizon, bleeding orange and crimson across the sky as Gee eased the Land Cruiser off the main road and into a rocky outcrop sheltered by a cluster of acacia trees.

“This is as good a spot as any,” he muttered, killing the engine.

Lorrisa climbed out, stretching her sore legs, boots crunching against gravel. “Not exactly the Ritz.”

“Yeah, well,” Gee replied, popping open the back, “no check-in desk, but the stars are free.”

Kong leaped out, hooting with excitement, immediately snatching up dry twigs to start building a makeshift nest near the fire pit Gee was assembling.

They worked in quiet rhythm—Lorrisa laying out sleeping mats, Gee starting the fire with a flint striker, Kong gnawing loudly on a piece of mango. As night fell fully, the desert air turned sharp and cold. Shadows deepened around them, the vast emptiness of the landscape suddenly feeling heavier.

Lorrisa sat by the fire, hugging her knees. “We should be fine out here, right? No jackals… no snakes?”

Gee snorted, sipping water from his canteen. “Just bandits. But don’t worry, we’re in the clear.”

“*Great* pep talk,” she muttered, shivering as she pulled her jacket tighter.

Kong curled up close to the fire, eyes half-closed, his breathing steady. Gee spread out the map again, tracing their route with a finger by firelight.

"If we make good time tomorrow," he murmured, "we'll reach the edge of the mountain pass by nightfall."

Lorrisa watched him silently, eyes catching the faint glow of the rings—tucked safely in a cloth pouch by Gee's side.

"Do you ever think about what we're really chasing here?" she asked quietly. "What if it's not treasure? What if it's a curse?"

Gee didn't look up. "Treasure. Curse. Either way… it's power. And someone's going to claim it. Might as well be us."

She stared into the flames, uneasy.

The desert was silent in the deep hours of the night. Only the crackle of the dying fire and Kong's soft snores filled the void.

Until…

A *snap*.

Lorrisa's eyes flew open. She strained to listen, heart thudding. Another sound—a scuff of boots on gravel. She grabbed Gee's arm, shaking him awake just as a low voice barked from the shadows.

"*Don't move!*"

Flashlights snapped on, blinding and sharp. Shapes materialized—five, maybe six men, faces hidden beneath scarves, guns leveled. One of them yanked Gee roughly to his feet, shoving the barrel of an AK into his chest.

"Get up! Hands up!"

Kong screeched, bolting upright, Gee lunged to protect him, but two of the men rushed forward, clubbing him with the butt of a rifle, forcing him into submission.

"*No!*" Lorrisa shouted, stepping forward, but a bandit grabbed her from behind, wrenching her arms back cruelly.

"Search everything!" the leader barked.

Within seconds, their camp was in chaos—bags ripped open, gear scattered. One of the men found the pouch with the rings and held it up, shouting in Arabic.

The leader stalked over, snatching the pouch. He opened it, examining the contents with a greedy gleam in his eyes.

"These," he said in broken English, "are worth *much*."

Gee spat blood. "You don't know what you're messing with."

The bandit backhanded him hard. “I know treasure.”

Two of the others were already hotwiring the Land Cruiser, revving the engine. Kong was dragged toward the vehicle, his hands bound with rough rope.

“*Wait!*” Lorrisa screamed, struggling against her captor. “Take whatever you want—*leave him!*”

The bandit leader sneered. “He’s worth something too.”

The last thing Lorrisa saw before the dust kicked up was Kong’s terrified eyes, locked onto hers, and the rings disappearing into the bandit’s clenched fist.

The headlights of the stolen truck flared as it sped off into the night, the roar of the engine fading into silence.

Aftermath

The silence was deafening. Gee lay on his back, gasping, his lip split and one eye swelling shut. Lorrisa staggered to the fire pit, clutching her arms, shaking from adrenaline and rage.

“They… they took everything,” she whispered hoarsely. “The money. The rings. *Kong.*”

Gee sat up slowly, wiping blood from his mouth. “We’re still alive. That’s something.”

She rounded on him, eyes blazing. “That’s all you have to say?! They took *him,* Gee! And the rings! We are *done!*”

Gee’s jaw clenched, eyes glinting in the dim light. “We are *not* done.”

Lorrisa paced wildly, tears of frustration welling up. “We don’t even have a *ride!*”

He stood, wincing, but his voice was hard. “We’ll find another way. We *have* to.”

She collapsed onto a rock, burying her face in her hands. “We lost *everything.*”

Gee knelt beside her, placing a tentative hand on her shoulder. “Not everything.”

She looked up, eyes hollow.

Gee’s gaze was distant, cold fire in his veins now. “We know where they’re going. Bandits don’t steal something that valuable without selling it. We track them. We take it back.”

Lorrisa’s breath shuddered out. “And Kong?”

His jaw tightened. “Especially Kong.”

They sat there in the darkness, bruised and broken, staring at the empty road ahead. Somewhere out there, in the black void of desert night, their stolen future was slipping farther away.

But neither of them was ready to let it go. By dawn, they were already moving—on foot, sore, parched, and driven by sheer desperation. The bandits' tire tracks carved deep ruts in the sand, clear and easy to follow in the early morning light.

"They're heading east," Gee muttered, shielding his eyes from the rising sun. "Toward the next settlement."

Lorrisa's voice was raw. "How far?"

"Four, maybe five miles. If they stop there to trade... we've got a shot."

The desert was merciless, the heat rising fast, but they pressed on. Every step was fueled by images of Kong—tied up, scared—and the rings, shimmering in their stolen captors' filthy hands.

After hours of trudging, the outline of a small village emerged on the horizon. Mud-brick huts, a few ragged awnings, and a central square where locals gathered, selling goods and haggling in sharp bursts of Arabic.

"They'll be here," Gee said quietly, scanning the cluster of battered vehicles and market stalls. "This is the nearest place to offload stolen goods."

Lorrisa pulled her hat down low, eyes sharp. "Let's make this fast."

They split up, moving cautiously through the narrow alleys and across the square. Gee flagged down a wiry old man near a food stall and slipped him a few remaining coins for information.

"Bandits?" the man rasped, eyes narrowing. "Came at sunrise. Sold livestock, supplies. Paid well. But... not here long."

Gee leaned in, voice low. "Where did they go?"

The man pointed north, toward the rocky hills. "To the *waste lands.* Hiding there now."

Lorrisa reappeared at Gee's side. "They're close. We can catch them."

Gee's eyes flicked to the distant hills. "We need weapons."

They scoured the market until they found a **small arms dealer**, an old man seated behind a wooden stall covered in dusty relics—rusted revolvers, battered shotguns, and chipped knives. His hawkish eyes watched them carefully as they approached.

"We need weapons," Gee said, urgent.

The man squinted. “Money?”

Gee grimaced. “No cash. But we’ll pay you back double.”

The old man’s eyes hardened. “No money, no guns.”

Lorrisa stepped forward, desperate. “Listen—we’re chasing *bandits*. They robbed us blind. If we don’t move now, they disappear forever.”

The dealer shook his head, unimpressed. “Your problem. Not mine.”

A small crowd had started to gather, curious. One man, tall and broad-shouldered with a scruffy beard, stepped closer, overhearing. He spoke quickly to the arms dealer in Arabic, gesturing between himself and Gee.

“What’s he saying?” Lorrisa whispered.

Gee listened, jaw tightening. “He says… he’ll vouch for us. If we bring *him* along.”

The big man stepped forward, chest out, thumping a hand against his heart. “My name is Hamid. You borrow, I come. If you fail, I pay.”

Lorrisa blinked. “That’s crazy. Why would you—?”

Hamid grinned, flashing a row of white teeth. "I like the fight."

The old dealer grumbled but relented, shoving a battered shotgun and two revolvers across the table. "Three weapons. Six rounds each. No more."

Hamid grabbed the shotgun, loading shells with practiced ease. "We go now."

Gee nodded, gripping one of the pistols and tucking it into his waistband. "Deal."

Lorrisa took the other revolver, checking the cylinder with shaking fingers. "You sure about this?" she muttered to Gee.

He met her gaze, eyes dark and cold. "No choice."

Hamid slapped Gee's shoulder. "You owe me now, friend. Big debt."

"We pay it," Gee said grimly.

Hamid laughed, already striding toward the edge of the village. "We *better.*"

With Hamid leading the way, the three of them set off toward the hills, weapons tucked close, eyes scanning every dune and ridge. The terrain grew rougher, jagged stones and deep ravines swallowing the horizon.

"They'll be hiding in one of the old mine shafts," Hamid said, eyes sharp as he moved quickly over the rocky ground. "We catch them *before dark,* or they vanish."

Gee gritted his teeth, scanning the skyline. "Then we don't stop."

Lorrisa's breath was ragged, boots crunching over loose stones. "We're coming, Kong," she whispered under her breath, gripping her pistol tighter.

They moved deeper into the wilderness—three unlikely allies on a mission nobody thought they could pull off—driven by desperation, loyalty, and the burning need to reclaim what was stolen.

And ahead of them, hidden in the shadows of the desert hills, the bandits waited—unaware that the hunters were now coming for *them.*

The sun was brutal now, hanging high and merciless as they clambered over a rise and looked down into a craggy valley—a maze of gullies and caves, scorched dry and scattered with the bones of old mining equipment.

"They'll be here," Hamid said, pointing with his shotgun. "This place—good cover, easy escape."

Gee wiped sweat from his brow, squinting at the jumble of rocks and shadows below. "Yeah. Perfect for an ambush."

They crouched behind a boulder, catching their breath. The air was stifling, the silence thick except for the occasional cry of a hawk circling overhead.

Lorrisa slid down next to Gee, lowering her voice. "You trust this guy?"

Gee's eyes flicked toward Hamid, who stood a few feet away, scanning the horizon like a sentinel. "Trust? No. But we need him."

She frowned, absently fingering the grip of her revolver. "He's got skin in the game now, sure, but... he doesn't know what we're really after. The rings. Kong. All of it."

Gee nodded grimly. "We keep it that way. To him, we're just desperate tourists chasing stolen gear. No reason to complicate that."

Lorrisa's gaze lingered on Hamid's broad back, her voice low and tense. "We could use him, though. He knows the land. He knows *them*."

Gee exhaled slowly, eyes narrowing. "Exactly. He goes in first—makes contact, distracts, gets us a read on numbers and weapons. We move while they're looking at him."

Lorrisa bit her lip, hesitant. "It's risky. They could shoot him on sight."

Gee's expression hardened. "We don't have a choice. We're outgunned, outnumbered, and Kong's life is on the line."

She studied his face for a long beat, then nodded. "Alright. But if he tries anything..."

"I'm watching," Gee said firmly.

They crept down the ridge, sticking to the shadows, boots crunching softly over loose stones. Hamid crouched at the edge of a narrow ledge, peering down into a cavern-like entrance flanked by rusted metal beams.

He held up two fingers, then pointed left—then three more fingers, pointing right.

"Five men," Gee whispered, translating. "Split across both entrances."

Lorrisa's stomach clenched. "Do we know where they're keeping Kong?"

Hamid shook his head but whispered, "They keep animals and goods in the lower shaft. Likely there."

Gee rubbed his jaw, thinking fast. "We need a diversion."

Hamid grinned. "I go loud. Get their attention. You two sneak around back."

Lorrisa hesitated, glancing between them. "You sure about this?"

Hamid chambered a round in his shotgun with a smirk. "I *like* the fight, remember?"

Gee gave a tight nod. "Don't get killed."

Hamid's smile faded slightly. "Not the plan."

They crouched behind a rocky outcrop, nerves buzzing like live wires. Hamid moved into position, his figure shrinking as he approached the main cave entrance, weapon raised.

Lorrisa leaned close to Gee, her voice a whisper. "We pull this off, what then? We've got one truck, no cash, and a warlord's treasure. You think we just... *drive off* into the sunset?"

Gee's eyes stayed locked on Hamid's retreating form. "We get Kong back. We get the rings. We survive. After that... we figure it out."

She stared at him, heart pounding. "You really think we'll make it out alive?"

Gee's jaw clenched. "We have to."

The stillness around them seemed to thicken, the air hanging heavy with the promise of violence. Down below, Hamid's voice rang out, loud and sharp—challenging, taunting. The shouts of the bandits answered, chaotic and rising.

"Here we go," Gee whispered.

He grabbed Lorrisa's hand for half a second—quick, fierce—then nodded toward the far side of the cave. "Stay sharp. We move *now.*"

Together, they slipped into the shadows, circling around the rocky flank as the first shots echoed out across the desert, the fight for Kong—and everything else—about to begin.

Lorrisa pressed herself flat against the rock wall, breath shallow, every sense on edge. She'd slipped around the back of the bandits' camp while Hamid's shotgun blasts echoed like thunder through the canyon. Dust rose in thick clouds, and angry voices bounced off the stone.

She peered through a crack in the rocks, scanning frantically. The camp was more organized than she'd expected—tents pitched in a rough semicircle, crates and weapons stacked in haphazard piles. A rusted chain-link fence sectioned off a pen near the cave's mouth.

Her heart clenched.

There—inside the pen, huddled and tied, was Kong. His dark eyes were wild with fear and fury, rope biting into his wrists and ankles. Two bandits stood guard nearby, one lazily flipping a cigarette between his fingers, the other scanning the perimeter with a cheap pair of binoculars.

Lorrisa ducked back, heart hammering. Got him. She fumbled for the tiny radio clipped to her belt, pressing the talk button. "Gee, I found him. Kong's—"

But static answered her. No reply.

She hissed in frustration, adjusting the frequency, pressing again. "Gee? Come in—"

Still nothing.

Her gut twisted.

Gee crept along the eastern ridge, eyes locked on the commotion ahead. Hamid's wild assault was working—the bandits were pouring out of the main entrance, barking orders and returning fire. Gee edged closer, gun raised, scanning for a clear path toward the tents.

Then—footsteps. Fast, close.

Before he could react, a hand slammed onto his shoulder, wrenching him backward. A bandit, face covered in a filthy scarf, jammed the barrel of his rifle into Gee's ribs and barked something in Arabic, forcing him down the slope.

"Alright, alright!" Gee snapped, hands up, stumbling as the man shoved him roughly toward the heart of the camp. His mind raced—*Where's Lorrisa? Where's Hamid?*

The bandit dragged him, shouting for backup, as two more men turned from their posts near the supply crates.

Then, from the corner of Gee's eye, a *blur of movement.*

Hamid exploded out of nowhere—silent, fast, lethal. He grabbed the bandit by the back of the neck, yanked him around in a flash, and with a sickening *crack,* snapped the man's neck like a twig.

The bandit crumpled to the dirt, lifeless.

Gee staggered back, wide-eyed, adrenaline surging.

Hamid stood over the body, chest heaving, that same wild grin spreading across his face. He looked at Gee, almost childlike with excitement.

"I *like* fight," Hamid said, panting, his eyes bright with savage glee.

Gee, still catching his breath, stared at him—half grateful, half horrified. "Yeah," he muttered, voice hoarse, "I'm getting that."

Hamid grabbed Gee's arm and yanked him upright. "We keep moving. More to kill."

Gee nodded slowly, eyes flicking down to the bandit's lifeless form, then up to Hamid's blood-smeared hands. A shiver ran down his spine—not from fear of the bandits, but from the raw, ruthless force Hamid had just unleashed.

He steadied his breath, forcing himself to focus. "We need to regroup. Lorrisa's close. And she's found Kong."

Hamid's grin widened. "Good. We finish soon."

Gee gripped his pistol tighter, his nerves thrumming. The bandits were deadly—but right now, so was their ally.

And Gee couldn't shake the feeling that Hamid's help came with its own kind of danger.

Lorrisa pressed her back against the rock wall, heart hammering in her chest. She'd seen Gee from a distance—dragged like a prize toward the main camp—and her stomach had twisted when the bandit's body suddenly dropped like dead weight.

Hamid.

She recognized his hulking shape instantly as he stepped into view, looming over the fallen man, that unsettling grin stretched across his face like a victory banner.

"What the hell..." she whispered, eyes narrowing.

She wanted to breathe in relief—Gee was alive—but something in the way Hamid moved, so casual, so hungry for violence, made her stomach knot tighter. Gee looked rattled too, standing a little too still, gripping his pistol like it was the only thing tethering him to reality.

Lorrisa crouched lower, inching around the outcrop until she had a clearer view of the camp.

The chaos was escalating. Bandits were shouting from every direction, scrambling to regroup after Hamid's brutal assault. A few had started sweeping back toward the rear, dangerously close to Kong's pen. One of them pointed frantically toward the spot where Hamid had struck, barking orders in rapid Arabic.

Lorrisa cursed under her breath. They're tightening up. We're losing the window.

Her eyes flicked to Kong. The ape was thrashing now, pulling against his bindings, wild with fear. The guards at his pen were visibly spooked, guns drawn but hesitating—no one wanted to be the first to get too close.

She gripped her radio again, whispering into it, "Gee, I can see you. Kong's still in the pen, but they're closing in fast. We have to move *now.*"

Static. Then a crackle—just enough to know her message *might* have gone through.

She bit her lip, weighing her options. Running straight in would get her shot. Hanging back meant they might lose Kong—and Gee too, if Hamid went off-script again.

Her pulse spiked. Think. Think fast.

Across the camp, she saw Gee glance her way—just a flicker of recognition as his eyes swept the rocks—and she realized he knew she was close. Hamid was already prowling forward, shotgun raised, eyes scanning for his next kill, restless and eager.

"Damn it," Lorrisa hissed.

She could feel it now—everything teetering on a knife's edge. One wrong move, one crack of gunfire, and it would all come crashing down.

She slid her pistol from its holster, checked the cylinder—six rounds—and closed her eyes for half a second.

"Alright," she whispered. "Showtime."

Hamid crouched next to Gee, peering around a pile of crates. His grin was shark-like now, eyes glittering with a fevered edge. "We go fast," he hissed. "Kill more. Take back the monkey."

Gee glanced sidelong at him, pulse racing. "Yeah... but smart. We move *smart,* Hamid."

Hamid's eyes flared with impatience. "Smart is *slow*. I like *fast*."

Gee’s gut twisted. He could feel the coiled spring inside Hamid, the danger of an ally who *loved* this fight a little too much. It made the bandits seem like a lesser threat by comparison.

“Just... wait for my signal,” Gee muttered, ducking lower behind the crates, eyes scanning the far rocks where he *knew* Lorrisa had to be watching.

“We wait *too long,*” Hamid growled, his fingers flexing around the shotgun grip. “They run. We lose.”

Gee swallowed hard. He was right—but the thought of Hamid unleashed without a leash made his blood run cold.

In the distance, another shot rang out—someone panicking, firing blind into the rocks—and the whole camp tensed again, every gun shifting, every shout rising.

The clock was ticking.

And Gee knew: whatever happened next, it was going to be messy.

Lorrisa saw it—the split-second shift when the bandits' attention zeroed in on the crates where Gee and Hamid had been hiding. The danger was closing fast, and she didn’t have time to wait.

She broke cover in a sprint, pistol raised. "*HEY! OVER HERE!*"

Her shots rang out—*pop-pop-pop*—aiming at the two guards by Kong's pen. One cried out, dropping his rifle and grabbing his arm; the other ducked behind a crate, yelling in alarm.

Kong, tiny and frantic, was tied to the side of the pen—his small body squirming against the ropes, eyes wide and wild as he shrieked in terror.

"I'M COMING!" Lorrisa shouted, skidding to her knees by the cage.

From the crates, Gee heard the gunfire and snapped into action. "MOVE!" he shouted at Hamid, pushing forward as bullets kicked up dirt and debris around them.

Hamid's shotgun roared—*BOOM!*—blowing one bandit off his feet. Laughing manically, he rushed the next cluster of men, reloading with swift, brutal efficiency. "I LIKE FIGHT!" he bellowed, eyes gleaming.

Gee flanked wide, weaving between supply crates, his revolver barking out tight, controlled shots. He clipped one bandit in the shoulder and dove for cover as another returned fire.

At the pen, Lorrisa fought with the knot binding Kong's tiny wrists, her fingers shaking. "Hold still, hold still—dammit—"

Kong squealed, eyes locked on her, shaking uncontrollably as she finally yanked the rope free. He sprang into her arms, clutching her shirt with tiny fists, trembling but safe.

"Got you," she gasped, wrapping him tight against her chest.

"LORRISA! MOVE!" Gee's voice boomed across the chaos.

She looked up—Gee was waving frantically, pointing toward a battered pickup truck parked at the edge of the camp. "GO NOW!"

Lorrisa cradled Kong close, bolting toward the truck as bullets hissed past. Gee met her halfway, grabbing her arm to steady her as they both sprinted the last few yards.

Hamid barreled in after them, shotgun smoking, blood streaked across his knuckles. He hauled himself into the bed of the truck, slamming his palm down. “DRIVE!”

Gee dove behind the wheel, wrenching the door shut as Lorrisa scrambled in beside him, clutching Kong like he was made of glass. “I got him—I got him—he’s okay!”

Gee fired up the engine, tires shrieking as the truck lurched forward in a cloud of dust. Shouts and gunfire erupted behind them, but they were already speeding away, rattling over rocks and dirt, the camp shrinking in the rearview mirror.

Hamid whooped from the truck bed, banging on the roof with glee. “GOOD FIGHT!”

Gee’s knuckles were white on the steering wheel, eyes flicking between the road and the mirror. “Everyone okay?”

Lorrisa looked down at Kong—wide-eyed, shaking, but alive—then met Gee’s eyes with a fierce nod. “We’ve got him. We’ve got the rings.”

Kong squeaked softly and uncurled one tiny fist—revealing the cloth pouch with the rings still clutched tight.

Gee let out a shaky breath, smiling despite himself. "That little bastard's tougher than he looks."

Hamid pounded the roof again, laughing. "More fight next?"

Gee groaned, eyes fixed ahead. "Let's *hope not.*"

They roared across the desert, bruised and breathless but together again—Kong safe in Lorrisa's arms, the rings back in their hands, and the horizon wide open before them.

For now, they'd won.

The truck rattled along a winding dirt path, the engine groaning as Gee guided it into the shadow of a craggy ridge. He finally killed the ignition, the sudden silence slamming down around them like a hammer.

Lorrisa was still cradling Kong, whispering soothing nonsense as he trembled in her lap, tiny fists gripping her jacket.

Hamid leapt down from the truck bed, stretching with a wide grin. "*Good fight,*" he said, wiping sweat and dirt from his face. "We make good team."

Gee stepped out of the driver's seat, pacing, his fists clenching and unclenching as adrenaline faded. "Yeah. Great. Except we didn't *finish.*"

Lorrisa's head snapped up, eyes blazing. "We *did* finish. We got Kong. We're alive. That's the win, Gee."

Gee spun toward her, eyes sharp, frustration breaking through. "The *rings,* Lorrisa. They still have the rings."

She stood, still holding Kong tight. "I don't care about the damn rings! We almost *died*. Kong almost died. This has gone far enough."

Gee shook his head, pacing again. "No. You don't get it. Those rings—what they can do—if Sebastian's people get their hands on them, it's game over. For all of us."

Lorrisa's voice cracked, raw with exhaustion and anger. "I don't care! I'm not watching that little guy get dragged into another firefight. We're done."

Hamid, leaning casually against the truck, cleaned his shotgun with a rag and smirked. "I say we go back. More fight, more fun." He looked up, eyes gleaming. "But this time... I want money."

Gee frowned, rubbing his temple. "We don't *have* money, Hamid."

Hamid shrugged, unbothered. “No money, no more fight. You owe me already.”

The standoff stretched, thick with tension. Lorrisa stared down at Kong, then back up at Gee, her jaw tight. She stepped closer to Hamid, her voice softer now, almost teasing.

“Hamid... please, I can’t go with you. Watch over Gee for me? Keep him safe?”

Hamid blinked, caught slightly off guard. His grin faltered just a bit as he straightened, eyes narrowing in mock suspicion. “*Pretty lady* asks... hmm.”

He glanced at Gee, then back at Lorrisa, clearly weighing his options.

“Alright,” he said finally, grinning wide again. “For *you,* pretty lady, I watch him. No money this time.”

Gee let out a breath, half relief, half wariness. “We’re still going back.”

Lorrisa shook her head, stepping away, her voice tired but firm. “You’re making a mistake.”

Gee met her eyes, quiet and resolute. “It’s a mistake we can’t afford *not* to make.”

She looked at Kong—small, fragile, clinging to her—and said nothing more, simply turning away as Gee and Hamid began reloading their weapons. They worked in silence, the sky darkening to a deep bruised purple as Gee and Hamid loaded extra shells and checked the weapons they'd scavenged earlier. The tension was thick but unspoken now—everything had been said.

Lorrisa sat on the edge of the dirt road, arms wrapped around Kong, who clung to her chest, his tiny body pressed tight as if refusing to let her go again. She stared straight ahead, eyes hollow, watching the horizon without really seeing it.

Gee knelt down beside a crate, stuffing a last handful of ammo into his pocket, glancing her way more than once, as if waiting for her to say something. But she didn't.

Finally, he stood and walked over, holding out a pistol.

"Here," he said, voice low, tired. "Just in case. Until I get back."

Lorrisa looked at it without moving.

Gee hesitated, then gently pressed it into her hand, wrapping her fingers around the grip. "If… if something happens to me, you'll need it."

She closed her fingers loosely around the cold metal, still not looking at him. No reaction. No words. Kong's tiny arms clutched her tighter, his dark eyes watching Gee warily from beneath Lorrisa's chin.

Gee swallowed hard, searching her face for anything—anger, fear, regret—but there was nothing. Just that quiet, unreadable mask.

"I'll be back," he said softly, more to himself than to her.

She didn't answer.

He lingered one second longer, then turned and walked back to the truck where Hamid was already waiting behind the wheel, shotgun across his lap.

Hamid flashed a grin as Gee climbed in. "We get rings now, yes?"

Gee glanced back once, catching one last glimpse of Lorrisa and Kong framed by the fading light. Lorrisa sat motionless, the pistol resting limply in her lap, staring out across the empty road.

"Yeah," Gee muttered, eyes dark. "Let's finish it."

The truck roared to life, the tires spitting dust and gravel as they peeled away, disappearing over the ridge within minutes.

The sound of the engine faded into nothing, swallowed by the desert's vast silence.

For a long time, Lorrisa didn't move.

Kong shifted in her lap, nestling deeper against her chest, his breathing uneven, still shaken from the day's chaos.

She stared at the empty horizon, fingers loose around the pistol. Her jaw tightened slightly, but her eyes stayed dry, her face unreadable, as if she were holding back a tide of thought too deep to surface.

Minutes passed. The sky dimmed. The silence grew heavier.

Finally, with a slow breath, she stood—Kong still wrapped around her like a second skin—and brushed the dust from her pants. She slipped the pistol into her waistband, adjusted Kong on her hip, and without a word, turned toward the direction of the village.

She started walking, her boots crunching softly in the dirt, each step steady and sure, never looking back.

The desert stretched out before her—wide, empty, and waiting. The truck's headlights cut through the creeping dark, casting long, shaky beams across the uneven ground as they barreled back toward the bandit camp. Gee sat stiffly in the passenger seat, one hand gripping the door handle, the other resting on his pistol.

Beside him, Hamid was humming—a low, tuneless rumble—his eyes gleaming with excitement as he guided the truck across the rough track, wheels bouncing over rocks and ruts.

“You’re way too calm for this,” Gee muttered, breaking the silence.

Hamid grinned without looking over. “You worry too much. We have plan now.”

Gee’s jaw clenched. “Yeah. Plan.”

He stared out the window, the night racing by in jagged streaks of shadow and dust. His mind was a storm—images of Lorrisa’s face, blank and closed off; Kong’s trembling little body; the rings, glowing faintly with a promise of something bigger than all of them.

“This isn’t just about treasure,” Gee said quietly, more to himself than to Hamid. “Those rings—they’re… they’re part of something ancient. Dangerous.”

Hamid shrugged, eyes on the dark road ahead. “Treasure, curse… same thing. We take it. We win.”

Gee let out a slow, tense breath, staring down at his lap. “We win… or we die.”

Hamid barked a short laugh, slapping the wheel. “*Good fight*, either way.”

The camp lights came into view—dim flickers on the horizon, ghostly and small. Gee's stomach twisted.

"Kill the lights," he ordered sharply.

Hamid grinned and flicked them off, plunging them into near-blackness, the stars winking coldly overhead.

They coasted the last stretch in silence, parking behind a jagged rock formation a few hundred meters from the camp's perimeter. Both men climbed out, crouching low, the air sharp and dry around them.

Gee scanned the area through a small pair of binoculars, jaw tight. "Looks like they've doubled the guard. They're spooked."

Hamid loaded his shotgun with a quiet click, eyes bright. "Good. More to kill."

Gee lowered the binoculars, frowning. "Hamid... we need *stealth* this time. No crazy rush. Get in, get the rings, get out."

Hamid's grin widened. "Stealth first. Then kill."

Gee groaned softly, rubbing his temple. "Why do I feel like that's the *wrong* order?"

Hamid just laughed, slinging the shotgun over his shoulder. "Come, my friend. Rings are waiting."

Together, they moved out—two shadows against the dark, slipping down toward the camp like wolves on the hunt.

The bandit camp still smoldered with tension. Fires burned lower now, flickering like dying embers across the dark sand. The chaos from earlier had left the camp disordered—supplies overturned, vehicles half-abandoned, wounded men sprawled under tarps or leaning groggily against crates. Those who could still walk were patrolling in twos, rifles slung carelessly, nerves visibly frayed.

Gee crouched behind a stack of rusted fuel drums, his breathing slow and controlled. Hamid knelt beside him, shotgun resting across his thighs like a loyal dog awaiting command.

"Split up," Gee whispered. "You check the far tents. Quiet. Don't shoot unless you have to."

Hamid nodded once, slipping into the darkness like a shadow, unnervingly silent for a man of his size.

Gee waited three full breaths before he moved, skirting between crates and broken vehicles, every step measured. His eyes swept every corner, every flicker of movement. He didn't know where the rings were—only that they *had* to be here.

They were too valuable to abandon. Too ancient to understand.

He crept past two bandits arguing softly in Arabic over a torn map, then ducked into a shadowed tent lined with hanging fabrics and weapon crates.

Nothing.

He pushed deeper into the camp, slipping past the edge of the cave structure they'd fought near earlier. An open crate of cigarettes and stolen jewelry sat near a barrel fire. A glint of brass caught his eye, but it was only an old pendant tangled in a broken chain.

Every minute felt like five.

Gee's legs ached, but he pressed on—past a pair of sleeping guards, through a collapsed lean-to, into a central supply tent that had been partially burned. The heat still radiated off the metal beams.

His hand rested on the edge of a splintered table as he paused to catch his breath. His thoughts started to unravel.

Maybe Lorrisa was right.

Maybe this was too much—too big, too cursed. The rings, the deaths, the chase. It started with a dig site and a half-truth. And now? People were dying. A monkey was kidnapped. He hadn't even slept in two days.

He leaned against the frame of the tent, sweat dripping down his brow.

What the hell am I even doing here?

Then—he saw it.

Half-buried beneath a collapsed stack of canvas and an old rifle sling, a small leather pouch, cinched at the top, faintly humming.

He froze. The hairs on his arms lifted.

"...no way," he whispered.

He reached down, slowly, carefully—heart thudding—and picked it up.

The weight was familiar. Buzzing, like pressure behind his eyes.

He opened the pouch and stared down.

The rings!

Still intact. Still glowing faintly in the moonlight.

His breath caught. He clutched the pouch to his chest like it might vanish, heart hammering with a cocktail of disbelief, relief, and fear.

We still have a chance.

Gee tucked the pouch deep into his inner jacket pocket, fingers lingering for a second longer than necessary on the cool, ancient rings. He swallowed hard, forcing himself to focus.

Not over yet.

He moved quickly, scanning the remains of the camp for anything useful. He spotted a battered strongbox near the edge of a canvas tent and pried it open, rifling through until he found a few small trinkets—gold coins, a chipped silver pendant, a heavy ruby brooch. Enough to pay Hamid's due... and something extra for the old arms dealer back in the village.

He stuffed them into his pack, every nerve in his body still humming, and started toward the ridge, weaving through the shadows with smooth, measured steps.

Halfway to the rocks, a figure dropped down beside him from the dark.

Hamid.

Gee startled, hand darting to his pistol, but relaxed when he saw the man's huge grin—face streaked with dirt, clothes bulging with loot.

Hamid slapped his chest proudly, his pockets jingling with every move. "*Got my money now,*" he said with a wide grin, holding up a fistful of gold chains and rings. "You good. Now we find rings."

Gee shook his head, catching his breath. "We *have* the rings. I found them."

Hamid blinked, genuinely surprised, then grinned wider. "Hah! Very good. We *win*. Time to go, yes?"

"Yeah," Gee muttered, gripping Hamid's arm briefly. "Let's *get the hell out of here.*"

They moved fast, climbing up the ridge under cover of darkness, keeping low as the camp slowly shrank behind them.

But then—Gee froze.

"Wait."

Hamid ducked behind a boulder, squinting down where Gee was staring.

Below, three vehicles rumbled to life—headlights flaring as they rolled out of camp, engines roaring into the night. First a battered pickup, then a rusted van, and last *a jeep, armed with a .50 caliber M2 Browning machine gun,* its barrel gleaming under the moonlight as it swept side to side, manned and ready.

Hamid whistled low. “They hunt someone.”

Gee’s stomach dropped, ice water rushing through his veins. His breath hitched, his brain snapping together the pieces with brutal clarity.

Lorrisa.

She was still out there—on foot, vulnerable, between them and the village.

“Oh, no,” Gee whispered, eyes locked on the convoy as it sped toward the horizon. His heart pounded harder than it had all night.

“They’re not going after us,” he said hoarsely. “They’re going after *her.*”

Hamid straightened, eyes gleaming, shotgun resting across his broad shoulders. “More fight.”

Gee’s fists clenched, his mind racing. “Damn it—Lorrisa’s out there alone.”

He looked at the desert stretching between them and the distant lights of the village, realizing with icy dread how fast those trucks were moving.

"No time," Gee muttered, gripping Hamid's arm. "We've got to move *now.*"

Hamid grinned, already checking his ammo. "*Good.* I was bored."

Gee's face was set, eyes blazing. "Let's *go.*"

Without another word, they scrambled down the rocky slope, racing to their vehicle, every second feeling like a lifetime as the bandits' engines roared farther into the dark—straight toward Lorrisa.

Gee jammed the keys into the ignition, and the engine roared to life as Hamid leapt into the passenger seat, shotgun cradled across his lap. Gravel and dust sprayed in all directions as Gee slammed the truck into gear, spinning the wheel hard and barreling down the ridge.

"Faster!" Hamid barked, eyes locked on the distant taillights ahead.

"I *know!*" Gee snapped, teeth clenched, foot pressed to the floor.

The truck rattled and bounced over rocks and scrub, the suspension groaning in protest. Ahead, the convoy of bandits tore through the dark—three vehicles, weaving and jostling, with the machine-gun jeep trailing like a deadly viper at the rear.

Gee's breath came ragged, every nerve screaming. The .50 caliber M2 glinted under the moonlight, swiveling, hunting.

"We can't let them reach her," Gee growled, eyes locked on the moving targets.

Hamid chambered a shell with a grin. "We stop jeep first. Big gun—big problem."

The gap shrank fast. Dust clouds boiled around them as Gee swerved hard, the truck fishtailing before regaining traction. The bandits were shouting now, spotting their pursuers in the rearview.

Muzzle flashes burst from the jeep, and a trail of glowing tracers ripped through the night, shredding the dirt just meters from their tires.

"¡Mierda!" Gee jerked the wheel, narrowly avoiding a blast that sent gravel exploding upward.

Hamid cackled wildly, leaning out the window, shotgun booming. One shot shattered the rear window of the van ahead, sending shards flying.

Gee clenched his jaw, eyes flicking between the road and Hamid. "You're *enjoying* this way too much!"

"Good fight!" Hamid whooped, racking the shotgun again. "Keep close!"

The jeep's gunner adjusted, spraying another burst. Bullets punched through the hood, tearing jagged holes as Gee gritted his teeth and floored it.

"Come on, you bastard," Gee hissed, drawing his pistol. He leaned out just enough to fire three quick shots—pinging harmlessly off the jeep's armor.

"We need to hit the tires!" Gee shouted.

Hamid nodded, aiming low. Another blast from his shotgun, and this time the rear left tire of the van shredded, rubber flapping wildly as the van skidded sideways, spinning out in a cloud of dust and slamming into a boulder.

"One down!" Hamid roared.

The pickup ahead veered off the road, trying to flank them. The gunner on the jeep opened up again, and a hail of lead slammed into their windshield—cracks spiderwebbing across the glass.

"HAMID!" Gee yelled, gripping the wheel tight as he swerved. The pickup screeched closer, its driver leaning out with an AK, spraying rounds wildly.

Hamid fired back, and the shotgun's blast tore through the windshield, sending the shooter flipping backward. The pickup jerked, hit a rock, and rolled, flipping twice before slamming to a stop.

"YES!" Hamid whooped, reloading with lightning speed.

But the jeep remained, relentless and deadly.

Suddenly, the machine gun burst again, and a round tore through the side of Gee's truck, punching through the wheel well. The tire blew out, jerking the whole vehicle sideways.

"Hold on!" Gee bellowed as he fought the wheel, skidding through the dirt and barely keeping control.

"Closer!" Hamid yelled. "We take him now!"

Gee's eyes blazed. He slammed the pedal down, swerving in a wide arc to ram the jeep.

" YOU CRAZY?!" Hamid laughed, bracing himself as the distance closed.

"YEAH!" Gee shouted back.

The front of their truck *slammed into the side of the jeep,* metal crunching, the force nearly flipping both vehicles. The gunner on the .50 lost his balance, tumbling off the back as his machine gun tipped over with a shriek of twisting steel.

"YES!" Gee yelled, pistol drawn. He emptied his clip into the jeep's engine block at point-blank, sparks flying as the rounds ripped through.

Hamid jumped down, tossing something small—a grenade he'd picked off a dead bandit.

"BACK!" he shouted.

Gee barely had time to dive as Hamid hurled it into the shattered remains of the jeep. A heartbeat later—

BOOM!

The explosion tore the night apart—fire and shrapnel roaring skyward as the jeep erupted in a fireball, the force blasting them both off their feet. Gee hit the ground hard, ears ringing, dirt in his mouth, chest heaving.

Groaning, Gee dragged himself upright, blood trickling from a gash on his forehead. Hamid stood too, battered but grinning, wiping soot from his face.

“We win,” Hamid rasped, clapping Gee’s shoulder.

Gee staggered to the smoldering wreck, eyes darting, making sure the jeep was well and truly finished. Flames licked at the twisted metal, thick black smoke rising into the stars.

“Yeah,” Gee panted. “We won.”

Both men limped back to their battered truck, its windshield shattered, its body riddled with bullet holes—but still running.

Gee slid behind the wheel, wiping sweat and blood from his face. “We’ve got to get back.”

Hamid climbed in, cradling his shotgun like a trophy. “Good fight. Need drink now.”

Gee didn’t answer, slamming the truck into gear, tires spitting gravel as they tore back toward the village.

By the time they rolled into the outskirts of the village, the horizon was bleeding pink with early dawn. The streets were quiet, the market stalls closed, shadows long and empty.

Gee pulled the truck to a shuddering stop, staring hard at the place where they’d left Lorrisa.

Nothing.

His chest constricted. He jumped out, limping fast across the square, eyes scanning every corner.

“Lorrisa?!” he yelled. “LORRISA!”

Silence.

Kong’s blanket still lay folded by the spot where she’d sat.

Gee’s stomach twisted, dread clawing up his throat.

“She’s... gone,” he whispered, his voice cracking as the weight of it hit.

Hamid climbed out, frowning, looking around. “Pretty lady?”

Gee turned in a slow, panicked circle. “Damn it—DAMN IT!”

The village was empty.

And Lorrisa was nowhere to be found.

Elsewhere...

Miles away from the dust and chaos Gee and Hamid had left behind, the scene was a world apart.

A luxury hotel, polished marble floors and crystal chandeliers casting soft golden light across a hushed, opulent dining room. Waiters in crisp uniforms glided between white-linen tables, pouring wine, adjusting silverware, their movements rehearsed and perfect.

But beneath the elegance, unease rippled through the room.

Several guests stole nervous glances toward the large corner table, where armed guards in sleek black suits stood watch, eyes cold and alert. Their hands rested lightly on their weapons, scanning the room with quiet menace.

At the center of it all, Sebastian sat—impeccably dressed in a tailored black suit and silk tie, a gold watch glinting at his wrist. His posture was regal, a picture of control and power as he swirled a glass of deep red wine between his fingers.

He checked his watch, then the entrance.

“Soon,” he murmured, eyes sharp with anticipation.

The piano player continued softly in the background as conversation across the room remained hushed, the other diners doing their best to pretend nothing was out of the ordinary.

Then—movement by the grand staircase.

Every head turned as a woman descended gracefully, her emerald green gown hugging her figure perfectly, shimmering with each step. The fabric clung and flowed, wrapping around her curves with effortless elegance, the plunging neckline and high slit balanced by quiet sophistication.

Sebastian stood immediately, setting his napkin aside, his eyes locked on her with clear appreciation.

She approached, poised and calm, her chin lifted, eyes unreadable.

"Enchanting," Sebastian purred, taking her hand and bowing slightly. He brushed his lips across her knuckles with practiced charm. "You are even more stunning than I remembered."

She smiled faintly, her expression cool, eyes shimmering with quiet calculation.

The waiter rushed forward, pulling out her chair. She sat smoothly, crossing her legs, her gown settling like a silken wave around her.

Sebastian gestured to the sommelier to pour her wine, settling back into his chair with a smile full of secrets.

"I trust your experience wasn't... too difficult?"

The woman's lips curled into a small, knowing smile as she accepted the glass of wine.

And then the tension crackling—

Lorrisa.

Her eyes flicked up to meet Sebastian's, calm and razor-sharp.

"Not at all," she said smoothly. "I was... overdue for a change of scenery."

Sebastian's smile widened, the glint in his eye dark and pleased.

The guards relaxed slightly, and the pianist played on as the rest of the room buzzed with a tension no one could quite place.

Far away from the battlefield, the next game had just begun.

Gee and Hamid's Return to the Village...

The battered Jeep rattled into the village, its tires crunching over blackened debris. What had been a bustling market square now looked like hell itself—homes flattened, carts overturned, the air thick with smoke and the stench of charred wood and blood.

Gee slammed the door open and stepped out, his boots hitting the ground hard. His eyes swept across the carnage—bodies scattered like rag dolls, women wailing over lifeless forms, children clutching each other in fear.

"¡Madre de Dios!" Gee muttered, his chest tightening. His fists clenched at his sides as he stepped forward, struggling to take it all in.

Hamid was already out of the Jeep, his face pale under the soot-streaked sky. "Ya Allah... what have they done?" he whispered, eyes darting around frantically. He turned to Gee, voice sharp with rising panic. "This... this was no ordinary raid."

They moved quickly through the wreckage, dodging burning beams and collapsed walls. Near the far edge of the village, Hamid spotted a familiar crumpled figure beneath a pile of broken timbers.

"There!" Hamid shouted, sprinting over.

Gee followed at a run, heart hammering in his chest.

It was Mustafa—the old arms dealer. He was barely recognizable, his face battered, blood oozing from a cut above his brow. His chest rose and fell in shallow gasps.

Hamid dropped to his knees. "Mustafa!" he cried, gripping his shoulder. "Stay with us, old man!"

Mustafa's eyelids fluttered, his lips moving weakly.

Gee knelt down, voice urgent. "Who did this? Was it the bandits?"

Mustafa coughed, his hand trembling as he grabbed at Hamid's sleeve. "Not... the bandits," he rasped, his voice dry as dust.

Gee's eyes darkened. "Then who?"

Mustafa's breath rattled in his chest. "White men... soldiers... they... they had an English boss. Said they were looking... for you... or the ring."

Hamid cursed under his breath in Arabic, eyes flashing with fury. "Sebastian's men."

Mustafa gave a weak nod, eyes glassy now. "He... he brought death to us... because of you..."

Gee's stomach twisted. He glanced around at the wreckage, guilt flashing across his face—but it hardened quickly into anger. He placed a hand gently on Mustafa's shoulder. "Rest now, my friend. You did good."

Mustafa's head slumped, his breathing slowing to a whisper.

Hamid stood, wiping his brow with shaking hands. "We should leave. Before they come back."

Gee’s jaw clenched tight. He stared at the destruction—his fists curling until his knuckles went white. "No," he said coldly. "We’re not leaving. We’re hunting."

Hamid let out a bitter laugh. "Good. I was hoping you'd say that."

Gee’s eyes locked onto the horizon, the last wisps of smoke rising into the bruised sky. "Let’s get armed. And let’s make them pay."

The dining room was opulence wrapped in silk—crystal chandeliers casting soft light over polished silver and delicate china. Lorrisa sat, elegant in her emerald gown, her fingers lazily circling the rim of her wine glass as she watched Sebastian across the table. His smile was sharp, his eyes locked on her as if nothing else existed.

Until something did.

A shadow loomed beside them. One of Sebastian’s mercenaries appeared, dusty and streaked with grime, moving with practiced stealth. He bent low, a hand brushing Sebastian’s shoulder as he leaned in to whisper.

Lorrisa's eyes flicked upward, casual but focused. She leaned back just slightly, appearing disinterested—but her ears strained for anything she could catch. The mercenary's voice was a low murmur, too soft to make out over the muted clatter of dinner plates and conversation.

Sebastian's smile faltered—just a flicker—before his jaw clenched tight. Color rose up his neck and into his face, a dark flush of controlled fury. His hand gripped the stem of his wine glass with white-knuckled tension, the muscles in his jaw flexing visibly.

There it is, Lorrisa thought, a small spark of relief hidden beneath her calm facade. *Gee's alive! That is the face of someone that Gee has pissed off... I used to get that all the time,* she mused, her lips curling slightly as she looked away, feigning indifference.

Sebastian hissed something sharp to the mercenary, who gave a quick nod before retreating silently into the shadows.

When Sebastian turned back, his smile had returned but looked brittle now, forced, the cool mask slipping back into place. "Apologies, my dear," he said smoothly, rising from his chair, adjusting his cufflinks with precision. "A minor issue requires my immediate attention. I won't be long."

Lorrisa tilted her head, her eyes gleaming with mock sweetness. "Business never sleeps, hmm?"

His smile thinned. "No, but it dies eventually."

He bent, brushing a dry kiss across her knuckles, and without another word, strode away, his shoulders stiff and movements sharp with simmering anger.

Lorrisa watched him go, her eyes narrowing as her fingers tapped a slow rhythm on the table. As soon as he was out of sight, she exhaled softly, her mind already racing.

Gee's alive, she repeated to herself, her gaze drifting to the darkened window beside her. *And whatever Sebastian's cooking up now... it's going to be ugly.*

She finished her wine in one slow swallow, her jaw tightening with resolve.

Sebastian strode through the lavish corridor like a storm in a tailored suit, polished shoes clicking sharply on the marble floors. His bodyguards trailed behind, struggling to keep pace. Without a word, he pushed open the heavy doors of the private lounge, the murmur of the dining room vanishing as the doors thudded shut behind him.

Inside, his mercenary team stood at rigid attention. Their faces—grim, bruised, some still smeared with ash—told the story of their failure before a word was spoken.

Sebastian's eyes swept the room, cold and cutting. Silence thickened around them.

"Well?" he finally spat, his voice razor-sharp. "Nothing?"

The leader of the squad, a scarred man named Callum, stepped forward hesitantly. "We tore the village apart, sir. No sign of Jesus—uh, Gee—or the rings. Locals wouldn't talk."

Sebastian's nostrils flared. He stepped in close, his voice dropping to a hiss. "You *burned* the village. You killed half their men, destroyed their homes, terrorized them—and still you came back with *nothing*?"

Callum's jaw tightened. "They were hiding him, we're sure of it. But by the time we arrived, he was gone."

Sebastian's hand shot out, grabbing Callum's lapel and yanking him in close, eyes blazing. "Do you have *any* idea what's at stake here? Two pieces of the ring,

Callum. Two! One I risked my *career* to dig out of the earth, and the other I *ripped* from the hands of that old crone before I put a bullet in her skull. And now? Now they're both with him."

Callum held his breath, eyes locked on Sebastian's.

Sebastian shoved him back hard, pacing like a caged predator. His hands curled into fists, and for a moment he seemed to be restraining himself from outright violence.

"I want him *found,*" Sebastian snarled, spinning back to face them. "I don't care if you have to comb every damn grain of sand in that desert. If you don't bring me Gee or those rings—*both*—you'll be explaining your failure to Simean Mogull himself."

A ripple of unease passed through the room. The men exchanged quick glances, fear flashing in their eyes at the mention of Mogull's name.

Sebastian's voice dropped to a cold whisper. "And I promise you—Mogull won't be as forgiving as I am."

Callum nodded stiffly. "We'll find him."

"You'd better."

Sebastian straightened his cuffs, breathing hard, and gestured to the door. “Out. All of you. Get out of my sight”

Without another word, the mercenaries filed out, their boots echoing down the corridor.

Sebastian stayed still for a beat, staring at the closed door, chest heaving. Then, with a slow exhale, he smoothed his jacket and turned back toward the dining room.

Sebastian returned to the dining room minutes later, looking composed but deadly beneath the surface. Lorrisa was still seated, the picture of elegance, swirling the last of her wine as if she hadn’t a care in the world.

“Handled?” she asked smoothly, her eyes watching him over the rim of her glass.

Sebastian sat down, the corner of his mouth lifting in a tight smile. “For now.”

She tilted her head slightly. “Bad news?”

He shrugged, picking up his knife and fork, but the tension in his shoulders betrayed him. “A minor setback. It happens.”

Lorrisa didn’t press—at least not openly. She simply leaned back, her expression relaxed, but her eyes sharpened, watching every twitch of his jaw, every flicker in his eyes.

Sebastian cut into his steak with a little too much force, chewing in silence for a moment before he finally looked up. “Do you know what I keep thinking about?” he said, voice deceptively light. “The day we met.”

Lorrisa smiled. “Hard to forget.”

He leaned back, watching her carefully. “There you were, wandering through that little backwater village. Alone. Brave. Beautiful. And you’d just bought that monkey—what’s his name?”

“Kong,” she answered with a small laugh. “Funny little thing.”

“Yes,” Sebastian said quietly, his gaze narrowing. “From some trader passing through. And then... the bandits struck. Hell of a coincidence, wasn’t it?”

Her smile didn’t waver. “Very unfortunate timing.”

Sebastian set down his knife, folding his hands in front of him, eyes drilling into hers now. “I’ve been wondering... what was that trader *really* doing there? Besides selling monkeys?”

Lorrisa kept her expression perfectly neutral, her heart racing beneath her calm exterior. “Do you think I asked for his life story? He was selling a monkey. I wanted one. Seemed simple enough.”

"Simple..." Sebastian echoed, eyes narrowing. He leaned forward just slightly. "And you—pure coincidence that you were there, too? No interest in local legends? No whispers of lost artifacts?"

She laughed lightly, shaking her head. "I was on holiday, Sebastian. Not every trip is a treasure hunt."

Sebastian held her gaze for a long, charged moment, his fingers tapping slowly on the tablecloth. The tension stretched so tight it felt like a wire about to snap.

Then, finally, he leaned back again, the smile returning—sharp and thin. "Of course. Coincidences happen."

Lorrisa smiled right back, lifting her glass to her lips. "They do."

The waiter reappeared, pouring fresh wine and clearing plates, breaking the electric tension for a moment. Sebastian picked up his glass, swirling the wine as he stared into its dark depths.

"I'm just curious," he said quietly, almost to himself. "Sometimes... people aren't who they seem."

Lorrisa raised her glass. "That's what makes life interesting."

Sebastian's eyes flicked up, his smile brittle. "Indeed."

They drank in silence, each lost in their own thoughts, the dance of suspicion and secrets playing out behind their polite masks. Lorrisa's mind worked furiously, piecing together the puzzle, her instincts sharpening by the second. Sebastian's mind, meanwhile, churned with anger and obsession, plotting his next move.

And somewhere out there... Gee was still alive, still moving, still holding the pieces that everyone wanted.

The rest of dinner played out like a slow, careful game of chess. Sebastian's smile had returned, his charm polished back to its gleaming facade, but Lorrisa could feel the heat of his eyes on her—calculating, watching, *wanting*. Every word was measured; every glance, a test.

By the time dessert arrived—a delicate swirl of mousse and sugared fruit—Sebastian's hand had drifted casually over hers across the table, his fingers brushing her knuckles with slow intent.

"You've had quite the adventure," he said smoothly, his voice low and intimate. "A brave woman, traveling alone. I admire that."

Lorrisa smiled, leaning in slightly, letting her fingers linger just long enough to keep things light. "It's more fun that way," she said playfully, her voice silky. "You never know what you'll find."

Sebastian's eyes darkened, and his fingers curled gently around hers, his grip tightening just a touch too long. "Sometimes the best finds are... unexpected."

Lorrisa's heart thudded, but she kept her gaze steady, her smile cool. "Sometimes," she agreed, then slowly, gracefully slid her hand out from under his. She brushed her napkin to her lips as if nothing had happened, her tone light. "But you know what I've learned on these trips? Rest is *everything*. Long days, dusty roads... it really takes it out of you."

Sebastian's eyes glinted with something hungry, his smile lazy. "I can think of ways to help you relax."

Lorrisa let out a soft laugh, dipping her gaze demurely. "Tempting. Very tempting. But tonight..." she sighed, stretching just slightly in her chair, letting the fabric of her gown shift across her legs in a subtle, practiced move, "I think I'm just too drained. Maybe tomorrow, after a good night's sleep?"

Sebastian's eyes flicked down her body, his expression a mixture of frustration and amusement. He leaned back in his chair, swirling the last of his wine. "You are such a tease dear lady," he said, though his tone held a dangerous edge beneath the humor.

Lorrisa gave him a slow, dazzling smile. "If I weren't a tease, I wouldn't be a lady. That's why you like me."

He chuckled low in his throat, but the heat in his eyes was unmistakable. "I'll hold you to that."

She lifted her glass in a toast, clinking it gently against his. "Of course you will."

The moment stretched, but Lorrisa was already planning her exit. She dabbed at her lips with her napkin and let her smile soften. "You've been wonderful company tonight, Sebastian. But if you don't mind... I think I'll turn in."

Sebastian's jaw twitched, but he forced the smile back into place. "Of course, darling. I'll have one of my men escort you to your room."

"Very thoughtful." She stood slowly, smoothing her gown, and leaned down to kiss his cheek—lingering just long enough to leave a whisper of perfume and a promise of nothing.

As she walked away, she felt his eyes on her the entire time, a predator watching its prey. But her smile didn't falter.

Her room was elegant, high-ceilinged and cool, with thick curtains drawn across tall windows. The moment the door clicked shut behind her—and the guard posted outside—Lorrisa dropped the smile like a mask hitting the floor.

She moved quickly, slipping out of her heels and pacing the room in bare feet, her mind racing. *Sebastian's losing his grip. He's furious, desperate, and he's watching me like a hawk. I need to move—fast.*

Her eyes landed on her bag in the corner. She crossed the room, unzipping it, and pulled out her travel notebook—a battered leather thing she'd kept close throughout her expeditions. Inside, between sketches and scribbled notes, were the details Gee had once mentioned—clues, old maps, references to the ring's possible hiding places.

She tapped a pen against her lips, thinking fast. If Gee was still alive—and she *knew* now he was—he wouldn't be hiding for long. He'd be moving, fast and smart, staying one step ahead. And wherever he was going next, she had to get there *first*.

She glanced at the door, frowning. The guard would be no problem later... but she couldn't risk slipping away just yet. Not without tipping her hand.

Her fingers brushed the small burner phone she'd hidden inside the lining of her suitcase. Just one message. One signal to let Gee know she was still in the game—and maybe, just maybe, help him stay alive long enough for her to do something about it.

She hesitated, thumb hovering over the keypad. Then she typed quickly:

Stay sharp. He's hunting you hard. I'm working on my angle. Will buy time. Stay alive. —L

She hit send.

The message disappeared into the encrypted app. Silent. Clean.

Lorrisa closed her eyes for a moment, her pulse steadying.

Game on, she thought, slipping the phone back into hiding.

Outside, the hallway remained quiet, the soft footsteps of the guard passing by her door every so often. Lorrisa sat on the edge of her bed, staring out the darkened window, her fingers flexing restlessly.

I have to be smarter, she told herself. *Faster. Better.*

A ghost of a smile touched her lips. The room was quiet except for the soft shuffle of movement near the windowsill. Lorrisa, still perched on the edge of her bed, turned her head and smiled as Kong scurried up onto the small table near the curtains. He was pawing at a bowl of fruit—lured in by the bright color of grapes and sliced mango.

“Back to your old tricks, huh?” she murmured, rising from the bed and walking over.

Kong looked up at her, eyes bright and familiar now—alert, mischievous, and no longer haunted by the terror of their last encounter. He chirped once, tilting his head, then stuffed a chunk of mango into his mouth, juice dribbling down his chin.

Lorrisa crouched beside him, stroking the soft fur on his back. “You’re a tough little bastard, you know that?”

Kong blinked at her, then resumed his feast, flicking his tail happily.

Lorrisa's smile faltered as her fingers absently smoothed the fur between his shoulders. She stared out the window, her mind racing again.

"Gee's alive," she said softly, almost as if confirming it to herself one more time. "And we're stuck in this gilded cage while Sebastian is losing his damn mind."

Kong glanced up, chattering quietly, then leapt to her shoulder, his tiny paws gripping her gently. He nuzzled the side of her face, and she laughed softly despite herself.

"Well, you've bounced back fast," she whispered, standing up and letting him ride her shoulder as she paced to the other side of the room. "I wish I could say the same. But we've got work to do, little man."

She paused by the dresser and looked at her reflection in the mirror—her emerald gown still flawless, hair in place, but her eyes were sharper now. Harder. Determined.

"This is the part where we get clever," she told Kong, meeting her own gaze in the mirror. "Because if Sebastian catches even a whiff of what I'm planning... we're both screwed."

Kong squeaked, as if in agreement, and began tugging at her earring.

“Stop that,” she said with a laugh, gently swatting his paw. “Not the time for fashion advice.”

She turned and pulled her travel notebook from her bag again, flipping it open to the map she’d been studying. The desert routes, the old legends of hidden chambers... and notes from Gee’s wild theories, ones she’d scoffed at before but now clung to like a lifeline.

She traced a line across the page with her fingertip. “If Gee’s smart—and he is—he’ll head toward the Al-Kharif ruins next. There’s no other lead strong enough to risk.”

Kong hopped down onto the desk, tipping over a pencil and grabbing it between his tiny hands like a sword.

Lorrisa smirked. “You planning to fight your way out of here?”

Kong bared his tiny teeth and made a show of waving the pencil, squeaking proudly.

She laughed quietly but sobered quickly, her eyes flicking to the door. The guard was still out there. She could hear his footsteps occasionally, pacing, pausing.

She leaned close to Kong, whispering, "Okay, listen. Here's the deal. We can't make a move tonight. Too risky. But tomorrow... tomorrow we slip out. I'll create a distraction. You—" she tapped his tiny chest, "—you stay close and keep your eyes open. No heroics, understood?"

Kong squeaked in response, dropping the pencil and climbing back onto her shoulder.

"Good," she said, standing tall. "Because we're not just playing defense anymore."

Her gaze moved to the window, the night sky spread out above the city like a velvet curtain. Somewhere out there, Gee was fighting to stay ahead, alone and hunted. And here she was, stuck in Sebastian's web—but not for long.

"We're coming for you, Gee," she whispered. "And we're bringing hell with us."

Kong chattered, tugging at a strand of her hair, and Lorrisa smiled. "Yeah... you too, monkey."

Lorrisa spent the next hour fine-tuning her plan. She moved with silent precision, checking the door, listening to the guard's patterns, and carefully hiding her essentials—maps, burner phone, a small knife—within the folds of her luggage and under the mattress. Every move was deliberate, every step taken with the grace of someone who knew the stakes were life and death.

Kong, for his part, explored the room with relentless curiosity, climbing the curtains, leaping onto shelves, and occasionally chattering at shadows. It was a strange comfort—his energy, his resilience—a reminder that survival wasn't just about strength. It was about adaptability.

At one point, he tugged at the edge of her notebook, flipping it open to a sketch of the ancient ring.

Lorrisa crouched down beside him. "That's the prize," she whispered, tapping the page. "The thing everyone's killing each other over. And we're going to make sure it doesn't end up in the wrong hands."

Kong poked at the drawing with a tiny finger, then looked up at her with wide eyes.

Lorrisa smiled faintly, brushing her fingers through his fur. "You're my partner now. Got it?"

He squeaked and leapt onto her lap, curling up comfortably.

She sighed, leaning back against the bedframe. “Tomorrow,” she whispered into the quiet room. “Tomorrow we stop playing nice.”

The night pressed in around them, silent and heavy, but Lorrisa’s mind stayed sharp, focused. The wheels were in motion, and the game was changing.

By the time she drifted off to sleep, Kong nestled beside her, her hand resting protectively over her notes, she was no longer just a pawn in Sebastian’s game.

She was ready to flip the board.

The night air was thick with heat and the smell of scorched earth. The village was eerily quiet now, save for the occasional crackle of dying fires and the soft shuffle of survivors gathering what little they had left.

Gee sat in a battered wooden chair inside one of the least-damaged huts, eyes on the map spread across the table in front of him, but his mind miles away. Hamid was outside, keeping watch, pacing near the Jeep. The adrenaline of the day’s horrors was wearing off, leaving behind only exhaustion and a gnawing sense of dread.

Then—a faint sound.

Beep... beep...

Gee's head snapped up, eyes narrowing. He stood abruptly, scanning the room. The sound came again—short, sharp, unmistakable.

"Damn it," he muttered, eyes darting around. "Where the hell..."

He shoved aside a pile of blankets, rifled through a dented metal crate, overturned a bucket. The beeping grew louder as he moved toward a cracked shelf in the corner.

Hamid poked his head in. "What is it? Trouble?"

"Hang on," Gee muttered, kneeling and pulling aside an old tarp. There, wedged under a broken clay pot, was the burner phone—half-dead but still blinking.

He snatched it up, heart racing as he unlocked the screen.

One new message.

Gee's eyes skimmed it fast:

Stay sharp. He's hunting you hard. I'm working on my angle. Will buy time. Stay alive. —L

He exhaled, a deep, shuddering breath of relief, sinking down onto the floor. His head tipped back against the wall, eyes closing for a beat.

“Thank God,” he whispered. “She’s alive.”

Hamid stepped inside, brow furrowed. “Good news?”

Gee held up the phone, shaking his head with a crooked smile. “Lorrisa. She made contact.”

Hamid let out a breath of his own, tension easing from his shoulders. “Alhamdulillah. And Kong?”

Gee’s smile widened slightly. “She didn’t say, but... if she’s alive, that little furball is probably hanging off her shoulder.”

Hamid crouched beside him, frowning. “What now? Do we keep moving? Or... do we go back for her?”

Gee’s smile faded, and he stared at the phone, thumb brushing over the screen. His instincts screamed to *go back*—to storm whatever fortress Sebastian was hiding behind, drag Lorrisa and Kong out of there, and burn it all to the ground.

But he knew better.

"She says she's buying time," Gee said slowly, thinking it through. "That means she's still in play. If we go back now… we blow everything."

Hamid arched a brow. "And if you keep moving forward?"

Gee rubbed his jaw, eyes distant. "Then we pray she catches up. Or that we get strong enough to force the next move."

They sat in silence for a long moment, the weight of it settling between them.

Finally, Hamid spoke, voice low. "These rings… why are they so important? I mean, enough to kill villages for? Enough for men like Sebastian to throw everything at them?"

Gee stared at him for a beat, then leaned back against the wall, exhaling hard. "You ever hear of King Solomon's Seal?"

Hamid's eyes narrowed. "A legend. Old stories. Magic rings and demons."

Gee smirked without humor. "Yeah. That's what I thought, too. Until I found the first piece."

He leaned forward, voice dropping. "The legend says King Solomon had a tablet, that bore a ring design, a seal—a powerful one, inscribed with the name of God.

It gave him dominion over spirits, control over nature, wisdom beyond imagination. Some say it was forged by angels; others claim it was stolen from heaven itself."

Hamid crossed his arms, listening.

Gee continued, eyes distant now. "The stories were passed down, twisted, turned into myths. But the truth? That seal was *real*. And when Solomon died, the tablet was broken—shattered, some say, to keep its power from falling into the wrong hands."

Hamid's brow furrowed. "And these pieces...?"

"Each one holds a fraction of that power." Gee's eyes burned now, intensity crackling under his exhaustion. "The one I stole from the dig site—Sebastian's site—it resonated. Did things I can't explain. And the second piece? It *called* to it. When I brought them close together, it was like magnets—like they wanted to be whole again."

Hamid whistled low. "So this... this is real magic."

Gee shrugged. “Call it what you want. But whatever it is—it’s powerful. Too powerful to end up with someone like Sebastian.”

Hamid’s eyes darkened. “What happens if he gets all the pieces?”

Gee’s jaw clenched. “I don’t know. And I don’t want to find out. But I’ll tell you this—Sebastian doesn’t just want power. He wants control. Over everything. If he is able to put that tablet back together...”

He shook his head, eyes hardening. “We’re screwed. All of us.”

Hamid was silent for a moment, processing. Then he looked Gee dead in the eye. “So what’s the plan?”

Gee stood, slipping the burner phone into his pocket, his jaw set with new resolve. “We keep moving. Fast. We get to the next site before Sebastian does. And we find the next piece.”

Hamid grinned, standing as well. “Good. Because I was getting bored.”

Gee chuckled, shaking his head. “You’re insane.”

Hamid clapped him on the shoulder. “Takes one to know one, my friend.”

They stepped outside into the cool night, the stars bright above them, and climbed back into the Jeep. The road ahead was dark, uncertain—but for the first time in days, Gee felt a sliver of hope.

He pulled out the map, spreading it across the dashboard. "Al-Kharif ruins," he murmured. "That's our best shot."

Hamid started the engine, headlights cutting through the darkness. "Then let's not waste time."

The Jeep rumbled to life, bouncing over the rough terrain as they sped off into the night—two men, chasing shadows, trying to stay one step ahead of a storm that was closing in fast.

And somewhere, not far behind, the pieces of Solomon's legend waited—ancient, powerful, and deadly.

Morning sunlight filtered through gauzy curtains, casting golden streaks across the room. Lorrisa stood by the dresser, focused and precise as she packed her bag. She moved with calm efficiency—maps folded, essentials tucked into hidden pockets, burner phone secured.

Kong sat on the bed, eyes bright and curious, pawing at the laces of her rugged climbing boots.

"Easy, little man," Lorrisa said with a smile, slipping into a pair of khaki shorts and a sleek, fitted black top that clung to her like armor. Her boots thudded solidly against the floor as she laced them up tight. "We're almost out of here."

She pulled out a small collar and crouched down beside Kong, fastening it gently around his neck—a soft tether clipped to her belt.

"Not taking any chances with you wandering off," she murmured. "We stick together today."

Kong chattered, leaping up to her shoulder as if ready for battle.

Lorrisa straightened, slinging her bag over one shoulder, eyes darting to the door. She could hear faint footsteps in the hall—the rhythm she'd studied last night. The guard would shift his post soon. Her hand tightened around the doorknob.

"Okay," she whispered, pulse quickening, "time to move."

She cracked the door open—

Knock-knock-knock.

Her heart lurched as the sharp raps came first—before she could step out. She froze, every nerve on high alert.

Then a familiar voice, smooth and deadly: “Lorrisa... it’s Sebastian.”

Her eyes snapped to Kong, who let out a low, warning chirp. Lorrisa exhaled through her nose, composing herself in an instant. She stepped back, setting down her bag, and opened the door just enough to see him.

Sebastian smiled, sharp as ever, but this time... he wasn’t alone.

Marta stepped into view—tall, striking, her dark eyes cool with triumph. Her arms folded tightly across her chest, a smirk tugging at her lips.

Lorrisa’s stomach dropped.

“May we come in?” Sebastian asked politely, but his tone left no room for refusal.

Lorrisa stepped back silently, opening the door wider, her mind racing.

Sebastian strolled inside with Marta close behind, his eyes sweeping the room—the packed bag, the climbing boots, the leash clipped to her belt.

"Going somewhere?" he asked lightly.

Lorrisa forced a smile. "Early hike. Wanted to stretch my legs."

Sebastian's gaze hardened. "Ah. Well, before you wander off..." He turned, smile tight. "There's something you should know."

Marta stepped forward, her eyes cold and triumphant. "Hello, Lorrisa."

Lorrisa arched a brow, keeping her voice cool. "Marta. You're a long way from your last tantrum."

Marta's jaw tightened, but Sebastian cut in, his tone silken. "I imagine you've been wondering how I put all the pieces together... how I knew who you *really* were. Turns out... Marta here was quite helpful."

Lorrisa's stomach twisted. "Of course she was. Bitch."

Sebastian's eyes gleamed. "Seems jealousy's a powerful motivator. She told me all about your little... history with Gee."

Marta's lip curled, arms still folded. "You should have stayed out of it, Lorrisa. But no—you just *had* to be near him. Typical."

Lorrisa's fingers twitched at her side, but she kept her face composed. "So what now? You hold me hostage until Gee shows up?"

Sebastian's smile sharpened. "Exactly. You and the monkey. You're leverage. And from what I hear... Gee's the kind of man who won't leave you behind."

He stepped closer, eyes narrowing. "And now, we wait."

No, Lorrisa thought, every instinct flaring. *Not today.*

She backed up slowly, step by step, until her heels hit the balcony door. Her heart thudded hard against her ribs, but her face stayed calm, voice airy. "Smart plan, Sebastian. Very smart."

His smile deepened. "I thought so."

And then Lorrisa *moved.*

She spun, yanking open the balcony door in one fluid motion. Sebastian shouted, lunging forward, but she was already over the railing—Kong clinging tightly to her shoulder—grabbing hold of a long strip of decorative fabric fluttering down the side of the hotel.

"LORRISA!" Sebastian roared from behind her.

She slid down fast, the fabric burning her palms, heart in her throat as the street rushed up to meet her. Kong squealed but held on tight, his tiny paws gripping her vest.

Halfway down, the fabric *tore*—a sharp rip that made her stomach drop—but she twisted, kicking out hard to push herself away from the wall, landing with a rough *thud* on a vendor's fruit stand below.

Apples and oranges exploded around her, and Kong sprang clear, chattering wildly.

One of Sebastian's men, stationed on the street, was already lunging toward her.

"Stop her!" he bellowed, reaching out.

But Lorrisa was ready. She planted her boots, twisting her body with precision—and *snap!*—her knee shot up into his gut, knocking the wind out of him. As he staggered, she spun, landing a sharp elbow to his jaw.

He stumbled back, dazed.

"Kickboxing," she muttered, ducking under his wild swing. "Worth every damn penny."

She pivoted on her heel, slamming a roundhouse kick into his ribs. He went down hard, groaning.

Kong leapt onto her shoulder, chittering triumphantly.

"Come on!" Lorrisa hissed, grabbing her bag off the wrecked fruit stand and bolting into the maze of narrow streets.

Behind her, shouts rang out—Sebastian's men flooding from the hotel entrance, sprinting after her.

But Lorrisa was already weaving through the crowd, boots pounding the pavement, Kong clinging tight, her pulse hammering in her ears.

She didn't look back.

No more waiting. No more games.

She was free—and now, the hunt was on.

Lorrisa sprinted through the twisting alleyways, Kong gripping her shoulder, his claws digging in with each sharp turn. The narrow streets were alive with noise—vendors shouting, kids playing, the distant blare of a car horn—but over it all, she could hear them:

Shouts. Boots pounding. Sebastian's men, hot on her heels.

"There! She went down that way!"

Lorrisa cursed under her breath, pushing herself harder, weaving through a market stall, sending crates of vegetables crashing down in her wake. Kong screeched in warning as a hand shot out from behind a cart, grabbing at her arm.

She twisted fast, driving her elbow into the man's throat, a clean strike that sent him reeling. Before he could recover, she stepped in, slamming her knee into his gut and yanking free.

"Keep moving," she muttered to Kong, ducking into a shadowy side street.

But there was no time to breathe. Two more mercenaries rounded the corner ahead of her, cutting her off.

"End of the line!" one of them shouted, drawing a baton.

Lorrisa's eyes narrowed. "Not even close."

She sidestepped the first swing, catching his arm and twisting sharply. He grunted in pain, and she shoved him into his partner, sending them both stumbling back. Kong leapt off her shoulder, hissing and baring his tiny teeth, lunging at the second man's face.

"Atta boy, Kong!" Lorrisa barked, using the moment of chaos to deliver a hard punch to the first man's jaw. He went down like a sack of bricks, groaning.

Kong somersaulted off the second man's head and landed back on Lorrisa's shoulder just as she spun and delivered a side kick straight into his chest, knocking him into a pile of crates.

She didn't wait to see if they got up.

"Go, go, go," she muttered, darting down another alley, Kong clutching tight again. Her breath came fast, her pulse pounding in her ears, but her eyes stayed sharp, scanning for an opening.

They emerged onto a busy street, horns blaring, people everywhere. She ducked low, weaving through the crowd, trying to put as much distance between them and Sebastian's men as possible.

But the shouts behind her told her they were still on her trail.

She slipped into a small side market—a cramped shop overflowing with clothes, scarves, and cheap jewelry. The shopkeeper barely looked up as she grabbed a long, flowing skirt, a colorful headscarf, and a pair of oversized sunglasses.

"Pay later," Lorrisa muttered, tossing a few bills onto the counter as she ducked into a corner and stripped off her boots and shorts fast, yanking on the skirt and wrapping the scarf expertly around her head.

"Kong, come here," she whispered, quickly unclipping his collar and tucking him inside the wide folds of the scarf, positioning him so only his little eyes peeked out. She tossed on the sunglasses last, stuffing her old clothes deep into a bin behind the counter.

By the time Sebastian's men thundered past the shop's entrance, she was strolling casually down the opposite side of the street—head high, pace unhurried, just another tourist browsing the markets.

Her heart pounded, but she didn't let it show.

Almost there, she thought, eyes scanning for the bus depot.

She spotted it up ahead—old, rusted buses idling, a cluster of locals boarding and disembarking. She picked up her pace slightly, weaving through the crowd, careful to keep her head down just enough to avoid notice.

Kong wriggled under the scarf, letting out a soft chirp.

"Shh," Lorrisa whispered, scratching his chin lightly through the fabric. "Almost free, little guy. Hold on."

She stepped up onto a waiting bus, flashing a polite smile at the driver and slipping a few more bills into his hand. No questions asked. Just how she liked it.

The doors hissed shut behind her. She sank into a seat near the back, eyes still scanning the streets as the bus rumbled to life and began to pull away.

On the sidewalk, she saw two of Sebastian's men glance her way—but their eyes slid right over her, not recognizing the woman in the bright scarf and skirt.

Her pulse slowed as the bus turned the corner and the hotel, the mercenaries, and the chaos faded into the distance.

She exhaled slowly, leaning back in her seat. Kong poked his head out of the scarf, blinking up at her.

She smiled, brushing his fur back. "We did it."

Kong chirped, snuggling into her side, eyes closing as the bus jostled them gently down the dusty road out of town.

Lorrisa stared out the window, her eyes sharp and unblinking. The city rolled by, noisy and vibrant, but her mind was already ahead—thinking, planning, calculating.

She was free for now. But she knew better than to relax.

Sebastian wouldn't give up easily. He'd be hunting, harder than ever. And Gee—wherever he was—would need her sharp, fast, and ready.

Her fingers tightened around the edge of her seat, and a fierce smile touched her lips.

The room was heavy with silence, broken only by the distant shouts of Sebastian's men still scrambling in the streets below. Sebastian stood by the balcony, eyes locked on the flapping strip of fabric that Lorrisa had used to make her escape. His face was stone, but his clenched fists and ragged breathing betrayed the storm raging inside.

Behind him, Marta hovered near the door, arms crossed tightly over her chest. Her eyes darted to the broken fruit stand far below, then back to Sebastian, her breathing quick and shallow.

"She just... she *jumped,*" Marta whispered, her voice shaking. "I—I didn't know she'd do something like that."

Sebastian didn't answer, his stare cold and murderous. He moved slowly, deliberately, gripping the balcony rail so hard the veins in his forearm bulged.

"I thought you said you *knew* her," he said at last, his voice low and deadly.

Marta flinched. "I—I do! I mean, I did! But she—Gee said she was always reckless, but this—this is insane!"

Sebastian turned, his eyes drilling into her like ice picks. "No. What's insane is me trusting the jealous rantings of a woman scorned."

Marta's breath caught. She stepped back instinctively, pressing herself against the wall. "I—I only told you what I knew," she stammered, her eyes wide with fear now. "They rented a car from me! They said they were headed for the hills, that's all! I thought— I thought you'd catch them!"

Sebastian's smile was slow, sharp, and terrifying. "And you thought that would bring you closer to him, didn't you?"

Marta's eyes filled with tears, her voice breaking. "I just wanted him to pay attention! He—he left me for her! I thought... I thought if you stopped them—"

Sebastian stepped toward her, and Marta shrank back, pressing herself tighter against the wall. He leaned in close, his voice a venomous whisper. "You miserable skank, you thought wrong."

He straightened, brushing his jacket sleeve like she was a speck of dust. "And now you're useless to me."

Marta's face crumpled, her fear spilling over into tears. "Please—I didn't mean—"

"Get the fuck out," Sebastian barked, his voice slicing through the room like a whip.

Marta flinched, tears streaming down her face as she stumbled toward the door. She looked back once, eyes wide and pleading, but Sebastian had already turned away, dismissing her as if she didn't exist.

She fled, her sobs echoing down the corridor as the door slammed behind her.

Sebastian stood there for a long moment, staring at the closed door, his chest heaving with fury. In a moment of uncontrolled rage, he kicked a table across the room, flung items at the mirrors, completely destroyed lamps. Then he exhaled slowly, running a hand down his face, trying to pull himself together.

Callum and two other mercenaries stood near the balcony entrance, stiff and silent, eyes avoiding his.

Finally, Sebastian turned, eyes sharp and deadly. "Well?"

Callum cleared his throat carefully. "We... we lost her in the market, sir. We think she slipped onto one of the buses. We've locked down the depot, and we're sweeping the stations now."

Sebastian's eyes blazed. "A bus? You let her get on a *bus?*"

Callum swallowed hard. "We're setting up roadblocks. We'll catch her."

Sebastian stalked forward, each step measured, eyes burning with cold rage. He stopped inches from Callum, his voice dropping to a lethal whisper. "You keep saying that. But every time, I get *nothing*. First Gee. Now Lorrisa.   Do you think I care about your excuses? You think Mogull's going to care about your excuses?"

Callum paled but kept his ground. "We're doing everything we can."

Sebastian's lip curled. "Clearly not enough."

He spun away, pacing, chest heaving. For a moment, it looked like he might smash something again—his hands flexing, searching for something to destroy. But instead, he stopped cold, pulling out his sleek black phone and dialing quickly.

The men stayed dead silent, tension crackling in the air.

The line clicked. A deep voice answered: “Yes?”

Sebastian’s tone was hard as steel. “We’ve got a problem.”

A pause. “I know.”

Sebastian’s jaw tightened. “I want reinforcements. Every route out of this city, every checkpoint—covered. I want drones, cameras, eyes everywhere. No more slip-ups.”

The voice on the other end was calm but cutting. “You sound desperate, Sebastian.”

Sebastian’s eyes narrowed dangerously. “I’m focused. And I’m warning you—the pieces are slipping through our fingers. If we lose them, we lose *everything*.”

Another pause. Then: “Fine. I’ll send more men. But you’re on thin ice. Mogull is watching.”

Sebastian’s jaw flexed. “I’m aware.”

The line went dead.

Sebastian lowered the phone slowly, staring at it like it might burst into flames. Then he turned to Callum and the others, his voice ice-cold. “You heard him. I want lockdowns on every route. No excuses. No failures.”

The men nodded sharply, turning to leave.

"And Callum," Sebastian added, his tone a razor's edge.

Callum froze, glancing back nervously. "Yes, sir?"

Sebastian's smile was deadly calm. "If you screw this up again... it will be your bones people will be looking for".

Callum's face drained of color. "Understood."

They left fast, boots echoing down the hall.

Sebastian stood alone in the room now, the city stretching out beyond the balcony, alive with oblivious noise and movement. He stared at the horizon, fists clenching at his sides.

"Run all you want," he muttered, eyes narrowing to slits. "But you can't hide forever."

His reflection stared back at him in the glass—hard, cold, relentless. He'd lost the upper hand tonight, but it wasn't over.

Not by a long shot.

He turned back into the room, already mapping his next move. The hunt was far from finished. And next time... there would be no mercy.

The Bus Ride...

The old bus rattled and shook as it wound its way out of the city, dusty roads stretching endlessly ahead. The inside was humid and packed, a tangle of locals, travelers, and their belongings—plastic bags, sacks of grain, and the occasional wandering chicken pecking at the floor.

Lorrisa sat near the back, a map stretched across her lap, her brow furrowed in concentration. Her finger traced a winding route, lips moving soundlessly as she worked through the best way to cross into Somalia without drawing attention.

"Desert trail here... maybe a ferry if the roads are blocked..." she muttered to herself, chewing the end of her pencil.

Kong, meanwhile, had found entertainment of his own.

Curled in Lorrisa's lap just minutes ago, he had quietly slinked across the aisle to the seat occupied by a stout man in a worn brown jacket, who was half-dozing, a paper bag of food resting lazily in his lap.

Kong's eyes gleamed with delight. He crept closer, paws delicate as feathers, and—*snatch!*—his tiny fingers darted into the bag, pulling out a fat sandwich. In one swift motion, he slipped it behind his back, scooted a little farther under the seat, and began munching noisily.

The man stirred, blinking awake, sniffing the air and patting his lap absently.

"Eh?" he muttered, lifting the now very empty paper bag. He frowned, turning it upside down. Nothing.

He looked around, puzzled, peeking under his seat, between the cushions—his brows furrowing deeper.

Lorrisa, oblivious, muttered to herself, "Cross-reference with the old ruins... coordinates line up, but..."

The man scratched his head, still bewildered, when a soft *crunch* caught his ear. He turned slowly—and locked eyes with Kong.

Kong, sandwich halfway in his mouth, froze. Big innocent eyes blinked up at the man. Slowly, very slowly, Kong set the sandwich down, folded his paws politely, and gave the man his sweetest, wide-eyed look.

For a moment, the man just stared.

Then he smiled, shaking his head with a little laugh. "Ahhh, clever little thief," he muttered in his native tongue, amused despite himself.

Kong chirped proudly, lifting the sandwich again as if toasting his victim, then crammed the rest into his mouth, chewing happily.

The man's eyes narrowed playfully. He leaned in closer, wagging a finger. "I see you now. Next time... I keep both eyes open."

Kong burped quietly and nestled back into his spot, licking his fingers, looking utterly pleased with himself.

The man chuckled and leaned back, closing his eyes. "Hmph. You win this round, little monkey."

Lorrisa finally looked up from her map, frowning thoughtfully. “Alright, Kong, we’ll need to head east once we hit the border town—then it’s a long haul south to the coordinates.”

She glanced down, noticing Kong curled contentedly in his seat, licking the last crumbs from his paws.

Her eyes narrowed. “What’ve you been up to?”

Kong gave her his most innocent face, tilting his head and chattering sweetly.

Lorrisa squinted, glancing across the aisle—and spotted the man now fast asleep, his empty paper bag crumpled sadly beside him.

Lorrisa sighed, pinching the bridge of her nose. “Kong...”

Kong yawned, stretching luxuriously, utterly unrepentant.

She shook her head, laughing despite herself. “You’re going to get us in trouble one day.”

Kong chirped and climbed back onto her shoulder, nuzzling under her chin as if to say, *worth it*.

Lorrisa glanced out the window, her smile fading as the landscape rolled by—dry hills, scattered villages, the horizon shimmering with heat.

"Almost there," she murmured, half to herself, half to Kong. "If we can make it to Somalia without Sebastian catching up..."

Her eyes dropped to the map again, tracing the route with precision. "We'll hit the ruins in three days if all goes well. And if Gee's moving the same way..." She exhaled slowly, eyes narrowing. "We'll meet him there." Kong settled into her lap, curling up like a tiny sentinel, one eye still on the man across the aisle—just in case more snacks became available. The hours dragged on, the bus rattling through endless countryside, but the tension in Lorrisa's chest never eased. Every time the bus slowed or passed a checkpoint, she held her breath, waiting for the worst. But so far... nothing. No sign of Sebastian's men. No red flags.

She allowed herself a small flicker of hope.

Kong snored softly, tail wrapped around her wrist like a living bracelet. His mischievous antics had lightened the moment, but Lorrisa's mind was already racing ahead—plotting, planning, preparing for whatever came next.

She glanced at her watch, then back at the map.

"Hold tight, Gee," she whispered, her fingers brushing Kong's fur. "We're coming."

Chapter 5

Outside, the sun dipped lower, casting long shadows across the dusty road. The bus kept rolling, miles slipping away behind them, each one taking them closer to the next chapter of the hunt—and whatever dangers lay waiting ahead.

The sun was just beginning to rise, casting long, skeletal shadows across the endless expanse of sand. The landscape was desolate—rolling dunes, jagged cliffs, and nothing but silence stretching for miles.

Gee leaned forward in the passenger seat of the battered Jeep, eyes narrowing as the horizon shimmered with heat. Ahead of them, barely visible, the first crumbling pillars of the Al-Kharif ruins rose from the earth like the bones of a long-dead giant.

“There it is,” Hamid said, his voice breaking the heavy quiet. He downshifted, guiding the Jeep over a jagged slope, engine grumbling in protest. “Doesn’t look like much.”

Gee squinted, scanning the half-buried temple, its ancient stones cracked and blackened by centuries of sun. “It never does—until you start digging.”

Hamid grunted. “I’ve got a bad feeling about this place.”

Gee glanced over, a crooked smile tugging at his lips. “Do you always say that?”

“This time I mean it,” Hamid muttered, gripping the wheel tighter as they crested the last dune. The ruins loomed larger now, eerie and imposing in the dawn light. “Feels… wrong. Heavy.”

Gee didn’t answer right away. He sat forward, eyes locked on the ruins, heart thudding with a mix of dread and excitement. The stories, the legends, the pieces of the ring… it all led here.

And something—he couldn’t explain it—*called* to him.

“Let’s keep it tight,” Gee said at last, voice low. “We get in, scout the site, and see if we can find anything before Sebastian’s crew shows up.”

Hamid snorted. “Assuming they’re not already here.”

Gee’s smile faded. He reached down, checking his sidearm. “We’ll find out soon enough.”

The Jeep rolled to a stop at the base of a crumbling staircase carved into the rock. The two men sat in silence for a moment, the weight of the place pressing down on them.

Finally, Hamid killed the engine. “Well,” he said, clapping his hands on the steering wheel, “ready to poke the sleeping giant?”

Gee opened his door, stepping out into the dry, whispering wind. He looked up at the towering stones, eyes narrowing, jaw tight.

“It’s not the giant I’m worried about,” he muttered. “It’s what’s guarding it.”

Hamid climbed out after him, grabbing a pack from the backseat. “More fight?” No response.

They slung their gear and began the slow ascent up the cracked steps, boots crunching over centuries-old dust. Overhead, a hawk circled lazily, its cry echoing across the empty valley.

Gee paused halfway up, turning to look back at the Jeep, at the wide sweep of desert stretching endlessly beyond it.

Somewhere out there, Lorrisa was moving too. He could feel it in his gut.

“Hold tight,” he whispered under his breath. “We’re almost there.”

And with that, he turned back to the ruins—where secrets waited, buried deep, and danger was sure to find them first. The wind whispered through the ruins, stirring the dust that had lain undisturbed for centuries. Gee and Hamid moved cautiously, boots crunching on crumbled stone, eyes sharp as they scanned the shadows of broken pillars and collapsed walls.

For a long while, neither spoke. The only sounds were the hush of the wind and the distant cry of a lone hawk circling high above.

Finally, Hamid broke the silence, his voice low and conversational. “You ever think maybe… some things are buried for a reason?”

Gee glanced at him sideways, a small smile playing at his lips. “Every day.”

Hamid stepped over a broken slab of stone, running his hand along an ancient, faded carving. “So why chase it? These rings, this… legend. You risk your life. For what? Glory? Gold?”

Gee stopped, staring at a half-buried archway, considering his answer. “Not glory. Not gold.” He crouched down, brushing away sand from a series of strange symbols, eyes narrowing. “It’s… bigger than that.”

Hamid stood quietly beside him, arms crossed. “How much bigger?”

Gee let out a breath, leaning back on his heels. “Too big. Imagine if a despot got his hold on a power like that. The anarchy caused, the lives in danger”.

Hamid’s eyes flickered, watching him closely. “Sebastian would do this?”

Gee nodded without looking up. “Him. Or anyone like him.”

Hamid was silent for a moment, then crouched down as well, tracing the carvings lightly with his fingertips. “I’ve worked with men like Sebastian before. They always want control. Power. And they’ll burn everything down to get it.”

Gee’s eyes met his, sharp and searching. “And you? What do *you* want?”

Hamid’s brow furrowed, and he leaned back, thoughtful. “I want to survive. Maybe make some money. But mostly...” He shrugged, his eyes distant. “I don’t like bullies. And Sebastian—he’s a bully with too many toys.”

Gee studied him for a long moment, then stood, dusting off his hands. “So what’s your angle? You stick with me, you're in the middle of a storm. Doesn't sound like the easiest way to survive."

Hamid chuckled quietly, rising to his feet. "No, it doesn't. But you're... interesting. I think you might actually have a shot. And if you don't?" He grinned. "Well, at least it'll be one hell of a ride."

Gee's smile was tight, wary but amused. "You're a strange guy, Hamid."

Hamid tipped an imaginary hat. "Takes one to know one, my friend."

They moved deeper into the ruins, passing towering stone columns and half-collapsed archways. The air grew cooler, thicker, the weight of history pressing down on them.

Gee paused by a narrow entrance to a dark tunnel, peering inside. "You've been awfully helpful. No questions asked. That doesn't happen much."

Hamid raised a brow. "You think I'm playing an angle?"

"I think everyone plays an angle," Gee replied calmly, pulling out a flashlight and flicking it on. The beam cut through the darkness, illuminating more carvings, ancient and worn. "Question is... what's yours?"

Hamid smiled, stepping beside him. “Trust is a tricky thing, isn’t it?”

Gee’s gaze didn’t waver. “It is.”

Hamid leaned against the wall, folding his arms. “Let me ask you something. Say we find all the pieces. Say you put the ring back together. What then?”

Gee’s jaw tightened slightly. “I keep it out of the wrong hands.”

Hamid tilted his head, eyes sharp. “And the right hands... are yours?”

Gee’s eyes narrowed, the flashlight beam steady. “You got a problem with that?”

Hamid’s smile was slow, almost lazy. “Not yet.”

For a long moment, they stood in silence, the air thick with unspoken tension.

Then Hamid gestured toward the tunnel. “Well? Shall we see what secrets your ring is hiding?”

Gee’s smile returned, small but genuine this time. “After you.”

They descended slowly into the darkness, the tunnel sloping down deeper beneath the ruins. The air grew colder, the smell of earth and old stone surrounding them.

Hamid's voice echoed softly off the walls. "Do you believe in the stories? Solomon's power? Angels and demons?"

Gee's flashlight flicked across an ancient mural—depictions of strange creatures bowing before a robed figure, a glowing ring held aloft. "I don't know," he admitted quietly. "But something's here. Something real."

Hamid nodded slowly. "The old world was full of mysteries. Power we can't explain. I've seen things—things that shouldn't exist."

Gee glanced at him, intrigued. "Like what?"

Hamid smiled faintly, eyes distant. "Another story. For another time."

They moved deeper, the tunnel widening into a vast chamber. Stalactites hung from the ceiling like jagged teeth, and in the center of the room stood an altar—stone, ancient, and cracked down the middle.

Gee stepped forward, his breath catching slightly. "This is it."

Hamid circled the altar, eyes sharp. "Looks empty."

Gee knelt, brushing away the thick layer of dust. His fingers found grooves—shallow but deliberate. A symbol. His eyes narrowed.

"It's a marker," he said quietly. "A clue."

Hamid watched him closely. "To what?"

Gee stood slowly, staring down at the altar, his mind racing. "The next piece."

Hamid's eyes glinted. "Then we're close."

Gee's jaw tightened, eyes hard. "Closer than I like."

They stood in silence, the weight of their mission settling heavy between them.

"Whatever happens next," Gee said finally, his voice low, "you sure you're in?"

Hamid's smile was slow, eyes sharp. "I'm in. Until I'm not."

Gee laughed softly, shaking his head. "Good enough."

As they turned to leave the chamber, Hamid glanced at him sideways. "By the way... what if Sebastian catches up before we find the next piece?"

Gee's smile was grim. "Then we make sure he regrets it."

Hamid chuckled darkly. "Now *that's* the kind of plan I like."

They started back up the tunnel, boots crunching over stone, shadows dancing on the walls.

Above them, unseen, a small stone dislodged from a crumbling ledge—tumbling down, echoing faintly into the dark.

And far in the distance, just beyond the edge of hearing… another echo answered. The deeper they went, the quieter it became—no birds, no wind, just the sound of their boots crunching through centuries of dust and the faint creak of their packs. The tunnel branched twice, but both paths led into the same cavernous chamber—cool, dry, and wide enough to hold a dozen horses.

Gee adjusted his flashlight and approached the far wall. Ancient etchings, barely visible under layers of grime, whispered across the stone in curling lines and faded pictographs.

He slid his pack off and knelt, pulling out a small leather notebook and a pencil.

Hamid watched him, leaning lazily against a column. “You always take notes? Even when running for your life?”

“Especially when running for my life,” Gee muttered, squinting as he began sketching a worn symbol—two concentric rings flanked by a vertical staff. “Memory gets fuzzy under pressure. Notes don’t.”

He paused to rub a smudge from the page with the edge of his thumb, then resumed. “Besides, half the places I’ve been don’t stay upright long. Collapsed tombs. Looted dig sites. It’s all gone before you can sneeze.”

Hamid gave a short, low chuckle. “So you’re the kind of madman who plans to come back to these death traps?”

Gee glanced up, smirking. “I’m the kind who thinks knowing what was here might help me survive the next one.”

He tapped the notebook thoughtfully, eyes returning to the wall. “These symbols match the ones from Morocco... but this layout’s older. Cruder. Maybe a different scribe or priest.”

Hamid wandered further into the chamber, kicking a rock. “It all looks like scribbles to me.”

Gee looked over his shoulder, his voice a little softer. “Did you ever study archaeology? History?”

Hamid barked a laugh. “Only thing I studied was how not to die in a trench.”

Gee stood, stretching his back. “Soldier?”

Hamid nodded once. “Seven years. Local forces. Border duty, mostly. Nothing glamorous.”

Gee’s pencil paused on the page. “What happened?”

Hamid didn’t answer right away. He wandered toward another wall, where a small basin had been carved into the floor. His fingers traced the edge absently.

“Sniper,” he said finally. “Wasn't even aimed at me. Just bad timing. Took a graze to the helmet. Rattled my brain a bit. Doctors said I was lucky. My captain said I was slower afterward. Couldn’t focus as well.”

Gee turned to face him fully, watching him in the shifting beam of the flashlight.

Hamid offered a crooked smile. “Didn’t trust myself to carry a rifle after that. Figured it was time to… find another path.”

Gee was silent for a long beat, then said quietly, “That explains a lot.”

Hamid arched a brow, half-amused, half-defensive. “Yeah? Like what?”

“Like how you’re two beats behind when we’re moving, but still manage to step in at the right moment when things go sideways.”

Hamid shrugged, a little awkward. “Brain’s slower than it used to be. But the instincts? Still sharp.”

Gee gave a small nod, his tone warming. “And reliable.”

Hamid looked at him curiously. “That a compliment?”

Gee returned to the wall, flipping to a new page in his notebook. “It’s a start.”

The two men worked quietly for a while—Gee sketching markings, jotting observations, occasionally murmuring something about sediment or seismic drift. Hamid mostly kept watch, his eyes scanning the shadows, his body always leaning slightly toward alert.

"I wasn't always this twitchy," Hamid said suddenly.

Gee looked up.

Hamid gave a faint grin. "The soldiering. It sticks with you. Even when you leave. I walk into a room, I clock the exits before I see the furniture."

Gee nodded. "That's not paranoia. That's survival."

Hamid's expression turned thoughtful. "And you? What did you do before chasing relics?"

Gee chuckled. "Ah, the classics: university dropout, part-time translator, full-time problem."

Hamid raised a brow. "You dropped out of school and still read ancient writing like it's a cereal box?"

Gee held up the notebook. "Dropped out. Didn't stop learning. Most of the best lessons happen in places like this."

He paused, gazing at the wall.

"This one," he said, pointing, "talks about a test. A 'Trial of Burden'—a phrase used in a few ring legends. Usually means there's a trap or a puzzle nearby. Something meant to keep the unworthy out."

Hamid stepped closer. “Unworthy?”

Gee gave a small, tired smile. “Yeah. Usually us.”

They both laughed, quiet in the dark.

Later, sitting near a cracked cistern at the center of the chamber, Gee was flipping through older notes from Morocco while Hamid studied him.

“You write like a man who expects to be read someday,” Hamid said.

Gee shrugged. “Maybe I will be. Or maybe I’ll die in a place like this, and some grad student will find my notes and wonder what the hell I was thinking.”

Hamid leaned back on his elbows. “You ever think about stopping? Settling down?”

Gee glanced up, surprised.

Hamid grinned. “Yeah, I know. Funny coming from me.”

Gee smirked. “More than you’d think. I’ve had moments. Even tried. But…”

“But the ring calls,” Hamid finished.

Gee’s eyes drifted to his satchel, where the two pieces of Solomon’s ring were wrapped in cloth, hidden deep in a side pocket.

"Something like that," he said.

Hamid looked at him a long moment. "I think you want to protect it. Not use it."

Gee looked up sharply.

Hamid shrugged. "I've seen men chasing power. You don't look like them. You look tired. Like you're carrying something heavy you didn't ask for."

Gee stared at him, then nodded slowly. "Yeah. That's closer to the truth."

For a moment, the silence between them wasn't tense. It was understanding.

Hamid stood, brushing dust from his pants. "Well. Now that we've both admitted we're broken, wanna go poke at whatever cursed relic is next?"

Gee laughed, standing with him. "Absolutely."

Gee ran his hand along the cold stone wall, fingers brushing over the ancient carvings that hinted at deeper danger. The phrase kept circling in his mind: *Trial of Burden*. The further they moved through the ruin's twisting corridors, the more certain he was that they were walking straight into something designed to hurt them.

“This place gives me chills,” Hamid muttered, sweeping his flashlight across the passage. The beam caught on strange indentations—grooves and worn edges—as though countless others had passed this way and never returned.

“It’s supposed to,” Gee replied, adjusting the strap of his satchel. “The people who built this wanted to scare off anyone who wasn’t serious.”

“Remind me again why *we’re* serious?”

Gee grinned, but it didn’t reach his eyes. “Because the alternative is letting Sebastian find whatever’s hidden here. I’d rather face ghosts than him.”

Hamid snorted but said nothing more, falling into step beside him.

Minutes later, they came to a wide stone doorway—unmistakably a threshold to something important. Massive pillars flanked each side, cracked but still imposing. Across the lintel, carved deeper than any other markings, were words Gee translated aloud, almost reverently:

“‘Strength fails, wealth falters, but the burdened heart endures.’”

Hamid frowned. “That’s... ominous.”

Gee examined the carvings more closely, pulling out his notebook again to jot down notes. Symbols repeated themselves—burdens, balance scales, a figure bent under weight but pressing forward.

"It's a test of endurance," Gee murmured. "Not just physical... mental. Maybe moral."

Hamid cocked an eyebrow. "Any idea what's on the other side?"

Gee looked at him, serious. "Pain. That's my guess."

Hamid chuckled dryly. "Of course."

They stepped through the doorway cautiously, their flashlights flicking over the vast space beyond. It was a cavernous hall, with high ceilings supported by thick columns and a cracked mosaic floor depicting ancient battles and strange, serpent-like creatures.

At the far end stood a pedestal—a stone table with a depression carved in its center, clearly meant to hold *something*.

But between them and the pedestal... lay a gauntlet.

Boulders. Shifting stones. Heavy, rusted chains hanging from above. And a series of worn platforms across a deep chasm, as if daring them to cross.

Hamid let out a low whistle. “You ever feel like these ancient architects were *too* clever for their own good?”

Gee stared at the setup, his eyes narrowing. “Or just clever enough.”

He stepped forward, kneeling near the edge of the chasm. His flashlight swept across the platforms, revealing strange grooves—almost like hidden weights embedded in the stone.

“Weighted,” he muttered. “Pressure-based. They want you to carry something... heavy.”

Hamid looked around. “Yeah, well, unless you want to carry me, we don’t have anything that—”

Gee’s eyes landed on a pile of ancient bricks stacked near the entrance—placed there centuries ago, perhaps as part of the test.

“Found our burden,” he said.

Hamid groaned. “Of course.”

Gee slung his pack off, setting it down carefully. “We each take one,” he said, grabbing a hefty brick, dust rising as he lifted it.

Hamid eyed him warily. “Why not just one of us?”

Gee shook his head. "The markings—two scales, two figures. This trial's meant for a pair."

Hamid sighed, grabbing his own brick and hoisting it over his shoulder. "You better be right about this."

Gee grinned. "Aren't I always?"

Hamid muttered something in Arabic that sounded suspiciously like a curse.

They stepped onto the first platform together, their combined weight causing the stone beneath them to groan—and then *lock* into place with a loud, grinding *click*.

"Good start," Hamid muttered, stepping to the next.

They moved cautiously, balancing the weight of the bricks and each other, each step deliberate. The platforms rocked slightly underfoot, threatening to tip if they lingered too long or shifted their burdens.

"Keep moving," Gee urged, sweat beading on his forehead.

Halfway across, the floor beneath Hamid's feet *shuddered*—a section giving way suddenly, dropping a stone block that smashed into the depths below.

Hamid froze, eyes wide. “You said keep moving, but I’d really like to stand still right now.”

Gee grabbed his arm to steady him. “We move together. Even pace.”

Slowly, step by step, they made their way across—Gee’s mind racing with each groan of the stones, every ancient mechanism creaking back to life.

Finally, breathless and drenched in sweat, they reached the pedestal. Gee set his brick into the depression carved at its center, stepping back cautiously. Hamid did the same, both of them watching as a *click* echoed through the chamber.

For a long moment, nothing happened.

Then, with a deep rumble, a section of wall near the pedestal *shifted,* revealing a narrow passage—lined with more carvings and faint glimmers of something metallic deeper inside.

Hamid exhaled hard, hands on his knees. “You were right. Again.”

Gee smiled, wiping dust from his brow. “We’re not done yet.”

Hamid straightened, eyes flicking to the dark passage. "Think there's another trap in there?"

Gee's smile faded. "Always."

They grabbed their gear, flashlights slicing through the dark, and stepped into the new corridor—hearts pounding, minds sharp.

And somewhere deep inside, both men knew: this was only the beginning of the real test.

The corridor beyond the pedestal was narrow, its walls damp and streaked with mineral stains. Gee's flashlight picked out more carvings—warnings of trials ahead, each more ominous than the last.

Hamid's breath was still ragged. "How many damn tests did Solomon think we needed?"

"Enough to make sure no one unworthy got through," Gee replied grimly.

They advanced cautiously, boots scraping over cracked stone. After a sharp bend, the tunnel opened into a circular chamber—a dome of ancient stone, the air dense and heavy.

At the center: a long bridge, maybe twenty feet across, suspended over a yawning pit. But the bridge wasn't stone—it was lined with brittle, crumbling planks, each no wider than a handspan.

Hamid groaned. “You’ve *got* to be kidding me.”

Gee stepped closer, shining his light down. The planks stretched across the pit, some broken entirely, revealing spikes and jagged rocks far below.

“Balance test,” Gee muttered. “Classic.”

Hamid stared. “Any idea how deep that is?”

“Deep enough.”

Gee scanned the sides of the pit—no hidden ledges, no ropes left by past travelers. It was all or nothing.

“You first,” Hamid said dryly.

Gee smirked. “We stay light. One at a time. Slow and steady.”

He stepped out onto the first plank, testing his weight carefully. The wood *creaked,* but held.

Gee moved with the precision of a tightrope walker—each step slow, controlled, his arms slightly out for balance. Sweat beaded on his forehead as the ancient wood flexed under his boots.

Halfway across, a plank *cracked* beneath his left foot. Gee froze, shifting his weight back just in time.

"Careful!" Hamid barked from the edge.

Gee exhaled hard, adjusted, and kept moving. With a final step, he reached the far side, kneeling to catch his breath.

"Okay!" he called. "Your turn."

Hamid cursed under his breath but stepped onto the bridge, moving cautiously. He was heavier, each plank groaning louder beneath him.

Gee kept his light steady, eyes locked on Hamid. "Slow. Don't rush."

Halfway across, one of the planks *snapped completely*, dropping away into the pit.

Hamid froze, arms flailing slightly—but managed to catch himself on the remaining plank, wobbling but upright.

"Damn thing!" he hissed, regaining balance.

Step by painstaking step, he crossed the rest of the way, finally collapsing beside Gee.

They both sat there for a long beat, breathing hard.

“Two down,” Hamid said between gulps of air. “One more, yeah?”

Gee nodded grimly. “Yeah.”

The next corridor sloped downward, narrow and claustrophobic. After several minutes, they reached a door—a massive slab of stone etched with new symbols: a ring of eyes, each staring outward.

Gee frowned. “This is new.”

He ran his fingers over the carvings, eyes narrowing. “Says something about… the watcher’s gaze. Something about reflection.”

Hamid stepped back warily. “I don’t like that.”

Gee studied the mechanism near the door—an ancient pressure plate with a tarnished mirror fixed above it.

“I think… it’s a light puzzle. We trigger the plate, and we have to reflect the light to open the door.”

Hamid glanced around. “Only problem? No light down here.”

Gee dug through his pack, pulling out his flashlight and a compact mirror. “We make our own.”

He handed Hamid the mirror and stepped onto the plate. The moment his weight pressed down, *clunk!*—a faint glow sparked in the walls, channels of phosphorescent paint lighting up along etched lines. The beam was weak but visible.

“Follow the lines,” Gee instructed. “We have to direct it back to the door.”

Hamid angled the mirror, catching the faint light. Slowly, they bounced it from reflective spots around the chamber—each time the light beam *clicked* against a new set of symbols, another lock disengaged on the door.

Gee moved fast, his breath quickening as he shifted position. “Almost there—one more reflection—”

Hamid twisted the mirror sharply, catching the last bit of glow and reflecting it onto the final glyph.

With a deep *rumble,* the massive door slid open, revealing a wide, dark chamber beyond.

Hamid sighed in relief, lowering the mirror. “I hope we never have to do that again.”

Gee laughed quietly, stepping through the threshold. “Agreed.”

The Final Room.

The chamber beyond was immense—a natural cavern reinforced with stone arches and ancient scaffolding. Dust hung thick in the air, glittering in the flashlight beams.

Gee's eyes swept the room. "This is it."

At the far end, half-buried in a mound of dirt and rubble, was a raised stone platform—an altar carved with deep-set grooves and concentric circles.

"The ring should be here," Gee whispered, stepping closer.

Hamid stayed at the edge, scanning the shadows warily. "Let's just grab it and go."

Gee knelt by the platform, brushing dirt aside with shaking fingers. His breath caught—there, peeking through the soil, was the unmistakable glint of metal.

"I see something," he murmured, heart pounding.

Together, they dug—hands scraping, dirt falling away in chunks. Every movement sent tiny echoes through the vast, silent room.

They were so focused, they didn't hear the footsteps behind them—soft but deliberate.

"Looking for this?"

Gee froze, every hair on his neck standing up. Hamid spun around, flashlight raised—its beam landing on the figure standing in the chamber's entrance.

Lorrisa.

She leaned casually against the stone frame, dusty and travel-worn but unmistakably in control. Kong perched on her shoulder, munching something happily, his bright eyes gleaming in the dark.

Gee's jaw dropped. "Lorrisa?"

Hamid blinked in disbelief. "*You?* How—"

Lorrisa stepped forward, her eyes twinkling. "You're not the only one who knows how to read a map, Gee."

Kong squeaked, waving what looked like a stolen snack at Hamid.

Gee rose slowly, brushing dirt from his hands, shaking his head in amazement. "I... I thought—how the hell did you find us?"

Lorrisa grinned, coming to stand beside them. "Let's just say, *I had a good guide.*"

Kong chirped proudly, puffing up his little chest.

Hamid stared at them both, then looked at Gee. "You didn't tell me she was bringing a monkey."

Lorrisa laughed, eyes scanning the half-exposed ring. "Looks like you've been busy."

Gee exhaled, grinning despite himself. "You have *no* idea."

She clapped him on the shoulder, smiling warmly. "Then let's finish this."

For the first time in days, Gee felt something he hadn't dared hope for.

Hope.

Gee couldn't stop staring at Lorrisa, still trying to wrap his head around the fact that she was actually standing there—dusty, sweaty, but alive and grinning like she'd just come back from a spa day instead of a death trap.

"How—" he started, shaking his head in disbelief, "—how did you *get in here?* We had to cross a bridge of death, solve a damn light puzzle, and dodge falling rocks. What, did you do it all backwards?"

Lorrisa arched a brow, amused. "Traps?"

"Yeah," Hamid added, wiping dirt from his face, "serious ones. We almost died twice."

Lorrisa exchanged a look with Kong, who chirped and licked his paw.

She smirked, brushing some stray hair back from her face. “We didn’t see any traps.”

Gee frowned. “Wait, what?”

She tilted her head, matter-of-fact. “There’s a tomb raider’s hole blasted through the side wall. Big enough for me and Kong to walk right in. We skipped the front door.”

Hamid blinked. “You’re kidding.”

“Nope.” Lorrisa grinned. “Breezy walk. Even found a snack stand halfway in.”

Kong squeaked happily, holding up a crumbly bit of stolen food.

Gee groaned, rubbing a hand down his face. “Unbelievable.”

“That’s why you bring a *woman,* boys,” Lorrisa teased, smirking.

Hamid looked at Gee, deadpan. “We almost died for nothing.”

“I heard that,” Lorrisa said sweetly.

As the laughter settled, Gee bent to check the exposed stone where they’d been digging. He was about to say something when he froze—eyes widening slightly.

Hamid caught it first. “Uh... Gee?”

Gee stiffened, a sudden look of alarm flashing across his face.

“Gee?” Lorrisa stepped forward, noticing his strange, tense posture. “What’s—”

And then they both saw it.

From Gee’s pants pocket, a long, unmistakable *bulge* was slowly pushing outward—rigid and...well, *pointed.*

For a split second, there was stunned silence.

Gee’s face turned bright red. “Oh... *hell.*”

Lorrisa’s eyes went wide, then she clapped a hand over her mouth, trying—and failing—to hold back a laugh. “Gee... *oh my God.*”

Gee stepped back, waving frantically at his pocket, the awkward lump jutting forward stubbornly. “It’s the *rings!* I swear to God—it’s the *rings!*”

Hamid doubled over, laughing so hard he could barely breathe. “Oh, man... this is *priceless.*”

Gee glared at both of them, flustered and panicked, trying to press the offending bulge back down. “Stop! It’s reacting to *something!*”

Lorrisa, still snorting with laughter, wiped tears from her eyes. “Reacting? Sure. Real *strong reaction,* Gee. You must’ve missed me a *lot.*”

Gee shot her a deadly look, eyes darting down at the rings practically *yanking* toward the far corner of the room.

Suddenly, realization hit. His expression sharpened, and the awkwardness disappeared in an instant. “Wait... no, this isn’t that. This means—”

Lorrisa straightened, laughter dying in her throat. “What?”

Hamid was still chuckling but watching now, intrigued.

Gee pulled the two ring pieces from his pocket—both glowing faintly, trembling in his hand, their edges *pulling* toward the corner of the chamber like magnets gone wild.

Gee’s eyes narrowed. “There’s *another piece here.* Close.”

Hamid’s grin faded. “A third piece?”

Gee nodded, heart pounding now. “It has to be.”

Lorrisa’s humor vanished too, her eyes darting around the room, suddenly alert. “Where?”

Gee moved fast, following the invisible pull of the rings, his hand outstretched like a dowsing rod. Kong jumped down, sniffing excitedly at the dirt floor near one of the cracked pillars.

“Here,” Gee said breathlessly, kneeling beside Kong. “It’s here.”

Hamid grabbed a small spade and began to dig, Lorrisa dropping to her knees to help. Dust flew as they scraped and clawed through the dry earth, all of them driven by adrenaline and the electric sense that something big—*really big*—was seconds away.

And then—

Clink.

Lorrisa’s hand hit something solid. Metal. Cold.

She froze. “I’ve got it.”

Gee and Hamid leaned in close as she brushed dirt aside, revealing a smooth, ancient curve of gold and etched symbols that gleamed faintly even in the low light.

Another ring piece.

Gee reached out, hands shaking as he lifted it free from the earth. It was heavy, warm, almost humming with energy.

The three of them sat back, staring at it in awe.

Hamid broke the silence first. "That's... number three."

Lorrisa exhaled slowly, smiling despite herself. "Guess it's a good thing we found the shortcut, huh?"

Gee looked at her, his eyes softening with deep gratitude—and something more. "Yeah," he said quietly. "It's a damn good thing."

Kong squeaked, snatching the third ring out of Gee's hand for a brief second before scurrying in circles triumphantly.

Gee laughed, shaking his head. "Careful, Kong. That thing's older than both of us put together."

Lorrisa smiled, leaning back on her heels, watching the tiny monkey parade around like a champion.

For a moment, they all just breathed, savoring the rare feeling of a win. Gee hugged Lorrisa and unceremoniously kissed her. Catching her off guard. She responded by kissing him back initially, then backing off quickly with a stunned look on her face.

And then, as if on cue... the ground beneath them trembled.

Hamid's eyes widened. "Oh, no."

Gee's head snapped up, already stuffing the ring pieces into his satchel. "Time to go."

Lorrisa grabbed Kong mid-strut and leapt to her feet. "I swear, you two never do *anything* quietly."

Together, they sprinted for the exit—three explorers, a monkey, and a stolen treasure of legend—running straight into whatever came next.

The ancient ruins groaned and trembled, dust raining from cracks above as the ground shuddered beneath their feet.

"Not again!" Hamid shouted, clutching the straps of his pack as he stumbled after Gee and Lorrisa.

"Move!" Gee barked, waving them forward. "Lorrisa—lead the way!"

"On it!" she called back, sprinting toward the side of the chamber, where Kong was already darting ahead like a tiny scout.

They reached the jagged hole in the wall—a ragged, bomb-blasted opening that looked nothing like the precision of the rest of the ruin's architecture. Lorrisa ducked through first, Kong leaping effortlessly after her, and then Gee and Hamid scrambled through, just as a section of ceiling behind them *collapsed,* sending boulders crashing down where they'd stood seconds before.

Out in the open, the bright desert sun hit them like a slap. Heat and wind roared across the dunes, blinding and endless.

Lorrisa was already jogging down the slope, panting hard. "We can cut around the east side—there's a ridge we can follow to—"

"Stop right there!" a voice thundered.

All three of them froze.

Gee's heart plummeted.

They turned slowly, and there—cresting the dunes, fanning out like a net—was a squad of Sebastian's men. At least a dozen, dressed in desert gear, their machine guns leveled and ready.

Hamid cursed under his breath, raising his hands immediately. "Oh, this is bad."

Lorrisa's jaw tightened, her eyes flicking around for options—there were none.

Gee exhaled sharply, raising his hands, too. "No sudden moves."

Kong hissed and bared his tiny teeth, gripping Lorrisa's shoulder tightly.

"Easy, buddy," Lorrisa murmured, slowly lifting her arms.

The mercenaries closed in quickly, rifles trained on them from every angle.

"Well, well," a gruff voice sneered. One of the squad leaders stepped forward, smirking as he eyed them. "Looks like we caught ourselves some tomb raiders."

"Funny," Lorrisa muttered. "I don't *feel* caught. Must be the adrenaline."

The leader's smile widened. "Cute. Tie them up."

Gee, Lorrisa, and Hamid were quickly frisked and disarmed—the satchel with the ring pieces ripped from Gee's shoulder, their hands *bound tight* with rough plastic ties. Kong screeched in protest, biting one of the mercenaries on the hand before being grabbed roughly by the scruff.

"Hey!" Lorrisa barked, twisting uselessly in her bonds. "Be *gentle* with him!"

The mercenary chuckled, stuffing Kong into a small animal carrier and latching it shut. The little monkey howled, shaking the cage violently.

"Dammit," Gee muttered, eyes flashing. "Leave him alone—he's harmless!"

"Yeah, yeah," the leader sneered. He pressed a finger to his earpiece, speaking into the radio. "Boss, we've got them. All three. And the monkey."

A pause.

Then: "Understood. We're bringing them in."

The leader snapped his fingers. "Let's move. The boss wants a chat with our little treasure hunters... before we put them down."

Gee and Hamid exchanged a look, grim but unsurprised.

Lorrisa glared at the squad leader, her voice cold as ice. "You tell Sebastian I'm *done talking.*"

The leader grinned, shoving her forward. "You can tell him yourself, sweetheart."

The mercenaries loaded them into the back of a dusty transport truck—hot, cramped, the smell of oil and sweat thick in the air. Kong's cage was shoved between the crates, his little hands gripping the bars as he whimpered softly.

Gee leaned back against the rattling metal wall, eyes locked on Lorrisa across from him. "I'm sorry," he said quietly.

She shook her head, her eyes fierce but resigned. "Not your fault. We were never going to outrun him forever."

Hamid let out a bitter laugh. "Well... at least we found the ring piece before dying. That's something, yes?"

Lorrisa glanced down at her tied hands, then at the satchel the mercenaries had taken—now sitting just out of reach near the front of the truck. "Too bad we don't get to keep it."

Gee's jaw clenched. "We're not dead yet."

Hamid arched a brow. "Optimistic."

Gee's eyes stayed sharp, scanning the truck's interior, always searching for an angle. "No. Just stubborn."

Kong whined quietly, eyes flicking between them.

Meanwhile, at a makeshift encampment several miles away, Sebastian paced impatiently inside a large canvas tent, phone pressed to his ear.

“Confirmed?” he barked.

“Yes, sir,” Callum’s voice crackled over the line. “We have all three of them. They’re on their way now.”

Sebastian’s lips curved into a slow, vicious smile. “Good. Bring them straight to me. I want to see their faces one last time... before we finish this.”

He ended the call, his eyes gleaming with cold satisfaction. The trap had finally sprung—and soon, everything he’d fought for would be within reach.

“Checkmate,” he murmured.

Back in the truck, the dunes rolled by, the sun high and merciless overhead. Time dragged, but the weight of what was coming pressed down on all of them.

Gee sat motionless, his mind racing.

Lorrisa’s eyes stayed locked on Kong’s cage, her jaw tight.

And Hamid—sweating, tired, but still half-smiling—leaned back and muttered, “So... anyone got a miracle up their sleeve?”

No one answered.

Gee sat slumped against the side of the rattling truck, wrists bound tight behind his back, the plastic biting into his skin. His jaw clenched, muscles twitching uselessly as he shifted to get some feeling back in his fingers.

The weight in his pocket was gone. Empty. His rings—*their* rings—had been taken. Stripped away when Callum's men patted him down back at the capture site.

Across from him, Lorrisa sat close to Kong's cage, eyes hollow but burning. Her hands were tied too, her fingers gripping the edge of the cage like it was an anchor in the chaos.

Hamid leaned his head back against the metal wall, sweat running down his temples in slow streams. His voice cut through the tense silence, dry but tinged with grim humor.

"ماذا الآن؟" he muttered. (*What now?*)

Gee's eyes stayed on the floor, his chest heaving with frustration. "Ahora... we wait," he bit out. (*Now... we wait.*)

Kong chattered softly, agitated by the swaying and heat. Lorrisa leaned in to stroke his tiny head through the bars, whispering, “Shhh, tranquilo, pequeño. Stay calm.”

Hamid shifted forward slightly, his dark eyes scanning Gee’s bound hands. “Your magic tricks, Rodriguez... I don’t see them working this time.”

Gee gave a bitter laugh, shaking his head. “Yeah... me neither.”

The truck hit a deep rut, jolting hard enough that Lorrisa nearly toppled over, catching herself just in time. Her hair clung to her face, damp with sweat, but her voice was sharp and steady.

“They took everything?”

Gee’s eyes lifted to hers, cold and hollow. “Sí. All of it. The rings, the map... gone.”

She cursed under her breath, her shoulders sagging for just a second before the fire returned to her eyes. “Bastards.”

“Agreed,” Hamid muttered, flexing his shoulders. “And now they have everything they need.”

The truck began to slow, a grinding sound as the driver downshifted. Shouts rang out outside—orders barked, feet crunching in the sand.

“They’re stopping,” Lorrisa said softly, her eyes locked on the back doors.

Gee sat up straighter, eyes narrowing. “Esto es.” (*This is it.*)

The doors flew open with a bang, and hot daylight streamed in, blinding them for a moment. Armed guards waved their rifles.

“Descend! Now!”

Hamid climbed out first, steady and calm, eyes scanning the horizon as though already counting escape routes. Lorrisa followed, clutching Kong’s cage with her bound hands, her jaw set. Gee slid down last, landing hard on his boots, his hands still lashed behind his back.

They were marched across a flat expanse of sand, toward the center of a bustling encampment where vehicles, gear, and tents sprawled under the sun’s merciless glare. Sebastian stood at the entrance to the largest tent, sunglasses on, one hand lazily in his pocket, the other holding a sat-phone.

His smile grew as they were shoved to their knees before him.

“Well, well,” Sebastian drawled, stepping forward, the desert wind tugging at his tailored shirt. “The prodigal treasure hunters return. Looking a little worse for wear.”

Gee stared up at him, breathing hard through his nose, his wrists raw and red.

Sebastian crouched in front of him, his smile ice-cold. “Missing something, Rodriguez?”

He held up his hand, and in his palm gleamed the three rings—gleaming gold and ancient, shining with that strange inner glow. Sebastian’s eyes glittered with triumph.

“I must say, you did the hard part beautifully,” he murmured. “And now... it’s mine.”

Lorrisa’s voice lashed out, sharp as a whip. “You won’t get what you want. The tablet’s secrets... you don’t even understand what you’re messing with.”

Sebastian laughed, slipping the rings into a small velvet pouch and tucking it into his jacket pocket. “Oh, but I intend to find out. And you—my dear—are going to help me.”

Gee struggled against his bindings, veins standing out in his forearms. “Over my dead body.”

Sebastian leaned in, almost nose to nose with Gee, his voice a venomous whisper. “Indeed, that’s the point.”

He stood, brushing sand from his knees, and nodded to his men. “Holding tent. Keep them close. We’ll move at dawn.”

Callum grabbed Gee roughly by the arm and hauled him to his feet, while two others dragged Lorrisa and Hamid after. Kong screeched in his cage, his tiny fists banging against the bars.

Sebastian’s gaze lingered as they were led away, his smile razor-sharp. “Rest up. Tomorrow, history changes.”

The guards shoved the trio into a low canvas tent at the edge of camp, zippered the entrance, and posted two men at the flap with rifles slung across their chests.

Inside, it was dark and stifling. Gee stumbled to a corner and sat hard, breathing fast, sand clinging to the sweat on his face.

Hamid dropped beside him, exhaling in frustration. “They have everything now.”

“Not everything,” Lorrisa said quietly, placing Kong’s cage down and kneeling beside Gee. Her eyes searched his face, fierce and alive despite it all. “We’re still breathing.”

Gee’s lips twitched into a humorless smile. “For now.”

He flexed his fingers behind his back, testing the zip ties, his voice low and hard. “But it’s not over. No jodidamente way.” (*No f***ing way.**)

Hamid’s brow arched slightly. “You have a plan?”

Gee’s eyes locked onto his. “No. But I’ve got anger. And sometimes… that’s enough to start.”

Kong let out a soft chirp, eyes bright in the dark.

Lorrisa nodded, her expression like flint. “Then let’s figure out the rest.”

Outside, the sun was dipping lower, casting long, ominous shadows across the camp—while inside the tent, the clock on their survival had already started ticking. The inside of the tent was stifling, thick with the smell of dust, sweat, and canvas. Light leaked through small cracks where the rough fabric didn’t quite meet at the seams, casting slashes of gold across their faces.

Gee sat propped against a crate, arms twisted painfully behind his back, the zip ties biting deeper with every tiny movement. Lorrisa crouched beside Kong’s cage, her eyes dark, sharp. Hamid paced like a caged tiger, every few steps pausing to glance at the tent's entrance where two guards stood silhouetted against the fading sunlight.

Outside, the sounds of the camp were loud and clear—engines idling, the clatter of weapons being checked, occasional bursts of laughter. And then… footsteps. Confident. Measured.

Sebastian.

They could hear his voice before they saw him. Arrogant, smooth as silk.

"Secure the perimeter. I want no surprises tonight," he was saying to Callum, who grunted in response. "And double-check the rings—I don't want any of my men getting ideas."

The flap of the tent snapped open, and Sebastian stepped inside, hands behind his back, eyes gleaming with that same predatory light.

"Well, well," he drawled, looking around as though he were visiting old friends. "How are my guests settling in? Comfortable?"

"Chingate," Gee muttered, not even bothering to look at him. (*Go screw yourself.*)

Sebastian laughed, clapping his hands once. "Ah, the fighting spirit! I have to admit, Rodriguez, you've impressed me. Really, I thought you'd be dead by now."

He circled them slowly, his boots crunching softly in the sand scattered across the tent floor. His gaze lingered on Lorrisa, head tilting slightly.

"And you, my dear Professor Santos-Rodriguez... quite the transformation. From lecturing halls to crawling through tombs... you wear it well."

Lorrisa's eyes narrowed, voice cutting like ice. "I'll wear your guts like a necklace if you touch me again."

Sebastian's smile thinned. He turned sharply to Hamid, pausing in front of him. "And our silent soldier... ever loyal. I wonder—are you in this for the money, or have you developed a taste for lost causes?"

Hamid's eyes met his calmly, his voice low but edged with steel. "I have a taste... for justice."

Sebastian snorted. "Justice. What a quaint idea."

He pulled the velvet pouch from his jacket pocket and untied the string with deliberate slowness, tipping the contents into his palm—the three rings, shimmering and ancient, seemed to glow even in the dim tent light.

"Beautiful, aren't they?" he murmured, admiring the way the carvings caught the fading sun. "So much power... locked away for so long. And you..." he glanced at Gee, "you were just too weak to unlock it."

Gee's jaw clenched. "You don't understand what you're holding. You think you can control it, but you're wrong."

Sebastian's eyes glittered with amusement. "Oh, I understand plenty. Power is power. You just have to be willing to seize it. And I am."

He tucked the rings away again with a smirk. "The best part? Tomorrow morning, when I complete what you all started, the world will change... and no one will even remember your names."

He stepped back, brushing his hands together like wiping away dust. "Sleep well, my friends. Tomorrow's a big day."

Turning on his heel, he strode out of the tent, barking orders to his guards as he went. The flap zipped shut behind him, and they heard the muted thump of his boots fading into the night.

For a moment, the tent was silent except for the faint hum of the rings, now muffled but still pulsing somewhere nearby.

Hamid exhaled slowly. “Bastard.”

“No argument here,” Gee muttered, leaning his head back and closing his eyes briefly. “We’ve got to get out of here. Fast.”

Lorrisa sat down beside him, brushing hair from her face, her voice low and urgent. “You saw where he put the rings?”

Gee nodded without opening his eyes. “Jacket pocket. Left side.”

Hamid crouched beside them, dropping his voice even lower. “Guards out front... two that I counted. Maybe more around the perimeter. No weapons inside here. We have nothing.”

Kong gave a tiny chirp, his eyes wide and twitching between the three of them as if sensing the weight of the moment.

Gee’s voice was grim. “We have nothing—yet.”

Lorrisa’s eyes glinted. “But we have each other. And we know this terrain better than they think.”

Hamid shook his head, lips pressed tight. “Still... those zip ties...”

Lorrisa's eyes scanned the tent, sharp and searching. Her gaze landed on a broken crate in the corner, a jagged splinter of wood poking out at just the right angle.

She nodded toward it. "Gee. Over there."

He followed her eyes, and despite the pain in his shoulders, began the slow, inching crawl toward the crate, dragging himself across the rough ground like a wounded animal.

Lorrisa and Hamid kept watch by the flap, shoulders tense, every nerve alive.

"Apúrate," Lorrisa whispered fiercely. (*Hurry.*)

Gee gritted his teeth and worked his wrists against the splintered wood. Every scrape sent a bolt of pain through his arms, but he pressed on, sawing back and forth, breath shallow.

Outside, the guards muttered to each other, laughing at some crude joke, oblivious to what was brewing inside.

Gee's breathing quickened. The zip tie frayed—slowly, agonizingly—then, with a soft snap, gave way.

"Got it," he hissed, sitting up fast, rubbing his raw wrists.

Hamid grinned. "الله أكبر." (*God is great.*)

Gee rolled his shoulders, shaking out his arms. His eyes locked on Lorrisa's, fierce and ready.

"Now," he said, his voice low and full of purpose, "let's make them regret keeping us alive."

Kong gave a quiet, approving chirp, eyes bright and wild.

The night deepened outside, shadows stretching longer, as the trio prepared for whatever came next—because they knew the clock was ticking, and there was no room left for failure.

Gee flexed his wrists, the sting from the broken zip ties sharp but satisfying. He crouched low, rubbing the raw skin, already thinking ahead.

"We need a clean exit," he whispered, eyes darting around the dim tent. "Fast and quiet if possible. Loud if it comes to that."

Hamid nodded, moving closer. "Two guards out front. Maybe more on a perimeter sweep. There's no way we can just walk out."

Gee's brow furrowed. "What about weapons?"

Hamid shook his head. “Nothing. I saw a few crates near the vehicles, but between here and there... we’re exposed.”

Lorrisa wiped sweat from her brow, eyes sharp and thoughtful. “We’re tied up in here, but the guards—lazy. Too comfortable. You saw how relaxed they were.”

She looked at Kong, who was clutching the bars of his cage, watching them intently.

A slow smile spread across her face. “He’s small enough. If we can get the cage open...”

Gee followed her gaze, catching on. “And send him out.”

Hamid frowned. “That little monkey?”

“Not just *little monkey*,” Lorrisa said, grinning now. “Kong’s clever. He’s unlocked handcuffs before. He can easily unlatch a tent flap.”

Gee’s eyes gleamed. “Yeah... and while he’s out there, he can stir the pot—bite, scratch, distract the guards. Cause chaos.”

Lorrisa leaned in, her voice quick and urgent. “We wait until one of the guards gets curious—maybe comes in to check on us if Kong’s causing enough of a scene. We ambush him, grab his weapon, and take down the other guard fast."

Hamid's eyes narrowed in thought. "That's two. But what about the others? They'll hear the commotion."

Gee nodded. "We've got a small window, maybe a few minutes. Once we're out, we make a beeline for the trucks. Create a diversion—something big. Blow up a fuel drum if we can find one."

Hamid smirked. "You think like a soldier."

Gee shrugged. "I think like a guy who wants to stay alive."

Lorrisa crouched by Kong's cage, speaking to him in soothing tones. "Okay, pequeño, listen to me... necesito que seas muy valiente ahora. (*I need you to be very brave now.*) When we open the cage, you slip out quiet and fast. Go to the tent flap... and get it open. Make noise. Get their attention. But be ready to run."

Kong stared at her, wide-eyed, then gave a determined little screech, as if understanding every word.

"Dios mío, he's really in," Gee muttered, shaking his head in awe.

Lorrisa worked fast on the cage latch, using a broken strip of wood to jimmy it loose. With a soft click, it popped open just a crack.

"Ready?" she whispered, looking at Gee and Hamid.

Gee crouched by the flap, muscles tense, ready to spring. Hamid gripped a jagged piece of crate wood, eyes locked on the entrance.

Lorrisa kissed Kong's tiny head. "Ve, Kong. Ahora." (*Go, Kong. Now.*)

Kong slipped out, low and nimble, scuttling across the tent floor. He paused at the flap, pressed a tiny hand to the zipper—and, with surprising strength, tugged it upward just enough to slip through.

Seconds later, the muffled sound of a guard's sharp curse drifted in.

"Damn thing—get back here!"

Then a yelp.

Kong screeched, louder this time, and the sound of shuffling boots followed—one of the guards clearly flailing, caught off guard.

Inside, Gee whispered, "That's our cue. Wait for it..."

Another yelp. A thud. The flap rattled violently, and then one of the guards stumbled halfway inside, rifle dangling as he tried to swat at Kong, who had scrambled up his back like a wildcat.

"¡Ahora!" Gee roared, launching himself forward.

Hamid slammed the guard in the temple with the broken crate wood, dropping him like a stone. Gee snatched the rifle and spun toward the flap, just in time to catch the second guard aiming his weapon.

"¡Atrás!" Gee shouted, firing a warning burst into the sand near the guard's feet. (*Back off!*)

The guard froze, eyes wide, hands up.

Hamid rushed out, tackling him to the ground and silencing him with a swift punch. He dragged him inside the tent, stripping the rifle from his slack hands.

Gee knelt beside Kong, who was shaking but unharmed. "You good, pequeño?"

Kong chattered proudly, gripping the hem of Gee's sleeve.

Lorrisa was already moving, grabbing the fallen guard's utility belt, checking for keys and weapons. She tossed a pistol to Hamid and kept one for herself.

"Truck yard is due west," Hamid whispered, scanning the shadows. "We go fast."

Gee nodded. "We make noise at the yard, draw everyone there... then we slip into the dunes and vanish."

Lorrisa gave Kong a quick cuddle and tucked him into her bag, peeking out just enough for him to breathe. "Stay quiet now, chiquito."

The three of them crept to the edge of the tent, ears straining.

"Ready?" Gee asked, voice low.

"Siempre," Lorrisa said fiercely. (*Always*.)

Hamid gave a single nod, eyes sharp.

Gee drew a slow breath. "Let's disappear."

And into the night they moved—silent, deadly, and ready to set the camp ablaze if that's what it took to escape. They slipped out of the tent like shadows, low to the ground, eyes flicking constantly for movement. The camp was alive but relaxed—guards chatting by fires, others smoking near parked trucks, their rifles slung lazily over shoulders. The sense of false security hung thick, and Gee knew that was their only advantage.

They moved west, sticking to the deepest pools of darkness between tents and crates. Kong's tiny head peeked out from Lorrisa's bag, his bright eyes darting around, whiskers twitching.

Gee crouched behind a battered water barrel, holding up a fist to halt the group. He jerked his chin toward the far side of camp, where a trio of guards laughed near an open fire pit, their backs to the truck yard. A flickering oil drum sent long shadows dancing across crates of ammo, fuel, and stacked supplies.

"Truck yard's just beyond them," Hamid whispered, leaning in close. "But we can't sneak past. Too exposed."

Gee nodded, voice barely audible. "We need to create a crack in their focus. Get their eyes somewhere else."

Lorrisa's eyes scanned the cluttered camp. "Fuel drums. If we can knock one over near the back row—quietly—we might pull a few of them away."

Hamid pointed toward a stack of crates balanced precariously on a rusted trailer. "Those crates too. If they fall, it'll sound like an earthquake."

Gee's smile was thin and calculating. "Kong."

Lorrisa reached into her bag and stroked the little monkey's head. "You up for another job, chiquito?"

Kong let out a faint chitter, eyes bright, tiny hands gripping her thumb.

She whispered urgently in Spanish, pointing to the crates. "Deslízate allí... empuja eso. Suave primero. Luego corre rápido." (*Slip over there... push that. Slow at first. Then run fast.*)

Kong wriggled free, scampering across the sand like a wraith. They watched, breath held tight, as he darted under trucks, around barrels, finally climbing onto the trailer's rusted axle.

"Casi..." Lorrisa whispered. (*Almost...*)

Kong reached the edge of the stacked crates, his little body pressed flat, tail flicking nervously. He gave one final look back at Lorrisa, as if for confirmation.

She nodded once, firm.

Kong pushed.

The top crate wobbled, scraped—and suddenly crashed down with a tremendous, echoing *BANG*.

A second crate tumbled after it, shattering on impact. Loose metal tools and supplies spilled everywhere, clanging like a car crash in the silent desert air.

"¡¿Qué diablos?!" one of the guards shouted, scrambling to his feet, rifle raised. (*What the hell?!*)

The others leapt up, circling the noise with shouts and frantic orders.

Gee grabbed Lorrisa and Hamid by the arms. "Move. Now."

They sprinted low and fast across the clearing, using the chaos as cover. Kong was already flying back toward them, tiny feet kicking up dust as he scrambled into Lorrisa's bag, panting hard.

Behind them, guards fanned out, flashlights slicing through the darkness. Angry voices barked orders in Spanish and Arabic.

"¡Verifica el perímetro!"
"!ابحثوا هناك"
(*Check the perimeter! / Search over there!*)

Gee and Hamid reached the edge of the truck yard first, flattening themselves against the side of a fuel truck. The faint smell of diesel filled the air.

"We've got minutes—maybe less—before they realize," Hamid whispered, eyes darting. "What's the diversion?"

Gee's eyes scanned frantically, then landed on a half-empty fuel drum with a rag sticking out of its spout.

A grin spread across his face. "Good old-fashioned fireworks."

Lorrisa's eyes widened. "You're going to light that?"

Gee was already digging into the guard's stolen utility belt, pulling out a weatherproof match pack. He flicked one alive, the tiny flame hissing in the desert breeze.

"Everyone clear?" he asked, voice tight.

Hamid and Lorrisa were already dragging crates to create makeshift cover behind a nearby truck, Kong clinging tightly to Lorrisa's bag strap.

"Do it!" Lorrisa hissed.

Gee yanked the rag loose, doused it with the trickling diesel, then shoved it halfway back into the drum. He lit the end, watching the flame creep along the soaked fabric like a snake, flickering and hissing.

He ran, sliding into cover beside the others.

"Any second now," he muttered, heart hammering.

Shouts rang out behind them—guards returning from the crate collapse, flashing lights now arcing toward the truck yard.

Then—

BOOM.

The drum exploded in a fireball, a shockwave blasting through the yard, setting off a chain reaction as other fuel drums and crates went up in secondary blasts. The night turned orange and red, smoke billowing high into the sky.

Screams, gunfire, and wild shouts filled the air as chaos engulfed the camp.

"Go!" Gee roared, grabbing Lorrisa's hand as they bolted toward the far perimeter, Hamid covering their rear with the stolen rifle, firing bursts to keep guards' heads down.

Kong shrieked, peeking out from Lorrisa's bag as firelight and smoke blurred together behind them.

The desert opened up beyond the camp—a sea of dunes and darkness.

"Into the dunes!" Hamid yelled, eyes scanning the horizon. "We can lose them in the sand!"

They ran, adrenaline burning, hearts pounding, fire and smoke rising behind them like a dying monster's roar.

And as the camp faded into the night's chaos, Gee glanced at Lorrisa, a ragged smile breaking across his face.

"Not bad for no plan, huh?"

She laughed breathlessly, tears streaking from the smoke. "Not bad at all."

But even as they ran, Gee's mind circled back to the velvet pouch—the rings still with Sebastian, somewhere in the flames.

And he knew: their fight was only just beginning.

The dunes swallowed them whole.

Breath ragged and legs burning, the trio finally slowed their sprint, ducking into the shelter of a narrow ravine between two towering ridges of sand. The fire from the camp was still visible in the distance, a distant orange smear against the black sky, but the shouts and gunfire had faded into the night.

Lorrisa slumped down against the slope, pulling Kong from her bag and cradling him close. The little monkey was shaking, his chest heaving with tiny breaths.

“Está bien... ya pasó,” she whispered, stroking his fur. (*It’s okay... it’s over.*)

Gee dropped to his knees a few feet away, chest rising and falling like a bellows, sweat cutting rivulets through the dirt on his face. He turned and sat heavily, wiping his forehead and staring back toward the chaos they’d left behind.

Hamid stayed standing, rifle cradled in his arms, eyes on the distant glow. He said nothing, just breathing quietly, watchful.

For a while, no one spoke. Just the wind across the sand, the sound of breathing, and the distant crackle of burning debris.

Finally, Lorrisa broke the silence, her voice shaking but resolute.

“That’s it.”

Gee looked over at her, brow furrowed. “What?”

She met his eyes, fierce and tired all at once. “I’m done. We barely made it out alive, Gee. This isn’t some academic scavenger hunt anymore—this is war.”

Gee didn’t answer, his gaze heavy.

She pressed on, voice rising. “You saw what Sebastian’s capable of. You *know* what he’s willing to do. We’ve been lucky, but sooner or later, luck runs out. I’m not dying out here.”

Gee let out a long breath, leaning forward, elbows on his knees. He stared at the sand, chewing his lip in thought.

Hamid sat down beside them, resting the rifle across his lap. His eyes bounced between them, but he said nothing—waiting.

Lorrisa kept going, her voice softer but no less intense. “Look… I get it. The rings are important. Maybe they *do* have power, maybe it’s not just legend. But we’re outmatched. We have nothing. You need to let me go back.”

She paused, swallowing. “I’ll get back to the States, find help if I can… but this? This isn’t my fight anymore.”

Kong made a soft whimper, burying his face in her shoulder.

Gee’s jaw flexed. His eyes flicked to Hamid, who sat silent, patient. Then back to Lorrisa, who stared at him with a kind of desperate calm.

For a long moment, all he could hear was the wind.

"I don't blame you," Gee said finally, his voice low and even. "I can't."

Lorrisa blinked, surprised by his calm.

He looked at her now, his eyes tired but searching. "You're right. We've been running blind, and we've been *damn* lucky. I should've... I should've sent you home the moment this got ugly."

Lorrisa shook her head. "Don't do that. Don't pin this on yourself."

Gee sighed, looking out across the endless dunes, his voice dropping to almost a whisper. "You're not a soldier, Lorrisa. Neither am I, really. We were never meant for this."

He rubbed his raw wrists absently, eyes distant. "But those rings... if Sebastian figures out how to use them, if he finds more... I don't know. I don't know what happens."

Lorrisa stayed quiet, watching him, her breath catching just a little.

Hamid finally spoke, his voice quiet but steady. "We all have reasons to fight. Or not to. I wait for your choice."

Gee looked at him, a wry smile tugging the corner of his mouth. “You don’t say much, Hamid.”

Hamid shrugged. “Enough has been said tonight.”

Gee exhaled deeply, leaning back against the sand, eyes tracing the stars above. “We’ll rest here until first light. Then we figure out the safest way to get Lorrisa out.”

Lorrisa nodded, holding Kong closer. “Thank you.”

Gee’s eyes were hard now, his voice turning cold. “And after that... I’m not letting Sebastian walk away with those rings. Not while I’m breathing.”

Meanwhile...

Back at the camp, Sebastian stood amid smoldering wreckage, the acrid smell of burning fuel hanging heavy in the air. His sunglasses were gone now, his eyes sharp and dangerous, jaw clenched in rage.

Callum stood beside him, looking grim. “They’re gone. Vanished into the dunes.”

Sebastian’s fingers curled into fists. “Idiots. I *told* you to tighten security.”

"They had help," Callum muttered. "That monkey of hers—he's a damn menace."

Sebastian let out a long breath, trying to calm the boiling fury inside. He patted the pocket of his jacket where the velvet pouch—miraculously unharmed—rested against his chest.

The rings. Still his.

And that was all that mattered.

"Fine," he said at last, his voice like steel. "They're running scared now. Let them. We have what we need."

He turned toward the remaining vehicles and equipment, eyes cold and calculating. "We break camp. Immediately. There's another lead—another potential ring. We pursue that."

Callum hesitated. "And Rodriguez?"

Sebastian smiled thinly, eyes glittering. "He'll come to us. Trust me. The fool can't help himself."

He barked orders, his voice sharp and crisp. The camp roared to life, men scrambling to pack up what was left. Engines revved, tires bit into the sand.

Sebastian stood still for a moment, watching the horizon where the dunes stretched endlessly into darkness.

“Checkmate,” he muttered under his breath, gripping the pouch tighter.

Back in the dunes, Gee, Lorrisa, and Hamid sat in tense silence, each lost in their own thoughts, the desert night cold and vast around them.

The next move loomed—and none of them knew just how fast the game was still shifting beneath their feet.

The Town.

The first light of dawn crept across the dunes, painting the sand in hues of pink and gold. Gee, Lorrisa, Hamid, and Kong had trekked through the night, their bodies pushed to the limit but driven by sheer will.

After hours of endless sand and searing quiet, the distant shimmer of rooftops finally came into view—a small border town, tucked between jagged cliffs and the vast desert.

“Finalmente,” Lorrisa breathed, gripping Kong tighter. (*Finally.*)

The streets were dusty and narrow, lined with faded buildings and stray cats weaving between the shadows. Market stalls, half-awake, began opening as locals set out their goods, eyeing the ragged trio with curiosity but little concern.

They found a cheap hotel near the main square—a battered old place with a crooked neon sign buzzing faintly in the daylight. Inside, the air was thick with incense and old sweat, but the rooms were clean enough.

Gee tossed his backpack onto the floor, collapsing onto the bed, arms flung wide, eyes on the cracked ceiling.

Lorrisa slid down against the wall, still clutching Kong, who now snoozed against her chest, finally calm after hours of being jostled.

Hamid sat cross-legged on the floor, resting the rifle across his lap.

"Half-day rest," Gee muttered, eyes closing briefly. "Then we get you out of here."

Lorrisa didn't answer. She just stared at him, a thousand words sitting heavy behind her eyes.

The Airport

By late afternoon, they'd made their way to the airport—a small, aging terminal buzzing with travelers, soldiers, and tired tourists trying to get through customs as quickly as possible.

The three of them stood at the entrance to the departure gate, Lorrisa holding Kong's crate now—checked in as a service animal, papers hastily arranged thanks to Hamid's contacts in town.

Her flight was boarding soon. Time was running out.

Gee stood stiffly, hands shoved in his pockets, eyes flicking from her to Kong and back again.

"You're sure about this?" she asked softly, voice trembling just a bit now that it was real. "You could come with me. Both of you."

Gee shook his head, jaw clenched. "I can't."

"Gee—"

"I *want* to," he said quickly, stepping closer, lowering his voice. "But if Sebastian's still out there... if he finds another lead... I can't leave it. You *know* I can't."

Lorrisa's eyes shone, her knuckles white against the crate handle. "Damn it, Gee. You're going to get yourself killed."

He smiled, tired and sad. "I've been trying to avoid that part."

A silence stretched between them, loud and full of all the things they couldn't say.

Finally, Lorrisa let out a shaky breath, blinking fast. "I don't want to say goodbye like this."

Gee took her face in his hands, gently, like it was the last fragile thing he'd ever hold. "Then don't."

And he kissed her—long, deep, desperate. Like lovers of old. Like people who knew the odds but kissed anyway.

When they pulled apart, her forehead rested against his, tears slipping free now. Kong let out a soft whimper from his crate, sensing the tension.

"You stay alive, Rodriguez," she whispered fiercely. "Promise me."

Gee's voice was low, steady. "Te lo prometo." (*I promise.*)

She lingered a second more, eyes memorizing every line of his face, then grabbed Kong's crate and turned—quickly—before she lost her nerve.

She strode to the check-in gate, handing over her boarding pass, barely looking back.

Gee stood there, hands in his pockets again, shoulders tense. He watched her until she disappeared around the corner, swallowed by the terminal.

Gone.

Gee and Hamid exited the airport terminal into the humid dusk, the low roar of planes overhead. They didn't speak for a long time as they walked across the lot toward their rental jeep.

"She'll be safe," Hamid said finally, quiet but sure.

Gee nodded, jaw tight. "Yeah."

They climbed into the jeep, fired up the engine, and pulled away from the curb—dust trailing behind them.

Neither of them noticed the sleek black car pulling up near the entrance.

Inside the airport, Sebastian stepped out of the vehicle, sunglasses on, jacket crisp, the velvet pouch of rings still tucked snug against his chest. He moved through the terminal smoothly, blending with the crowd, his eyes scanning the boarding signs.

His lips curled into a thin smile as he spotted the gate.

Flight 742—nonstop to New York.

He adjusted his cuffs and made his way calmly through security, ticket in hand, stepping into line for the same flight Lorrisa had just boarded.

As he passed through the final checkpoint, his smile deepened.

The jet engines started to turn, outside the sun dipping low over the runway. The last boarding call echoed through the terminal. Flight 742—nonstop to New York.

Lorrisa adjusted Kong's travel crate, her fingers trembling just slightly. Her chest still burned from the goodbye with Gee, and the dull ache of leaving everything behind weighed heavier than she'd expected.

She followed the stream of passengers toward the tarmac. The late evening sun threw long shadows across the plane's side, heat shimmering off the pavement. At the back stairwell, an attendant checked her boarding pass quickly and waved her on.

"Rear cabin, aisle five," he said with a smile.

Lorrisa nodded absently, clutching Kong's crate, feeling Kong stir inside—quiet now, drowsy from exhaustion and the sedative she'd tucked into his treats earlier.

The air inside the plane was stale and cool, a contrast to the thick humidity outside. She made her way to her seat, squeezing into the narrow row of the economy cabin, settling Kong's crate at her feet. A middle-aged woman with too much perfume slid into the window seat beside her, already flipping through a magazine.

Lorrisa let out a long breath, leaning her head back. *Just a few more hours,* she told herself. *Then it's over.*

She bent down and opened the crate just a crack to check on Kong. He blinked up at her, those dark little eyes filled with quiet trust.

"We're going home, pequeño," she whispered, brushing her fingers across his fur. "Almost there."

The plane was still boarding when a flicker of movement caught her eye—shadows and bodies filing down the aisle.

She glanced up… and froze.

Sebastian.

He strode down the aisle, polished as ever: crisp jacket, sleek shoes, dark glasses concealing his eyes. One hand tucked casually into his jacket pocket—the other rolling his carry-on smoothly behind him. He didn't look around. Didn't even hesitate as he passed row after row, eyes locked straight ahead.

Arrogant. Confident. Completely unaware.

Lorrisa shrank back instinctively, heart slamming against her ribs, her breath catching in her throat. Her fingers tightened on the armrest, knuckles whitening.

What the hell...?

He was on *her plane*.

Her pulse roared in her ears. She kept perfectly still, eyes following him as he moved forward, oblivious. He never looked her way—not once—as he turned up toward the business-class section and disappeared behind the curtain.

Her mind raced. *The rings. He's taking them out of the country. That son of a bitch...*

She looked down at Kong, who blinked up at her, somehow sensing the shift.

"No me jodas..." she muttered under her breath. (*You've got to be kidding me.*)

She sat frozen for a moment, wrestling with a hundred thoughts at once. She was supposed to be leaving this behind. Safe. Done.

But the rings... the damn *rings*... were right here. Just *rows away*.

She clenched her jaw, fingers digging into her thighs. Her breath hissed out between her teeth.

"Hijueputa," she whispered fiercely. (*Son of a bitch.*)

Her eyes darted toward the front of the cabin. The boarding was nearly done, passengers buckling in, the buzz of conversation rising and falling like waves. Flight attendants moved briskly, closing overhead bins, checking seatbelts.

Suddenly, she saw him.

Sebastian—rising from his seat. Calm, precise. Slipping down the aisle toward the bathroom near the cockpit.

Lorrisa's pulse quickened. Her body tensed like a coiled spring.

This is it. Right now, or never.

She stood abruptly, grabbing Kong's crate and stowing it under her seat, whispering softly, "Quedate aquí, pequeño. Be still."

Kong gave a soft grunt, curling back into the blanket.

Lorrisa slid into the aisle, heart hammering, her eyes sharp, locked onto Sebastian's tall frame as he disappeared into the lavatory, the door clicking shut behind him.

She moved fast—quiet, smooth, weaving past flight attendants who were too busy to notice one more passenger stretching her legs. Step by step, she made her way toward the front, her mind narrowing into a single, razor-sharp focus.

The bathroom light above the door blinked: *Occupied*.

She waited—hands shaking slightly but her eyes cold and sure now.

Seconds stretched like hours.

The captain's voice crackled over the intercom: "Flight attendants, prepare for departure."

The bathroom door clicked. Sebastian stepped out, adjusting his cuffs, glancing down at his watch.

He never saw it coming.

Lorrisa's fist shot out, a clean, brutal punch—straight to his jaw.

CRACK.

Sebastian's head snapped to the side, eyes wide in shock as his knees buckled.

She shoved him back hard, using every ounce of strength she had, slamming him into the narrow bathroom stall. He crumpled backward, dazed, his tall frame folding awkwardly into the tiny space.

"No tan rápido, cabrón," she hissed, slamming the door shut behind him. (*Not so fast, bastard.*)

Her breath came in gasps now, adrenaline pumping as she fumbled through his jacket. Her fingers hit something hard—*there.* She yanked out the velvet pouch, slipping it quickly into her own bag.

Voices drifted toward her—the nearest flight attendant turning, about to notice.

Lorrisa smoothed her hair, straightened her jacket, and walked quickly, calmly, back down the aisle, heart thundering, barely breathing.

Kong's bright eyes watched her as she slid back into her seat, fingers trembling. She bent down, clutching his crate, whispering fast.

"We're leaving. Now."

The attendants were distracted with final preparations; the door was still unlocked, last checks in progress. She stood up fast, grabbing Kong's crate, weaving quickly toward the exit.

"Miss?" a flight attendant called behind her.

Lorrisa threw a glance over her shoulder, feigning sickness. "Lo siento—I'm—I'm sick. Need off. Ahora!" (*Sorry—I'm sick. Now!*)

Without waiting for approval, she darted down the stairwell, her feet hitting the tarmac hard, breath gasping as she ran clear of the plane.

The door hissed shut behind her.

She ducked into the terminal, eyes wild, clutching Kong's crate tight. Behind her, the plane's engines roared louder, the vibrations shaking the floor as the flight finally began its slow crawl toward the runway.

Lorrisa turned to the tall windows, watching, chest heaving, as the plane taxied, then accelerated down the strip, and finally lifted—disappearing into the darkening sky.

She stood frozen for a long moment, her heart pounding in her ears.

Kong whimpered softly from his crate, and she crouched down, opening it enough to stroke his soft fur. He blinked up at her, confused but safe.

Lorrisa smiled gently, eyes stinging with tears of relief.

"We're not done yet, pequeño," she whispered.

Her other hand slid into her bag, fingers closing around the velvet pouch. She pulled it out slowly, holding it up to the flickering airport lights.

The three rings gleamed—ancient, powerful, shimmering with mystery.

Lorrisa stared at them, her lips curving into a slow, wicked grin.

"Not even close."

She stood, squaring her shoulders, Kong's crate in one hand, the rings in the other, eyes burning with new resolve.

Behind her, the empty terminal hummed with quiet indifference, oblivious to the small, fierce woman who had just shifted the balance of the entire game.

And far above, on the now-airborne plane, Sebastian stirred, groaning softly, still crumpled on the bathroom floor—oblivious to how badly his luck had just turned.

Chapter 6

The payphone buzzed softly in Lorrisa's ear, the metal receiver cold and a little sticky against her temple. Outside the cramped booth, the bustling sounds of the small desert town filled the air—market stalls clanging open, vendors shouting over each other, the distant hum of motorcycles weaving through narrow streets.

She adjusted Kong's crate at her feet, wiping sweat from her brow with a shaky hand. Kong's dark eyes peered out through the mesh, blinking sleepily but ever-watchful.

"Come on, come on..." she muttered under her breath, fingers tapping the grimy glass of the booth.

Finally—a click.

"¿Hola?" a sharp, familiar voice came through, crackling slightly on the line.

"Xenia—it's me," Lorrisa breathed, relief flooding her chest like water over cracked earth.

"¡Dios mío, Lorrisa!" Xenia's voice rose, part shock, part scolding. "Where have you *been*? I've been losing my mind!"

"I know, I know. I'm sorry." Lorrisa shut her eyes briefly, head falling back against the booth wall. "Listen, I need your help."

"Of course. What's wrong?" Xenia's tone shifted instantly, sharper, more focused.

"I need you to wire me some money. Enough to get by for a bit. I swear I'll pay you back the moment I land in the States."

"Don't even *say* that. How much?"

Lorrisa exhaled, giving her the amount and the name of the local wire office. Silence fell for a moment before Xenia spoke again, her voice lower now.

"Lorrisa... what's going on?"

Lorrisa's eyes fluttered shut, exhaustion dragging at her bones. "It's... a lot."

"I'm listening."

Lorrisa sighed and glanced down at Kong, who tilted his head, as if urging her to speak.

"Okay," she began, voice a little hoarse, "you remember the whole Tablet of Solomon mess? The rings Gee was obsessed with?"

"Of course. The 'big find.' What about it?"

"It was real," Lorrisa said, her voice tightening. "All of it. Gee got hold of one ring—stole it, actually. Then found a second. We thought we were chasing some myth, but it spiraled fast. Mercenaries. Gunfights. A psychopath named Sebastian Reicht—he funded the dig and turned out to be a complete lunatic."

Xenia made a sharp noise. "You're kidding."

Lorrisa shook her head, even though Xenia couldn't see her. "We got captured twice. Escaped twice. Barely. Hamid—our guide—he's been incredible. And Kong..." she laughed quietly, brushing her fingers over the crate, "has been braver than half the people I know."

Xenia's voice tightened, disbelief creeping in. "You're telling me your *monkey* was part of this?"

"You wouldn't believe half of it," Lorrisa whispered, her smile fading. "Anyway... Gee and I—he wanted me out. Said it was too dangerous. I listened. I was coming home."

She paused, eyes narrowing as the next words spilled out. "But... Sebastian was on my flight. He was smuggling the rings out of the country."

Xenia gasped audibly. "What?!"

"I saw him board. Right past me, didn't even notice. I followed him when he went to the bathroom... and I—I knocked him out."

"Lorrisa." Xenia's voice dropped to a whisper, full of shock.

"I took the rings. Got off the plane before it took off." She swallowed hard, the weight of it all settling over her. "He doesn't even know yet."

The line went dead silent. For a long beat, neither spoke.

Then Xenia's voice, small but steady: "Mija... what have you *done?*"

Lorrisa leaned her head against the booth wall, eyes fluttering shut, exhaustion creeping in. "I don't know. But it was the right thing. I *know* that."

Xenia let out a shaky breath. And then, without warning, her voice dropped into prayer:
"Virgencita Santa, por favor protege a mi amiga Lorrisa. Guíala por la oscuridad, dale fuerza y valor, y tráela sana y salva a casa. Amén."
(*Holy Virgin, please protect my friend Lorrisa. Guide her through the darkness, give her strength and courage, and bring her home safe and sound. Amen.*)

Lorrisa's throat tightened, her eyes burning. "Gracias, Xenia," she whispered. "Te lo agradezco con todo mi corazón." (*Thank you, Xenia. I appreciate it with all my heart.*)

The line crackled.

"This call will be terminated in thirty seconds," the automated voice announced coldly.

"Okay, I'll get the money out ASAP," Xenia said quickly. "Promise me you'll call me when you're safe."

"I promise."

"Te quiero, mija."

"Te quiero más."

The line clicked, the tone going flat.

Lorrisa lowered the receiver slowly, her hand resting on it for a long moment before she hung up. She stood there, staring through the smeared glass at the bustling market, the distant noise of life pushing forward as though nothing had changed.

She crouched, stroking Kong's little head through the bars. He looked up at her, blinking slow and calm.

"We're not done yet, pequeño," she whispered, her voice low but sure.

She glanced at her bag—the velvet pouch heavy inside—and felt a deep, rising determination settle in her chest.

She was in this now.

And there was no turning back. Lorrisa's phone buzzed with a single line of text:
"Funds sent. Be safe. XO – Xenia."

Relief swept through her like a crashing wave. She let out a breath she hadn't realized she'd been holding and tucked the phone into her vest pocket. Kong, perched on a rickety chair in the corner, watched her with curious eyes, munching absently on a piece of dried fruit.

"Looks like we're back in business, little man," she said, brushing sweaty strands of hair from her forehead.

It was mid-afternoon, and the air in the market town was thick with heat and dust. The old wire transfer office—little more than a shack with a flickering neon sign—sat on the edge of a busy square. Outside, scooters and battered pickup trucks rattled by, and the scent of roasting meat mixed with diesel fumes in the stagnant air.

Armed with fresh cash, Lorrisa moved quickly. No time to waste.

First stop: a supply stall. She bought:

- Bottles of water,
- Non-perishable rations,
- A coil of climbing rope,
- Flashlights and extra batteries,
- A new canvas backpack to replace her worn one,
- And, on impulse, a small machete.

Next: fuel and transport. She found it in a dusty side alley—a faded green jeep, sun-bleached and patched in places with scrap metal. The owner, a leathery-faced old man missing two front teeth, assured her it ran "good enough."

"It'll get you there," he said with a wink, counting the bills she pressed into his hand.

She climbed into the driver's seat, Kong jumping in beside her, and turned the key. The engine coughed to life after two sputtering tries. Not exactly a chariot, but it would do.

"Not bad, huh?" she muttered, giving Kong a glance. He bared his teeth in what looked suspiciously like skepticism.

Back at her rented room—a cramped, concrete-walled space with a single fan spinning lazily overhead—Lorrisa laid everything out on the bed:
Maps, old books, photos of artifacts she'd taken on her phone, and a few scraps of handwritten notes.

She opened her notebook and traced a finger along a line she'd circled twice:
"Third ring points to the shadow of the Serpent's Crown."

Lorrisa took the three rings from the pouch and attempted to study the mineral composite to determine the possible origin, when the three rings bound together like the previous two did before. This time all three pieces slid across the map toward each other over one location on the map.

"Serpent's Crown..." she murmured, eyes narrowing. Her gaze flicked to a topographical map of the surrounding region. Rocky hills and plateaus stretched to the horizon, pockmarked with ruins both famous and forgotten.

She flipped pages, cross-referencing, piecing together what she'd learned over the past weeks.
An ancient legend kept popping up—a temple complex built beneath a jagged rock formation locals called *La Corona del Serpiente—The Serpent's Crown*.

"Could be nothing," she said, thinking aloud, "but it's the best lead we've got."

Kong jumped onto the table, scattering loose papers. He pawed at a black-and-white photo of the formation, almost as if pointing.

She smiled, brushing her hand over his little head. "Good eye."

Outside, the sun was sinking low, casting long shadows across the town's narrow streets. Lorrisa knew she couldn't waste the night. She packed her gear methodically, double-checking every item, every knot.

With the last of her gear stowed, she stood in the doorway, looking out at the quieting square. The jeep waited at the curb, engine ticking faintly from its last run.

"Alright, Kong," she said, hefting the pack over one shoulder, "Let's go find that tablet."

Kong scrambled up her arm and perched on her shoulder, gripping tightly as they stepped into the fading light—toward the unknown. The jeep roared through the dusk, the cracked road snaking into the hills as stars began to pepper the sky. Lorrisa kept one hand tight on the wheel, the other gripping the map spread across her lap, eyes flicking between the road and the spot where the rings had pointed.

Every bump and dip sent Kong jolting in his seat, but he stayed sharp, scanning the horizon with those quick eyes.

"We're close," Lorrisa muttered, teeth clenched as the terrain grew rougher. The Serpent's Crown loomed in the distance now—its jagged peaks black against the starlit sky.

Suddenly, a hard *thud*. The jeep lurched violently, almost fishtailing off the narrow trail.

"Shit!" Lorrisa barked, wrenching the wheel as Kong screeched, grabbing her shoulder. She slammed the brakes and jumped out, boots kicking up gravel.

The front tire was a mess—blown out, shredded by a jagged rock embedded in the road.

She cursed under her breath, scanning the deserted trail. No lights, no movement. Just the whisper of wind through the rocks.

"Great," she muttered, glancing at Kong. "Of course it couldn't be easy."

Digging out the spare, she kept her eyes on the darkness—acutely aware that things had a way of going wrong out here. Kong hissed once, ears flattening, but the night stayed quiet.

Finally, with the spare in place, Lorrisa climbed back in and revved the engine, pushing forward, every nerve tight with anticipation.

By the time she rolled to a stop at the base of the Serpent's Crown foothills, the moon was high, casting silver light over the rock spires.

She stared up at the looming silhouette, heart pounding with equal parts fear and excitement.

"Tomorrow," she whispered to Kong, who curled up beside her. "We find out what's waiting."

The fused ring in her pouch seemed to hum faintly—almost as if it, too, was waiting.

Gee Rodriguez leaned on the bar, sweat-soaked and exhausted, staring down at the untouched glass of water in front of him. His shirt was stiff with dust and sweat, boots caked with dried mud from hours of chasing dead leads. Hamid slumped into the seat beside him, wiping grime from his brow with the back of his hand.

"Third place tonight," Hamid muttered, eyeing the bartender's wary glance. "Third time we've been treated like lepers."

Gee cracked a wry grin but didn't look up. "Yeah, well, we're a little... ripe."

"Little?" Hamid laughed, sniffing his own shirt and recoiling. "We smell like goats."

The bar—if you could call it that—was little more than a hole-in-the-wall joint on the outskirts of the city, the kind of place where bad things happened after midnight. A ceiling fan clicked overhead, spinning slowly, doing nothing to move the stifling heat.

Gee finally looked around. "You'd think a place like this wouldn't care how we look."

"Not about the look," Hamid muttered, nodding toward the bouncer near the door. "It's the smell, hermano. We stink like we've been dead two days."

Gee chuckled darkly, finishing his water in one gulp and slamming the glass down. "Well, they can hold their noses. We're not leaving until we get a name."

Hamid sighed. "And what if Sebastian's not in the country anymore?"

Gee's jaw tightened at that. "Then we keep looking until we're sure."

They'd spent the entire day hitting every spot they knew Sebastian Voss might have connections to—exclusive clubs, shady warehouses, private dockyards. Each lead turned out cold, and more than once, they were **refused entry outright—**not just because they were outsiders, but because they looked like they'd been through hell.

And, well... they had.

Hamid flagged down the bartender, slipping a few crumpled bills across the counter. "Come on, brother, little information." His voice was smooth, practiced. "White man. Blonde hair. Sharp suit. Name of Voss. He comes here?"

The bartender eyed the bills, then looked them both up and down, nose wrinkling. “Not here,” he said in thickly accented English. “Maybe the casino down the road. But you… you clean up first.”

Gee leaned in, his smile all teeth now. “Casino, huh?”

The bartender shrugged, pocketing the bills. “Maybe. Maybe not. But you smell like dead animals. No casino let you in.”

Hamid groaned. “Told you.”

Gee rubbed his temples, trying to stay calm. “Alright,” he said, standing up and tossing a few more bills onto the counter. “One last try tonight. If Voss has a gambling habit, we’ll catch a whiff of it.”

“Yeah,” Hamid said, eyeing Gee’s shirt with mock disgust, “but let’s be real… unless that casino’s got a ‘feral animal’ section, we’re not getting past the front door.”

Gee sighed, clapping Hamid on the shoulder. “Then we crash their party from the back.”

Hamid grinned, shaking his head. “You and your crazy ideas.”

They stepped back into the thick night air, the city humming around them—lights glowing, engines revving, the pulse of nightlife beating through the streets. But under it all was the same frustration, the same empty trail.

As they trudged down the street, Gee glanced up at the sky. Somewhere out there, Lorrisa was doing her thing. He just hoped to God she was safe.

Because tonight?
He was no closer to finding Voss than when he'd started.

The whiskey burned going down—sharp, cheap, and exactly what Gee needed after the day from hell. He slammed the glass back onto the table and motioned for another. Across from him, Hamid wiped his mouth, eyes already glassy, grinning from ear to ear.

"This..." Hamid slurred, raising his refilled glass, "...this is the only good decision we've made all night, hermano."

Gee laughed, the sound raw and loose. "Hell yeah. To bad ideas and worse plans."

They clinked glasses, downed their drinks, and stumbled out into the warm night air, the city's glow twisting and shimmering around them. Lorrisa wasn't there to keep them in check. Tonight, it was just two beat-up men, chasing shadows and losing track of time.

"Where to now?" Gee asked, squinting down the street.

Hamid pointed—wildly, vaguely—toward a flickering neon sign up the block. "More whiskey!"

Gee didn't argue.

The bar was a tiny, grimy dive, darker and sweatier than the last, with a handful of rough-looking locals hunched over tables. Gee and Hamid crashed through the door, laughing too loudly, reeking of old sweat, dirt, and spilled booze.

Heads turned. Noses wrinkled. A heavy silence fell.

Gee stumbled up to the bar, slapping it with his palm. "Whiskey. Two."

The bartender gave them a long look. "You smell like something died."

Hamid cackled, swinging an arm around Gee. "It's part of our charm!"

A thick-set local at the corner table—beefy, bald, with a scar cutting across his eyebrow—pushed back his chair with a loud scrape. He stood, nostrils flaring, eyes locked on Gee and Hamid.

“Hey,” the man growled, voice low and dangerous. “You two… stink. Get out.”

Gee blinked, trying to focus, swaying slightly. “Wasn’t aware this place was… a perfumery.”

Hamid grinned, raising his glass in a sloppy salute. “More whiskey! More fight!”

The local’s chair hit the floor as he lunged, knocking Hamid’s glass flying. Hamid dove straight at the man’s legs, tackling him like a linebacker.

“Aw, dammit—” Gee started, but it was too late.

Chaos erupted.

Tables toppled. Bottles shattered. Gee found himself grappling with a second guy who came in swinging—a blur of fists, curses, and clumsy dodges. He caught a punch to the ribs but landed a solid right hook of his own, sending his opponent crashing into the bar.

Hamid whooped, still wrestling the first guy across the floor, knocking over stools and kicking up a storm.

“Yup,” Gee muttered between punches. “Fantastic plan.”

Later... In Jail..

Gee sat slumped against the cold concrete wall of a tiny holding cell, shirt torn, eye swollen, head pounding. Hamid sprawled beside him, one arm draped dramatically across his face, breathing like a man who'd run ten miles uphill.

"Worth it," Hamid mumbled, eyes closed.

The jailers, fed up with the stench of sweat and booze, dragged a hose across the floor, opened the cell, and *blasted them with freezing cold water* without so much as a warning.

"God dammit!" Gee shouted, staggering to his feet, gasping for breath as the torrent soaked him from head to toe.

Hamid yelped, scrambling for cover behind the bench, but it was useless—the water hit him square in the back.

"Now you smell better," one of the guards muttered, slamming the door shut with a smirk.

Shivering, soaked, and miserable, Gee sank onto the bench, running a hand through his wet hair, heart still thumping from the cold shock.

Silence settled between them, except for Hamid's wheezy breathing.

Gee stared at the wall, jaw tight, lost in thought.

Lorrisa...

She was probably asleep right now, safe and sound back in the U.S., far away from this mess. Away from the dirt, the danger, the madness.

He closed his eyes, leaning back against the wall, water dripping from his chin.

"She's out of it," he muttered to no one in particular. "She's fine."

A beat of quiet.

But even as the words left his mouth, a flicker of doubt wormed into his gut. He couldn't shake the feeling—the twist of instinct—that maybe, just maybe, she wasn't as safe as he wanted to believe.

Hamid, half-asleep, groaned, "Shut up and get some rest, hermano."

Gee exhaled sharply, staring up at the flickering light overhead.

Please be okay, he thought, before letting his eyes close at last.

The harsh clank of the cell door echoed like a hammer in Gee's skull.

He groaned, blinking against the stabbing daylight that cut through the barred window. His head throbbed in sync with his heartbeat, and his throat felt like sandpaper. Every muscle ached, and he was **freezing** in his still-damp clothes.

Across the cell, Hamid lay sprawled on the bench, one arm over his eyes, muttering curses in three different languages.

"Wake up," Gee croaked, rubbing his temples. "We're not dead yet."

Hamid cracked one bloodshot eye open. "Feels like death. But wetter."

The guard appeared, looking as unimpressed as ever. "You're free to go. Try not to come back."

Gee stumbled to his feet, grabbing his backpack and nudging Hamid hard enough to get him moving. They staggered out of the cell block, squinting into the harsh sunlight like a pair of vampires emerging from a tomb.

On the street, they paused, taking in the morning bustle of the city: scooters weaving through traffic, vendors shouting over each other, the smell of grilled meat and exhaust hanging in the air.

Hamid leaned against a lamp post, groaning. “Remind me again why we do this.”

Gee shielded his eyes, scanning their filthy clothes—ripped shirts, stained pants, boots falling apart—and grimaced. “Because we’re stubborn idiots.”

Hamid sniffed himself and recoiled. “And still stink.”

Gee nodded. “Yeah. That’s problem number one.”

Hamid straightened, rubbing his temples. “We’ve been hitting all these places looking like hell. No wonder no one takes us seriously.”

“Exactly.” Gee pointed down the street. “First order of business: get clean. Real clean. Then we hit a shop and buy something that doesn’t make us look like...”

“Homeless pirates,” Hamid finished, deadpan.

Gee grinned despite his headache. “Right. And once we look like we belong, we go back to that casino lead from last night. If Voss has any kind of habit, someone there will know.”

Hamid nodded slowly, working through the plan with a hangover squint. "Alright. Bathhouse first. Then clothes. Then casino."

Gee clapped him on the back, wincing as pain flared through his bruised knuckles. "You read my mind."

Hamid glanced sideways, grinning. "Also… coffee. Gallons of it."

"Non-negotiable," Gee agreed.

They limped down the street, still looking like hell but with a renewed sense of purpose.

The bathhouse was tucked behind a quiet alley, the kind of place only locals knew—*no-frills, all steam and stone*.

Gee and Hamid stepped inside, blinking as thick, humid air wrapped around them, the scent of soap and hot water almost overwhelming after weeks of dirt, sweat, and grime.

A gruff attendant pointed them toward the washing area, muttering in broken English, "Private tubs. Over there."

They stripped down without ceremony, too tired and sore to care about modesty, and each sank into their own deep stone tub, the water scalding hot and tinged with the faint smell of minerals.

Gee gasped as he lowered himself in, the heat hitting every bruise, every scrape, every aching muscle. For a long moment, he just sat there, eyes closed, letting the water seep into his bones.

Hamid, in the next tub over, let out a groan—half agony, half bliss. “By Allah… I think I’m dying,” he moaned, leaning his head back, eyes rolling shut.

Gee cracked an eye open, watching the murky water around him turn a sickly gray-brown as layers of sweat, dirt, and dried blood floated free. He ran his hand through his hair and winced, feeling the grime practically peel off in strips.

“Jesus,” he muttered, lifting his arm to see a line of filth swirling away from his skin. “We were disgusting.”

Hamid laughed weakly, eyes still closed. “Were? Look at this water, man. We’re melting.”

Both tubs frothed with soap as they started to scrub—hard. Gee grabbed a rough cloth and worked it over his arms, chest, face, neck—gritting his teeth as raw skin emerged beneath the dirt.

Hamid cursed as he tried to untangle a knot of sweat-clumped hair. "I don't think I've been properly clean in... what, weeks? Months?"

Gee grunted, splashing his face. "Too long."

Hamid reached down and stirred the water with his foot, grimacing. "I think we've single-handedly turned this place into a biohazard."

The heat softened their muscles, and for a while neither man spoke—just the sound of scrubbing and dripping water, the steam curling lazily around them like ghosts. The filth lifted away in layers, until at last the water began to clear, the worst of it washed down the old stone drains.

Gee leaned back, staring at the cracked ceiling, letting the heat work its way deeper, draining the ache from his bones.

Hamid let out a long, contented sigh. "This... this might actually be worth it."

"For once," Gee agreed, finally feeling human again.

The attendant came back, wordlessly dropping two clean towels and small cakes of rough soap on a bench beside them. Gee gave a tired nod of thanks.

“Fifteen minutes,” the man grunted. “Then out.”

Gee sat up, splashing water from his face and glancing at Hamid, who was now fully reclined in his tub, arms splayed out like he’d sunk into paradise.

“Fifteen minutes,” Gee echoed, smirking. “Enjoy it while it lasts.” After the Bath

They dressed in their old clothes, now sticky and clinging awkwardly to their freshly cleaned skin. Both men felt the difference immediately—lighter, sharper, awake.

Outside the bathhouse, Gee took a deep breath of the fresh air, eyes narrowing as he scanned the busy street. For the first time in days, he felt focused.

Hamid shook out his damp shirt and made a face. “Now we just look like two clean guys in rags.”

Gee cracked a grin. “One problem at a time. Next stop: new clothes.”

Hamid nodded, grinning despite himself. “Damn right.”

The bathhouse had worked wonders—they looked human again, if still a little ragged around the edges. But their clothes? Another story entirely. Gee’s shirt was barely holding together, and Hamid's pants looked like they'd been mauled by a wild animal.

They stood outside a small clothing shop tucked between two cafes, eyeing the display of crisp shirts, fresh pants, and clean boots in the window.

"This is what we need," Gee said, wiping a bead of sweat from his brow. "Get us back in the game."

Hamid patted his pocket and frowned. "Yeah... except we're broke."

Gee exhaled, running a hand down his face. "Damn, now what?"

Hamid started to turn away, then paused, a flicker of memory lighting his eyes. He reached into his bag, rummaged around—and pulled out a small, worn pouch.

"What's that?" Gee asked, frowning.

Hamid untied the string and poured a few gold pieces into his palm. They gleamed in the sunlight, unmistakably real.

"From the bandits' camp," Hamid said with a grin. "I forgot all about these."

Gee's eyes widened. "Hamid, you big beautiful bastard."

"Hey, it's not Fort Knox, but it should get us something decent."

They pushed through the door, a little bell jangling overhead. The shopkeeper—a thin man with sharp eyes—glanced at them skeptically, but the flash of gold changed his tune fast. He welcomed them in, gesturing broadly at the racks of clothes.

Hamid was all business. He strode straight to a shelf, grabbed a pair of sturdy khaki pants and a plain button-down shirt, and held them up. "Fits. Done."

Gee, though, stood still, eyes tracing the rows of shirts, jackets, and boots, his fingers trailing over the fabrics without really seeing them.

His mind drifted.

Lorrisa...

He remembered the way she used to drag him to shops when they had downtime between digs—how she'd tease him for always picking the same tired look, how her eyes would sparkle as she held up shirts against his chest.

"This one brings out your eyes," she'd say with that half-smile that always disarmed him.

He could still feel her fingers brushing his shoulders, the

gentle tug as she buttoned a shirt for him, the way her hair smelled—clean, soft, with that hint of jasmine—when she leaned close to smooth out a collar.

And when she found a jacket she liked? She'd slip it over his shoulders and give him that little neck massage, like it was the most natural thing in the world. Like she knew every inch of him—and cared for it all.

Gee swallowed hard, shaking off the memory, but the ache lingered—a knot in his chest that no bath or new clothes could ever wash away.

Hamid reappeared beside him, holding up his haul. "You find something yet, or you gonna stand there daydreaming all day?"

Gee smirked faintly, blinking himself back to the present. "Yeah... yeah. Just looking."

He ran his hand over a rack of shirts and finally picked out a dark blue one, simple but well-fitted. He added a pair of rugged pants and a worn leather jacket—practical, nothing flashy. But as he held them, he couldn't help thinking: *She'd pick better.*

Hamid handed over the gold, and the shopkeeper wrapped their new clothes in neat bundles, smiling wide.

"See?" Hamid said as they stepped outside, the sun blazing overhead. "Easy."

Gee nodded, adjusting his bag on his shoulder, but his eyes were distant again, drawn to some far-off thought, some far-off face.

"Yeah," he said quietly. "Easy."

But deep down, he knew nothing about this was easy—not without her.

Lorrisa at the base of the Serpent's Crown...

The Serpent's Crown loomed above her—jagged rock spires piercing the morning sky, casting long, jagged shadows down the rugged slope. The cliffs shimmered faintly with heat as the sun crept higher, and every crevice seemed to dare her to climb.

Lorrisa adjusted the makeshift wrap slung across her back, where Kong nestled in tight, eyes wide and alert. His little fingers clutched at the fabric, and she felt his tiny breath puff warm against her neck.

She craned her head up, tracing the route she'd picked out: a narrow vein of rock and scrabble, zigzagging upward along the sharp incline toward the summit.

"Alright, Kong," she muttered, gripping the first jagged handhold, "no turning back now."

The rock was warm and rough beneath her fingers, crumbling in places, solid in others. Each pull sent a shiver of strain through her arms and shoulders, but she kept moving—slow, steady, precise.

The jagged outcrops bit at her gloves and boots, threatening to catch and tear. She moved deliberately, testing each foothold twice before committing.

Her breathing grew ragged as she climbed, the weight of Kong and her gear pressing down with every upward shove. Sweat trickled down her temples, stinging her eyes.

This is insane, she thought.
What the hell am I doing out here alone?

Her fingers fumbled slightly on a thin ledge, and her boot slipped, sending a shower of loose stones skittering down the cliff face.

“Shit,” she hissed, heart jackhammering as she pressed herself close to the rock, breath shallow. Kong whimpered softly in her ear.

“It’s okay,” she whispered, forcing calm into her voice. “We’ve got this.”

She blinked up at the next handhold and couldn’t help but think back—*the climbing wall at her gym*. Clean, color-coded grips. Bright fluorescent lights. Always a harness, always someone spotting her. And even then, she’d struggled—never the best climber, always a little too cautious, a little too slow.

But this?

This was real. No harness. No spotters. No second chances.

She gritted her teeth, refocusing. “That wall had nothing on this,” she muttered under her breath. “And I sucked at that wall. But I’d better not suck now.”

Hand over hand, foot over foot, she pressed upward. Every muscle trembled, but she locked into a rhythm—reach, pull, push, breathe.

Minutes stretched endlessly, the wind whipping her hair across her face as she neared a narrow ridge. The summit gleamed just ahead, taunting her.

Finally—with a grunt and one last desperate push—she hauled herself over the final ledge. Her knees hit the ground hard, grit biting into her palms as she gasped for air.

"We made it," she rasped, rolling onto her side, her chest heaving. "Holy hell... we made it."

Kong wriggled free of the wrap and hopped onto the rocky surface, shaking out his limbs like a tiny champion. He chattered softly, pacing in a little circle before plopping down beside her, panting from the ride.

Lorrisa pushed up on one elbow, unhooked her water bottle, and took a long, grateful drink. She tipped the bottle down toward Kong, who greedily lapped at the cool stream, chittering his thanks.

For a moment, they both just sat there, basking in the thin air and dizzying height, looking out over the endless expanse of scrubland and rock below.

Lorrisa wiped sweat from her brow and pulled out the creased, sweat-stained map. She flattened it across her knee, eyes scanning for the next clue.

The Serpent's Crown summit was marked with a tiny symbol—an *X* near the north side, labeled in faded ink: *"Fang's Shadow—Entry Below."*

She squinted, lowering the map and glancing around the rocky ridge. The jagged peaks rose around her like a crown of broken teeth, shadows stretching long and sharp across the ground.

"Fang's Shadow," she murmured, standing slowly, legs shaking. "Alright, let's find out what that means."

Kong chattered, hopping up onto her pack, ready for the next step.

Lorrisa slipped the map back into her pouch, taking one last deep breath of the thin summit air, her eyes narrowing as she scanned the ridge for any sign of an entry point.

"Not done yet," she muttered, setting off along the ridge, boots crunching on gravel.

The summit wind had picked up, tugging at Lorrisa's hair as she paced the jagged ridge, eyes locked on the ground. Kong clung to her shoulder, his little head swiveling as he sniffed at the air, ears perked.

She followed the shadows cast by the towering rock spires, circling slowly, reading the map over and over.

"Fang's Shadow," she muttered under her breath, scanning every crevice, every jagged slit in the stone. Nothing.

Hours seemed to crawl by. She checked the angle of the sun, watched the shadows shift, waited for something—anything—to stand out.

Frustration crept in, gnawing at her resolve. The climb had been brutal; her muscles still burned. She felt the sting of sweat and grit in every pore.

"Where the hell is it?" she hissed, dropping to a knee and tracing her fingers over the rough ground. Kong slid down beside her, pawing at loose stones.

She was about to curse again when something—a sharp glint—caught her eye.

She froze.

There, across a narrow ravine—a flash of light, quick and precise, as if sunlight had bounced off glass.

Her pulse quickened. Binoculars?

She narrowed her eyes, staring hard at the spot, but the glint was gone—swallowed up by the rocks and haze.

Kong let out a low growl, eyes darting to the same place.

“Yeah,” she whispered. “Someone’s watching.”

She scanned the ridge, but saw no movement, no sign of who—or what—it might’ve been. Voss’s men? Or... someone else?

No time to dwell.

She forced herself to refocus, turning back to the map. The sun had shifted further west, and as she squinted at the longest shadow—a jagged spear of darkness stretching from a spire shaped like a curved fang—she saw it:

A narrow crack in the rock, barely visible from where she stood, half-hidden beneath a spill of loose scree.

“There,” she breathed.

Kong darted forward, chittering excitedly as he pawed at the loose rocks. Lorrisa scrambled after him, dropping to her knees and pulling the rubble aside, revealing a narrow entrance, no wider than a crawlspace.

She clicked on her torch, its flickering light cutting through the darkness. Cool air whispered out of the opening, carrying the scent of age and damp earth.

"Looks like we're in business."

Kong climbed up onto her back, gripping tight as she lowered herself into the narrow shaft, sliding down into the gloom. The tunnel sloped steeply downward, the walls slick with moisture, carved with faded symbols and ancient script. Her torch danced across the stone, revealing fractured glyphs—images of serpents, crowns, and strange, coiling patterns.

Kong stayed quiet now, ears twitching at every drip of water, every shift of loose gravel beneath their boots.

The passage opened into a small chamber, its walls etched with intricate carvings—figures kneeling before a serpent-headed king, hands raised in supplication. Dust choked the air, swirling in the dim light.

Lorrisa stepped carefully, eyes scanning every surface, every crack in the floor.

At the far end, something caught her attention: a small pedestal, toppled and broken, its surface bare.

She crouched low, examining it closely.

"No ring," she muttered, frowning. "Just more damn clues."

Her torchlight flicked upward, tracing a series of carvings—an ancient map, maybe, or a coded message. She snapped a few photos with her phone, breathing hard.

"This better be worth it." Kong suddenly went rigid on her shoulder, eyes wide, ears flat.

"What is it, buddy?" Lorrisa whispered, her own nerves flaring as she swept the torch around the room.

Then—the sound of a faint metallic click.

Her breath caught.

Kong hissed, leaping from her shoulder to the far side of the chamber, eyes locked on the floor beneath her feet.

Lorrisa's eyes darted downward—the stone beneath her heel had sunk slightly.

"Oh no..."

The walls seemed to groan, ancient mechanisms grinding to life, echoing through the dark.

Her pulse hammered.

"*Run,*" she breathed. The grinding roar of ancient gears filled the chamber, vibrating through Lorrisa's boots as the walls shuddered to life.

She spun, torchlight flicking wildly across the carved walls. Stone panels began sliding open, revealing rows of jagged spikes and—worse—a deep rumble beneath her feet.

Kong squealed from his perch by the exit, bouncing anxiously as dust rained down around them.

"Not good," Lorrisa breathed, heart pounding.

The pedestal at the center of the room snapped downward like a pressure plate, and from above, a low mechanical *clunk* sounded—a counterweight.

She looked up—just in time to see a massive stone slab descending from the ceiling.

"MOVE!" she shouted, sprinting for the exit. Kong was already ahead, scrambling up her leg as she lunged for the narrow tunnel.

The stone crashed down behind her, sealing the chamber with a deafening boom. Dust choked her lungs as she slid down the sloped tunnel, gripping the torch with one hand and shielding Kong with the other.

She hit bottom hard, gasping, blinking into the dim light of the entrance she'd come through hours earlier.

Safe. Barely.

Outside, the sun was sinking low again, casting the Serpent's Crown in bloody gold. Lorrisa leaned against the rock face, chest heaving, sweat streaking her dust-caked face.

"Okay," she rasped to Kong, "time to get out of here."

She reattached her makeshift harness, tucking Kong securely against her back, and peered down the cliff face.

It looked steeper than before—a sheer wall of jagged rock and loose scree. Her legs trembled, but she gritted her teeth, grabbed the nearest handhold, and began the descent.

Every movement was slow, deliberate. Her hands ached, muscles screaming with every stretch and pull. Stones crumbled beneath her boots, tumbling down into the vast silence below.

"Steady girl," she muttered, "you've got this."

Halfway down, her foot slipped—rocks skittered away, and she slammed hard into the cliff, scraping her forearm raw.

Kong squeaked, tightening his grip.

“Shh, it’s okay,” she panted, fingers digging desperately into the rock.

Her heart hammered. No harness. No second chances. Just gravity and grit.

She paused, hanging there, every limb burning, and glanced downward—her jeep still a speck far below.

“Almost there,” she whispered.

But suddenly—a voice.

“Need a hand?”

Her head whipped around, eyes wide.

Standing on a narrow outcrop a few feet away was a man—tall, dark-haired, wearing a windbreaker and mirrored sunglasses. Calm, collected.

He extended a gloved hand, bracing himself.

“Carlos Conchata,” he said smoothly. “Special Agent.”

Lorrisa’s breath hitched. *F.B.I.*

“Seriously?” she gasped, fingers cramping. “How...?”

"Cliff talk later," he said, leaning out slightly. "Come on. You're about to lose your grip."

Gritting her teeth, Lorrisa shifted her weight, stretched—and grabbed his hand.

He hauled her up onto the ledge with surprising strength, steadying her as she collapsed to her knees, panting hard. Kong leapt free, chittering in alarm but circling quickly.

Carlos crouched, offering a small, knowing smile. "Rough day?"

She shot him a glare but didn't answer, pulling off her harness and shaking out her cramping hands.

The jeep rattled down the winding dirt road, its battered frame groaning with every bump and rut. Lorrisa gripped the wheel tightly, knuckles white, eyes locked on the narrow track ahead as dusk deepened around her.

Kong was curled in the passenger seat, fur damp with sweat and dust, dozing fitfully after the harrowing day.

In the rearview mirror, a pair of headlights bobbed steadily, keeping pace.

Lorrisa's jaw clenched.
Carlos Conchata.

She hadn't invited him. Hadn't even asked for his help. Yet here he was—trailing her all the way back to town like a patient wolf.

She downshifted as the road twisted around a rocky outcrop, her eyes flicking back to the mirror again. The headlights stayed close—never aggressive, never backing off.

What the hell is the FBI doing out here? she wondered, sweat slicking the back of her neck.
And better yet... how the hell did they track me?

Her mind raced through every step of the past few days—every move she thought had been off the radar. But clearly, someone had eyes where she didn't expect them.

She thought back to Carlos's timing—appearing on that ledge just when she'd needed help the most. Coincidence? Or had he been watching the entire time, waiting for the right moment to make his entrance?

Her fingers drummed restlessly on the steering wheel. This wasn't a chance encounter. This was a message.

Kong stirred, blinking up at her with a sleepy grunt. Lorrisa glanced down, giving his fur a quick ruffle. "Yeah, buddy," she muttered. "I don't like it either."

The jeep crested a rise, and the small town came into view below—a scattering of lights, low buildings, and dusty streets just starting to stir with the cool of evening.

She guided the jeep toward the main road, choosing a small inn at the far edge of town. The jeep rattled into town, its battered frame shuddering with every dip in the road. Lorrisa kept her eyes on the quiet streets ahead, but her focus kept darting to the rearview mirror.

Carlos Conchata's SUV shadowed her the whole way, never too close, never too far—a silent predator on her tail.

Why now? she wondered, every nerve on edge. *Why here?*

She guided the jeep toward a low-slung inn at the edge of town, its neon vacancy sign buzzing faintly in the gathering dark. She killed the engine and sat for a beat, heart still racing from the day's ordeal.

Across the street, Carlos's SUV rolled to a smooth stop.

Lorrisa grabbed her pack, scooped up Kong, and stepped out of the jeep, locking it with a sharp *snap*.

She didn't look over—not right away. But she heard the SUV door swing open, boots crunching on gravel.

"Ms. Santos," Carlos's calm voice drifted across the narrow street.

She turned, meeting his gaze as he stepped into the yellow glow of the lamplight. He had shed his sunglasses now, revealing sharp eyes—dark, calculating, impossible to read.

"Are we really doing this?" Lorrisa asked, exhaustion sharpening her tone. "You followed me all the way here just to... what? Spy?"

Carlos raised a hand, palm out in a mock gesture of peace. "Nothing so sinister. Just... concerned. You've had a busy day."

She crossed her arms, jaw tight. "What do you want?"

Carlos stepped a little closer, his voice low and steady. "Let's just say the Bureau has a... vested interest in certain artifacts—especially ones that seem to draw international attention."

Lorrisa's eyes narrowed. "I'm not handing anything over."

He smiled faintly, almost amused. "We're not asking. Not yet."

They stood in silence a moment, the quiet of the town pressing in around them.

Carlos tipped his head slightly, voice dropping just enough to send a chill through her.
"Careful, Ms. Santos. The rings don't just attract treasure hunters—they attract governments."

He held her gaze a beat longer, then stepped back, calm as ever.

"Enjoy your stay," he added smoothly, before turning and climbing back into his SUV.

The engine purred to life, and he pulled away into the dark, leaving Lorrisa standing in the lamplight, Kong gripping her shoulder tightly.

She exhaled slowly, eyes fixed on the empty road where the SUV had disappeared.

"Fantastic," she muttered, turning back toward the inn. "Just what I needed.

Chapter 7

The soft hum of air conditioning and the low murmur of voices hit Gee the moment the polished glass doors swung open. He stepped inside, Hamid close behind, and took a slow breath, soaking it all in.

Bright chandeliers glinted off marble floors. The sharp snap of cards, the roll of dice, and the distant clink of slot machines filled the sprawling space. Waitresses in crisp uniforms glided between tables, trays of cocktails balanced effortlessly in their hands.

This was the kind of place they'd never have been let near the night before—two filthy wrecks reeking of sweat and whiskey. But tonight? Different story.

Gee tugged at the collar of his new button-down shirt, the fabric still stiff from being fresh off the rack. His boots were clean, his hair combed back, and he looked—if not exactly high-roller ready—at least like someone who belonged.

Hamid, slick in his sunglasses and pressed shirt, gave a low whistle, eyes scanning the tables. "Now this is a step up."

“Don’t get distracted,” Gee muttered, eyes sharp as they swept the room. “We’re here for Voss.”

“Yeah, yeah,” Hamid said, tucking his hands in his pockets, “but if we find a winning streak along the way, I’m not gonna argue.”

They moved deeper into the casino, weaving through clusters of gamblers and tourists, keeping their heads on a swivel. Gee’s eyes flicked to every corner, scanning for blonde hair, tailored suits, any sign of Sebastian Voss’s signature style.

Nothing.

Yet.

They approached the main bar—sleek, dark wood, bottles lined up like soldiers. Gee leaned in casually, catching the bartender’s eye.

“Two whiskeys,” he said, sliding a bill across the counter, “and a quick question.”

The bartender poured without comment.

Gee kept his voice low. “Tall guy, blonde, sharp dresser. Name’s Sebastian Voss. You seen him around here lately?”

The bartender's hands never paused, but his eyes flicked up—just for a second—before he set the drinks down.

"Maybe," he said noncommittally. "Lots of guys like that in here."

Gee smiled thinly, sliding another bill across. "This one's hard to miss. Big spender. European. Likes the tables that matter."

The bartender hesitated, eyes darting down the bar, then leaned in a little closer. "He used to come around. Same crew, same habits. But it's been... quiet lately."

"Quiet how?" Hamid asked, finally setting his glass down.

The bartender shrugged. "Like he disappeared. Word is, he left town a few days ago. Maybe longer."

Gee's jaw tightened. "He say where?"

"Not to me." The bartender straightened, wiping his hands on a towel. "But he's got... connections. You want to find him, you gotta think bigger."

Gee exchanged a look with Hamid, eyes dark with frustration.

“Thanks,” Gee muttered, grabbing his drink and stepping back.

They moved to a quiet corner, sipping the whiskey, eyes still scanning the room.

“Dead end?” Hamid asked.

Gee shook his head slowly. “No. He was here. Which means someone around here knows where he went.”

Hamid smirked, raising his glass. “You thinking what I’m thinking?”

Gee’s eyes narrowed, locking onto a table of sharp-dressed men in the corner, laughing a little too loudly, watching the room a little too closely.

“Yeah,” Gee said quietly. “We start asking the right people.”

He set his glass down, rolling his shoulders loose. “Let’s make some friends.”

Gee was halfway through his drink when he noticed her.

She moved like liquid silk across the casino floor, every step deliberate, every sway of her hips measured. Tall, elegant, with an hourglass figure poured into a deep crimson dress that hugged every curve. Her skin was warm and golden, her legs long and sculpted beneath the slit of her gown.

But it was her eyes that caught him first—light brown, almost amber, bright but cool, pulling you in while flashing a quiet warning: *Look too long, and you'll regret it*.

"Damn," Hamid muttered, following Gee's gaze. "That's trouble."

Gee said nothing, but his posture straightened as she approached, heels clicking softly on the polished floor. She moved like she owned the room—and maybe she did.

"Good evening, gentlemen," she said, her voice a low, honeyed murmur with just the faintest trace of an accent. Middle Eastern, Gee guessed. Smooth, refined—but sharp underneath.

She rested one hand lightly on the edge of their table, nails perfectly manicured, a delicate gold bracelet sliding down her wrist. Her eyes flicked between them, slow and assessing.

"I couldn't help but overhear," she said, smile curling like smoke, "that you're looking for a man."

Gee's eyes narrowed, cautious but intrigued. "We're just socializing."

Her smile deepened, and she leaned in slightly—just enough for her perfume to tease the air between them. Something floral, but with a dangerous undertone.

"Socializing," she echoed, her gaze sharp now, "about Sebastian Voss?"

Gee's pulse jumped, but he kept his expression even. "The name's come up."

She tilted her head, studying him. "It's... unusual. Most people here know better than to ask about Mr. Voss."

"Guess we're not most people," Hamid said smoothly, eyes roaming up her figure but with a flicker of caution behind the charm.

She laughed softly, the sound low and velvet-smooth. "No, you're not."

She pulled out the chair beside Gee and sat with slow grace, crossing her legs. Gee caught the flash of a dagger's curve at her thigh—a hint, almost invisible, but deliberate.

“I’m Inaya,” she offered, eyes gleaming with something between mischief and warning. “And I make it my business to know… certain things.”

“Nice to meet you, Inaya,” Gee said carefully. “And what exactly is your business tonight?”

Her gaze lingered on him a moment too long, then slid to Hamid with equal weight.

“I’m curious,” she said softly, fingers tracing the rim of a martini glass the waiter set down without her even asking. “Men like you—cleaned up, but with dirt under the nails—you don’t just stumble into this place and ask about Voss unless you have a reason.”

Gee’s jaw tightened. “Let’s just say we’re old friends.”

Inaya’s smile twitched. “I doubt that.”

She sipped her drink, eyes sparkling. “But… I might know where your friend has gone.”

Gee leaned forward slightly, matching her cool tone. “For free?”

Inaya laughed—a musical, dangerous sound. “Nothing is free, Mr…?”

“Gee,” he said. “Just Gee.”

"Just Gee," she mused, tapping her glass thoughtfully. "Well, Just Gee, maybe we can… trade favors."

Gee's gut tightened. There was something coiled behind her polished exterior—a snake beneath the silk.

"What kind of favors?" Hamid asked, his voice low and measured.

Inaya's eyes flicked to him, playful but hard-edged. "Nothing too difficult. Yet."

She rose smoothly, smoothing her dress, and stepped back from the table.

"Enjoy your evening, gentlemen," she said with a smile that didn't quite reach her eyes. "I'll be in touch."

And just like that, she turned and disappeared into the crowd, her hips swaying hypnotically as the crowd seemed to part around her.

Gee stared after her, jaw tight, mind racing.

Hamid drained his glass and muttered, "Yep. Trouble."

Gee nodded slowly, eyes still scanning where she'd gone. "Yeah. The useful kind."

Inaya moved smoothly through the maze of casino tables, her smile fading the moment she was out of sight. Her eyes sharpened, her movements no longer seductive but purposeful, swift.

She slipped past a pair of bored-looking security guards and down a quiet side corridor, heels tapping briskly on the marble floor. At the end of the hall, she pressed a keycard to an unmarked door, and the lock clicked open.

Inside: a small, stark office.
No windows. A desk, a leather chair, and a single corded phone.

She closed the door behind her, locking it with a soft *snick*. The hum of the casino fell away, replaced by cold silence.

Inaya crossed to the desk, sat gracefully, and picked up the phone, her fingers moving quickly over the keypad.

It rang twice before connecting.

"Report," came the voice on the other end—sharp, clipped, unmistakably *Sebastian Voss*.

Inaya's lips curled into a smirk, eyes gleaming as she settled into the chair. "Your American friends are here. Right on schedule."

“Both of them?” Voss’s tone was cool but laced with urgency.

“Yes,” Inaya said smoothly. “Your rugged Mr. Rodriguez and his... robust friend.” She let the smile slip into her voice. “They’ve been asking around—subtle at first, but they’re hungry. Very eager to find you.”

A pause on the line. Then Voss’s voice, low and calculating: “They’ve cleaned up their act?”

“Showered, shaved, and looking sharp.” Inaya’s gaze flicked to the security monitor on the desk, showing the casino floor. She zoomed in on Gee and Hamid at their table, nursing their drinks, eyes alert. “But they’re not subtle. Not really.”

Voss gave a quiet, humorless chuckle. “That’s Rodriguez. All muscle, little finesse.”

His tone darkened. “And the girl? Any sign?”

Inaya’s eyes narrowed slightly. “No. Not yet. But if they’re here, she won’t be far behind.”

Another pause. Then Voss’s voice dropped to a steely whisper:
“Find her. I don’t care what it takes.”

Inaya's fingers drummed lightly on the desk. "And the two men?"

A beat of silence.

"Keep them close. Reel them in—slowly. I want them distracted... occupied. But not dead. Not yet."

Inaya's smile returned, slow and sharp. "Understood."

"And Inaya," Voss added, voice tight now, "don't underestimate Rodriguez. He's a hammer—but even hammers break things I care about."

Her smile didn't waver. "I'll be careful. And what about your return?"

A low sigh from Voss. "I'm... delayed. Complications. But soon. When I'm back, we settle everything."

Inaya's eyes glittered with amusement. "I look forward to it."

"Good. Keep me updated." The line went dead.

Inaya replaced the receiver slowly, her smile lingering. She stood, smoothing the folds of her dress, and glanced once more at the screen—Gee and Hamid still at their table, still searching, still clueless.

"For now," she murmured to herself, brushing a stray lock of hair behind her ear, "let's see how deep you're willing to go."

She slipped back out of the office, her face once again a mask of seduction and charm, heels clicking softly as she rejoined the glittering maze of the casino floor.

Gee leaned back in his chair, eyes still locked on the space where Inaya had disappeared into the crowd. His jaw was tight, fingers drumming a slow, steady beat against his glass.

Hamid broke the silence first, swirling the last of his whiskey. "Well... that was interesting."

Gee didn't answer right away, scanning the casino floor as if expecting her to reappear at any moment.

"You thinking what I'm thinking?" Hamid added, setting his glass down with a quiet *clink*.

"That she's trouble?" Gee muttered. "Yeah. Big trouble."

Hamid smirked. "The good kind of trouble or the kind that gets us killed?"

Gee's lips twitched—half a smile, half a grimace. "Both, probably."

He finally looked at Hamid, eyes sharp again. “She’s connected. No way she just *happens* to stroll over after we start asking questions.”

Hamid nodded, wiping his palms on his thighs. “You think Voss put her on us?”

“Feels like it.” Gee’s gaze returned to the crowd, brow furrowed. “Or she’s got her own angle. Either way, she’s not playing straight.”

Hamid leaned in, voice low. “You believe her? That she might know where he went?”

Gee exhaled slowly. “I believe she knows something. Whether she tells us the truth… that’s another story.”

They fell silent, both men watching the room. The casino was alive with laughter, the soft clatter of chips, the hum of slot machines, but beneath it all, Gee felt the undercurrent—the pulse of something bigger moving in the shadows.

Hamid finally leaned back, stretching. “So… what’s the play, hermano?”

Gee rubbed the back of his neck, thinking hard. “We wait. She said she’d be in touch—and I’ve got a feeling we don’t have to wait long.”

Hamid grinned, his eyes gleaming with mischief. “In the meantime, maybe we actually gamble. Blend in a little.”

Gee gave him a dry look. “Yeah, because we’re so good at subtle.”

Hamid laughed, standing and straightening his shirt. “Come on. What’s the worst that could happen?”

Gee shook his head, smiling despite himself, and followed him toward the nearest table. But as they moved, Gee’s eyes swept the casino floor one last time, his gut tight with instinct.

Something was coming.

And when Inaya returned...
They’d better be ready. Gee had just laid down his bet—a modest stack of chips—when he felt it:
that shift in the air.

The subtle scent of jasmine and danger.

“Miss me already?” Hamid muttered under his breath, eyes flicking up with a grin.

Inaya was back.

She stood at their table like she’d never left, a new drink in hand, her red dress hugging every curve, catching the low lights just right. Her smile was the same—slow, smooth, but her eyes? Sharper now. Calculating.

"Gentlemen," she purred, sliding into the seat between them, crossing her legs in that deliberate way that made heads turn nearby. "I hope you weren't too bored without me."

Gee's eyes narrowed, every nerve on alert. "We were wondering if you'd disappeared."

"Oh, I never disappear," Inaya said lightly, her gaze holding his a second longer than necessary. "I've been… thinking."

Hamid arched a brow. "Thinking about what?"

She traced the rim of her glass with one fingertip, eyes thoughtful. "About your friend, Voss. And… options."

Gee's jaw tightened. "We're listening."

She leaned in slightly, her tone dipping to a near-whisper—meant only for them, even in the hum of the busy casino. "Sebastian Voss isn't here. He's out of the country… and let's just say, some people think it's better if he stays that way."

Gee exchanged a quick glance with Hamid, pulse kicking up. "That right?"

Inaya smiled, slow and dangerous. "Men like Voss... they collect enemies as easily as they collect riches. And sometimes, those enemies are closer than they think."

Her eyes gleamed, full of unspoken meaning.

Hamid folded his arms, leaning forward. "You're saying you want him gone?"

She gave a delicate shrug, her smile never faltering. "I owe Sebastian a great deal. My... status here, for one. But power has a way of shifting, doesn't it? And frankly..." she looked around the opulent room, her fingers brushing the stem of her glass, "...I like what I have. I'd like to keep it."

Gee's voice was low, steady. "You're saying if we help you—get rid of Voss—you'll help us?"

Inaya's smile deepened, playful but razor-edged. "Let's not be so blunt, Gee. I'm saying... we may have mutual interests. Interests that align—for now."

She leaned back, her amber eyes locking onto his. "But make no mistake—this isn't charity. If I help you find Voss... if I feed you the right information... I expect something in return."

Gee held her gaze, reading the sharpness beneath the softness. “And what’s stopping you from turning us in? Or playing both sides?”

Inaya’s laugh was soft, but it carried weight. “I *am* playing both sides. That’s the point.”

She rose smoothly, brushing her dress into place, her smile lingering. “You two… you’re useful. And I think you’re just desperate enough to take the help.”

She stepped back, eyes glittering under the dim lights.

“I’ll be in touch,” she said, her voice honey-smooth but cool as stone. “Soon.”

With that, she turned and slipped away, hips swaying, disappearing once again into the glittering crowd.

Gee sat still, staring after her, jaw tight.

Hamid let out a low whistle. “That woman… is poison.”

“Yeah,” Gee muttered, knocking back the rest of his drink. “Let’s just hope she’s the kind we can use and not the kind that will kill us.”

The small town was quiet by morning, the heat already rising off the dusty streets as Lorrisa stepped out of the inn, Kong perched on her shoulder. She adjusted her backpack, eyes sharp beneath her sunglasses, scanning the quiet scene in front of her.

Her jeep sat in the lot, dusty but ready.

Carlos Conchata's words from the night before echoed in her head:

"The rings don't just attract treasure hunters—they attract governments."

She exhaled sharply, brushing a lock of hair from her cheek. "No kidding."

Kong chirped softly, eyes darting around as if he, too, sensed the invisible threads tightening.

The town seemed normal—vendors setting up stalls, kids running through narrow alleys, the distant hum of old engines. But underneath it all, Lorrisa couldn't shake the feeling: she was being watched.

She slid into the jeep and pulled out her map, spreading it across the steering wheel. Three rings in her possession—and no closer to assembling the full puzzle.

The ruined chamber at the Serpent's Crown had been another dead end—no fourth ring, just more riddles. She traced her finger along the lines she'd sketched last night: the strange carvings, the half-deciphered symbols, the crude coordinates she'd pieced together.

"Where the hell are you pointing me now?" she muttered.

Kong pawed at the edge of the map, chittering quietly.

She sighed, pulling out her notebook, flipping to the notes she'd made after escaping the trap. One symbol kept nagging at her—an engraving of a lion's head with what looked like a crescent moon above it.

Not part of the original trail. Something new.

"Maybe a marker," she whispered, snapping a quick photo of the page and cross-referencing it against a dusty old book she'd kept in the jeep—an ancient symbols field guide.

Her finger hovered over the page as she found it. "Lion's Gate. Middle Kingdom. Carved at—"

She froze.

A location flickered to life in her head—an old fortress ruin two days' drive east, rumored to have ancient ties to trade routes and lost treasures.

She sat back, breathing hard. "You've got to be kidding me."

It was remote. Dangerous. And too good of a lead to ignore.

She folded the map quickly, tossing her bag onto the passenger seat. Kong scrambled over her shoulder and settled in beside the gearshift, eyes bright with curiosity.

“Alright, little man,” Lorrisa muttered, starting the engine. “Time to move again.”

As the jeep rumbled to life and rolled out of the lot, her eyes flicked once to the rearview mirror.

No sign of Carlos.

No sign of anyone.

But her gut still twisted tight. She wasn’t alone—not really.

The hunt was far from over—and the next piece of the puzzle was waiting.

Somewhere out there. The sun was a molten disk hanging low in the sky, baking the endless sea of sand and stone. Lorrisa’s jeep rumbled along the narrow, uneven track, its tires kicking up thin plumes of dust that disappeared almost as soon as they rose.

Kong sat in the passenger seat, pawing absently at the air vent, eyes squinting against the glare. Lorrisa sipped from her water bottle, eyes scanning the horizon for any sign of the Lion's Gate ruins.

Nothing but dunes and jagged outcrops in every direction.

She checked the map again, biting her lip. "We're close," she muttered, mostly to herself. "We've got to be."

Just ahead, a movement—a shimmer—cut across the road. She squinted, slowing the jeep as shapes emerged from the haze.

A caravan of camels, ten or more, loaded with packs and supplies, made its way across the barren landscape, shepherded by five men in traditional desert garb. Long robes, headscarves wrapped tight, faces shaded by the sun's brutal rays.

Lorrisa pulled over, cutting the engine, and stepped out, shielding her eyes with one hand.

"Salam!" she called, raising her other hand in greeting.

The leader—a tall man with weathered skin and sharp eyes—raised a hand in return, motioning for the caravan to halt. The camels grunted and shifted, stirring up dust.

"Where are you headed, traveler?" the man asked in accented English, voice rough but not unfriendly.

Lorrisa approached cautiously, Kong perched on her shoulder, sniffing the air.

“I’m looking for Lion’s Gate,” she said, unfolding her map and holding it out. “The ruins... I’m close, but I want to be sure I’m on the right track.”

The man stepped forward, glancing at the map, eyes sharp and assessing. He pointed east, his finger tracing a winding path through the rocks.

“Another twenty kilometers,” he said. “You’ll find a dry riverbed—follow it. The ruins sit at its end.”

“Thank you,” Lorrisa said, tucking the map away, her eyes flicking over the other men—quiet, watchful, eyes hidden behind layers of cloth. “You’ve been a big help.”

The leader gave a small smile. “Not many foreigners out here alone. Be careful.”

“I will.” She offered a nod and turned back toward her jeep, Kong chittering softly.

As she drove away, kicking up a fresh plume of dust, the leader watched her until she was a distant blur.

Then, without a word, he reached into his robe and pulled out a *satellite phone.*

He dialed a number, lifting the receiver to his ear. The line clicked once—twice—then connected.

"Yes?" came the cold, familiar voice.

"Sebastian," the man said in a low tone, eyes still on the fading trail of dust, "The American woman you were looking for, she's here. She's looking for the Lion's Gate."

A pause. Then Voss's voice, sharp and controlled: "You've done well. Follow her. Don't engage. Report everything."

"Yes, sir."

The man ended the call, slipping the phone back into his robe. He turned to his men, gesturing toward the camels.

"Let's move."

The caravan shifted, wheels already in motion, a quiet shadow on Lorrisa's trail.

Sebastian Voss exhaled slowly, forcing himself to relax into the deep leather chair. His fingers toyed absently with the edge of the massive desk in front of him, trying to look composed—*but his pulse was still racing.*

Across from him, Simean Mogull sat like a stone idol, hands folded neatly, his eyes—dark, unblinking—

watching Voss with the quiet patience of a predator. Behind him, a floor-to-ceiling window framed the skyline, the late afternoon sun painting the room in streaks of gold.

It would have been beautiful, Voss thought—if it didn't feel like his execution chamber.

Mogull didn't speak. He just watched. Waited.

Voss cleared his throat, forcing out words. "I... appreciate your time, Mr. Mogull."

Mogull said nothing, his gaze hard as granite.

Voss shifted, straightening his tie. "As you know, I've... had a complication. After the—" his voice hitched slightly "—incident on the airline, I was detained."

Still silence.

Voss pressed on, fingers digging into the armrests. "To secure my release, I had to give... something. I informed the authorities about the situation unfolding in Northern Africa—the pursuit of the Rings of Solomon."

Mogull's nostrils flared—a subtle but dangerous shift. He leaned back slightly, the chair creaking under his bulk.

“And in doing so,” Mogull said at last, his voice a low, deadly rumble, “you compromised the entire operation.”

Voss’s mouth went dry. “It was… necessary. They were closing in. Without that leverage, I wouldn’t be sitting here right now.”

Mogull’s eyes narrowed. “And perhaps that would have been better.”

Voss’s stomach twisted. He pushed forward, desperate. “But I’m back in control. I’ve already set countermeasures in place—Inaya is monitoring the situation on the ground, and… and the Bureau has dispatched a Special Agent—Carlos Conchata. He’s there to clean things up.”

Mogull’s fingers tapped slowly on the desk, the only sound in the cavernous office.

“You invited the FBI into my affairs,” he said, each word precise, like a hammer driving a nail. “Like I do not have enough problem here with law”.

Voss swallowed hard. “Not invited—manipulated. I fed them just enough to keep them chasing shadows. Conchata thinks he’s on the trail of an international smuggling ring. He doesn’t know the full picture.”

Mogull's eyes burned. "And yet, the full picture is exactly what I *own*. The moment the Bureau got involved, you handed over control of this entire operation to *others*."

Voss tried to breathe, heart thudding in his chest. "I… I can fix it. The search is still ongoing. The rings have not been united yet. We are close—so close—to assembling the tablet."

Mogull stood suddenly, the massive chair scraping back, and stepped around the desk. His presence filled the room, oppressive and inescapable. He loomed over Voss, hands clasped behind his back, eyes boring down like a vise.

"You know what your value is to me, Sebastian?" Mogull asked quietly.

Voss dared a glance upward, voice small. "Information. Access."

"Exactly." Mogull's lips twitched—a smile, but one colder than ice. "And when you lose control of that—when you leak my business to governments, to fools and treasure hunters—you become a liability."

Voss's breath quickened. "I—I can still deliver. I swear it."

Mogull circled slowly, like a lion around a wounded animal. "Then listen carefully. There's only one path to redemption now."

He leaned in, voice like a whisper of death:
"Find the tablet. All of it. Every piece. And deliver it to me… or you won't walk away from this alive."

Voss's heart hammered, his mouth dry. He nodded quickly, words tumbling out. "Yes, yes, of course. I—I'll make it right. I'll get it done."

Mogull straightened, stepping back to the window, looking out over the city.

"The girl—Lorrisa Santos," Mogull said thoughtfully. "She's the key, isn't she?"

Voss's eyes flashed. "Yes. She has the rings. She's ahead of the others. But I've got people tracking her. Even now."

Mogull nodded slowly. "Then focus there. No more distractions. No more mistakes."

Voss stood, legs shaky, clutching his briefcase. "I understand."

Mogull's eyes slid back to him, sharp and final. "Do you?"

Voss hesitated, then gave a quick nod. “Yes, sir.”

Mogull turned back to the window, dismissing him with silence.

Voss hurried to the door, heart still pounding, sweat slicking his back despite the coolness of the room. His hand shook as he grasped the handle.

Behind him, Mogull’s voice rumbled one last time—soft but unmistakable:
“Redemption or death, Sebastian. Choose wisely.”

Voss stepped out into the hallway, the door clicking shut behind him. He leaned against the wall, gasping for breath, his mind racing.

Redemption or death.

And time... was running out.

Sebastian Voss sat stiffly in the back of a sleek black sedan, his fingers tapping anxiously against his thigh as the car glided through the city streets. The sun had set, casting long shadows that flickered across his pale face.

He still felt Mogull’s words burning in his ears:
Redemption or death.

His jaw clenched as he reached into his coat pocket and pulled out his phone, scrolling quickly through his contacts until he found the name he'd been dreading—and yet needed most.

Lazlo.

He hesitated a heartbeat, then hit *call.*

It rang twice before a voice—low, gravelly, and unmistakably dangerous—answered. "Haven't heard from you in a long time, Voss."

"Lazlo," Voss said tightly, "I have a job. One I need handled fast."

A soft chuckle. "You're calling me directly. Must be serious."

Voss stared out the window, his reflection sharp and pale in the glass. "It is. Africa. I'm flying out tomorrow. I need backup—someone who can get their hands dirty."

"Who's the target?"

Voss's grip on the phone tightened. "A woman. Lorrisa Santos. She's... persistent. Resourceful. And she's got something I need."

A pause. Then Lazlo's voice, curious now: "And you want her dead?"

Voss hesitated. He could picture her—the fire in her eyes, the way she'd struck him down with no hesitation. His jaw tightened.

"No," he said slowly. "Not yet. I want her followed, pressured. If you get a clean shot—if she becomes a threat—then yes. But not before I say."

Another pause. "And the package?"

Voss's eyes narrowed. "The Rings of Solomon. Three of them. She's hunting the fourth and beyond. I need all of them."

Lazlo let out a low whistle. "Big game. What's the payout?"

"Triple your usual fee," Voss said quickly. "Plus bonuses if we secure everything before the Bureau tightens their grip."

A hum of approval. "Tempting."

"I'm not asking," Voss snapped. "This is a done deal."

Lazlo's laugh was slow and cold. "You don't get to give orders, Voss. But… I'm intrigued. I'll meet you at the airstrip."

The line went dead.

Voss exhaled sharply, shoving the phone back into his pocket. The car rolled to a stop outside a private terminal, the lights of a jet gleaming in the dark. His driver stepped out and opened the door, but Voss lingered a moment, staring at the jet, his pulse hammering.

This is it, he told himself.
Redemption or death.

He climbed out, smoothing his coat, eyes sharp now—cold, focused.

Tomorrow, he'd be back in Africa. And this time, he wouldn't be alone.

The bar was a dump—half-lit, half-empty, smelling of old smoke and stale beer. Lazlo sat alone in a back booth, a scarred hand wrapped around a glass of dark liquor. He nursed it slowly, eyes flicking occasionally to the door out of habit, but mostly watching his phone, which sat facedown on the sticky table.

The message came through ten minutes after Voss's call.
One attachment.

Lazlo's lips curled into a lazy smirk as he picked up the phone and thumbed it open.

A photo appeared—low-res, but clear enough:

Lorrisa Santos.
A university headshot—her hair sleek and dark, eyes sharp but warm, a soft smile just touching her lips. Official-looking, no hint of the dirt, sweat, and danger she was apparently wrapped up in now.

Lazlo let out a low whistle, leaning back in the booth.

"Well... well... this is the infamous Ms. Santos."

He zoomed in a little, studying the lines of her face—the high cheekbones, the curve of her lips, the softness around the eyes that hinted at something a little too smart, a little too confident.

"Sebastian," he murmured, shaking his head with an amused grin, "what the hell kind of mess have you gotten yourself into?"

He glanced at the message thread—coordinates, travel plans, a brief note from Voss:

"Target is highly mobile. Persistent. Dangerous. Do not underestimate."

Lazlo's grin widened. "Dangerous, huh?"

He studied the picture again, letting his eyes linger—longer than necessary.

“Beautiful,” he muttered. “But I don’t see deadly. Yet.”

He set the phone down, tapping one finger thoughtfully against the glass.

What was it about this one that had Sebastian Voss—slick, ruthless Sebastian—so tied up in knots? Enough to risk everything, enough to hire a man like him.

Lazlo’s eyes narrowed, sharp now, the playful smirk fading just a little. Beauty was one thing. Survival... that was another.

He took a slow sip of his drink, still staring at the phone, her image frozen on the screen.

“Alright, Ms. Santos,” he murmured, voice low and rough, “let’s see what you’ve really got.”

The sun hung low and heavy by the time Lorrisa finally spotted it—a jagged silhouette against the glowing horizon. The ruins of Lion’s Gate rose like broken teeth from the rocky earth, jagged walls and crumbled towers half-swallowed by shifting sands.

She pulled the jeep to a stop at the edge of the ancient site, killing the engine. The sudden silence pressed in, broken only by the ticking of the jeep's cooling engine and the faint whisper of the desert wind.

Kong stirred, stretching on the passenger seat, blinking blearily at the ruins ahead.

"We're here," Lorrisa murmured, brushing hair from her face, eyes locked on the massive stone archway that still stood—weathered but proud, its keystone carved with the head of a lion.

The same symbol that had haunted her notes, her dreams.

She stepped out, boots crunching on gravel, and stretched, scanning the perimeter. No signs of life. No vehicles. No watchers. Just the endless desert stretching out in every direction.

Kong hopped onto her shoulder as she grabbed her gear—torch, rope, water, the map—and started toward the ruins, each step heavy with anticipation.

The closer she got, the more immense it felt—ancient stones towering above her, scarred by time and sandstorms, yet still holding onto their secrets.

At the base of the arch, she paused, running her hand across the rough surface, fingers tracing the deep-cut lines of the lion's mane. The stone was cool beneath her touch, solid and unyielding.

"This is it," she whispered.

Kong sniffed the air, ears perked, eyes darting to every shadow.

She unrolled the map, flattening it against her thigh, eyes flicking over her notes.
The carvings from the last ruin had pointed her here—but now? No clear next step. No obvious entry point.

Her eyes roamed the ruined complex—half-collapsed corridors, fallen columns, darkened doorways swallowed in shadow.

"Well," she muttered, rolling up the map, "time to get to work."

She made her way through the first corridor, stepping over crumbled stones and shattered pottery. Her torch flickered across the walls—more carvings, more symbols, too eroded to read clearly.

Every sound seemed magnified—the scrape of her boots, the whisper of wind through broken archways, the occasional creak of ancient wood deep within the ruins.

Kong stayed tight to her, nose twitching, body tense.

After an hour of **searching—careful, methodical—**Lorrisa found herself at a sunken courtyard, the stones slick with age, half-covered in sand. She paused, catching her breath, eyes narrowed at the far end where a half-buried statue jutted from the earth—another lion, its eyes worn hollow.

She moved closer, brushing sand away from its base, revealing a patch of weathered script.

Her heart skipped. She snapped a photo, leaning closer to study it.

"'When the Lion drinks, the Gate opens,'" she read aloud, frowning. "What the hell does that mean?"

Kong pawed at the sand, stirring it restlessly.

She stood, scanning the area again—no fountains, no obvious mechanisms. But she'd learned by now: nothing was ever obvious.

"Okay," she whispered, stepping back, eyes narrowing. "Let's figure out how to make the Lion drink."

Lorrisa sat back on her heels in the quiet courtyard, the sun sliding lower, casting long shadows across the ancient stones. Her fingers absently sifted through the sand at her side, eyes locked on the half-buried lion statue as the words echoed in her mind:

"When the Lion drinks, the Gate opens."

She exhaled slowly, wiping sweat from her brow, and sat down fully, leaning back against a broken column. Kong nestled at her side, his small chest rising and falling in the growing hush of the ruins.

Silence. Stillness.

Her eyes traced the statue's worn face, but her mind began to drift—further back, to another life.

She could see it now as clear as day—one of her first digs, the blistering sun of Cairo, the endless trenches, and the constant frustration of coming up empty-handed. And then there was him.

Gee.

That cocky grin as he leaned over the edge of a trench, hat pushed back, wiping sweat from his brow.
"You know," he'd drawled, "you could dig all day and not find anything. Or... you could let me figure it out in half the time."

She'd rolled her eyes, but couldn't help laughing.
"Got it all figured out, huh?"

"Of course," he'd said with a wink. "The trick is not just thinking like a treasure hunter—you've gotta think like the people who *hid* it."

She smiled faintly now, eyes distant.

God, he'd been insufferable sometimes—but brilliant. The way he'd solve the toughest puzzles, piecing together fragments of clues like a magician pulling rabbits from hats. And when they hit dead ends, when exhaustion crept in and morale dropped, he'd keep her laughing with the stupidest jokes, always finding light in the darkest digs.

She remembered late nights poring over maps, falling asleep on his shoulder, and... other nights, when maps were forgotten altogether, and the only thing that mattered was the way he'd pull her close, murmuring something ridiculous that made her laugh even as she melted into him.

Her fingers tightened on the sand, her breath catching slightly as the memory pressed closer—too close.

Kong stirred beside her, letting out a small, questioning chirp.

She blinked, dragging herself back to the present. "Yeah," she whispered, voice rough, "no time for that."

She looked at the lion statue again, her mind still humming with Gee's words.

"You've gotta think like the people who hid it."

Her eyes narrowed. The riddle... the Lion drinks.

She scanned the area again—the statue, the carvings, the half-sunken stones. Dry. Empty. Nothing about this place had seen water in centuries.

But—what if it wasn't about real water?

She stood slowly, brushing herself off, eyes sharp now. She circled the statue, running her hand along its base, her fingers tracing the faint, ancient grooves.

Suddenly, she paused—a hollow, narrow indentation at the lion's mouth. A small depression running down from its jaw into the earth.

Her heart pounded. "Gee... you'd love this."

She knelt quickly, digging around the lion's base, clearing centuries of sand until the shallow channel revealed itself—a primitive aqueduct, leading from the lion's mouth toward the ground.

She laughed softly, shaking her head. "It wants to drink."

Pulling out her canteen, she unscrewed the top and poured a slow, steady stream of water into the lion's open mouth. The water trickled down, disappearing into the ancient channel.

For a beat, nothing happened.

She held her breath, heart hammering.

Then—a deep, low *click,* followed by the faint grinding of stone.

Kong leapt to his feet, eyes wide, chittering with excitement.

Lorrisa spun around just in time to see a section of the courtyard's far wall begin to shift, a crack widening, sand spilling out as an ancient door—hidden in plain sight—slid slowly open.

Her pulse raced. She grabbed her pack, scooping up Kong, eyes locked on the dark passage now yawning before her.

"Okay," she whispered, adrenaline surging, "here we go."

And with that, she stepped into the shadows, leaving the dying daylight behind.

The hidden door creaked open just wide enough for Lorrisa to slip through, revealing a narrow stone passage, dark and cool, the air inside thick with dust and the weight of centuries.

She stood at the threshold for a moment, breathing steady, eyes adjusting to the gloom.

“Alright,” she muttered, slinging her pack off her shoulder and kneeling to check her gear.

She ran through the mental list:
a. Flashlight—click. A sharp, bright beam cut through the darkness.
b. Spare batteries.
c. Rope, utility knife, notebook, chalk for marking the walls.
d. Extra water.
e. Matches—just in case.
f. And... the rings, safely tucked in their pouch.

Kong, already sensing the adventure ahead, scampered onto her shoulder, his little claws gripping lightly through her shirt. He chattered softly, peering into the darkness, alert but fearless.

“Instincts, huh?” she whispered, giving him a quick scratch behind the ear. “Good boy.”

She stood, cinching her backpack tighter, and swept the flashlight across the entryway. The walls were rough-hewn stone, marked with faded carvings—snakes, lions, and symbols she didn't immediately recognize. The floor sloped downward, the tunnel seeming to disappear into the earth itself.

She hesitated only a second longer.

"Let's do this."

With Kong pressed close, she stepped inside. The heavy stone door began grinding shut behind them, the sound echoing deep into the tunnel until it sealed them in total darkness—except for the bright, narrow beam of her flashlight.

Her boots crunched softly on the ancient floor as she moved deeper, eyes darting across the walls, every muscle tense. Each breath tasted of old stone, dust, and secrets.

Far up on a rocky ridge, just out of sight, the camel caravan had stopped. The leader—the man who had given Lorrisa directions earlier—stood with a small pair of binoculars pressed to his eyes, watching her every move.

He saw her slip through the hidden entrance, watched as the stone door groaned shut behind her.

"Foolish girl," he murmured in his native tongue, lowering the binoculars.

He reached into his robe once again, pulling out the satellite phone.

"Update," he said quietly when the line connected. "She has entered the ruin. Alone."

A pause on the other end—Voss's cold, familiar voice: "Good. Stay back. Report anything unusual."

"Yes, sir."

He ended the call, slipping the phone away, and glanced at his men. They were already settling down, building a small fire as the desert night crept in.

"She won't come out soon," he said calmly. "But we wait."

Lorrisa pressed forward, deeper into the ruin. The tunnel widened gradually, leading into a vast, cavernous chamber. Her flashlight swept across the space, revealing massive stone columns and fragmented mosaics half-buried in sand and debris.

She stepped carefully, eyes darting from floor to ceiling. The silence pressed in around her, broken only by

Kong's quiet breathing and the distant drip of water from somewhere deep within.

Her hand brushed against a raised carving—a sunburst design. Familiar. It tugged at the edge of her memory, but she kept moving, her instincts telling her this place had more layers than met the eye.

"Stay sharp," she whispered to Kong, adjusting her grip on the flashlight as she ventured further into the shadows, unaware of the silent eyes watching from above, waiting.

Lorrisa's breath hitched as her flashlight beam swept across the far side of the chamber.

There—half-buried beneath a fallen column—was a *stone slab etched with deep, precise carvings*. She stepped closer, crouching, brushing sand away from its face. Kong clung tighter to her shoulder, eyes darting nervously around the echoing space.

She leaned in, eyes tracing the ancient symbols, the flowing lines of script. Something clicked in her memory—a fragment she'd seen in her research, buried in a forgotten archive.

"Coordinates," she whispered, heart racing. "This... this marks another site."

She snapped a quick series of photos, fingers trembling with excitement, her mind already racing ahead. A new lead—a major piece of the puzzle.

Kong let out a sharp, nervous chirp, twisting on her shoulder.

“What’s wrong?” she murmured, glancing around.

Then she felt it—a faint vibration through the soles of her boots.

Click... click...

Her eyes shot up just as the floor beneath her began to tremble, ancient mechanisms grinding to life. Before she could react, the slab lurched sideways, revealing a narrow passage and from deep below, a sudden rush of water roared upward.

“Shit!”

The torrent hit her hard, knocking her off balance. Kong scrambled to cling to her as the water surged fast, filling the chamber with frightening speed. In seconds, it was up to her knees—then her waist—rising fast.

Lorrisa fought to stay upright, gasping as the cold gripped her.

“No, no, no—”

She spun, looking for the exit, but the way she'd come in was already sealed tight—solid stone, no visible mechanism.

"Kong—hold on!" she shouted, shoving her flashlight into her backpack and hugging it close to her chest, wading toward the new passage the slab had revealed.

The water was waist-high now and climbing fast—gushing from hidden vents along the walls, ancient traps sprung to deadly life.

She ducked into the narrow passage, her boots slipping on slick stone, the tunnel pitch black except for the thin beam of light slicing ahead.

The water rose—chest-deep. Then her shoulders. Kong clung to her neck, shivering, his claws digging in.

"Keep it together," she panted, pushing forward, one hand on the wall, the other gripping the edge of her pack.

But the tunnel sloped downward—the water surging higher, faster.

Suddenly, the floor dropped out—a plunge into deep, freezing blackness.

Lorrisa screamed, gulping a mouthful of air before she was pulled under. Kong gripped tight as she kicked furiously, fighting the surge, her flashlight beam swinging wildly beneath the surface.

She surfaced once—gasping, eyes wild—then went under again as the tunnel twisted and churned.

Her lungs burned, her mind raced.

There's got to be a way out—there's always a way out—

She spotted something—a faint shimmer of light ahead, barely a flicker through the swirling water.

Kong's weight shifted as he tried to climb higher, squealing in panic.

"Almost... there—"

Her hand slammed into something—a grate. Metal, corroded but solid—blocking the tunnel completely.

"No!" she screamed, slamming her fists against it, the water now up to the ceiling, leaving her no space to breathe.

Desperation surged. She kicked at the grate, fingers scrabbling for purchase, eyes stinging, chest on fire.

Kong screeched, his claws raking at the bars, frantic.

Then—her hand found a weak point. A crack in the frame.

She grabbed the knife from her pack, jamming it into the crack, levering with all her strength, legs braced against the slick tunnel walls.

The metal groaned, warped.

She pressed harder, teeth gritted, eyes squeezed shut—every muscle screaming—

And suddenly, the grate gave way—snapping open with a surge of water.

Lorrisa was flung forward, tumbling through the narrow gap, Kong screeching in her ear, water roaring around them.

She surfaced in a new chamber, gasping, dragging herself onto a ledge, coughing and shaking, drenched and shivering.

Kong collapsed beside her, panting hard, fur soaked and eyes wild.

For a long moment, she just lay there, breathing ragged, staring up at the crumbling ceiling.

“Jesus,” she rasped. “That... was too close.”

She rolled onto her side, gripping Kong gently, pressing her forehead to his.

“We’re okay,” she whispered, her voice breaking into a laugh. “We’re okay.”

She sat up slowly, blinking around the dimly lit chamber—new walls, new carvings, another step deeper into the mystery.

Her heart still thudded hard in her chest, but her eyes sharpened with resolve.

“Alright,” she muttered, wringing water from her shirt, “let’s see what the hell we almost drowned for.”

Lorrisa sat slumped against the cold stone wall, breathing in deep, shaky gulps of air. The chamber was dim and silent now, the roar of rushing water just a distant memory echoing in her ears.

Her clothes clung to her like a second skin—soaked, heavy, cold. She shivered, brushing wet hair back from her face, blinking away the grit and exhaustion clouding her eyes.

Kong pressed close, his tiny body trembling, water dripping from his soaked fur. He let out a soft, uncertain chirp, staring at her with wide, worried eyes.

She gave him a weak smile and gently ruffled his fur. “Yeah,” she whispered, her voice rough, “we really know how to find trouble, huh?”

She peeled off her backpack and dumped it beside her, unzipping it fast. Half the contents were drenched. She cursed under her breath, pulling out the flashlight—amazingly still working—and a small emergency blanket, shaking it out and draping it around her shoulders.

Kong climbed onto her lap, burrowing under the silver sheet for warmth, his tiny paws gripping her shirt.

“Easy, buddy. We made it,” she whispered, more to convince herself than him.

Her hand brushed across her side—the pouch. Her stomach clenched as she unfastened it, breathing a sigh of relief when the rings inside shimmered faintly under the flashlight beam.

“Still with me,” she muttered. “Good.”

She leaned back against the wall, closing her eyes briefly, letting the quiet wash over her. For a moment, just a moment, she let herself feel it all—the exhaustion, the fear, the raw pulse of survival.

And underneath it... the burn of frustration.

She thought of Gee—how he'd have teased her for nearly drowning, how he'd have cracked a joke, maybe offered a sly smile and said something like, *"You always had a flair for the dramatic, Santos."*

She smiled weakly at the thought, shaking her head.

But the smile faded as the weight of it all pressed in—the clues, the danger, the watchful eyes she couldn't see but could always feel.

Her gaze swept the chamber, flashlight beam dancing over ancient carvings and symbols she didn't yet understand. Another puzzle. Another risk.

"Not stopping now," she whispered, her eyes hardening.

She sat up straighter, pushing Kong gently off her lap and digging through the bag again. She found a small energy bar, tore it open, and took a few quick bites, tossing a piece to Kong, who devoured it greedily.

"Alright," she said, her voice firmer now. "Dry off, eat something, and get back on track. We're not done here."

She wrapped the blanket tighter, forcing her breath to steady, her mind already calculating next steps. Whatever lay ahead, she wasn't turning back.

The chamber was waiting—quiet, ancient, heavy with secrets.

And Lorrisa Santos? She was ready to uncover every damn one of them.

The hiss of the jet's door opening cut through the humid night air as Sebastian Voss stepped out onto the tarmac, sunglasses perched on his nose despite the dark, his expression tight and unreadable. He inhaled slowly, taking in the sharp scent of jet fuel and heat-soaked asphalt.

Lazlo followed close behind, a canvas duffel slung over one shoulder, his sharp eyes scanning the perimeter out of habit.

At the foot of the stairs, a black SUV idled, a driver waiting with military precision.

"Back in paradise," Lazlo muttered dryly, eyeing the surrounding buildings and floodlights with a flicker of disdain.

Voss ignored the comment, descending briskly. He slid into the backseat without a word, Lazlo settling in beside him. The door slammed shut, and the driver pulled away smoothly, merging onto the dark road that led out of the airport complex.

For a moment, the car was silent, the hum of the tires filling the void.

Then Voss spoke, low and measured. "We don't have time to waste. The girl—Santos—is already deep in the Lion's Gate ruins. She's ahead of us."

Lazlo's lips twitched in amusement. "She's really got you spooked, doesn't she?"

Voss's jaw clenched. "Not spooked. Focused. She's smart, determined—and she's got three of the rings in her possession. If she finds the tablet before we do, we lose everything."

"And Rodriguez?" Lazlo asked, pulling out a small blade and idly twirling it between his fingers. "You still worried about him?"

Voss shook his head. "He's a distraction. Useful, maybe, but not the priority."

Lazlo arched a brow, smirking. "You saying he's not a threat? After everything?"

Voss's eyes flashed, cold and sharp. "I'm saying he can wait. Right now, all that matters is Lorrisa—and the rings."

He leaned forward, tapping the driver's shoulder. "Get me to the safehouse. I want a crew assembled within the hour—five men, armed, no questions."

"Already in motion, sir," the driver replied crisply.

Lazlo chuckled, glancing at Voss. "A little overkill for one woman and her pet monkey, don't you think?"

Voss's stare was icy. "She's survived more than she should have. I'm not taking chances."

He pulled out his phone, scrolling through live updates. A small blip on a tracking map flashed—her last known location, deep within the Lion's Gate ruins.

"She's still inside," Voss murmured, eyes narrowing. "We move now, we catch her before she surfaces."

Lazlo stretched, cracking his knuckles lazily. "Sounds like fun. Haven't had a good hunt in a while."

Voss's lips curled into a tight, humorless smile. "Good. Because this is your hunt now. I want her caught, cornered—and if necessary..." He paused, eyes flashing. "Eliminated."

Lazlo's smile was all teeth. "Understood."

The SUV disappeared into the night, engine humming as it sped toward the safehouse—toward the next move in a deadly game already in motion.

The casino's neon glow flickered behind them as Gee and Hamid stepped outside into the thick, dry night air. The distant hum of engines and chatter cut through the relative quiet of the street.

Hamid paused mid-stretch, squinting across the plaza. "You seeing what I'm seeing?"

Gee followed his gaze. A small crowd of men—rugged, broad-shouldered, some in military-grade gear—were gathering near a row of off-road vehicles. Cargo was being loaded. Radios buzzed. Boots stomped in tight formation.

No shouting. No fanfare. But this was organized movement.

"Locals don't roll that deep unless something serious is about to happen," Hamid muttered.

Gee's jaw tightened as he took in the scene. "They're not locals. Look at the gear. Too clean. Too new. Those guys are either ex-military... or getting paid like they are."

"You thinking what I'm thinking?"

Gee gave a single, deliberate nod. "Sebastian's on the move."

Hamid adjusted the strap of his bag, eyes sharp now. "So what's the play?"

Gee watched as the group split into teams, climbing into blacked-out trucks and sand-caked Land Cruisers. The vehicles rumbled to life, headlights off, moving out in formation.

He gave Hamid a smirk. "We follow the crowd." Twenty minutes later, their borrowed jeep crawled to a quiet stop on the edge of an old industrial yard. The moon lit the space in fragments—rows of rusting shipping containers, broken fences, and crumbling warehouses.

But what caught their attention was at the center:

A makeshift staging zone.

Dozens of men—all armed, armored, and moving with clockwork precision—were loading weapons, ammunition, climbing into trucks and dune buggies outfitted for desert travel. Engines idled. Radios crackled with coded chatter. Tension hung in the air like static.

"Holy shit," Hamid breathed. "What are they gearing up for—war?"

Gee didn't answer at first. He scanned the perimeter, then looked across at Hamid. "We've been trying to find Sebastian. We just did."

Hamid glanced at him. "You sure?"

"Voss never gets his hands dirty," Gee said quietly. "Not unless the prize is close. Whatever's going down, it's big—and it involves the rings."

Hamid's expression darkened. "Then what are we waiting for?"

Gee threw the jeep into gear and rolled them slowly around the edge of the compound. As they moved, he spotted a parked supply truck with two men smoking and laughing off to the side. Their gear was stacked beside the vehicle—helmets, body armor, weapons, radios.

"Opportunity," Gee said, pulling into the shadows. "We blend in."

Hamid raised a brow. “You’re talking infiltration. No plan. No backup.”

“Just instinct,” Gee said, stepping out and popping the trunk to grab whatever improvised gear they had. “And if Sebastian’s heading into the desert, that must mean he found something.”

They locked eyes, a silent agreement passing between them.

“Alright,” Hamid said with a shrug. “Let’s crash this party.”

The stolen uniforms itched like hell, but they did the job.

Gee adjusted the tactical vest over his chest, the name patch reading *“S. Ortiz”* half-torn and faded. Hamid was already fitting a comm earpiece into place, glancing at himself in the cracked side mirror of the supply truck they’d slipped into.

“You know,” Hamid muttered, “for a group of supposed professionals, these guys suck at securing their gear.”

“Lucky us,” Gee said quietly. “Keep your head down. Say little. Watch everything.”

They’d parked their own vehicle behind a rusted-out container and had slipped into the flow of activity under cover of darkness. Now they moved among the crew like they belonged—just two more soldiers in black fatigues and dusty boots.

The staging yard buzzed with tension. Crates of weapons were being strapped down. Satellite gear and survey equipment were checked. Maps were being passed around.

From one corner of the camp, a small group of higher-ups gathered around an LED-lit table. Voss was among them—elegant despite the desert grit, issuing orders with clipped precision.

Gee froze at the sight of him.

"That's him," he whispered to Hamid. "No doubt about it."

"Looks smug for someone who's got the desert crawling up his ass," Hamid replied.

Gee's eyes narrowed. "He found something."

"You still think it's a ring?"

Gee didn't answer right away. He just watched. Voss wasn't reacting like someone chasing a myth. He moved like a man making final adjustments—like a man who'd already won.

From the conversation fragments around them, Gee picked up snippets:

"...coordinates locked..."
"...ruins buried under the canyon line..."
"...no resistance expected, but keep eyes open..."

He grabbed a clipboard from a nearby gear crate and pretended to double-check it, just to stay mobile. His ears strained.

"Convoy leaves in twenty," someone barked. "Load the last unit and prep the east-bound route."

Gee moved closer to Hamid, speaking low. "They're going to a ruin site. East. Canyon terrain."

"Perfect terrain for an ambush," Hamid noted.

"Or a dig site," Gee muttered. "Either way, we're riding with them."

"Copy that."

As they passed behind one of the armored transports, Gee looked to the distant vehicles—at least six trucks, two sand runners, and a covered cargo van.

"Pick one near the back," he said. "In case we need to disappear."

Hamid flashed a grin. “You mean when we need to disappear.”

Ten minutes later, Gee and Hamid climbed into the rear of one of the transport trucks, wedging themselves between crates of supplies and rough canvas sacks. The truck’s engine rumbled beneath them.

Gee glanced down at his borrowed rifle, then out through the gap in the canvas as the convoy began to roll.

“You really think he’s onto something?” Hamid asked.

Gee’s voice was tight. “He wouldn’t move this many men unless he was certain.”

Hamid leaned his head back, eyes narrowing. “Still wish we knew what Lorrisa thought of all this.”

Gee gave a faint smirk. “She’s probably halfway back to her apartment. by now, writing a lecture about how reckless we are.”

“Yeah,” Hamid chuckled. “She’s the lucky one.”

Neither of them noticed the ridge in the far distance—where the camel caravan watchers were just beginning to break camp, following another path that converged with the same canyon terrain.

Or that further ahead, beneath the ground, Lorrisa Santos was already breaking history wide open. The tunnels were colder than expected—stone sweat lining the walls, the kind of damp that whispered old things in the dark. But the silence didn't last long.

It shattered with the low thud of boots. Five men, armed and armored, moved with predator-like precision, rifles raised, beams cutting through the black.

Their comms crackled with a command:

"Target is female. Mid-thirties. Capuchin monkey with her. Do not kill unless absolutely necessary. Voss wants her alive."

The lead man—a square-jawed mercenary with a scar running down his cheek—signaled the others with two fingers. They split, two taking a left bend, two flanking wide, the last trailing center behind their lead.

Their footfalls fell silent over dust-covered stone.

Elsewhere in the Ruins...

Gee crouched near a jagged pillar of ancient limestone, eyes tracking the mercenary team's movements from the shadowed crevice of a collapsed archway. Beside him, Hamid lowered his binoculars with a frown.

“They’re not moving like they’re here for relics,” Hamid whispered. “These guys are after something breathing.”

Gee didn’t answer.

His jaw clenched as he stared at the mercs. His gut churned—not from fear, but something worse. Instinct.

“These guys aren’t treasure hunters,” Gee said, his voice gravel. “They’re hunting someone.”

Hamid’s voice was low. “And I don’t think it’s Voss anymore.”

Gee squinted down the corridor. A faint beam of light flickered—just briefly—then vanished.

A memory flickered, uninvited:
Lorrisa’s flashlight bouncing along the dig site in Cairo, her soft laugh echoing over the sand.

Hamid grunted. “You think that’s...?”

Gee nodded, breath hitching. “It can’t be.”

“You said she went back to the States.”

“I thought she did.”

Both men rose slowly, rifles raised.

The scarred merc rounded a turn, pausing just before a junction chamber.

Then all hell broke loose.

The moment was sudden.

Gee squeezed the trigger—*pop pop pop!*—and the lead merc dropped hard, his armor thudding against stone. The rest shouted in clipped formation talk, scattering to cover.

Hamid opened up from the side angle, catching one with a controlled burst that slammed the man against a crumbling column.

“Contact! We’ve got hostiles!” one of the mercs shouted.

Gee rolled into new cover, shifting his fire toward the corridor mouth. “They don’t know who they’re fighting. Let’s keep it that way.”

But he wasn’t thinking about tactics.
He was thinking about that flashlight.

Lorrisa moved swiftly, sweeping her own beam over the moss-laced carvings of a side chamber. Kong remained crouched on her back, gripping her tightly, every muscle in his tiny frame tense.

The walls here felt closer. Ancient, but disturbed.

She turned to mark a symbol when the crack of gunfire roared through the tunnel like thunder.

Kong screeched in alarm. She ducked instinctively, flashlight beam swinging violently.

Gunfire. Close.

Adrenaline surged.

She spun, weapon drawn—but shadows darted fast in the smoke of ancient dust.

A figure emerged—tactical armor, masked, weapon lifted.

She didn't think.
Didn't aim.
Didn't breathe.

She just *moved*.

CRACK!

She grabbed the thick, broken stalactite she'd spotted earlier—a jagged spire of calcite. Her grip tightened, and she swung with everything she had.

THWACK!

The weapon collided with the figure's temple. The man crumpled sideways, groaning. His helmet clattered off, rolling to her feet.

Lorrisa's breath caught as her flashlight beam fell across the man's face.

Familiar jawline.
Five o'clock shadow.
Eyes—dazed but unmistakably furious and surprised.

"...Gee?!" she gasped.

He blinked, squinting up at her, blood trickling from his temple, his speech a bit garbled.
"Did... did you just brain me with a stalactite?"

Her mouth opened, but no words came. Then:

"You shot at me!"

"No I didn't!"

"You—"

More gunfire snapped past them, one round punching into the wall behind her.

"Later!" Hamid's voice rang out as he slid into view, laying down cover fire. "Move or die!"

Lorrisa slung one of Gee's arms over her shoulder, still stunned. Kong scampered across her back to peer at Gee in confusion.

"You were supposed to be in D.C.," Gee groaned.

"You were supposed to be smart enough not to sneak up on someone with a rock in her hand," Lorrisa snapped back.

Hamid emptied a clip, ducked behind a column, and reloaded. "We've got three more moving in. The fourth's flanking."

"Path to the left?" Lorrisa asked.

Gee nodded. "Collapsed earlier. Still passable."

"Then that's our out."

Together, the trio rushed the left tunnel. Kong leapt ahead, scampering to scout while bullets tore through the cave behind them. The mercs' shouts faded with distance, their heavy gear slowing them down.

A ricochet sent a chunk of rock exploding beside Gee's head. He ducked instinctively.

"That better not be Lorrisa's aim again," he muttered.

"She only misses when she cares," Hamid said, grinning as he fired blind behind him.

They emerged into a forgotten side shaft, ducking under a massive stone beam. Gee collapsed against the wall, breathing hard, cradling his skull.

Lorrisa dropped to a knee beside him. “Let me see it.”

“It’s not that bad,” he muttered.

“It’s bleeding.”

“It’s not the worst head job you’ve given me.”

She smirked—then, in spite of everything, she laughed. Exhausted. Shocked. Relieved.

Kong let out a tired warble and collapsed in her lap.

Hamid scanned the rear with his rifle, still on edge.

“More will come,” he said. “This was just the first wave.”

Gee looked to Lorrisa. “We’ve got a lot to talk about.”

She nodded slowly. “Yeah. Starting with why the hell you’re here.”

“Let’s survive the next ten minutes,” Hamid muttered. “Then we’ll get into love letters.”

Lorrisa pulled out her map, unfurled it between them.

“Then let’s find our way out. And maybe… toward the next piece.”

אפיה
דזן
אפזיון
ועייזן
נייעון
עמיעון
ימצון
יהד
יוידהן
רמיעון
יהוֹהה
מעזנן
רמעון
שידען
רעאון
ידה
ישחון

Chapter 8

The passage was narrowing. The ancient stone walls closed in on both sides, rough and uneven, their surfaces damp from centuries of moisture. Footing was treacherous—wet sand and crumbled rock concealed slick edges—but Lorrisa pressed forward, guiding the group with Kong clinging to her back.

Gee limped behind her, one hand pressed to the side of his head where the stalactite had made its unfortunate introduction.

Hamid brought up the rear, rifle steady, eyes checking every shadow. The echo of gunfire had faded behind them, but none of them dared to relax.

They'd gone silent for the last hundred feet, words too heavy and breath too short.

Finally, they reached the sloping chamber—a natural cavern that led up and out, where filtered moonlight spilled through a half-collapsed section of ceiling. Vines crept through the cracks. A breeze touched Lorrisa's face.

Air. Fresh air.

“We’re close,” she whispered.

Gee grunted. “If I pass out, leave me next to something with a nice view.”

Lorrisa smiled faintly. “You’ll live. I didn’t hit you that hard.”

Hamid muttered, “Not what it looked like from my angle.”

They climbed, hand over hand, Kong leaping from Lorrisa’s back to the higher ledge ahead, chittering urgently. It took effort—raw and desperate—but they finally emerged from the ruins into the cool desert night.

They barely had a moment to feel the relief when a burst of gunfire echoed in the distance—just beyond the rise.

The sound was sharp, military, too clean to be random.

Gee ducked behind a stone outcropping, pulling Lorrisa with him. “That’s not our guys.”

Hamid crept forward, just enough to get eyes on the ridge. He froze. “You’re not going to believe this.”

“What?”

“Feds.”

“What?”

Hamid pointed. Down below, a dust-hazed firefight had broken out—a squad of FBI tactical agents in desert fatigues returning fire against Voss's black-clad mercenaries.

It wasn't a large team, but it was aggressive. The feds were moving smart—covering fire, coordination, clear rules of engagement. A command SUV with government plates sat hidden behind a low dune.

Gee blinked. "They've been tracking someone."

Lorrisa exhaled, bitter. "Me."

"Friend of yours?" Hamid asked.

"Not exactly."

They didn't wait to watch the outcome. Under cover of the chaos, the trio veered east along the ridge, staying low as bullets zipped below and shouts rose in the dark.

The agents and mercenaries were fully engaged now, too focused on each other to notice the silhouettes slipping out over the rocks.

Two hours later, they were well away—deep in the desert basin, tucked beneath a collapsed stone arch half-covered in drybrush. The stars above them were sharp and cold.

Lorrisa leaned back against the rock, Kong curled against her chest. Her flashlight lay beside her, dead. They'd made it out on instinct and fragments of memory.

Gee sat across from her, face still bruised, a dark bandage over his temple. He looked tired—but alert.

Hamid kept watch, seated a short distance away, his rifle across his knees.

Finally, after the silence stretched too long, Gee spoke.

"You were supposed to be on a plane home."

"You were supposed to be minding your own business," she shot back softly, but without malice.

Kong shifted, blinking at Gee, then reached out a paw to touch his boot.

Gee grinned faintly. "Hey, buddy. Missed you too."

Hamid tossed a canteen toward them. "Drink up. You're both going to need your strength."

Lorrisa nodded slowly. "This thing's bigger than I thought."

Gee's expression sobered. "We've been chasing Voss thinking he had a lead on the tablet."

"Well," she said, reaching into her jacket and pulling out the photo she'd taken of the stone carving—coordinates etched into ancient script, still visible even on her dirt-smeared screen. "He wasn't wrong."

Gee leaned in, eyes widening.

Hamid whistled low. "Tell me that doesn't say what I think it says."

Lorrisa nodded grimly. "It does. That was just one chamber. There's more."

The three of them sat in the dark, dust in their lungs, moonlight on their faces. A temporary ceasefire in a war none of them had fully understood until now.

But they knew one thing with certainty:

The hunt wasn't over. It had just escalated.

Nightfall – Hills Beyond the Tunnels

They stumbled through a break in the brush and into the silence of open terrain. For the first time in what felt like hours, the gunfire had faded into a memory. Only the rustle of wind through dry leaves and the faint wheezing of exerted lungs remained.

The abandoned mission house stood like a ghost in the clearing—crumbling stone walls, roof half collapsed, its bell tower long silenced. Whatever missionary zeal had once lived there had long since packed up and died.

Gee dropped to a crouch behind a low stone wall. “Nice place,” he muttered, brushing a smear of blood from his cheek. “Five stars. Great views. Smells like snake piss.”

Lorrisa didn’t respond. She’d already slipped past him, scanning the dark interior with a practiced eye. She moved like she had something to prove. Or hide.

Hamid arrived last, bent nearly in half, sweat pouring down his face. He leaned one hand against the wall, the other gripping the butt of his pistol.

“No welcome mat,” he wheezed, “but I’ll take it.”

Gee finally looked at Lorrisa as they stepped inside the building’s main chamber, lit only by slivers of moonlight cutting through cracks in the roof. Her frame was tense, shoulders hunched too high.

“You know,” he said, brushing past her, “when I said I’d kill to see you again, I didn’t think you’d take me so literally.”

Lorrisa dropped her pack to the floor. “Trust me, you weren't on the list.”

Gee smiled without showing teeth. "That hurts."

"Only if you care," she shot back.

Hamid flopped against a low bench and held up a hand, palm out. "Enough. You two sound like angry parrots. Just admit it."

"Admit what?" Lorrisa asked, eyes narrowing.

"That you're both thrilled the other's not dead," Hamid said plainly. "But you're both too damned proud to say it."

Kong chose that moment to leap from Lorrisa's shoulder to the bench beside Hamid, stealing a half-eaten energy bar from the man's pocket with a chirp.

Gee took a deep breath, leaning against a pillar. "Alright, well… now that we've made it out of the underworld, what's next? We go after Sebastian? He's probably halfway to a private island with those rings by now."

Lorrisa didn't answer right away. She crouched by her pack, fishing out a canteen, her fingers lingering a beat longer than necessary before she zipped it open and pulled something else from beneath the flap.

Three small cloth-wrapped bundles.

She placed them carefully on the ground, each one unspooling with a whisper of fabric until their contents shimmered in the firelight: three ancient, unmistakable rings.

Gee stared at them as if they'd materialized from nowhere. His brow furrowed, then lifted in disbelief.

"Wait… what the hell—?"

Lorrisa didn't look up. "I took them. From Sebastian. On the plane."

"You what?"

She straightened slowly, brushing dust from her hands. "He didn't even notice. Too busy *sleeping* one off. Typical."

Gee blinked. "So, you've had them *this whole time*?"

"I didn't see a reason to advertise," she said flatly. "Last time I checked, you weren't exactly on my team."

"You didn't trust me."

She gave a dry chuckle. "Gee, I barely trust Kong."

Kong screeched in protest from his perch.

Hamid gave a long, low whistle. "You two make romance look like warfare."

The air shifted. The gravity of what sat between them—those three rings—began to settle in.

Gee approached the artifacts slowly, as if afraid they'd disappear. "I thought he had all of them. I thought we were behind."

Lorrisa's voice was low now. "We're not behind. We're ahead. And that's what scares me."

Gee looked at her then—not the ring, not the building, not the fading bruises along her jaw—but her.

"So what now?"

Lorrisa bent and carefully re-wrapped the rings, placing them back into the pack. "Now we stay ahead."

Outside the ruins, something moved.

Not the wind. Not an animal.

A figure watched from the dark, eyes locked on the flickering light within the old mission house. No sound. No rush. Just patience.

And purpose.

Inside the Mission House...

The old wooden table in the center of the chamber groaned beneath the weight of damp, curling papers, faded topographic maps, crumpled field notes, and two opened books—one in Arabic, the other in English.

A rusted lantern flickered on the sill, throwing long shadows across the stone walls.

Hamid pressed his palms against the tabletop and leaned in. "Here. The *First Book of Kings*," he said, tapping the English Bible with a fingertip. His voice dropped into something almost reverent, yet sharp with precision. "Chapter 4, verse 21. It says: *'Solomon ruled over all the kingdoms from the Euphrates River into the land of the Philistines to the border of Egypt.'*"

He looked up, dark eyes serious beneath the low glow. "If that's where his domain stretched, then another piece—the rest of the Tablet, or the last few Rings—must lie somewhere within those ancient borders."

Gee gave a noncommittal grunt as he scanned one of the worn maps. "Except no one's found a shred of credible archaeological evidence to support that claim. Megiddo? Lachish? Even Hazor—those were strongholds, sure, but nothing pointing to a centralized kingdom. And nothing definitively tied to Solomon. It's more biblical lore than history."

"Biblical lore or not," Hamid countered, "this verse has persisted for millennia. People have died over less."

"That's exactly the problem," Gee shot back, running a hand through his sweat-matted hair. "People read that line and start digging in the wrong deserts. You want my bet? Whatever kingdom Solomon had, if it even *was* his, was probably regional—tribal, fragmented, barely worth writing down outside his own scribes."

Lorrisa sat at the far edge of the table, legs crossed, arms resting loosely on her thighs. She hadn't said much while the men talked. Instead, she kept her eyes on the third ring she'd just re-wrapped. It seemed heavier now, like each piece grew in mass the closer they got to the truth.

"Gee's not wrong," she said finally, lifting her head. "There are no documents confirming the existence of a large Israelite kingdom stretching from Egypt to Mesopotamia in the 10th century BCE."

Both men paused, glancing at her.

"Assyrian records, Egyptian trade archives, Mesopotamian accounts—none of them mention Solomon by name. Not even obliquely." She leaned forward and picked up a sepia-toned parchment filled with her own notes from a dig in northern Jordan. "But that doesn't mean the *rings* are fake."

Gee raised a brow. "You're saying the Bible exaggerated, but the magic rings are legit?"

"I'm saying myth and artifact don't always follow the same logic trail."

She placed the parchment down beside a dog-eared copy of a translated Phoenician trade log, then pointed to a mark she'd circled in red months ago.

"This—here—is the link."

Hamid leaned in. "The coastal exchange ledgers?"

"No. *The seal.*" Lorrisa pulled a separate scrap of vellum from her bag and laid it beside the ledger. The faint impression of a crescent, framed by what looked like winged lions, was etched in charcoal. "We found this near the cave in Qasr Abu Rummaneh. Guess what was carved into the chamber wall next to the vault?"

Gee looked closer. "A winged sun? Or—no, a lion gate?"

"Both," Lorrisa said. "Overlapping. Like a dual dynasty stamp."

Hamid's eyebrows shot up. "Phoenician?"

"Or something that borrowed from them." She flipped one of the pages in the Book of Kings and tapped a margin note she'd scribbled months earlier: *Ophir—Tarshish—ships of gold.*

"This isn't just about Solomon's political kingdom. It's about his trade empire—his *network*."

Gee's jaw tightened. "So you're thinking coastal. Sidon? Tyre? Maybe further west?"

"Too obvious," she said. "Too excavated. What if the real trail wasn't inland, or coastal, but somewhere overlooked because of the warzones?"

Hamid's eyes darkened. "Syria."

Lorrisa nodded. "Specifically, the Orontes Valley."

Gee leaned back in his seat. "You're kidding. That place is a goddamn minefield. Half the area's still off-limits to foreign researchers."

"Which is why it's still hiding secrets," she replied, her voice cool and steady. "And if the ring inscriptions are right—'three to summon, one to command'—then that piece of the Tablet has to be protected somewhere ancient, forgotten, and politically inconvenient."

She rose from her seat and crossed to her bag. Digging deep into the bottom, she pulled out a folded paper marked with grease stains and age—*a centuries-old*

Crusader map, annotated with scribbles in Latin and Arabic.

"The Monastery of Saint Kasian. Half-buried. Located where the Orontes crosses what used to be the old caravan trail near modern Hama."

Gee studied the map. "That monastery was destroyed."

"The surface structure was," she corrected. "But old monastic catacombs don't collapse unless something *wants* them to."

Kong gave a nervous trill from his perch as if he understood the ominous tone.

Hamid exhaled and crossed his arms. "So let me get this straight. We flee gunfire and mercenaries, dodge an FBI agent with more secrets than we can count, and now we're planning to infiltrate a war-damaged zone to find a buried vault that may or may not contain the rest of a tablet connected to an undocumented empire?"

Lorrisa smiled. "You forgot the part where we have to do it without getting killed."

"Or arrested," Gee added.

Hamid gave a tired shake of his head. "Wonderful. I'll start packing the body bags."

The lantern had been snuffed. The three of them moved quietly beneath the stars, repacking their gear with grim efficiency. Kong darted back and forth, collecting small trinkets and snacks like a one-monkey militia.

As the wind whistled through the broken tower above, Lorrisa paused and looked out over the dark hills.

Gee joined her. “You sure about this monastery?”

“No.”

He nodded. “Good. At least we’re back on familiar ground.”

She smirked faintly, not looking at him. “Familiar doesn’t mean safe.”

Gee’s voice softened just a notch. “Neither do you.”

She finally turned, meeting his eyes with that same unreadable gaze she always wore when she wanted to say something—but wouldn’t.

Hamid’s voice called from behind them. “We leave before dawn.”

They both turned without another word and walked back inside.

Far behind them, far beyond the ridgeline, a small drone glided in the darkness—silent, watching, transmitting.

Mission House – Pre-dawn

The maps had been rolled up, the gear mostly repacked. But the three rings still sat between them on the stone table, glinting like they were made to attract more than just light.

Hamid was the first to break the long silence.

"Let me ask something," he said, tugging the half-empty Bible back toward him. "How many *rings* are we actually looking for?"

Gee raised an eyebrow. "I thought the number didn't matter as much as the *one* they unlock."

"It matters," Hamid replied. "We've been guessing there were maybe six. Maybe ten. But I remember reading something in Lorrisa's earlier notes about the Tablet of Solomon being shattered."

Lorrisa slowly nodded. "Into fragments. The oldest surviving legends say it was written in a language not spoken by man. Passed down to Solomon from 'the Watchers.'"

Hamid tapped the table. "You wrote it was broken into *thirty-two fragments.*"

Gee gave a short, humorless laugh. “You’re telling me someone took a tablet and forged it into rings?”

“I’m saying,” Hamid replied, “it would make sense. Pieces of the original Tablet scattered, but disguised. Hidden as something valuable, but not obviously powerful.”

Lorrisa’s brow furrowed. She moved to her pack again and retrieved a small digital caliper and scale—tools of the field. She gently picked up one of the three rings and began measuring.

“Each ring is roughly the same weight—1.25 ounces,” she murmured. “Diameter matches ceremonial signet rings from the 9th–10th century BCE. Consistency like this implies they were made as a set.”

Gee crouched beside her, intrigued despite himself. “Let’s say the original Tablet was, what, twelve inches long, six wide, an inch thick?”

Hamid nodded. “That’s a plausible estimate. Limestone or black basalt. Both would’ve been used in that era for sacred inscriptions.”

Lorrisa picked up her journal and began sketching a rough outline of a tablet. “Volume of the stone would be roughly—" she paused, writing down dimensions, "—about 72 cubic inches."

Hamid's fingers tapped on a small, solar-powered calculator he'd pulled from his jacket. "And each ring, melted and reforged from the original stone-metal composite, would contain about..." He glanced at the reading on the scale again. "A tenth of a cubic inch of material."

Gee looked between them. "Wait a minute. So—"

Lorrisa finished the math aloud:
"Seventy-two divided by 0.1... gives us 720. But that's assuming no loss, no forging waste, and that the entire Tablet was used. Which isn't likely."

Hamid added, "Now factor in ancient forging inefficiencies. High loss rate, say 90% of the stone survived the melting and casting. That gives us usable material of about 7.2 cubic inches."

Lorrisa was already scribbling again. "At 0.225 cubic inches per ring—"

Gee ran a hand through his hair. "That's—what—*thirty-two* rings exactly?"

Hamid's calculator beeped softly. "*Precisely.*"

They all looked down at the three in front of them.

Lorrisa whispered, “So we’re looking for twenty-nine more.”

Gee gave a low whistle. “And they’re *not* all in one place.”

“Far from it,” Hamid added. “If this was deliberate—designed to scatter knowledge, not just hide it—then the rings are distributed globally. Planted in temples, tombs, royal collections. Maybe even melted into heirlooms, or auctioned off as artifacts.”

Lorrisa slowly picked up one ring and turned it between her fingers. “Thirty-two rings forged from one forbidden text.”

Kong snatched a beetle off the table nearby and chewed thoughtfully.

Gee stood and crossed to the door, looking out toward the faint edge of dawn. “Then this isn’t a scavenger hunt,” he said. “It’s a map in thirty-two parts.”

Hamid joined him. “And we’ve only just begun the journey.”

Outside, the sky bruised with the first signs of daylight. A golden hue touched the horizon.

Far above, the high-altitude drone that had been circling the region for hours banked slowly and returned to its path. Its operator—somewhere deep in a windowless control room—marked the GPS location of the abandoned mission house.

Back inside, Lorrisa unwrapped the rings again, setting them into the shape of a triangle on the table.

Three down.

Twenty-nine to go.

The fire had long since burned to embers. The final traces of their night in the mission house had been packed away, save for a few crumbs Kong refused to abandon and the chalk outlines Gee had scribbled on the stone wall as a joke about "Solomon's football playbook."

Outside, the first light of dawn began spilling between the trees, soaking the horizon in copper and gold. The ruined bell tower cast a long, narrow shadow that pointed east—toward ancient ground, old blood, and secrets waiting under centuries of dust.

Gee slung his pack over one shoulder and adjusted the strap on Kong's harness. "Let's hope this monastery is half as intact as your math was last night."

Lorrisa checked the hidden pocket where the rings were stored, now wrapped and sealed in layers of oilcloth. "Or we'll just be adding more ruins to the itinerary."

Hamid stepped out last, taking one final look at the room they'd worked in. There was something different in his posture now—calmer, more centered.

Gee caught it, then cocked his head. "You know, not to get sentimental, but when I first met you, you were all gun-handling, adrenaline, and shouting."

Hamid smirked, securing the flap on his holster. "Still am, depending on the day."

"Yeah, well," Gee said, squinting at him, "last night, you started quoting scripture and calculating mass distribution like some Oxford professor. What gives?"

Hamid paused in the doorway, one hand resting on the crumbling frame. His smile thinned but didn't disappear.

"I was trained to fight because my homeland didn't leave room for anything else," he said. "But my father—before he was taken—he taught me about ancient texts.

He said, 'Understanding the past is the only way to survive the future.'" He looked back into the mission house. "I guess... I didn't forget as much as I thought."

Lorrisa gave a quiet nod. "You didn't sound like a fighter last night. You sounded like someone who belonged to something older."

Hamid shrugged. "Maybe both things are true."

Gee smiled slightly and started walking. "Well, remind me to stay on your good side, Professor."

The three of them moved out, boots crunching softly over gravel and broken leaves, Kong leaping from rock to rock ahead of them like a scout on a mission. The old world was waiting.

Behind them, the bell tower remained silent, standing watch over a secret once buried, now chasing the wind.

Chapter 9

They didn't steal the van, though it looked like they had.

It came courtesy of a man Hamid only referred to as "Uncle Kamal"—a fixer of sorts who operated on the southern edge of Tripoli. The kind of man who didn't ask questions as long as you paid in cash, bartered in favors, or had a story worth listening to over tea. Hamid offered all three.

Uncle Kamal called it a "delivery vehicle," but the stripped paint, mismatched panels, and faint bloodstain on the ceiling told a less innocent tale. Still, it ran, and that was more than could be said for most of the rusted corpses littering the region's backroads.

Now they were halfway to the Syrian border, crawling through a half-forgotten smuggler's trail that didn't exist on any map made after 1987.

Hamid drove with the discipline of a man who had once lived through convoys where the rearview mirror mattered more than the windshield. His eyes stayed forward. Hands steady. Every turn was taken with care—not from caution, but memory.

Lorrisa sat in the middle row, knees pulled up, field journal open on her lap. Its pages were overrun with cross-referenced notes, dog-eared pages, and ancient transcriptions scratched in four different languages.

In the back, Gee had a laptop balanced on his knees, its battery wheezing with every satellite image he tried to load. Kong, more alert than he let on, sat curled beside him—occasionally looking out the cracked window like he too understood how close they were getting.

“So,” Gee muttered, not looking up, “this monastery—if it even exists—should be buried somewhere near the Orontes trade route. But nothing in the official satellite archive has it listed.”

“That’s because it was delisted in 1983,” Lorrisa replied without glancing away from her notes. “The Syrian Ministry labeled it a contaminated site. No civilian access.”

Gee snorted. “Contaminated. Right. That’s Cold War lingo for ‘don’t dig where we hid the bodies.’”

“Or something more valuable,” Hamid offered, adjusting the wheel as the van groaned over another gully.

“And how exactly did *Uncle Kamal* get us this far without raising flags?” Gee asked.

"He still owns the paper trail for the van—technically it's a Lebanese Red Crescent vehicle. Washed clean. Good reputation. No one asks questions when you look like aid workers."

Kong reached up and playfully tugged on Gee's scarf.

Lorrisa finally looked up. "Besides, the route we're taking hasn't been monitored regularly since the 2019 air corridor collapse. We've got one day, maybe two, before someone notices."

Gee gave a low whistle. "I hope your geography's better than your optimism."

Checkpoint – Border Fringe near Al-Qusayr

The border was unofficial, manned by unofficial men.

Militia. Or former militia. The kind of soldiers who never quite took the uniform off.

The gate was iron, welded crooked, and rusted to hell. Their guard wore half a military uniform and civilian boots, but the American-made rifle was in perfect condition.

Hamid eased the van to a stop. He leaned out the window, greeted the man in fluid Arabic, and handed over a small envelope and a carton of cigarettes.

The man nodded. Opened the gate.

Nothing else was said.

Once again the Van was Moving Again.

Lorrisa tapped on her notebook. “I did some deeper work before we left. There’s no monastery in official Christian records. But some Coptic scrolls reference a cursed site—Kasian’s Tomb.”

Gee leaned forward. “And the math still holds?”

“Thirty-two rings total,” she said. “We’ve only located three. This site—Kasian’s Tomb—matches the tri-point references when the rings are placed in the correct geometric alignment.”

Hamid glanced in the rearview. “You think the next piece of the Tablet is buried beneath the monastery?”

“No,” Lorrisa said. “I think the *assembly chamber* is.”

Gee raised a brow. “As in—where the rings were forged?”

“Or where they’re meant to be brought together.”

Near the Orontes Valley – Approaching Kasian’s Tomb

They left the van behind at first light, its wheels buried halfway beneath a slope of thistle and chalkstone, disguised beneath a dusty net and the drooping limbs of a dead olive tree. It was a six-mile hike from the drop point, but Hamid insisted they do it on foot.

“Nothing with wheels makes it past the last shepherd’s path,” he said. “And even if it could, we’d be questioned—or worse.”

The terrain grew uneven quickly—low ridges and collapsed terraces where villages had once stood. Bombed-out homes and weed-choked ruins marked the distance between what had been and what barely remained. The silence here wasn't peaceful. It was carved out of war.

Lorrisa moved ahead of the others with a quiet grace, her figure mostly concealed beneath a long charcoal-colored *abaya*, the hood of which was drawn low over her forehead. Beneath it, her face was partially veiled with a scarf she’d wrapped in careful layers—eyes exposed, but nothing more.

She blended in.

Or more accurately, she vanished into the landscape.

Gee took a moment to study her and murmured to Hamid, “When did she get the wardrobe change?”

Hamid didn't break stride. "She borrowed it from the woman at the checkpoint. Traded her a solar charger and a flask of French perfume." He paused. "Smart. In this region, a foreign woman walking uncovered would be seen. Not admired. Not questioned. *Seen*. That's more dangerous."

Gee grunted his agreement. "Still weird seeing her quiet."

"She's not quiet," Hamid said. "She's listening."

Lorrisa snapped at both men. "Will you two shut up!"

They crossed a sunbaked valley and followed the spine of a narrow ridge. Far below, the lazy green ribbon of the Orontes River wound through the land like a forgotten vein. At its highest crest, the ruins appeared—half-swallowed by earth and time.

Kasian's Tomb.

It didn't look like much.

A collapsed entry arch. Crumbled limestone steps. Dead shrubs growing between shattered columns that had once held up a Byzantine facade.

But Lorrisa stood still as soon as they reached the ridge and stared down with a gaze so focused it almost frightened them.

“I’ve seen this in a dream,” she whispered.

Neither man spoke.

She stepped forward. The closer she got, the more the air changed. The heat was still there—dry and oppressive—but now it carried something behind it. Not scent. Not sound. A *vibration* she felt in her teeth and the soles of her feet.

Kong hissed softly from Gee’s shoulder.

Lorrisa descended the slope in measured steps, moving like someone approaching an altar. She paused at the base of the staircase, fingers brushing the stone. Her hand moved across a panel mostly hidden beneath overgrowth, revealing a carved disc—nearly invisible—etched with a ring of script and geometric symbols.

Hamid joined her, breath short from the climb. “This wasn’t made by monks,” he said. “This is older. Much older.”

“Pre-Christian,” Lorrisa said, voice flat with awe. “Maybe even pre-Canaanite.”

Gee crouched beside the disc and ran his hand over the design. “That symbol again—the split ring inside the sunburst. Just like on the ring base.”

Lorrisa nodded. “This was never a monastery. It was a cover. Maybe adopted by monks later, but originally...”

“A forge,” she said.

Hamid added quietly, “A vault.”

Within the Tomb Ruins – Minutes Later

They descended carefully into what remained of the interior—half-rotted stairs giving way to compacted soil. Light dimmed as they moved inward, the temperature dropping sharply as stone overtook the walls.

The structure inside wasn’t large—more like a chapel than a cathedral—but it had symmetry. Arched alcoves. Masoned corners with mathematical precision. And in the center, a circular depression, about four feet in diameter and sunken into the floor.

Lorrisa stepped forward and knelt at its edge.

“It’s a mount,” she said. “Something was once placed here. Something round. Like—”

“Like a disc?” Gee said, already checking his pack.

She shook her head. "Not a full disc. A *socketed* disc. Multiple insertions."

Hamid's brow furrowed. "Like... rings?"

Lorrisa didn't answer. Instead, she pulled the three she'd brought and unwrapped them slowly, reverently.

The moment she placed the first one near the floor depression, it moved.

Just slightly.

Like the chamber had breathed.

The second ring echoed it. A harmonic vibration. Faint, but undeniable.

The third ring clicked faintly in her hand.

"I think we're standing in the site where the rings were either forged or assembled," she whispered. "This whole building... is tuned to them."

Gee crouched beside her, scanning the floor more closely now. "This slot here—it's got carvings. Inlaid channels. Like circuit paths."

"Or ritual channels," Hamid added. "Mystics believed geometry itself had spiritual conductivity."

Lorrisa gently held all three rings over the depression.

They began to vibrate—soft, circular pulses, no louder than a heartbeat.

But what happened next none of them expected.

A low, humming tone resonated through the floor. Faint glyphs—previously invisible—illuminated along the floor edge, spiraling out from the circle like a star-map. Glowing pale blue.

Lorrisa gasped, her breath catching. "They're *activating*."

Gee was stunned. "What the hell is this?"

"A memory," Hamid said softly, eyes wide. "This place is remembering."

They stared down as the glyphs flickered like a silent whisper from the past.

Then—abruptly—the light faded.

Darkness returned.

The silence after it was deafening.

They didn't speak for a long time.

Only when Lorrisa wrapped the rings again, and the last flicker of glow vanished from the chamber floor, did

Hamid finally whisper, “We’re not the first to stand here. But we might be the last.”

Inside Kasian’s Tomb – Beneath the Monastery.

Dust settled in the wake of the vanished light, hanging in the stale air like ash. No one moved for a long moment. The rings were now still—quiet as stone—but what they had triggered left behind an undeniable truth: they had activated something ancient. Something *alive* in its own strange way.

Hamid finally broke the silence. “Whatever that was, it’s older than anything we’ve touched before.”

Lorrisa remained kneeling at the edge of the depression, her fingers absently tracing the faint lines on the stone. “These weren’t just ceremonial artifacts,” she said, voice low and steady. “They’re mechanical. Ritualistic. Coded.”

Gee stood and scanned the chamber, his eyes catching on the alcoves spaced evenly along the walls. “How deep does this place go?”

“Hard to say,” Lorrisa replied, rising to her feet and brushing dust from her knees. “This could be one chamber of many.”

Gee approached one of the alcoves. “Think the others hold rings?”

Lorrisa followed his gaze. “Maybe. Or worse—what protected them.”

Hamid glanced toward the narrow corridor they had entered through. “We need to decide. Dig or leave. Every second we stay here, we increase the chance of someone noticing. Satellites, sensors, informants… not even a ghost town stays ghosted for long.”

Kong let out a chirp and jumped from Gee’s shoulder to a jagged stone ledge, sniffing at something embedded in the wall. It looked like a thin seam—a possible door, almost indistinguishable from the masonry.

Lorrisa crossed the room, gently brushing the surface near Kong’s perch.

“Help me,” she said to Gee.

Together they pushed. Kong imitated the action as well.

With a groan of ancient hinges and a puff of stale air, the seam gave way. The wall shifted inward by inches, revealing a passage no wider than a closet—choked with darkness, but unmistakably man-made.

Hamid sighed. “Of course there’s another door.”

Lorrisa turned. "You can wait here."

"I said I'd go," he muttered. "Doesn't mean I have to like it."

Gee retrieved a headlamp from his pack, passing another to Lorrisa. "Let's make it quick. If we're going in, we mark the path, stay within fifty meters, and get back out in twenty minutes."

Lorrisa nodded, pulling a grease pencil from her bag. "Standard cave walk. Left marks. Trail rope. Don't separate."

She looped the nylon cord through her belt, tied it around Hamid's, then Gee's. Kong, watching from above, dropped down and landed lightly on Gee's shoulder again.

"Guess he's in too," Gee muttered.

The hallway stretched downward at a slight incline. The floor transitioned from stone to packed earth, but the walls remained unnaturally smooth—hand-carved with obsessive symmetry. Faint lines of geometric symbols appeared along the corners. Some were similar to glyphs they had seen earlier. Others were entirely alien.

"The architecture's wrong," Lorrisa said softly. "This isn't Roman. Not Greek. Not even Mesopotamian."

“Then what is it?” Gee asked.

She shined her light on the wall. “It’s *intentional*,” she said. “This wasn’t built for aesthetics. It was built for function. As if every line, every angle was calculated for purpose—spiritual, energetic, maybe even technological.”

Hamid adjusted the scarf around his mouth. “You’re saying the chamber’s *designed* to interact with the rings?”

“I’m saying it’s more than just a tomb,” she replied. “It’s part of a network. A system. The rings don’t just *fit* here. They *belong* here.”

Chamber Below – The Altar of Dust.

They emerged into a larger space at the bottom of the ramp—a circular vault about twenty feet across, its ceiling rising like a dome, lined with starburst carvings.

In the center stood a flat, wide stone altar. Not a sacrificial slab. Something more refined. There were thirty-two shallow indentations, evenly spaced around the outer rim.

Each slot was shaped with precise curvature. Almost like a calibration unit.

"Oh my God," Lorrisa breathed. "It's the Ring Array."

Gee stepped forward, incredulous. "You're saying... this is where they go?"

"All of them," she whispered. "This isn't just symbolic. It's literal. Thirty-two slots. And if I'm right..."

She took one of the rings and slowly lowered it toward the nearest indentation.

As the ring reached proximity, it *clicked into place* on its own, gently drawn by unseen magnetism. The slot lit with a faint blue glow.

Lorrisa swallowed.

Gee leaned close, barely daring to speak. "We're standing in the keyhole of an ancient global mechanism."

Hamid looked around warily. "Which means *someone* will want the key."

That sobering thought hung in the chamber as the faint blue glow shimmered outward from the ring—*not fading*, but waiting.

One of thirty-two.

Only one.

And they had *twenty-nine left to find.*

Kong whimpered, pulling on Gee's sleeve.

"What is it?" Gee asked.

Then they all heard it.

A *sound*—distant, mechanical, metallic—somewhere above them.

Not local.

Not friendly.

Lorrisa took the ring back and wrapped it quickly.

"We're not alone anymore," she said. The sound came again—metallic and subtle, like boots on distant stone or the weight of machinery shifting overhead.

Lorrisa instinctively dimmed her headlamp. Hamid was already backing toward the corridor, his hand on his sidearm, though he didn't draw it.

Gee knelt, reaching into his pack for a compact motion sensor, then paused. "No signal. Could be a drone. Could be something else."

They all froze.

The sound wasn't constant. It came in irregular intervals. Not the smooth sweep of surveillance equipment. More like *someone—or something—searching*.

Lorrisa motioned with two fingers and silently guided them into a small recess along the edge of the chamber—an uneven outcrop in the wall that partially obscured their position.

They crouched in total silence.

Kong clung to Gee's neck, uncharacteristically still.

Above them, the sound moved again.

A scraping. Faint.

Then silence.

For nearly three minutes, nothing happened.

No breath. No echo. No motion.

Then—without warning—the same soft, humming vibration returned.

But this time, not from the rings.

From the walls themselves.

A low-frequency pulse, like sonar or a heartbeat transmitted through the stone.

Lorrisa's eyes widened. "We activated something," she mouthed.

Hamid shook his head. “We need to leave. Now.”

Lorrisa hesitated—just for a second—then nodded.

They moved in silence, retracing their path, tying off each section of the guide rope, brushing over their footprints as they went. The humming gradually faded behind them, swallowed once more by the chamber’s eternal stillness.

Outside the Tomb – Midday.

They emerged squinting into harsh daylight. The tomb’s shadow gave way to a vast, exposed hilltop. The wind had shifted—dry, heavy with dust and the acrid scent of burning rubber.

From the ridge, they had a clear view of the valley beyond.

It was a scar.

The remnants of a bombed village stretched across the basin like scattered bones. Caved-in roofs, broken stone homes, and the twisted shells of vehicles long since burned out. Smoke trailed from a crater where a shell had recently struck. The trail of black char traced toward a thin column of refugees—families—walking east on foot, carrying what little they had in sacks and water jugs.

No press. No rescue teams.

Just survivors.

Hamid lowered his binoculars. His jaw clenched. “Three kilometers. Maybe four. They're trying to reach the next aid station. But they'll never make it in this heat without transport.”

Lorrisa didn’t speak. Her eyes stayed locked on the line of human figures moving in single file. She counted at least four children. An old man walked with a limp. One woman was cradling an infant, wrapped in stained linen.

Gee exhaled slowly. “And here we are. Hunting rings of ancient power while they’re just trying to find a place to sleep tonight.”

No one answered.

The wind shifted again.

Lorrisa finally spoke. “We could carry a few of them in the van.”

Gee looked at her. “And then what? Drive them across militia checkpoints? Feed them, hide them, risk blowing our cover entirely?”

“They’re human beings.”

"So are we," he snapped. "And if we're caught, those rings are gone. The Tablet's gone. Everything we've discovered ends up in someone else's hands—probably someone worse than Sebastian."

Hamid stared into the distance, visibly torn.

Then he said, quietly, "You know what the worst part is?"

They both looked at him.

"It doesn't matter how many people we help here. It won't stop this war. But those rings? That Tablet? It *might.* Maybe not tomorrow. Maybe not this year. But if it contains what the legends say—knowledge, energy, control over the balance of power—then it could matter."

Lorrisa turned back toward the van. "So we have to choose. Rescue a few. Or find the key that could stop this from happening to entire generations."

They all stared at the carnage before them. Thoughts racing. Eyes welling up, but not a tear was shed.

Kong let out a soft, sad whimper.

Gee turned, slowly following her. "Let's find the key. And then decide how to use it."

Hamid didn't move right away.

But when he did, he whispered a quiet prayer in Arabic, picked up his gear, and followed.

Behind them, the war smoldered on. The van creaked along the fractured trail leading away from the ridge, slowly weaving between collapsed rock walls and rusted fences. Inside, the mood was hushed, somber—not because of fatigue, but the sheer weight of what they'd just touched.

Lorrisa sat with her journal open on her lap, back hunched over the glowing screen of her tablet. The light glinted across her eyes, focused and sharp.

"What are you looking for?" Gee asked, glancing at her from the passenger seat.

"The glyphs," she said. "From the altar chamber. They weren't just decorative. They formed a sequence."

Hamid, at the wheel, muttered, "What kind of sequence?"

"Celestial geometry," she replied. "Starmap-like, but not fixed to the night sky. More like *transits*. Intersections of specific locations—mapped by harmonic resonance."

Gee leaned back. “I hate how much sense that doesn’t make.”

Lorrisa held up the tablet, zooming in on one of the sketches she’d made. “Each ring slot on the array was flanked by paired glyphs. Like a binary coordinate system—placeholders or references. I cross-checked three of them against locations tied to the three rings we already have. And this one—” she pointed to the fourth slot—“matches a known site.”

Hamid’s fingers tightened on the steering wheel. “Where?”

Lorrisa tapped the screen. “Beneath the ruins of an Ethiopian church complex in Lalibela.”

Gee blinked. “Lalibela? That’s not just a ruin—it’s a UNESCO site. Constantly surveyed, monitored, crawling with tourists.”

“Which is why no one would think to look *beneath* it.”

Hamid frowned. “You’re saying they buried a ring under a *sacred site*?”

“I’m saying the builders of Lalibela might have inherited something ancient. There are legends that the churches were ‘built by angels overnight’—carved directly from rock in ways we still can't explain with 12th-century tools."

Gee nodded slowly. "I read something about that once. Subterranean tunnels. Ceremonial catacombs sealed off during the Italian occupation."

"Exactly," Lorrisa said. "And if this mapping from the altar is correct, the fourth ring isn't inside the churches—but under the oldest chapel: *Beta Medhane Alem.*"

Hamid raised a brow. "The House of the Savior of the World?"

"Fitting, isn't it?" Lorrisa murmured.

Inside the Van – Minutes Later.

Gee flipped open his notebook, jotting down logistics. "We'll need aliases again. And documentation to even get close. The Ethiopian government doesn't let foreign archaeologists poke around under their heritage sites without permission or bribes."

Lorrisa was already ahead of him. "I know a fixer in Addis Ababa. I can get Xenia to wire the funds and the paperwork through a shell foundation. We pose as a historical preservation team studying foundation stress fractures."

Hamid looked skeptical. “And we think no one else will notice?”

She glanced at him. “The fourth ring is below a church carved from volcanic stone by unknown methods. In a chamber no one even acknowledges exists. It’s not about being seen. It’s about *not being understood*.”

Kong chirped, clearly uninterested in geopolitics, and pulled a date from Lorrisa’s bag.

Gee looked to Hamid. “You in?”

Hamid nodded once. “We go to Ethiopia.”

SKYLINE of ETHIOPIA

Far away, beyond the fractured borderlands, the African continent turned gold in the sunset. The wind danced across high plateaus and dipped into the ancient stone veins of Lalibela’s sacred city—where time moved slowly, and faith ran deep.

Beneath Beta Medhane Alem, buried under centuries of prayer and secrets, something old stirred in the dark.

It was waiting.

Chapter 10

The air in Addis Ababa carried a texture unlike anywhere else—thin and dry at the high elevation, but alive with motion. It was a city of contrasts: gleaming towers rising from colonial bones, internet cafés beside churches carved a thousand years ago. The altitude made everything feel sharper—colors, sounds, even the jet lag.

They stepped off the private commuter plane under a blazing afternoon sun. A government-chartered flight, secured through Lorrisa's contact posing as a cultural liaison, had brought them in discreetly.

Gee stretched and squinted up at the hazy sky. "You know," he said, dropping his bag onto the hot tarmac, "I remember a *Superman* movie where the bad guys go to Addis Ababa. Whole city looked like a set from a villain's monologue."

Hamid snorted as he passed. "And you wonder why people don't like Americans."

Lorrisa, already adjusting her satchel and sunglasses, didn't break stride. "You mean the one where Lex Luthor buys land in Africa? That wasn't Addis Ababa, genius. That was Namibia. And it was a cartoon."

Gee raised his hands in mock surrender. "Well, forgive me for confusing international villainy."

She shot him a dry look over her shoulder. "Let me guess, you think Wakanda is west of here too?"

He grinned. "I mean... technically—"

She quickly raised her index finger. "*Don't.*"

They moved quickly through the smaller terminal where a contact—a wiry man named *Dagmawi*—waited beside a sign that read: *EARTH HERITAGE STRESS SURVEY TEAM.*

"Miss Lorrisa?" he asked.

"Doctor," she corrected gently.

He smiled. "Of course. This way."

ADDIS ABABA – STREETS – AN HOUR LATER.

The city rolled past in a stream of visual poetry—vivid murals on concrete walls, women in white *habesha kemis* balancing clay jars, taxis weaving between donkeys, mopeds, and suit-clad businessmen talking into Bluetooth headsets. Minarets rose between modern high-rises. Orthodox crosses crowned ancient rooftops.

Dagmawi briefed them in hushed tones from the driver's seat. "Lalibela is quiet right now. Tourism is lower than usual. Security is posted near the primary churches, but underground areas? Not watched unless there's movement."

"Perfect," Lorrisa said.

"You'll have two days, maybe three. After that, someone *will* ask questions."

Hamid looked out the window. "Any unrest in the region?"

"There was a clash north of Woldiya two weeks ago. Border tensions. Nothing recent. But if anyone sees you taking equipment into restricted areas... the Church can summon federal authorities within an hour."

"Understood," Gee said. "And what about the Foundation cover?"

Dagmawi handed them a manila envelope. Inside were laminated ID badges marked with the logo of a fictitious structural preservation group. The names were false but clean.

"Your hotel is near Bole. Quiet. Unremarkable. I'll take you to the airport in the morning. From there, it's a short flight north to Lalibela."

"Good," Lorrisa said, taking the IDs and sorting them. "We'll be ready."

That night at the hotel, the room was modest, clean, and cool. Gee unpacked slowly while Kong explored the curtains, pulling on the drawstrings like they were vines in a jungle.

Hamid sat on the edge of the second bed, unrolling a local map.

Lorrisa stood by the window, looking out into the city lights. Her reflection, faint in the glass, mirrored her tightly-drawn features.

"This is it," she murmured. "If the pattern holds… the fourth ring is beneath *Beta Medhane Alem*. The layout of the altar chamber back in Syria suggested directional alignment. The glyph next to the fourth ring's socket translated loosely to *'rock sanctuary to the east.'*"

Gee walked over and looked at the map. "And it lines up?"

“Perfectly,” Hamid confirmed. “The church’s layout even mirrors the circular vault. Like it was carved with *the array* in mind.”

Gee gave a low whistle. “So whoever designed the church may have known about the rings?”

“Or used the site to hide one. Either way, it survived centuries of conflict, empire, and colonization. That means the ring is *very* well hidden.”

“And if it's not?” Gee asked.

Lorrisa looked at him. “Then we’re in the wrong story.”

The conversation had wound down. Maps were rolled, equipment stored, IDs checked and double-checked.

Hamid didn’t bother with ceremony. The moment he kicked off his boots, he collapsed face-first onto the first bed. Within seconds, he was out cold, arms and legs spread diagonally like a starfish—blanket untouched, boots forgotten, breath deep and even.

Gee stared at him. Then stared at the other bed. Then glanced sideways at Lorrisa.

“One bed left,” he said, rubbing the back of his neck. “And two of us.”

Lorrisa didn’t even turn around. “Don’t get any ideas.”

He lifted his hands in mock innocence. “I’m just saying, it’s a big bed. We’re both adults. You might hate me, but you’re not going to kill me in my sleep, right?”

She finally turned to face him, expression neutral. “You think so?”

“Come on, Lorrisa. My spine’s been compressed by three countries’ worth of cave systems. I need a flat surface and a pillow that isn’t made of stone or guilt.”

She gave him a long look. Just as he opened his mouth again, she stepped forward and—without warning—gently pressed a single finger to his lips.

“Shhh,” she whispered seductively, her beautiful eyes locked on his. Gee blinked.

Then her voice dropped into a low, velvety murmur. “I know how to solve this.” He raised an eyebrow in anticipation.

She leaned in slightly closer, almost conspiratorially. Whispering softly in his ear .“Perfect solution.”

He waited.

She smiled sweetly. Then shoved a pillow into his chest.

“Floor’s all yours, Romeo.”

Gee staggered back a half step, laughing quietly. “You’re cruel, Santos.”

Lorrisa was already peeling back the covers. “No, I’m just tired. And I don’t have time for your sick little fantasies. Besides you snore like a chainsaw”

“Only on high altitudes,” he protested as he grabbed a spare blanket and a throw cushion from the corner chair.

“And we’re at seven thousand feet,” she replied, slipping under the sheet with a satisfied sigh.

Kong, ever the opportunist, scampered up from his perch on the windowsill and curled himself at the foot of the bed like a furry nightlight.

Gee arranged himself on the floor with mock dignity. “Don’t worry about me. Just the guy who carried you out of gunfire. Crawled through a snake-infested tomb. Shared his last protein bar with your monkey.”

“You can add martyr to your résumé tomorrow,” she murmured, already drifting into sleep.

The Next Morning – Pre-Dawn Light.

Hamid stirred first, blinking blearily in the blue glow of the rising sun. For a moment, he couldn’t quite remember where he was. Then the aching stiffness in his shoulder and the unfamiliar ceiling brought it all back.

He turned his head slowly.

Lorrisa was sound asleep, back turned toward him, the blanket pulled up neatly over her shoulders.

At the foot of her bed, Kong was sprawled belly-up, one tiny arm across his face like a drunken child after a party.

Hamid yawned—and then noticed Gee, curled like a castaway on the floor, using a rolled-up hoodie for a pillow.

Hamid shook his head, a smirk forming as he reached for his canteen.

"Romance," he muttered to himself, "is wasted on the clever."

Zippers rasped. Velcro sealed. Gear was being packed with well-practiced precision.

Lorrisa was rolling up the last of her map copies while Kong stuffed himself with the remnants of a fig bar he'd found at the bottom of Gee's pack.

Gee stood with one hand on the small of his back, stretching awkwardly.

“Ugh,” he groaned, wincing dramatically. “I think I slept on a jagged dream last night. That floor had a personal vendetta against my spine.”

Lorrisa didn’t look up. “Good. Maybe it straightened you out.”

Hamid chuckled softly as he double-checked his documents. “She’s got a point. You complain more than the monkey.”

“Hey,” Gee said, pointing a finger at Kong. “Kong got the bed.”

“And yet,” Lorrisa added dryly, “he managed not to whine about it all morning.”

Gee muttered something about betrayal and monkey favoritism as he slung his pack over his shoulder.

Hamid grabbed his scarf and looked toward the door. “We have time for food? Even just coffee and something flat and round?”

“No,” Lorrisa said. “Yes,” Hamid said at the same time.

They both looked at each other.

Hamid raised a hand. “I’m just saying—flying over the highlands on an empty stomach is the fastest way to throw up on someone's boots.”

Gee clapped him on the shoulder. “Fine, I vote with Hamid. Coffee and carbs. Democracy.”

Lorrisa rolled her eyes, then relented. “Fifteen minutes. Something fast. No sitting. And if it delays the flight, I swear I’m leaving both of you behind.”

“Understood,” Hamid nodded, already halfway to the door. “One pastry to rule them all.”

BOLE DOMESTIC TERMINAL – ADDIS ABABA – ONE HOUR LATER.

Their flight to Lalibela wasn’t glamorous. The twin-engine prop plane had more duct tape than legroom and made odd sounds during takeoff that even Kong didn’t seem to trust.

But the flight was short. Just under an hour north, across mountain ranges etched into the continent like claw marks, to a place built in silence and devotion—a city carved from stone and hidden in time.

As the aircraft dipped toward the horizon, Gee looked out the small oval window. The vast ridges of northern

Ethiopia stretched into the distance like the spine of some buried giant.

Lorrisa leaned forward from the row behind him. “You ready to go underground again?”

He glanced back with a crooked smile. “Sure. Just as long as I don’t sleep on stone again.”

The plane’s wheels hit the tarmac at Lalibela airport, with a jarring bounce, dust curling into the mountain air as the aircraft slowed along the single airstrip. Beyond the airfield, hills rolled into ridges, and ridges gave way to steep gorges cut deep into the earth—guarding the hidden city of stone. Northern Ethiopia.

Inside the terminal—a small, sunlit building that smelled of incense and diesel—the trio waited with their gear lined up at their feet.

Then she arrived.

She moved through the terminal with the kind of grace that didn’t belong in an airport. Tall, wrapped in a flowing ochre shawl, with tightly braided hair and skin the color of warm bronze. Her smile landed softly on everyone she passed, but her eyes flicked like radar—reading, measuring, cataloging.

She stopped in front of them. “Doctor Lorrisa Santos?” Her accent was lilting Amharic, overlaid with perfect English. “You’re earlier than I expected.”

Lorrisa straightened but didn’t extend a hand. “And you are?”

The woman offered a dazzling smile. “I am called *Meskela*. Dagmawi sent me. He said you’d need someone who understands the terrain and the Church.”

Gee blinked. “Meskela. That’s... a beautiful name.”

“It means ‘cross,’” she replied. “Very old. Very sharp.”

“I think I’m in love,” Gee whispered to Hamid.

Hamid didn’t respond. He was too busy adjusting his collar and clearing his throat. “I—I mean, it’s good to have a local liaison. Very professional.”

Meskela smiled knowingly. “I’ve guided many foreigners through the stone churches. Most don’t listen. Some don’t return.”

Lorrisa crossed her arms. “And which are we?”

The guide tilted her head slightly. “That remains to be seen.”

Gee looked to Lorrisa. “Can we keep her?”

“We’re not buying a goat, Gee.”

“Still feels like we got the better end of the trade.”

Meskela chuckled. “I assure you, I am no one’s possession. I merely offer safe passage—for those wise enough to pay attention.”

Lorrisa’s eyes narrowed. “And what is it you expect in return?”

Meskela stepped closer, her smile never wavering. “Only that you treat Lalibela with the reverence it deserves. The city is alive. It remembers those who offend it.”

There was a long pause. Kong chittered once and then scampered behind Gee’s leg.

Lorrisa nodded slowly. “Let’s get moving. We didn’t come to flirt.”

Meskela's smile widened just a hint, then turned and led the way.

Gee watched her for a moment and muttered, "I'd follow her into a tomb full of snakes."

"You probably will," Lorrisa replied, brushing past him. "And if she pushes you in, I'm not pulling you out."

Lalibela Village – Late Afternoon.

The sun sat low behind the plateau, casting long shadows across the red rock and worn rooftops of Lalibela. They'd taken an old Toyota Hilux from the airport—a bouncing, dusty ride through narrow roads lined with children chasing goats, and vendors waving strings of onions or woven cloth from roadside stands.

The village near *Beta Medhane Alem* was quiet. Not abandoned, but hushed in a way that felt deeper than mere poverty or heat. Men sat in front of small shops sipping coffee. Old women in white shawls murmured to one another on stoops. Children stopped playing when the group passed, watching them with wide, unblinking eyes.

Meskela led them on foot through the narrow alleyways, pausing to greet an old man with a bowed back and rheumy eyes.

He looked past her to Lorrisa, then to Gee and Hamid. He said something low in Amharic.

“What did he say?” Lorrisa asked.

Meskela hesitated, then translated with a strange softness:
“He said, ‘The house of the Savior does not welcome strangers after sunset. The stones shift in the dark.’”

Gee’s brow furrowed. “Creepy. Is that, like, metaphorical? Or just a warning about falling rocks?”

Meskela looked back at him with a neutral expression. “The people here remember what scholars forget. They believe the church breathes. That it speaks. And sometimes... it hides things it no longer wants found.”

Lorrisa didn’t blink. “Convenient for a guide to say. Especially if you want us to walk away.”

“I want nothing but your safety,” Meskela said, voice like silk. “But safety and knowledge rarely walk together.”

They continued on in silence, past weather-worn homes and through an open courtyard where a group of boys played a game using smooth stones and marks in the dirt. One of the boys looked up and pointed at Lorrisa, then said something in a hushed whisper.

Meskela flinched—barely perceptible.

Lorrisa caught it. “What did *he* say?”

Meskela gave a practiced smile. “Children tell stories. It’s nothing.”

Hamid stepped in. “He said you carry death,” he translated flatly. “In your bag.”

Lorrisa and Gee froze.

Hamid met her gaze. “My grandmother was Amharic. I understand more than you think.”

Lorrisa’s hand tightened slightly on her satchel—the rings wrapped and buried deep inside.

Gee exhaled slowly. “Maybe we’ve lit up more than just ancient maps.”

The guide stopped in front of a low clay-walled house near the edge of the church complex. “We’ll stay here tonight,” Meskela said. “It’s quiet. Private. Close to the site.”

“Do we have permission?” Hamid asked.

“No one gives permission for what you seek,” she said. “But the caretaker’s blind and the priest is absent until morning. You’ll be alone with the stones.”

Lorrisa stepped past her, eyes scanning the hills beyond. “Good. We’re not here for their permission.”

Meskela’s voice followed her: “Then I hope you’re ready for their silence.”

At the Village House – Near Midnight.

The sound of the village had changed.

Earlier, it had been the murmuring of distant voices, the occasional clatter of dishes, the soft beat of sandals on packed earth.

Now, there was only stillness. Even the stray dogs had gone quiet.

Gee knelt by the open window, scanning the silhouette of the church complex under the moonlight. From this angle, *Beta Medhane Alem* rose like a fortress carved out of a single dream—a massive, sunken cathedral shaped into the earth itself, its walls squared with divine geometry and its windows like black eyes watching the sky.

“I’ve broken into tombs, temples, even a war museum in Belgrade,” he muttered, adjusting his gear. “But there’s something about this place...”

Lorrisa was tying her boots with silent precision. Her hair was braided tight and tucked beneath a dark scarf. She moved with an edge that said ritual more than routine.

Hamid was checking a compact radio near the front door. “You don’t have to go in tonight,” he said without looking at her. “Wait until morning. Use the official entry. You’ll get twenty minutes before anyone starts asking questions.”

“We don’t have twenty minutes,” she said. “Once the morning prayers start, there’s no way into the substructures without being seen.”

Gee pulled on his pack. “Besides, if someone’s watching for us—and I mean someone not exactly in a church robe—they’ll be looking *tomorrow*.”

Hamid raised an eyebrow. “You think Meskela’s a plant?”

Lorrisa didn’t answer. She just looked at Kong, who sat on a shelf by the window, watching her with wide eyes. He tilted his head, then let out a small, chattering whimper.

She walked over and placed a hand gently on his head. “You stay here.”

Kong responded with a low chirp, gripping the edge of her sleeve.

“No,” she said softly. “If something happens… you’ll listen to Hamid. Right?”

The monkey stared for another second. Then reluctantly let go.

Gee watched her and gave a lopsided smile. “Didn’t know we were leaving the monkey behind. Is that a bad omen?”

“It’s a decision,” she replied, adjusting the strap of her satchel. “Bad omens don’t need mascots.”

She turned to Hamid. “Stay inside. Lights off. If we’re not back in two hours—burn the notes.”

Hamid nodded grimly. “Got it.”

Gee slipped on his gloves and rolled his shoulders. “Well. Off to break into God’s basement.”

Hamid gave one last warning as they moved toward the side door. “Just don’t forget what the boy said.”

Lorrisa paused. “That I carry death?”

Hamid nodded once.

She looked him in the eye. “We all do.”

Then she and Gee stepped into the night.

The path leading to the great church was nothing more than a narrow stairway carved into solid rock. Walls rose on both sides, twenty feet tall, creating the sensation of walking down into a canyon sculpted by divinity and discipline.

Moonlight barely touched the bottom.

They reached the edge of the church's northern face. Lorrisa crouched, pulling a faded diagram from her jacket pocket—a 1950s French architectural survey she'd uncovered in a university archive years ago.

"There," she whispered, pointing. "That drain access. Leads to a maintenance crawlspace under the foundation."

Gee squinted. "You want to squeeze through *that*?"

"I'll take your silence as gratitude."

She pulled out a compact crowbar and began quietly loosening the iron grate. The metal gave way with a low groan.

They slipped inside.

BELOW BETA MEDHANE ALEM the tunnel was narrow, damp, and pitch dark. Ancient volcanic stone pressed in from all sides. Each movement echoed, swallowed quickly by the labyrinthine design.

As they advanced, the air thickened—not with dust or mold, but *pressure*.

Lorrisa slowed. “Feel that?”

Gee exhaled. “Yeah. Like something’s holding its breath.”

She paused and opened her satchel. The wrapped rings—three of them—shifted slightly in their linen pouch.

“They’re reacting again,” she whispered. “Just like in Syria.”

Gee unslung his flashlight, but hesitated to turn it on. “You ever wonder if we’re not *finding* these rings, but waking them up?”

Lorrisa looked back at him.

“I wonder that every time I touch one.”

Ahead, the passage widened into a chamber half-sunken in the rock, hidden completely from the church's visible layout. Pillars lined the space—marked with spiral carvings and faint, faded iconography.

At the far end stood a stone dais.

Lorrisa stepped forward, rings still in hand—drawn again by unseen pull.

Something was here.

Waiting.

Beneath Beta Medhane Alem

The air in the chamber had gone still—unnaturally so.

Lorrisa stepped cautiously toward the stone dais, its surface layered in centuries of soot and ceremonial wax. At its center sat an ornate circular plate, carved with interlocking spirals—similar to the ring array from Syria, but this one was sealed, fused into the stone.

The rings in her pouch twitched.

She knelt, brushing away centuries of dust.

"There," she whispered. "The socket's still intact. Just like the others."

Gee stayed a step behind, watching the doorway with one hand on his sidearm—even though a bullet wouldn't help them now.

Lorrisa reached into her satchel and drew out one ring. She hovered it over the plate.

Instantly, the carved grooves around the dais pulsed with a soft amber light. Not blue like before—this was warmer. Older. It seemed to thrum like a low chant beneath their feet.

And then the stone cracked.

Not a collapse—but a deliberate splitting motion, like a puzzle coming undone.

The central plate rotated, and a recessed compartment rose from within the altar. Inside, *the fourth ring* sat upright—suspended slightly above the pedestal, as if floating. The metal was darker than the others—almost black, like it had been tempered in fire.

Lorrisa reached for it.

Gee's hand shot out to stop her. "Wait." Too late.

The moment her fingers touched the ring—
the chamber screamed.

Not a noise from any one direction, but a sudden psychic vibration that erupted across every surface. The air rippled. The carvings along the pillars lit red for a split-second, and the shadows in the corners moved.

"Lorrisa!" Gee shouted. "We need to get out—"

But something was already happening.

From the carvings in the walls and floor, a black mist began to pour, rising unnaturally fast. It swirled like smoke underwater, tendrils forming and reforming—shapes almost human, but never whole. Each shadow had too many arms. Or none. Or faces with no mouths.

They circled the room.

Gee drew his pistol reflexively, but Lorrisa pulled him back.

"No," she said, breathless. "Weapons won't help. This is a trigger—a *guardian construct*. It's defending the ring."

"From who?" he snapped. "We're not raiders!"

"Doesn't matter."

The mist coiled tighter. The temperature dropped. Their breath came out in white clouds.

Suddenly, one of the shapes lunged—an armless shadow *exploding* toward them like smoke compressed through a blade.

Lorrisa shoved Gee aside as it passed through her—her body seizing in pain. She collapsed to one knee.

Gee fired instinctively into the mist. The bullet passed clean through. Nothing.

"Damn it!" he growled, grabbing her arm. "What do we do?"

Lorrisa looked at the fourth ring in her hand.

It was pulsing. Not randomly—but *rhythmically*.

Like a signal.

She grabbed the pouch with the other three and pressed all four together.

The moment the rings touched—the mist recoiled.

The shadows hissed in a voiceless shriek, pulling back from the glow of the unified rings.

"They recognize each other," she breathed. "The rings. They're not just keys. They're part of a containment system."

Gee helped her to her feet, eyes wide. "You're telling me they're anti-ghost repellents now?"

"Something like that."

The shadows began to collapse inward on themselves—drawn back into the stone, into the altar, into the carvings.

The temperature rose slightly.

The air became breathable again.

And the fourth ring—its glow now softened—sat quietly in her palm, no longer fighting her touch.

The chamber was silent once more.

They didn't speak as they exited the crawlspace and returned to the surface. Only when they reached the open air and the silver light of the moon did Gee finally break the quiet.

"So," he said, hands on his hips. "Next time we 'just grab the artifact,' remind me to check if it's booby-trapped by haunted geometry."

Lorrisa looked at the fourth ring, still warm in her hand. "We're not just unearthing history anymore, Gee."

He met her eyes.

"We're waking it up."

Village Perimeter – Late Night

The path back to the village was darker now. No lights in windows. No music. Not even the soft sounds of animals.

Just silence.

Lorrisa felt the stillness before she saw it. Her footsteps slowed. Her grip on the satchel containing the four rings tightened.

Gee moved beside her, a little more alert now. "It's too quiet."

"Too intentional," she whispered.

They rounded the final bend—and stopped.

The small courtyard before their lodging was lit by torchlight.

Dozens of villagers had gathered in a loose semicircle. Several carried tools repurposed as weapons—shovels, wooden poles, farming blades. Not angry. Just grim. Determined.

At the center of the group stood Hamid, arms tied behind his back, a bruise forming at his jawline.

Next to him, Kong was tethered with a thin cord around his middle, squeaking in frantic protest, eyes wide and panicked.

And at the front of the assembly stood Meskela, radiant in a blood-colored shawl, her face calm and unreadable.

Lorrisa took one step forward. "What the hell is this?"

Meskela turned toward her, serene. "A reckoning."

Gee tensed. "You said we had safe passage."

“I said I offered safe passage,” she replied. “But the *stones* decide. The *people* remember.”

She motioned to an older man near the back—one of the local elders Lorrisa had seen earlier whispering by the church steps.

“He saw you enter the sacred ground after the final prayer. He heard the mountain whisper. He knew something had been *taken*.”

Gee stepped closer. “Nothing was stolen. It was hidden there. Buried. Forgotten.”

Meskela’s voice hardened. “Forgotten by *you*. Not by us. That ring was not yours to awaken.”

Lorrisa glanced at Hamid. He looked back without panic—more tired than afraid. “They came in quiet,” he said. “Didn’t hurt me. Said they wanted answers.”

Meskela’s eyes narrowed. “And you owe them.”

Lorrisa slowly lifted her satchel and opened it.

She held the fourth ring up between her fingers. “Let them all see it.”

“It was meant to be found.”

There was a murmur in the crowd. Some stepped back. One old woman crossed herself.

Meskela's expression didn't change. "You desecrate what was sealed for generations. And now you bring it back here, to flaunt it? Do you know what this could unleash?"

Gee looked at her sharply. "Do *you*?"

Another voice rose from the villagers—a younger man, trembling but firm. "We've lost too much. You bring death with your knowledge. Like the others before you. Always digging. Always taking."

Lorrisa scanned the crowd, her voice steady. "Then don't help us. But don't lie to yourselves, either. This ring—this artifact—is older than Lalibela. Older than this valley. It was *buried* here to protect it from the world. But the world is catching up. You won't be able to keep it hidden forever."

Meskela said nothing. Her gaze locked with Lorrisa's. Both women locked in a combat. Each undeterred by the other.

For a moment, nothing moved. Even Kong stopped squirming.

Then the elder stepped forward, placing a hand on Meskela's arm. He said something in Amharic—soft but with finality.

Meskela blinked. Then nodded.

"The village will not take your blood tonight," she said. "But the mountain will remember what you've done."

She motioned for the ropes to be cut.

Hamid stepped forward, rubbing his wrists, and scooped up Kong, who immediately buried his face in his chest.

Gee let out a slow breath. "Well, that was a warm welcome."

Lorrisa said nothing. Her eyes spoke volumes.

Meskela walked past them as the crowd slowly dispersed. But before she disappeared into the shadows, she turned back.

"You carry four rings now, *Doctor Santos*."

Her voice dropped, almost inaudible.

"Be careful, when the fourth awakens, the mountain of salt will bleed again. The fifth ring will not be as quiet as the others."

And then she was gone.

After the Confrontation...

The door clicked shut behind them with a finality that felt louder than it should have. For a moment, no one moved.

Outside, the air was thick with tension. Whispers. Stares. The kind that didn't speak of welcome anymore. Inside, the air wasn't much better.

Gee peeled off his jacket and let it fall to the floor. "Well," he muttered, "that could've gone worse."

"They didn't burn us alive," Hamid offered. "That's something."

Kong skittered up to the bed and flopped down flat on his belly, tail twitching in irritation. The little capuchin had sensed the shift too—the crowd's silence at the end was not relief. It was *restraint*.

Lorrisa stood with her back to them, hands braced on the small dresser beneath the cracked mirror. Her jaw was tight.

"They didn't hurt us," she said quietly. "But they don't trust us anymore. Especially not me."

Hamid sat on the edge of the bed, carefully removing his boots. "That woman—Meskela—she kept them from doing anything. But you could feel they wanted us gone.”

“They’ll make sure we are by morning,” Gee said. “That place is done. We’ve outstayed whatever welcome we had.”

Lorrisa turned to face them, her expression unreadable. “It was the rings. They *felt* them. All four.”

Hamid nodded. “Fourth one still humming?”

“Like it wants to jump out of the pack and link up with the others,” Gee muttered, nodding toward the bag leaning against the table. “I don’t like it.”

“I don’t either,” Lorrisa admitted. “But we have them now. Four out of... thirty-two.”

Gee rubbed his face with both hands. “Still can’t believe that’s the number.”

“It makes sense, though,” Lorrisa said, crossing to the map spread across the table. “Solomon was said to have ruled over 72 spirits, commanded armies of men and djinn. He wouldn’t have bound all of that with just five rings.”

Hamid leaned forward. “And the inscription?”

"It didn't lie," she said. "Four rings formed the second quadrant of the sigil. It matched the arc in the tablet's outer layer."

Gee pointed. "Which means the tablet itself is broken into four quadrants—eight rings per section."

"Exactly," she said. "Eight rings per quadrant. Four quadrants. Thirty-two total."

"That's not a treasure hunt," Hamid muttered. "That's a war map."

Kong squeaked and pointed toward the pack, where the faintest metallic chime echoed, like a vibration with no source.

Gee stood, walked over, and unzipped it just far enough to peer inside. "They're doing it again. Look."

All four rings—each forged from different metals, each etched with ancient script—shifted subtly in place, like magnets reacting to an invisible force. Not clinking, not spinning—*aligning*.

"Trying to connect," Gee said.

Lorrisa didn't approach. "That shouldn't be possible. They're individually inert. I tested each one."

"They're not inert when they're together," Hamid said. "They're awake."

The room fell into silence for a long beat. The only sound was the occasional distant bark of a street dog and the slow, rhythmic hum from the rings in the bag.

Lorrisa folded her arms. "We were wrong. This isn't just a key or a cipher. It's *activation*. A sequence."

Hamid looked up. "And we only have the first four."

Gee zipped the bag shut. "Sebastian doesn't know we have the fourth yet. That's our only edge right now."

"Then we don't waste it," Lorrisa said. "We move fast. Tonight, we sleep. Tomorrow, we disappear."

"But where?" Hamid asked.

She pulled a journal from her satchel and flipped to a bookmarked page. "Meskela didn't want to help us. But she said something before we left. Barely audible—like she didn't want anyone else hearing."

Gee raised an eyebrow. "What'd she say?"

Lorrisa hesitated, then repeated the words slowly: *"When the fourth awakens, the Mountain of Salt will bleed again."*

Gee blinked. "That's... not ominous at all."

Hamid sat forward. “Mountain of Salt? That’s not just folklore. There’s a real formation—eastern border, closer to Djibouti. Locals call it the ‘White Spine.’ Used to be a salt trade route centuries ago.”

“Some believe Solomon built a prison complex beneath it,” Lorrisa added. “To bury what couldn’t be destroyed.”

Gee frowned. “That sounds like a place someone would hide more rings.”

“Or what the rings are meant to control,” Hamid said, dryly.

Kong chattered, unnerved.

Lorrisa met both of their eyes. “Meskela wasn’t trying to warn us away. She was pushing us *forward*. Quietly. Carefully. Because someone else is listening.”

Gee nodded. “Sebastian’s network?”

“Or worse,” Lorrisa said. “Whoever *first* hid the rings might still have guardians in place. If Meskela is one of them…”

Hamid exhaled slowly. “She didn’t stop us—but she didn’t exactly cheer us on either.”

“She knows more than she’s saying,” Lorrisa said. “But she pointed us in a direction. We take it.”

Gee nodded, then glanced at the bag again. "I hate to say this, but… the closer we get to the truth, the less I think we understand what we're holding."

"That's why we keep going," Lorrisa said. "Not for power. Not for fame. But because we *have to know*."

The rings in the bag gave one soft hum—then fell quiet.

As if they agreed.

The first light of dawn crept across the sky like a secret trying not to wake the world. Pale gold streaked through the thin curtains of the guesthouse window, brushing against dust and silence.

Inside, the group moved with deliberate quiet. Bags were packed, gear checked, boots laced tight. Even Kong seemed to understand the mood—alert, tail coiled, backpack slung over his small shoulders as he perched by the door, watching.

Outside, the village was still. But too still.

Gee slung the pack with the rings over his shoulder and adjusted the strap. "We need to be out before the market crowd stirs. No more eye contact, no more smiles. Just go."

Lorrisa gave a curt nod and did one last sweep of the room. Her fingers paused briefly over the folded note Meskela had left tucked beneath her bag—just a single phrase in ancient Ge'ez script, too weathered to fully translate. A riddle, most likely. Another breadcrumb.

She pocketed it without a word.

Hamid was at the table, double-checking the paper map folded beside his satphone. As he rolled it tight and tucked it into his vest, he glanced toward Lorrisa.

"You said something last night," he said, keeping his voice low. "That there were thirty-two rings, and someone deliberately scattered them across the world."

Lorrisa nodded, adjusting the collar of her jacket. "That's right."

Hamid hesitated, then asked, "Who would do that? I mean—thirty-two ancient artifacts, each forged for a purpose. Hidden. Guarded. *Why*? And more importantly... are there still people connected to whoever did that?"

The question hung in the air like a held breath.

Lorrisa looked at him, her eyes sharper than the sunrise. "I've asked myself that a thousand times," she said. "If Solomon really forged these rings—and evidence suggests he did—it's possible he never intended for them to remain united. Maybe he feared what they could do in the wrong hands. Or maybe he simply… lost control of what he created."

"Then someone else stepped in," Gee said, leaning against the doorway. "Priests. Scholars. A secret order—whatever you want to call them. People who knew what the rings were and took it upon themselves to protect the world *from* them."

"Or from what they were meant to control," Lorrisa added.

Kong let out a soft chuff, as if agreeing.

Hamid tilted his head. "So you're saying there's a lineage? Some kind of custodianship passed down over time?"

"That's the theory," she replied. "Whispers of them appear in old scrolls. The 'Sons of the Flame,' the 'Wardens of the Seal,' even the 'Ash Order' in Babylonian accounts. Different names. Same purpose: keep the rings apart. Keep them hidden."

Gee glanced around. "Which begs the question—where the hell are they now? Why didn't they stop us?"

"They might not know we're doing this yet," Lorrisa said. "Or... they're testing us."

"Testing us?" Hamid asked. "Like some ancient initiation?"

"Or a gauntlet," Gee said. "See who survives long enough to understand what's at stake."

Kong made a low grumbling noise and turned his head toward the window. Someone passed by outside, footsteps slow, deliberate. The group froze.

But the sound faded.

Lorrisa pulled her scarf higher over her face. "There *are* still people associated with Solomon's legacy. We've crossed paths with a few already—we just didn't recognize them. Meskela might be one."

"She let us leave," Hamid reminded.

"She *needed* us to," Lorrisa said. "If there's really a prison beneath the Mountain of Salt... then the rings might be the key not just to unlocking it—but to *containing* whatever's still sealed inside."

Gee pushed off the wall. "Let's not stick around long enough to find out if the villagers decide to bar the gates."

Lorrisa looked at Hamid one last time. “To answer your question—yes. I believe there are still people who serve Solomon’s cause. Guardians. Watchers. Maybe even deceivers among them.”

She pushed open the door, revealing the golden morning beyond. “We just haven’t figured out yet which ones are which.”

The road to the east twisted through terrain that grew more desolate with every mile. Low hills of dust-colored stone gave way to jagged flats of sunbaked earth, pocked by the occasional bramble of thornbush or bleached skeleton of a long-dead goat. The deeper they drove, the less life there was to see.

Kong sat between Lorrisa and Gee in the back of the rented 4x4, nose pressed to the window, eyes darting with twitchy energy. He didn’t like the silence. Neither did anyone else.

Hamid drove, hands loose on the wheel but posture alert. He hadn’t said much since they left the village—no jokes, no side comments, not even his usual low hum of a tune under his breath.

Gee noticed first. “You alright up there, captain?”

Hamid didn't answer at first. He was watching the rearview mirror.

"I've seen that same dust pattern behind us twice now," he finally said. "Different ridgelines, same motion."

Lorrisa leaned forward. "What kind of motion?"

Hamid glanced sideways. "Not animal. Not random. Measured. Timed. Like someone falling back to keep out of sight."

Gee frowned. "You think we're being followed?"

"I don't think. I *know*."

Kong let out a small hiss and ducked lower on the seat.

"How long?" Lorrisa asked quietly.

Hamid exhaled through his nose. "At least since the last fuel stop. Maybe earlier. I didn't want to say anything until I was sure."

Gee turned slightly in his seat, peering through the back window. Just dirt and heat haze. "I don't see anyone."

"That's the point," Hamid replied. "Whoever it is—they're good."

Lorrisa shifted her weight. "Sebastian?"

"Possible," Hamid said. "But if it *were* Sebastian, we'd have heard more by now. He doesn't do subtle."

"Then it's someone else," Gee muttered. "Another player."

"No one followed us directly from the village," Lorrisa said, thinking aloud. "The townsfolk wanted us gone, but they weren't organized. They don't have tail cars."

"What about watchers?" Hamid asked. "One person. Maybe two. Marked us, radioed ahead. Could've passed us off."

Lorrisa tapped a finger on the map in her lap. "There's nothing out here but rock and rusted trade routes. If someone's still back there, they're not just curious. They're *committed*."

Gee leaned back, arms folded. "Great. So we've got four ancient rings humming in our bag like a tuning fork from hell, a barely-sleeping monkey, and now a shadow we can't shake."

Kong gave a tired grunt, as if to object to being mentioned.

Lorrisa didn't smile. Her eyes stayed on the map, tracking their path toward the White Spine. "There's a pass here," she said, tapping the paper. "Narrow. Rocky.

If someone's following, that's where they'll have to show themselves. There's no other way around."

Hamid nodded slowly. "And if they do?"

"We take a picture. Maybe a license plate," Gee offered.

"Or we ambush them," Lorrisa said, without emotion.

That caught both men off guard.

She looked up. "We've been lucky so far. But that's not a strategy. If someone's tracking us this deep, they're either here to intercept the rings—or worse, make sure we never reach our destination."

Hamid's knuckles tightened slightly on the steering wheel. "I'll slow our pace just enough. Make it easier for them to keep eyes on us. If they're watching, they won't break off."

"Good," Gee said. "Then we'll know it's real."

"And not just paranoia," Hamid added.

Kong blinked and crept up onto Lorrisa's shoulder. He stared out the rear window again, body tense.

Lorrisa didn't turn around. She just muttered, "Let's find out who wants to be the ghost in our mirror."

They made camp just before the narrowest point of the pass—a place where the cliffs funneled the ancient trade road into a corridor barely wide enough for two vehicles. Jagged outcroppings loomed on both sides like broken teeth.

Perfect for an ambush. Or a trap. Depending on who walked into whose.

Lorrisa crouched low near the path, stringing a tension wire between two boulders. "This won't stop anyone serious," she said. "But it'll give us a few seconds."

Gee was twenty meters up on the ridge, laying out their signal flares and adjusting the angle of a compact mirror to reflect light downward. Hamid, rifle slung and eyes scanning the terrain, paced steadily, trying to anticipate angles of attack.

Kong stayed close to Lorrisa, tail flicking nervously.

"We're doing this for information," Lorrisa reminded them. "We catch them, we talk. We don't shoot first."

"Unless they do," Hamid muttered.

Gee called down from above. "Movement—south approach. Slow. Deliberate. One figure."

Lorrisa ducked behind a ridge as Hamid dropped into position. A few tense seconds passed. Then the figure emerged through the rising dust.

It was Meskela.

Alone.

She walked calmly through the trap zone, robes fluttering around her, head high. Her eyes didn't even scan for danger. She stopped where the wire was laid and stared at it—then deliberately stepped over.

No hesitation. No fear.

"I believe this belongs to you," she said, producing a folded scrap of paper. Lorrisa recognized it instantly—the old Ge'ez note Meskela had slipped beneath her bag.

"You followed us," Lorrisa said, rising slowly from her crouch. "You marked us back at the village."

"No," Meskela said coolly. "I *protected* you."

That's when the whistling started.

Low. Sharp. A kind of unnatural hush.

From behind every rock and ridge, men appeared—over a dozen, all cloaked in dark sand-colored fabric, rifles raised. A second later, Gee stepped up from his perch only to find one of the figures already flanking his path. Another man had a bead on Hamid from the ridge.

They were surrounded.

A perfect reversal.

"Damn," Gee whispered. "We just got counter-trapped by a gorgeous woman and a philosophy class."

Lorrisa raised her hands slightly, not in surrender—but recognition. "You're Ash Order."

Meskela gave a slight nod. "And I ask you now, Lorrisa Santos... will you die for curiosity? For arrogance? Because that's what it will take."

Hamid tensed. "We don't want a fight."

"But you've already brought one," Meskela said. "The rings never come without a price. Not for those who seek them."

"We want the truth," Lorrisa said. "Just the truth."

"And if the truth damns the world?" Meskela asked, voice rising. "Would you still dig?"

Before Lorrisa could answer, a *thump* cracked through the canyon air—followed by a *roaring blast* just beyond the southern ridge. Rock and dust exploded upward, and everyone ducked instinctively.

A second explosion rang out, closer this time—sending an echo down the canyon like thunder trapped in a bottle.

Then came the engines.

Growling. Mechanical. Heavy.

Tanks—two of them—rolled into view from the far end of the pass. Flanked by black-armored jeeps and soldiers in desert camo. The insignia on the side of the lead tank was unmistakable:

Sebastian Voss.

His mercenaries.

Gee swore under his breath. "You have *got* to be kidding me."

Meskela's people turned, weapons raised toward the advancing vehicles. Chaos teetered on the edge.

Meskela remained unmoved. She turned slowly back toward Lorrisa.

"I asked if you would die for your cause," she said. "Now I ask again—because *they* surely will."

Lorrisa looked at Gee. Then at Hamid. Then down at Kong, who clung tightly to her arm, eyes wide.

She didn't answer with words. She stepped forward.

And raised her voice.

"You're all looking in the wrong direction. The rings aren't weapons. They're keys. And we've unlocked something. If we don't stop it—*none* of us are walking out of here."

Sebastian's tank halted at fifty meters. The top hatch popped open. A single figure emerged.

Immaculate suit. Wind-tousled blond hair. Cold, calculating eyes that didn't blink against the sun.

Sebastian Voss.

He raised a bullhorn.

"Miss Santos," his voice crackled across the canyon, "I do hope you're not planning to give my rings away to the locals."

Lorrisa took one defiant step forward. "You're late, Voss. We've moved on."

He chuckled, humorless. "So I've heard. Four now, isn't it? My sources were surprisingly slow this time. No matter—I'll take them all now."

His soldiers raised their rifles.

Meskela's did the same.

Hamid leaned toward Lorrisa. "This is bad math."

Kong leapt from Lorrisa's shoulder and landed beside the pack that held the rings. His small hand hovered near the zipper.

"No," Lorrisa said firmly.

Everyone froze at her voice. Even Kong.

Sebastian's smile faded.

"Are we going to play fair," he called, "or is this going to get dramatic?"

Gee looked around. "It's already dramatic."

Lorrisa stepped into the narrow space between the opposing lines, arms slightly raised. "You want the rings? Fine. But know this—every person who's handled one of these has ended up either dead, possessed, or hunted. You think you can handle all thirty-two?"

Sebastian's eyes narrowed. "Thirty-two?"

There it was.

The flicker of *ignorance*—the moment he realized he didn't know as much as he thought.

Lorrisa saw it. Pressed the moment.

"Eight is a corner," she said. "One quadrant. There are three more. Didn't your misters Smith, Johnson and Williams tell you?"

Sebastian's face twisted, lips parting slightly as calculations began behind his eyes.

"That's not possible."

"It is," she said. "And the next set is already waking up."

That's when the third explosion hit.

Not from Sebastian. Not from the Ash Order.

But *beneath* the ground.

The canyon floor buckled. A tremor surged through the pass, knocking several soldiers and Meskela's men off their footing. One of the tanks screeched as it slid slightly sideways on the shaking gravel.

A fracture opened in the earth near the far ridge—steam and dust pouring out like the breath of something buried deep.

Everyone backed away.

Everyone... except Lorrisa. She stared at the opening.

The rings, still zipped in the pack, began to glow faintly through the fabric—hot white pulses syncing with the tremors below.

Gee muttered, "Well, I guess the mountain *is* bleeding now." The tremor ceased, but the silence it left in its wake was louder than any explosion.

From the earth's jagged wound, a steady column of white boiling steam billowed upward, twisting like a serpent into the dawn air. The scent that followed was metallic, ancient—like rusted blood and ash long buried.

The rumble was gone, but something *else* remained.

Meskela's men were the first to react. As if moved by one silent command, they lowered their rifles and fell to their knees in a sweeping motion. Heads bowed. Palms turned skyward. Prayers whispered in a language older than the kingdom of Aksum.

Even Meskela's sharp eyes softened. She knelt last, hands clasped. Her lips moved, not in fear—but in reverence.

Sebastian's mercenaries, however, stumbled backward. Guns held loosely now, feet crunching against gravel as they instinctively backed away from the crack, from the heat, from *whatever* was exhaling through that fault in the earth.

“Hold position!” Sebastian barked, his voice cracking through the chaos. But his men didn't answer. Not all of them. One dropped his weapon entirely. Another man crossed himself. Even the tank’s gunner slid down into the hatch, slamming it shut.

The ground had shifted—*not* just physically.

It was *spiritual*.

Gee’s jaw tightened as he scanned the ridge—but then he caught it. A movement. Small at first.

“Lorrisa?”

She didn’t respond.

Her eyes had locked onto the crack. Her body moved slowly—gracefully—toward the rising steam as if pulled by invisible strings.

“Lorrisa!” Gee called again, louder this time.

Still no answer.

Her expression was calm. Too calm. Her eyes glazed, unfocused, pupils dilated slightly. Her arms hung loose at her sides, feet crunching across stone as she descended the incline. She stepped over the debris without flinching, as if the dust and jagged rock weren't even there.

Hamid turned from the perimeter, noticing. "Gee—what is she doing?"

Gee didn't hesitate or respond.

He dropped the flare from his hand and sprinted down the slope.

"*Lorrisa!*"

Kong screeched from his perch, clearly agitated. He scrambled after them, leaping across the rocks.

The temperature changed as Gee neared the fissure—warmer, denser. The air shimmered in strange waves. Static hummed faintly against his skin, like standing beneath a thundercloud.

Lorrisa was already at the edge, now only feet from the crack where the steam hissed like breath from a sleeping beast.

Gee grabbed her arm. "Hey! Hey—snap out of it!"

She blinked slowly, as if surfacing from underwater. Her lips parted, voice dazed.

"I hear them..."

Gee pulled her gently but firmly back. “Who? What are you talking about?”

Her gaze slowly turned toward him. “They’re singing.”

“Singing?” Gee glanced toward the crack. “There’s *nothing* down there but heat and probably more death traps.”

“No,” she whispered. “It’s below. Deeper.”

Meskela stood again, just behind them. Her voice was like a distant bell. “She hears what you do not. The Seal is near.”

Gee turned, keeping his hand on Lorrisa’s shoulder. “The *Seal*? What are you saying?”

“The rings resonate,” Meskela said. “Not only with each other... but with what they were forged to contain. And something has stirred.”

Kong whined, ears flattening. He scrambled up Lorrisa’s leg and clung to her hip.

Lorrisa’s knees wobbled. Gee steadied her.

“Back up the hill,” he said quietly. “Now.”

But then, *another sound*—so low it barely registered at first. A hum. Then a pulse.

The ground beneath their feet gave one more low groan—not enough to open further, but enough to make dust fall from the cliffs.

Then it stopped. Everyone was still.

Then, Lorrisa took one deep breath and said clearly:

"It's not sealed anymore."

Hamid, watching from above, swore under his breath. "Time to *go*. Now."

Sebastian, eyes narrowed from the tank, saw to take advantage of the moment. The way the air had changed. The way Lorrisa had changed.

He barked an order to his men.

"Secure the site! Move in—*get the rings!*"

The spell snapped. The tension exploded.

Meskela's men rose in a fluid line and raised their weapons. Sebastian's mercs moved in response—fanning out, forming lines.

And in the center of it all, Lorrisa stood—eyes wide, steam curling past her face, the pack on her back trembling faintly.

Gee took her hand.

“Time to move, my little Tomb Raider. You found the door. Let’s not get buried in it.” She looked at him, fully aware now. Then she nodded. And the run began.

The air ignited with shouting, smoke, and then rifle fire.

The first shot came from one of Sebastian’s mercs—young, jittery, trying to assert dominance. It hit the rocks near Meskela’s feet. A warning. A mistake.

The second shot came from the Ash Order.

A mercenary dropped with a scream, shoulder blown wide open. Then chaos bloomed like wildfire.

Gunfire cracked in staccato bursts across the canyon. Meskela’s men, despite their spiritual fervor, fought with lethal efficiency—firing from elevated ground and crevices. No hesitation. No waste.

Sebastian stood atop his tank, shouting commands in multiple languages, each one sharper than the last. His radio crackled as orders ricocheted through frequencies.

“Tango positions, move up on both flanks—contain the ridge! Secure the archaeologist at all costs!”

His men scrambled, some diving behind the armored vehicles, others laying suppressing fire against the rocky cover.

Meskela ducked low behind a boulder, still issuing commands in an ancient tongue. The woman's eyes never blinked, even as bullets snapped past her ears.

"We are not meant to win!" she called to her people. "We are meant to *stall!*"

In the 4X4 TRUCK — SIMULTANEOUSLY

Gee jammed the stick into gear and floored the gas pedal. Dust exploded behind the tires as the vehicle rocketed away from the canyon mouth, skidding onto the cracked trade road that led deeper into the hills.

Lorrisa sat in the passenger seat, clutching the pack that contained the rings. Kong huddled in her lap, eyes darting, his tiny frame trembling with energy and fear.

Hamid leaned between the seats from the back. "They're engaging. Both sides. We just walked away from a *proxy war*."

Gee didn't glance back. "I'm okay with that."

Lorrisa finally looked over. Her voice was low, still distant. "You saw what happened."

"I saw you walking into a sulfur vent like a possessed hiker," Gee replied. "We can debrief later."

"I *felt* something. The rings were responding. There's something under that ridge—and it woke up."

Hamid grimaced. "And we just left it behind."

"No," Lorrisa said. "We're driving toward it. That crack? That was just the *edge*. The real site is ahead. The White Spine. That's where the keyhole is."

Gee adjusted the wheel as the terrain grew rougher. "Then let's just hope Sebastian's too busy eating bullets to follow."

THE CANYON

The sound of war choked the canyon. Smoke from flash grenades drifted into the upper ridgelines as two of Sebastian's jeeps exploded in fiery arcs—hit by well-placed shots or booby traps Meskela's people had hidden in the rocks.

Blood streaked the gravel.

Meskela crouched beside a wounded young fighter, pressing her hand to his chest.

"My daughter," he whispered, blinking through blood.

“She will know your name,” Meskela promised. She kissed his forehead and closed his eyes.

Then she stood again—her posture tall, unwavering despite the gunfire around her.

Across the battlefield, Sebastian scanned the ridge through binoculars.

“She’s still here!” he growled.

“No visual,” one of his lieutenants called.

“She won’t run,” he muttered, more to himself than anyone. “She *believes*. That makes her predictable.”

Then, over the comms: “The archaeologists have escaped. They’re heading east.”

His expression hardened. “Let them run. Let them lead us to the next ring.”

He stepped back into the tank hatch and pulled the radio to his lips.

“Activate drone pursuit. I want eyes on their convoy within the hour.”

DESERT ROAD – AN HOUR LATER

The sun climbed higher, bleaching the road ahead into shimmering waves.

Gee drove with one hand, scanning the horizon through narrowed eyes. Lorrisa stared at the horizon, tense.

"There's a fuel station up ahead," Hamid said. "Not marked on GPS. Probably off-grid."

"Perfect," Gee muttered. "Maybe we can fill up and *not* get shot at for a change."

Kong tapped on the window, pointing.

In the distance—beyond the fuel station—rose the jagged teeth of the *White Spine*, the mountain range that loomed like fossilized remains of a sleeping titan.

"Looks like our next tomb is right on schedule," Gee added.

Lorrisa unzipped the pack just slightly, allowing the faint hum of the rings to spill out.

They pulsed in sync—soft light thudding like a second heartbeat.

"The closer we get," she whispered, "the more they come alive."

Hamid leaned forward. "Then we'd better get there before Sebastian does. Because next time? I don't think we'll walk away clean."

THE CANYON — BACK TO THE CLASH...

Smoke blanketed the pass now. The fighting was dying out—but not because of victory.

Because of exhaustion.

Bodies lay sprawled on both sides. Sebastian's forces had driven back Meskela's men by sheer firepower—but not without bleeding for it. They were not unscathed.

Meskela, wounded but upright, limped through the haze with only five of her fighters still standing.

She reached the edge of the fracture—its steam now fainter, but still hissing. Still *alive*.

She stared down into it, whispering something unintelligible.

Behind her, Sebastian approached slowly, brushing dust from his suit. His pistol hung at his side.

"Old zealots always impress me," he said flatly. "Willing to die for a fairy tale."

She didn't flinch. "It's not a tale. You felt it. You *saw* it."

He raised the pistol. "What I saw was a distraction. But thank you—for buying me time."

She looked over her shoulder, serene. "You think the rings are your prize. But you are already too late."

Sebastian paused. “Too late for what?”

Meskela smiled, blood trickling down her chin.

“They’ve been chosen.”

Then, without fear, she stepped backward—into the fissure.

And vanished into the steam.

Sebastian stood still, silent for a long moment. Then he turned toward his men.

“Clean up. Burn the bodies. And find me that mountain.”

OUTSKIRTS OF THE WHITE SPINE – SUNSET

The vehicle crested the ridge overlooking a dry plateau flanked by dark, towering cliffs. The wind was stronger here—cooler, sharper. The terrain looked dead... but something about it pulsed with *intent*.

Lorrisa stepped out first, boots crunching against stone. She walked forward several paces and dropped to one knee.

There, half-buried in the dust, was a *symbol* carved in ancient script—one matching the rings’ inner lining.

She reached into the bag and removed one ring.

It pulsed stronger.

Gee and Hamid joined her, looking down at the mark.

“Tell me that doesn’t look like a lock,” Gee muttered.

“It’s a seal,” Lorrisa said.

She looked up toward the dark peaks of the White Spine, wind catching her hair, Kong pressing tightly against her side.

“Whatever’s in there... was never meant to come out.”

Entering the Mountain.

The wind howled as they stood before the carved seal at the mountain’s base. A symbol, chiseled deep into ancient basalt, shimmered faintly beneath the dust—subtle, but unmistakable.

Lorrisa ran her fingers over the lines. “This isn’t a marker. It’s an interface.”

Gee scanned the horizon behind them, eyes tight. “Let’s hope it’s also a door—because I guarantee Sebastian’s already rolling this way.”

Hamid crouched beside Lorrisa. “What do we need?”

Lorrisa unzipped the side compartment of the pack and carefully removed two of the rings. “A pattern. A sequence. These rings don't just open locks. They respond to each other. We just have to figure out how."

Gee kept the vehicle idling, its engine low and ready. "Be quick. We might've bought ourselves a head start, but it won't last."

Kong scrambled up onto a jagged boulder beside the carving. He stared down at it, then began tapping it curiously with his small knuckles.

Lorrisa looked up at him, amused. "If you open the gate before I do, I'm demoting myself."

She pressed the first ring into the carved depression that most closely matched its inner markings.

Nothing happened.

She tried a second location—this time, a faint *click* echoed inside the stone. Dust shifted. A low hum followed.

"That's one," she muttered.

Gee moved closer. "Try the next ring in that crescent groove—like a domino path."

She did.

This time, the seal rotated slightly beneath their hands. The symbol glowed faint gold.

Kong chattered excitedly, backing away as the earth beneath the stone began to tremble.

Hamid stood, rifle ready. “Uh, guys...”

The seal split down the middle with a hiss of ancient steam, and a hidden panel sank inward to reveal a narrow tunnel, descending sharply into darkness.

Cool air rushed out—moist, mineral-rich, untouched by time.

Lorrisa stared into it, suddenly breathless.

“It’s real,” she whispered. “It’s *all* real.”

Gee pulled a flashlight from the pack and flicked it on. “Guess we’re going in.”

Kong jumped back into Lorrisa’s arms as the team moved into the opening. Gee followed last, turning just before disappearing inside to sweep the horizon.

A dust cloud was rising in the distance—vehicles. Fast-moving.

“They’re coming,” he muttered, and ducked in after them.

The tunnel was tight at first, carved by hand with clear precision. Symbols lined the walls—some familiar, some impossible to identify.

"Ethiopic script," Hamid muttered. "But older than anything I've seen in museums."

Lorrisa ran the flashlight across a repeating motif—a circle broken into four equal quadrants.

"Same structure we saw on the tablet," she said. "The seal we activated outside was only one quadrant. There are three more."

"Inside this mountain?" Gee asked.

"Or connected to it," she replied.

They moved cautiously, the rings still pulsing softly from inside the pack. The path angled downward, and the further they went, the more the temperature dropped.

Then they reached a landing.

A massive stone door, over fifteen feet high, stood before them. In the center—a metal disc, exactly the size of the rings.

Lorrisa stepped forward, unzipping the pack. She pulled out the third ring and pressed it into the disc.

Nothing.

Hamid exhaled. "Maybe the sequence is wrong?"

"Maybe it needs all four," she said.

She placed the remaining rings around the disc—each at equal spacing. As the fourth slid into place, the disc began to rotate—slowly, methodically. Then a sharp *clang* echoed through the corridor.

The door split open, revealing a massive cavern beyond.

They stepped inside. The chamber swallowed them.

It was vast, lit by strange veins of glowing quartz that pulsed with faint blue light. Ancient machinery—half-alchemical, half-architectural—lined the walls in silent vigil.

And at the far end... another seal.

This one dwarfed the first. Thirty-two recesses encircled a central pedestal. Each recess bore a unique symbol—waiting for a ring.

Hamid let out a low whistle. "So it's true."

Gee took a step closer. "Thirty-two keys. One vault."

Lorrisa approached the pedestal and set the four rings they had onto the corresponding positions. The entire seal lit up—dimly, but clearly responding to their presence.

A sound echoed from deep within the mountain—a *groan*, like stone being shifted by breath.

Kong clung tighter to her arm.

Lorrisa looked around the chamber. “This was Solomon’s last vault.”

“Or his prison,” Gee said softly. “What if that seal isn’t meant to be *opened*?”

Lorrisa’s voice barely rose above a whisper. “Then we just walked into the place built to hold something even Solomon was afraid of.”

Meanwhile at the *mountain entrance,* The dust cloud was now close. Sebastian’s lead vehicle screeched to a halt at the opened entrance of the mountain. The cracked seal still glowed faintly.

He stepped out of the jeep, his eyes burning with fascination. “They went inside.”

One of his mercenaries raised a scanner. “Signal trace confirms. Four bodies. They’re descending.”

Sebastian smiled. “Then we follow,” he said. “But not too fast.” He turned to his team.

“They’ve opened the first chamber for us. Let’s see how far they get before it *closes* behind them. Meanwhile ready the explosives in case we need them.”

Lorrisa knelt before the massive seal, examining the thirty-two recesses around the central pedestal. The four rings they possessed now pulsed in unison—low and steady, like breath.

She brushed dust from one of the untouched recesses, revealing intricate filigree in the ancient metal.

“They weren’t just keys,” she murmured. “Each one was encoded. Calibrated.”

Gee paced behind her, eyes scanning the stonework above.

“What are the odds the rest of this place is booby-trapped?”

“High,” Hamid answered before she could.

Kong let out a nervous chirp and clambered onto a nearby plinth. He sniffed the air, then hissed, fur rising.

“What’s gotten into him?” Gee asked, turning.

But before anyone could respond—

A low *thrumm* vibrated through the floor.

It was faint at first, like a tuning fork resonating through stone.

Lorrisa's head jerked up. "That didn't come from us."

OUTER PASSAGE – SIMULTANEOUSLY

Back at the outer edge of the mountain's tunnel, Sebastian's squad had entered the threshold with calculated caution.

The flickering quartz veins along the walls still glowed, but the ambiance had grown colder—more aware.

Sebastian followed behind two of his more heavily armed men, scanning the walls with a thermal reader.

"No defenses triggered," he muttered. "Either they disabled them, or—"

"Sir!" one of his men called from up ahead. "There's a side chamber. Looks like some kind of alternate passage."

A younger merc, eager and overly bold, ducked inside the offshoot chamber, sweeping it with his flashlight.

"Wait!" another barked. "We don't know what that is—"

CLICK!

A small depression beneath the young merc's boot suddenly sank into the floor with a mechanical snap.

The quartz veins along the entire tunnel system immediately *flashed red*.

Then, from the far recesses of the tunnel, the walls began to move.

A *rumble*—deep and ancient.

Gears. Pistons. Something was waking up.

Sebastian's face twisted in disgust. "*Idiot!*"

The reverberating sound hit Lorrisa and Gee like a drumbeat from the underworld.

A *deep, hollow clunk*, followed by a violent tremor. Dust rained from the high stone ceiling. The seal beneath the rings momentarily surged with blinding gold light—then dimmed sharply. The rings spun in place and locked. "*Get back!*" Lorrisa shouted, pulling Hamid down with her just as a shaft of energy flashed across the pedestal.

A hidden mechanism near the eastern wall activated—a series of *iron blades* shot down from overhead in rapid succession, *SLAM—SLAM—SLAM*—before resetting themselves just as fast.

Kong screamed and bolted into Lorrisa's arms.

Gee had his weapon out, half-pointed toward the hall. "That wasn't us."

"No," Lorrisa growled. "That was *them.*"

SIMULTANEOUSLY...

The young merc screamed as the floor beneath him dropped out—instantly replaced by a bed of obsidian spikes. Two others grabbed him just in time and yanked him back, but not without a graze slicing into his thigh.

Blood sprayed the stone.

Sebastian's jaw clenched. "Amateurs."

Another vibration hit the corridor—this one different.

A wave.

A pulse of *energy*—not seen, but *felt*—raced down the quartz-lined walls, trailing deeper into the mountain.

Sebastian looked toward the tunnel's far end. "They'll feel that."

Within the *INNER CHAMBER*, they did.

The light along the walls changed—shifting from calming blue to a dangerous amber. The air grew heavier.

Lorrisa looked at the pedestal and the four rings. They were *glowing hotter* now, humming like electric circuitry pushed to its limit.

"They activated something further back," she muttered. "A defensive sequence, or maybe a signal."

Hamid looked around. "A signal to what?"

Kong clung to Lorrisa's shoulder and slowly raised one trembling finger to the far side of the room—toward a newly visible door that hadn't been there before.

It had no hinges. No handle.

Just a smooth obsidian surface, split down the center. Etched across it was an emblem:

A crown surrounded by a ring of chains... and beneath it, an eye—closed, but weeping flame.

Gee stared. "That... looks bad." Lorrisa stepped forward, compelled. She touched the symbol.

It *flared to life.* The eye opened.

At the *OUTER PASSAGE* ...

Sebastian and his team halted as the air around them shifted. One of the older mercs looked pale. "Did you feel that?" Sebastian didn't answer.

He just pressed two fingers to his temple and whispered, *"We woke it up."*

INNER CHAMBER.

The silence of the chamber was so complete it rang in their ears. The four rings set into the seal pulsed faintly, their glow illuminating the carved recesses around the circular pedestal.

Lorrisa crouched, brushing dust off the glyphs encircling the floor, studying the pattern for anomalies.

Gee was just behind her, running his gloved hand along the wall's outer curvature—fingertips sensing pressure differences, subtle airflow.

"This whole place was designed to breathe," he murmured. "You feel that?"

Lorrisa nodded. "A living vault. It responds to proximity. Pressure. Maybe even intent."

Kong sniffed the air near one of the rings and hissed softly before climbing back into Hamid's arms.

Gee tapped the metal rim of the pedestal with a knuckle. “Not reacting to the rings right now. You think we’re locked out?”

“No,” Lorrisa said quietly. “It’s waiting.”

They exchanged a look—mutual understanding. The kind that had once kept them alive in tombs beneath Petra, ruins in Peru, and a three-day standoff in eastern Turkey.

Hamid, posted at the entrance to the chamber, kept his voice low. “No signs yet. But we all know they’re coming.”

“They’ll move slow,” Gee said. “He’s smart enough to know this place isn’t just ancient. It’s trapped.”

Lorrisa stood. “And we can’t risk triggering something we don’t understand.”

“We need to scout the perimeter,” Gee added. “Divide and map. No guesswork.”

Hamid nodded. “I’ll keep watch. If I see flashlights, we’ll know.”

Lorrisa grabbed her pack. “Let's move quiet. Catalog everything. Look for any sign of how these rings interact with this chamber.”

They split into their pattern—practiced and precise. Lorrisa moved clockwise, examining carvings and inscriptions along the stone benches and alcoves. Gee moved the opposite way, stopping at what looked like an intentionally blackened groove in the stone floor—almost as if something had been dragged or burned in a slow, circular pattern.

Every step was deliberate. Measured. Not even Kong made a sound.

ELSEWHERE...

Sebastian and his men advanced with surgical discipline through the winding passageways, keeping formation tight.

They wore headlamps now. Their beams cut through the dark, throwing ancient murals and carvings into stark relief—beasts and kings, fire and rings, chains and seals.

One of the mercenaries, Diaz, glanced toward the wall. "These aren't just warnings. They're... blueprints."

"Keep moving," Sebastian said, checking a signal scanner. "The ring pulse is intensifying. They're close."

He turned to his demolitions expert, Khouri. "Contingency?"

Khouri tapped the case he carried, secured to his chest rig. “Low-yield. Precision-punch. Only if necessary.”

Sebastian gave a short nod. “We’re not here to blow holes in history. Just remember—we’re not the first to want what’s buried here. But we might be the last to get this far.”

No one spoke after that.

Every step deeper felt like crossing a threshold into something not meant for the living.

INNER CHAMBER

Lorrisa paused at a narrow slot in the stone wall—almost like a speaking tube or air duct. She leaned in slightly and heard it: a vibration, distant but rhythmic. Footsteps? Machinery? She couldn’t tell.

“They’re close,” she said softly to herself.

On the far side of the room, Gee called gently across the chamber. “Lorrisa.” She turned.

He was standing beside a second recess in the floor—flat, circular, ringed with gold.

“Looks like a pressure gate. Might be how the rings trigger the next mechanism.”

Lorrisa approached slowly. She examined the circular pad.

“Eight segments,” she murmured. “Each ring quadrant might align to one.”

Gee nodded. “Which means we’re only one-eighth ready to unlock this thing.”

“We’re still just scratching the surface,” she said. “There’s another layer below.” They were quiet for a beat.

Then Gee added, “He’s going to come down here thinking brute force will do the trick.”

“He’ll be wrong,” Lorrisa said. “This place doesn’t reward force. It tests judgment.”

“And it punishes ignorance,” Gee said, then looked down at the rings. “We should move before he finds his own way in.”

OUTER TUNNELS.

Sebastian’s team stopped at a collapsed stairwell—stones piled inward at an unnatural angle.

“Alternate entrance,” one merc whispered. “Looks recent. Could’ve been an old collapse.”

Sebastian crouched near it. “No. This was sealed *from inside*. Intentionally.”

He turned to Khouri. “Mark it.”

Khouri began prepping a shaped charge—compact, controlled. The others adjusted formation, spreading out with discipline.

No one panicked. No one rushed.

Sebastian glanced ahead toward the dark archways that extended like veins through the mountain.

“They’ve gone deeper. Good.” He stood. “We let them lead the way.” Khouri slid the final charge into place and stepped back, glancing at Sebastian.

“We’re clear,” he said. “Timer’s set for thirty. Controlled collapse. Should give us a tight crawlspace and preserve the structure.”

Sebastian gave a slight nod. “Do it.”

Khouri tapped the detonator. A muffled **crack** echoed through the stone as dust exploded outward in a brief cloud. A faint tremor shivered through the corridor—but nothing collapsed. Nothing fell.

Sebastian’s men approached the blast site and immediately began shifting debris.

The narrow tunnel they'd opened stretched downward at an angle—just wide enough for a single person at a time.

Sebastian was the first to slide through.

The air changed the moment he passed the threshold—cooler, heavier, tinged with iron and the strange sweetness of aged incense.

"Scan the walls," he said quietly.

Diaz and Moulier followed him in, sweeping lights along the corridor.

There were carvings here too—but different from the ones above. Less decorative. More... ritualistic. Patterns of coiled chains, eyes in flame, and something new:

A figure with no face—cloaked, crowned, and kneeling before a ring held in open air.

"See that?" Sebastian muttered.

Khouri came through last, the explosives case still secured to his chest.

Sebastian stared at the figure. "They sealed something down here. Not just a vault... a *presence.*"

They moved quietly, deeper. Their boots echoed against smooth stone, the path subtly descending with every meter.

The tunnel narrowed, then opened again—into a circular chamber.

No door. Just eight archways, each engraved with a different geometric sigil.

In the center of the room: a pedestal.

Not a seal this time. A flat slab with concentric grooves, empty but unmistakable.

Khouri knelt beside it. “Looks like something’s supposed to sit here.”

Sebastian stepped closer. “More rings.”

He looked around the room. “But no sign of Santos.”

Diaz called from one of the archways. “Boss—footprints. Light ones. Three sets. They passed through here, maybe half an hour ago.”

Sebastian turned slowly. “They’re still ahead.”

He paused at one of the sigils—shaped like a sun being eclipsed.

He ran his fingers along the groove.

The stone warmed slightly under his touch.

A faint vibration buzzed beneath the surface—just enough for his fingertips to feel it.

“I think these are gates,” he said. “The rings activate them. Like nodes.”

Khouri’s brows knit. “Want me to rig this one for insurance?”

Sebastian hesitated, thinking.

“No,” he said. “We need to see where it leads.”

He pulled out the partial ring he carried—a damaged fragment recovered from a black-market dealer months ago. Not functional. Not keyed.

But ancient.

He set it into the groove on the pedestal.

The reaction was instant.

A hum filled the room—low, resonant. Not hostile. Just *aware*.

One of the eight arches *glowed* faintly—its sigil now illuminated.

Sebastian smiled.

“Well,” he said, gesturing to the path now opened. “Let’s find our hosts.”

ELSEWHERE IN THE MOUNTAIN – SIMULTANEOUSLY

A faint ripple passed through the deeper levels of the mountain. A shift in temperature. A whisper against stone.

In the chamber beyond the pedestal, Lorrisa stopped mid-step. She turned.

Gee noticed it too. “You feel that?”

She nodded. “They’ve reached the second threshold.”

Hamid, behind them, muttered, “And they’ve got the mountain’s attention.”

Kong let out a low, warning hiss.

BACK TO SEBASTIAN

The archway they passed through was narrow, tunnel-like, the walls smooth and curved inward—almost *organic* in design. It twisted slightly, forcing them to walk in single file.

Diaz kept his rifle up, flashlight on.

"Something feels wrong," he muttered. "Like we're inside something... alive."

Sebastian didn't respond. His attention was on the walls, on the way the light refracted oddly—sometimes bending where there was no surface to bend around.

They reached a threshold—beyond it, a wide stairwell descending into what appeared to be a chamber filled with chains.

Chains hung from the ceiling, thick and unmoving, each affixed to stone columns etched with hundreds of unreadable names.

Sebastian stopped. "This... was not meant to be seen."

Moulier whispered, "What is this place?"

Khouri's voice was low. "Containment."

No one laughed.

Sebastian moved slowly into the center of the chained hall, tilting his head. "No vault. No treasure. Just locks."

Diaz said, "But what are they keeping locked *in*?"

Sebastian stopped walking. Turned.

And for the first time in hours—he looked unsettled.

"I think the real question is: *What happens when thirty-two keys are finally inserted?*"

The silence within the chained hall wasn't empty—it was *coiled*. Waiting.

Sebastian advanced slowly down the central aisle, boots echoing off cold stone. His men flanked him, weapons at the ready, eyes tracking the hanging chains. Each one thick as a man's wrist, suspended from blackened rafters and anchored into the floor like prison restraints.

Khouri whispered, "These were for holding something. Or *someones*."

"Be quiet," Sebastian snapped. "This isn't a temple. It's a warning."

From the far entrance of the chamber—opposite where Sebastian entered—a second group emerged, stepping cautiously from a shadowed arch:

Lorrisa. Gee. Hamid. Kong.

Gee was the first to spot movement. He raised a hand.

"Company."

Lorrisa froze. She recognized the crisp silhouette immediately—Sebastian, calm and deadly at the center of his men.

They locked eyes.

Sebastian smiled faintly. “Miss Santos.”

Lorrisa’s tone was flat. “You’re out of your depth, Voss.”

“I prefer to think of it as inherited confidence.”

Khouri’s rifle twitched upward. Hamid took one step forward, weapon raised to mirror.

Gee’s voice cut through the tension. “Don’t.”

Everyone paused.

Kong hissed from Lorrisa’s shoulder—ears twitching, body suddenly tense. His claws dug into her jacket.

Then he looked *up*.

So did Lorrisa.

So did everyone.

The chains were swaying. Not all of them.

Just a few—*slowly*, with no wind. No movement. Like something unseen had brushed past.

Gee whispered, “We’re not alone.”

Sebastian's smirk faded.

A low, grinding *groan* echoed from the rafters. Somewhere deep within the ceiling—*metal shifted*. The entire chamber seemed to inhale.

Then—something dropped. Something *fast!*

A blur of darkness *slammed* into one of Sebastian's forward scouts—Diaz—*ripping* him backward into the chains with impossible force. His scream was short. The sound of bone snapping—shorter.

Blood sprayed across one of the columns. Diaz was gone.

Gunfire erupted instantly—Khouri and Moulier opened up in every direction. Muzzle flashes lit the chamber like strobe lights.

"Visuals! Where is it?" Khouri yelled.

Nothing.

The chains were swinging violently now—slapping against columns. One snapped loose and struck the floor with a *crack*.

Lorrisa dropped to a crouch, shielding Kong.

Gee moved in beside her, weapon up, scanning fast. "It's using the chains. Moving through them."

Hamid fired a shot toward a blur on the far ceiling. It sparked—something metallic—then vanished.

"*It's not alone!*" he shouted.

A second merc screamed as he was lifted *straight up* into the air by something unseen. The chains snapped taut—then went limp. His body didn't come back down.

Lorrisa looked to Sebastian. "We can't shoot our way out."

Sebastian glanced around—calculating.

"Cease fire!" he barked. "You're hitting stone!"

His men reluctantly obeyed. Silence dropped again.

Then—a low *guttural rasp* echoed through the hall.

Lorrisa stood slowly. "There's more than one."

"Entities," Hamid said softly. "Guardians. Bound here."

"Until *someone* triggered the wrong sequence," Gee added dryly.

Sebastian turned toward Lorrisa, ignoring the blood at their feet. "You've been deeper than us. How do we stop this?"

She looked toward the central pedestal.

"We don't," she said. "Not without the rings."

Sebastian stepped closer leveling his pistol at her. “Then give them to me.”

Kong shrieked—suddenly launching off Lorrisa’s shoulder. He scurried toward the base of one of the columns, where a faint golden ring lay amid the dust.

“Kong, no—!” Too late.

A shadow burst from the floor—*like liquid smoke*—and *slammed* into Kong mid-dash, pinning him beneath a thick, slithering coil of chain.

He screeched—panicked—trapped.

Lorrisa screamed, racing forward.

Gee tackled her sideways just as a black claw struck the floor where she had been—cracking stone.

“*Hamid!*” Gee shouted.

Hamid fired three precise shots toward the smoky mass. The bullets seemed to *bend* inside the creature, slowing, evaporating.

“*It’s not solid!*” he shouted.

Sebastian’s men regrouped, forming a perimeter, breathing heavy.

Lorrisa scrambled toward Kong, now tangled and barely moving. The chain tightened.

She threw herself down beside him.

“Come on, come on—”

A glowing ring still pulsed beneath the chained coil—ancient, flickering gold.

Gee knelt beside her. “We’ll have to cut him out.”

“I don’t think this is about cutting,” she said. “It’s about finishing the pattern.”

She yanked one of the rings from her satchel and *slammed it* into the hollow groove where the fallen ring had come loose.

Instant response.

The chamber *shook*.

Chains rattled.

The smoky creature shrieked—high, unearthly.

Then vanished.

Kong coughed once. Then whimpered, still barely breathing.

Lorrisa scooped him up, tears hot in her eyes. “I got you,” she whispered. “I got you, my adorable monkey.”

Behind her, Sebastian stared at the glowing seal where the ring had been placed.

“They’re not weapons,” he muttered. “They’re *restraints*.”

Gee rose, helping Lorrisa up. “You’re learning.”

Hamid moved to cover the rear. “We’ve lost the element of surprise—and if those things come back...”

“They will,” Lorrisa said. “This place doesn’t care about alliances. It punishes all trespassers.”

She looked at Sebastian.

“For now, we work together. Or none of us leave alive.”

Sebastian stared at her. No expression.

Then, finally—he nodded. “One chamber at a time,” he said.

The chain-creature’s departure left the room humming with residual energy—static that crackled against the skin. The broken pedestal still glowed faintly, pulsing from the ring Lorrisa had locked back into place.

Kong, cradled in Lorrisa’s arm, shivered weakly but was breathing steadily. She held him close, her other hand pressed protectively over his fur.

Gee watched her, then turned toward Sebastian. “This is your mess now too. Hope you brought more than bullets.”

Sebastian didn’t take the bait. “I brought ambition. That’s more than most people ever survive with.”

Hamid stood at the far archway, scanning the exit routes. “We’re exposed here. And judging by what we just saw, this chamber was just the *reception room*.”

Lorrisa looked up. “If we go back, we die slowly. If we go forward… we might die faster, but at least we’ll know *why*.”

One of Sebastian’s mercs muttered, “Or we could just blow our way out and call it a day.”

“Try using C4 in a structure designed to collapse under pressure,” Gee said sharply. “See how far you get.”

Sebastian held up a hand, calming his man. “Let’s hear it. What’s your plan?”

Lorrisa stood now, gaze locked on the far hallway where the floor dipped into darkness.

“There’s a fifth ring somewhere deeper,” she said. “Every time we’ve found one, it’s been close to a convergence point—place of power, of confinement.

This chamber wasn't housing a ring. It was *reacting* to one nearby."

Hamid nodded. "And those... things? They're tied to proximity. They react when the rings shift."

Sebastian crossed his arms. "Then we're already in their territory."

Gee added, "And panic gets people killed."

He looked at Sebastian's remaining men—six now, two visibly shaken, eyes darting at every shadow.

Sebastian followed his gaze. "We move in pairs. No noise. No wandering."

Lorrisa turned toward the archway. "Then let's go."

DESCENDING CORRIDORS – MINUTES LATER

The walls changed as they descended. What had once been ritual stone carvings gave way to smoother black surfaces—volcanic rock polished until it reflected faint flickers of light like obsidian mirrors.

Each foot fall echoed oddly. The air became dense. Movement was dampened, as if the mountain itself were trying to slow them.

Gee and Lorrisa moved in tandem, both reading the walls differently but complementarily. He checked for structural weaknesses and trip hazards; she deciphered glyphs, trying to determine which paths were warded or mapped to specific energies.

Behind them, Hamid walked beside Khouri. The demolitions expert was sweating heavily despite the cold, fingering the clasp of his satchel every few seconds.

Two of the younger mercs—Jensen and Loire—whispered quietly behind the group.

“I don’t like this,” Jensen muttered. “Not natural. Not even haunted. Like we’re *inside something*.”

“Shut up,” Loire hissed. “Just keep moving.”

That’s when the passage narrowed again.

A shallow bridge crossed a chasm cut clean through the mountain—only about five feet wide, but no railing, and a sheer drop into darkness that seemed to stretch forever. The group paused.

Gee crouched low, testing the bridge. “Stable. Hand-carved.”

Lorrisa examined the sides. “No traps, but it’s pressure-activated. It records passage.”

“What does that mean?” Khouri asked.

Gee replied, “Means if you try to sneak across… it’ll know.”

Sebastian waved the first two men forward.

Jensen and Loire stepped carefully onto the bridge.

Loire made it halfway before something on the far wall—just at the edge of the light—*moved*.

Not much. Just a *shiver* in the stone. Loire stopped. “What was that?” Jensen turned. “What?”

Loire backed up too fast—heel caught, arms windmilling. He slipped. Gee lunged for him—but too far to reach.

Loire fell.

His scream echoed for what felt like minutes.

Then silence.

No thud.

Just the nothingness of bottomless black.

Lorrisa exhaled. “He panicked.” Sebastian said nothing.

But Jensen? He turned white. He stood there, frozen, not even breathing.

Then—

He *bolted*.

"No!" Lorrisa shouted.

He took off back across the bridge—but faster, noisier.

The far wall moved again—faster this time.

A ripple.

Then a dart of *black mass* streaked toward the bridge—like a thrown spear of smoke and shadow.

It hit Jensen mid-sprint.   And he was gone.

Not a scream this time.   Just... *erased*.

Kong shivered and buried his head in Lorrisa's jacket. Gee stepped onto the bridge. "We move. Now. Quiet. Fast. But *not* rushed."

They crossed in pairs, careful and silent. One by one, they made it.

Sebastian was last. He crossed alone.

When his boots touched the far side, the wall settled again—like it had been watching.

The corridor opened into a smaller, dome-shaped room. At its center was a pedestal, surrounded by four stone statues—each depicting a faceless figure holding a ring-shaped object in one hand and a torch in the other.

Lorrisa approached it slowly.

The pedestal held a recess, smaller than the seal chamber's—but designed to hold something specific.

She knelt and ran a thumb along the edges.

Gee joined her.

"That groove's fresh," he said.

Hamid asked, "One of the other rings?" Lorrisa shook her head. "No. *A fifth.*"

Sebastian stepped forward. "Then we're close."

Kong peeked out from Lorrisa's coat. He looked toward one of the statues—and hissed.

The torch in that statue's hand flickered. Once. Then stayed still. Gee whispered, "We're not done." Lorrisa looked at him. "We've only just begun."

MOMENTS LATER.

The four statues stood silently around the pedestal, each about eight feet tall and carved from dark stone veined with quartz. Identical in posture: heads bowed, left arms raised holding torch-shaped rods, right hands cradling a simple, hollow ring.

The pedestal at the center was smooth and octagonal, with a shallow bowl-like depression carved into it—precisely the size to house a single ring.

Lorrisa walked around it slowly, flashlight scanning each statue.

“Solomon’s seal,” she said. “Four corners, four watchers. Torch and ring.”

Gee knelt beside the pedestal. “You think the fifth ring goes here?”

“Eventually,” she answered. “But this isn’t just a display. It’s a mechanism. And a *test.*”

Sebastian eyed the chamber. “A puzzle, then. What's the trick?”

Hamid crouched near the fourth statue and gestured. “Look at their rings—each one is facing a different direction.”

Gee stood and began to circle with Lorrisa, inspecting. “They’re rotated. Not randomly.”

“Compass points,” Lorrisa said. “North, east, south, west.”

Hamid added, “And the torches?”

Lorrisa turned her light upward. “Tilted differently. One straight. One down. Two angled.”

Sebastian frowned. “There’s a pattern here, yes?”

“There always is,” Gee said. “That’s the rule.”

Lorrisa stared at the torch-bearing hands. “Four guardians. Four truths. The ring and the torch—the seal and the flame. Light and obedience.”

Gee added, “Each torch aligns to a virtue. One of Solomon’s laws.”

They moved around again, comparing postures. Then Hamid spoke:

“One torch points down. Toward the floor. As if rejecting something.”

Lorrisa looked up at that one. “Maybe humility.”

Sebastian snapped, “Enough talk. What activates it?”

Lorrisa turned slowly to him. “Rushing this could get you all killed. Again.”

Sebastian’s jaw twitched.

She turned back to the pedestal. “These statues weren’t just meant to be looked at. They’re *interactive.*”

Gee nodded toward the base of one. “Pressure plates.”

She looked closer. "Yes."

Then to the bowl in the pedestal. "And we place something in here—maybe one of the rings."

Gee took out one of the four. "You think it's keyed?"

"We test that *very* carefully," she replied.

They placed one of the rings gently into the bowl.

Nothing.

Then Lorrisa stepped onto the plate of the north-facing statue. Its torch raised *slightly* in response, casting a golden glint on the floor.

"Something's happening," Gee said.

Hamid stepped onto the east-facing plate. That torch dipped lower.

Sebastian stood back, arms crossed, observing.

"Wait," Lorrisa said. "Step off. Let's try another order."

She reset it—ring removed.

Then: Gee on the west. Hamid on north. Lorrisa herself on the south.

Nothing.

Then, a faint tremor beneath their feet.

The *east statue's torch flared*.

Lorrisa pointed. "That's it. That was the start."

"The east statue responds to the right alignment of people and ring," Gee muttered.

"Then it's order *and* symbolism," Lorrisa said. "They must be stepped on in the right sequence... with the ring placed for each attempt."

Hamid raised a brow. "So trial and error."

"No," she said, kneeling again. "Trial and *interpretation*."

They studied the symbols at the base of each statue—barely visible glyphs. Gee translated aloud:

"North: 'To lead with wisdom.'
East: 'To bear the burden of fire.'
South: 'To yield one's glory.'
West: 'To guard the shadowed truth.'"

Lorrisa inhaled sharply. "It's a riddle. A progression."

Sebastian finally stepped forward. "Say it."

Lorrisa looked up at the statues one by one. "First, the burden of fire must be taken—east. Then comes humility—south. Then wisdom—north. Finally... the one who guards the truth—west."

Gee nodded. “We follow that order.”

They took position:

Hamid at East.
Lorrisa at South.
Gee at North.
Sebastian—though clearly annoyed—at West.

Lorrisa placed the ring into the pedestal.

Silence.

Then, slowly, each torch glowed. One by one. A soft golden fire shimmered within each statue’s outstretched arm.

Then—the pedestal sank.

Grinding stone. A lock disengaging.

The wall behind the south statue split open, revealing a narrow alcove with a raised pedestal inside.

And upon it—

A fifth ring!

The ring shimmered in a faint, golden halo. Unlike the others, its surface was etched not only with symbols—but with faces. Four tiny visages encircled the band.

Gee muttered, “The Watchers.”

Lorrisa stepped forward. The air was heavier here.

Sebastian followed—but not too close.

As she reached toward the ring, the torches behind them dimmed.

Kong stirred in her pack.

Then...

She lifted the ring.

And the fire in all four torches extinguished at once.

They moved in silence now—every breath calculated, every step deliberate.

The fifth ring rested in a reinforced container strapped to Lorrisa's back. Unlike the others, it didn't glow. It pulsed softly with heat. Not aggressive, but alive.

Gee led the group through the same passages they'd entered hours ago. Sebastian and his men took the rear this time—tighter formation, weapons out but lowered.

No one spoke.

The mountain seemed to allow their exit. For now.

Kong stirred once in Lorrisa's satchel but remained silent—sensitive to the tension, the weight of what they carried.

Hamid whispered, “Still no movement. No more guardians.”

“Maybe they only guard the ring,” Gee replied, eyes forward. “Maybe they’re watching.”

“Or maybe,” Lorrisa said grimly, “they *want* us to leave.”

MOUNTAIN ENTRANCE – DAYBREAK

The mouth of the mountain yawned open like the jaws of a sleeping beast. Cool dawn wind licked at their faces as they emerged—squinting against the sunlight after hours in the dark.

For a moment, the fresh air felt like salvation.

Gee exhaled. “I’ve never been so happy to see dust and rocks.”

Lorrisa turned to glance back at the carved seal far behind them—now dimmed, silent.

“We shouldn’t have found it,” she murmured.

Sebastian stepped up beside her. “But we did.”

She turned slowly.

That was the moment everything changed.

Sebastian’s remaining men—three of them now—raised their weapons.

Sebastian extended one hand, palm open.

"Time to hand them over."

Gee tensed. "You can't be serious."

"Quite," Sebastian said. "You did the hard work. I thank you. Truly. But you're not meant to carry them forward."

Hamid stepped between Lorrisa and Sebastian. "You want to get into a shootout *now*?"

Sebastian's tone stayed smooth. "No. I want to avoid one. But I'm prepared for it. And frankly, you've all seen what these things can do. They belong with someone who can protect them."

"You mean exploit them," Lorrisa snapped.

"Semantics," he said with a shrug.

Gee raised his weapon. "Come any closer—"

But Lorrisa stopped him. Quietly. Calmly.

She reached for the container and unstrapped it.

Then held it out.

Sebastian approached slowly and took it from her hands.

"Very wise."

His men collected the others—the first four rings—still sealed in protective sleeves in Gee's pack.

Then Sebastian turned, walking toward one of the parked SUVs.

"Make sure their weapons are disassembled. Leave them the vehicle. We're not savages."

"I could argue that," Gee muttered.

But then—

From beyond the outer ridge—

A horn blew.

Low.

Ancient.

Followed by the rumble of approaching feet.

Everyone turned.

And then they saw her.

Meskela.

Striding from the slope above with nearly *one hundred forty armed men and* women behind her—robes blending with the dust, rifles in hand, blades at their sides.

They moved like desert ghosts.

Sebastian's men scrambled, raising their weapons—but Meskela raised her hand and her people *stopped.*

Silence.

Meskela stepped forward, her voice like iron wrapped in silk. "Return them now."

Sebastian turned, expression unreadable. "You're late."

"I was never gone," she said. "I've been watching."

Lorrisa stepped forward slowly, standing now beside Sebastian, facing the desert priestess. "You knew this would happen."

Meskela nodded once. "I told you: there is a price."

Sebastian barked a dry laugh. "And what is this, then? A reckoning?"

"No," Meskela said. "A crossroads."

She looked at all of them now—Lorrisa, Gee, Hamid, Sebastian. Her voice carried weight.

"You have five rings. Five is power. Five is temptation. Five... *unlocks.*"

Gee whispered, "She knows."

Meskela took one more step forward. "There are forces in this world that *must remain buried*. Those rings are not keys to riches. They are coils to a prison. One you've now weakened."

Sebastian scoffed. "You think I fear superstition?"

Meskela's eyes sharpened. "I think you've never met a god who *didn't* need worship to kill."

Her soldiers raised their weapons.

Sebastian did not retreat. But for the first time, his eyes darted—to his men, to Lorrisa, to the open road.

Hamid spoke up.

"Let us walk. All of us. If you want a war, none of us are walking away. But if you want the truth—let us decide what happens to the rings. Together."

Silence stretched.

Then Meskela lowered her hand.

But her eyes never left Sebastian.

Moments later...

The five rings now sat in the center of the assembled group—surrounded by stone, sky, and steel.

Sebastian's men, hopelessly, outnumbered.

Meskela's warriors surrounding.

Lorrisa and Gee side by side.

No one touched the rings. Not yet.

The fifth pulsed faintly. A heartbeat in gold.

Meskela spoke: "Now... we talk."

The rings lay between them, glinting under the growing sun—five artifacts of impossible age and silent danger.

They formed a loose circle on the warm stone, each casting faint ripples of heat into the air. Though inert, they radiated weight far beyond their physical form.

Meskela stood over them, flanked by her warriors. Neither she nor her people moved for some time. Just watching. Measuring.

Sebastian crouched nearby, arms resting on his knees, sweat darkening the collar of his shirt. One of his men nursed a twisted ankle. Another muttered prayers under his breath.

Gee, leaning against the dead hood of one of the SUVs, kept his hand near the hilt of a sheathed survival blade. His lips were dry. He said nothing.

Hamid sat cross-legged beside Kong, who still hadn't fully recovered from the chain-creature attack. The little monkey trembled occasionally, clinging to Hamid's scarf.

Lorrisa stood a few feet from Meskela.

"I'm not handing them to you," she said, her voice firm but low.

"You already did," Meskela replied without looking at her. "When you left the mountain alive."

Lorrisa stepped forward, eyes locked. "We can work together."

Meskela turned, her expression unreadable. "No. You *dug* for power. I guard what should never be *un*buried."

Sebastian stood now, brushing dust from his sleeves. "Then we're at a stalemate."

Meskela finally looked at him. "You believe you are owed something. You are not."

"You watched us die back there," Sebastian said coldly. "Watched them die."

"And I mourned them," she said. "But you were warned. You knew."

Silence again. Then Meskela knelt.

She began gathering the rings—slowly, reverently—placing each into a silk-wrapped pouch held by one of her lieutenants. One. Two. Three. Four.

She paused at the fifth. Then lifted it.

The air seemed to pull inward when she did. Wind passed over the ridge like a breath being held.

She placed the fifth ring in the pouch. Stood. Turned.

"Leave this place," she said, motioning for her group to retrieve their SUV's.

Sebastian stepped forward. "You're not taking our vehicles."

She faced him fully now. "You'll live. Which is more than many do."

Lorrisa's fists clenched. "You said we needed to talk."

Meskela nodded. "And now you understand. You weren't chosen. You were *tested*. And you barely passed."

She gestured to her warriors.

Without words, they moved swiftly—opening the hoods of both SUVs, removing the distributors, tossing the radios, even draining the water from every canister they found. The sound of punctured plastic echoed across the ridge.

Gee stepped forward. “Hey! We’re in the middle of the damn desert!”

Meskela’s voice was calm. “And you’re still alive.”

Sebastian’s men raised their weapons—but one sharp glare from Meskela’s second-in-command made them hesitate.

Hamid rose slowly. “This is how it ends?”

“No,” Meskela said. She turned to Lorrisa, then to Sebastian. “This is how it *continues*... without you.”

Then she and her people turned. Within minutes, they were gone—disappearing into the shifting light of the dunes, their passage as silent as smoke.

The five rings went with them.

The sun climbed higher.

The heat bore down like punishment.

The group sat beneath a torn cloth rigged between two ruined vehicle frames. Lorrisa knelt beside Kong, giving him the last drops from her canteen cap. Gee worked quietly beside her, turning a metal fan blade into a crude solar mirror—trying to reflect signal flashes upward.

Sebastian sat apart, a rifle laid across his lap, his face a mixture of fury and calculation.

Hamid paced slowly, eyes scanning the horizon. “We have maybe five hours before this turns dangerous.”

Gee glanced up. “It’s already dangerous.”

“No water, no comms, no rings,” Hamid muttered. “We are so screwed.”

Lorrisa didn’t respond. She reached into her jacket pocket, slowly removed the old parchment Meskela had slipped her back in the village—the one written in Ge’ez. She unfolded it again. For the first time, she *read it fully.*

It said: *“He who seeks the rings seeks to undo the chains of the fallen. But she who understands the burden... becomes the key.”*

Lorrisa looked at the horizon, eyes narrowing.

“Meskela’s not done,” she said softly.

Gee looked over. “What do you mean?”

“She didn’t take the rings to hide them,” Lorrisa said. “She took them to finish something. Something we started.”

Sebastian stood now, looking down at her. “Then where is she going?”

Lorrisa rose slowly. “She’s going to find the *next ring*.”

Chapter 11

The sun had scorched the backs of their necks by the time the thunder rolled in—not from clouds, but engines.

The whine of rotary blades broke the desert silence, followed by the shimmer of dark green vehicles emerging from the heat haze.

Lorrisa sat up first from where she'd been sheltering beside the gutted SUV. Gee stood slowly. Hamid waved his jacket overhead.

The trucks that approached were marked in Amharic and carried the insignia of the *Ethiopian Federal Rangers*—a special division of military intelligence. And trailing behind them: a light transport helicopter.

One of the rangers—a captain with a square jaw and dust-covered boots—approached, rifle slung but relaxed.

"We saw the fire," he said, nodding toward the distant smoke still curling skyward. "Tank explosion. Your work?"

"No," Gee answered. "But the guys responsible aren't far from here."

"We'll take it from here," the captain replied.

Then he gestured to his men.

"Get them to Mekelle. They look like hell."

Mekelle's base buzzed with controlled chaos when they arrived. A medic immediately pulled Kong away from Lorrisa and into a veterinary tent. Gee was led to a field surgeon. Hamid asked for bottled water before anything else.

Sebastian stood near the rear of the convoy, arms folded, one cheek freshly stitched from a flying shard. His remaining men flanked him, subdued but alive.

As the sun dipped low over the base, casting the yard in copper tones, Sebastian approached the trio one last time.

He didn't wear his usual arrogance.

Just calm.

Dangerous calm.

"You're no longer in possession of the rings," he said, voice measured. "That makes you irrelevant to me. For now."

Gee opened his mouth—but Sebastian held up a finger.

“We’re civilized people. Let’s not confuse civility with mercy.”

Then he walked away, boots silent on the concrete.

It was a modest hotel perched on a slope above Mekelle proper—stone façade, wrought-iron balconies, slow-spinning ceiling fans.

The military had arranged rooms—one each. After what they’d been through, no one argued.

Gee showered first. The water turned rust-red for the first minute.

Hamid fell asleep still half-dressed, shoes on.

Lorrisa stood under the water until it ran cold.

When she emerged, towel wrapped tight, she looked at herself in the mirror for a long time. Not studying her face—but her eyes.

Still there.

Still fighting.

The city of Mekelle the next morning was alive with noise and heat. Markets spilled into the streets, camels plodded alongside honking taxis, and children hawked dates and spiced bread to anyone who slowed down.

Gee stood outside the hotel with a bitter espresso and a borrowed newspaper.

Hamid reappeared first—fresh shirt, tactical pants, sunglasses.

Lorrisa arrived last, in a linen blouse and tan scarf wrapped around her hair.

“You look… not dead,” Gee offered.

“I feel worse,” she replied, sipping from his cup.

That’s when Hamid pointed across the square.

A massive white banner hung from a modern glass building two blocks away:

“Regional Diplomatic Forum – Hosted Gala: TONIGHT at 7PM – Invite Only”

“You thinking what I’m thinking?” Gee asked. “Crash it?” Lorrisa said.

“Make an impression,” Hamid clarified. “Find answers,” Lorrisa corrected.

They spent the afternoon gathering intel. The hotel concierge mentioned the guest list included ministers, European diplomats, and military attachés. No names, of course. But the event would be held at the Gheralta Conference Hall, a former colonial mansion-turned-venue near the hills above Mekelle.

Gee and Hamid would handle ingress. Lorrisa, blending easily, would scout inside.

A contact Hamid bribed with cigarettes produced two forged passes and a staff credential.

By dusk, they were dressed like half the security team—and one elegant cultural attaché.

Music filtered through the grand hall like honey. Strings and soft drums. Gold lighting cast long shadows across white-clothed tables. Champagne glasses clinked. People whispered in multiple languages.

Gee adjusted the collar of his tailored shirt—borrowed, slightly too tight.

Hamid remained near the bar, posing as liaison staff.

Lorrisa walked the perimeter, chin high, scarf replaced with a sleek braid. Then she stopped.

At the far end of the room, surrounded by generals, ministers, and at least one international ambassador, stood a woman in a midnight blue gown that shimmered like wet ink.

Her hair was pinned. Her earrings matched the stars.

Meskela.

She smiled, mid-conversation. Clinked glasses.

As elegant and commanding as any dignitary in the room.

Lorrisa stared. Gee stepped beside her. “Well,” he whispered. “She cleans up nice.”

Meskela noticed them at once—but didn’t acknowledge them.

She raised her glass toward a military attaché and gestured toward a regional map on the far wall. The crowd around her nodded. Listened.

Lorrisa's voice dropped low. "She's not just a guardian."

Gee nodded slowly. "She's a power broker." Then Meskela's eyes finally met theirs.

And she smiled.

The chamber shimmered with light. Crystal chandeliers reflected off marble floors, casting subtle kaleidoscopes over the bodies in motion—diplomats, dignitaries, officers, and opportunists moving through a carefully choreographed performance.

At the center of it all, Meskela stood radiant in midnight blue—laughing softly, her posture regal, utterly at home among the world's elite.

Then her eyes landed on Gee.

She expected tension. She expected confrontation.

She did *not* expect him to step directly into her space, offer a hand with a slight bow, and say: "Shall we?"

Before she could object, Gee's other hand was at her waist, and the two of them were in motion—sliding into the rhythm of the room's slow waltz.

"Bold," she said, lips not moving.

"I get that a lot," he replied smoothly. "But don't worry—I'm housebroken."

"Then why are you stepping into a lion's den?"

"Because lions don't hide in caves. They stand on marble and smile for cameras."

Meskela's mouth curved faintly. "You've improved your metaphors."

Gee's voice dropped lower, face still smiling. "Where are the rings?"

"Safe," she replied.

"Safe from whom?"

"From everyone—including you."

He pivoted her gently, hand tightening just enough to press a point. "You dressed for war in silk."

"You can't fight everything with bullets."

"Funny. That's what Sebastian thought."

Her body tensed just enough to feel it under his hand. "He's here?" "Not now, not tonight," Gee said. "But he will be."

The music swelled. Their feet glided. She asked quietly, "Why are you here?"

"To see if you're as dangerous as you looked in the desert. Or just as good at pretending."

Meskela's eyes locked on his. "The two are not exclusive."

ACROSS THE BALLROOM...

Lorrisa took a cautious sip of her champagne. Her eyes followed Meskela and Gee, with a hint of hidden jealously—dancing like old friends, but she could read the tension in their shoulders.

A voice behind her said, "You don't dance enough."

She turned.

Standing behind her in a sharply tailored dark gray suit and a wine-red tie was Carlos Conchata-FBI.

Smooth. Smiling. Coiled like a spring under silk.

"I didn't realize I was on your schedule," Lorrisa said coolly. Carlos extended a hand. "You are now."

Lorrisa hesitated.

But the music was already shifting. And the room was watching.

She placed her hand in his. They moved to the floor.

Carlos's movements were perfect—measured, suave, unassuming.

His voice stayed low. “I assume you’ve had a busy week.”

“I assume you’re still pretending to be my friend.”

Carlos chuckled. “I’m a lot of things, Dr. Santos. Friendly is just the easiest one to fake.”

Lorrisa studied him as they turned. “What’s your angle here?”

“I found out about these rings you and your ex-husband have been chasing. I don’t have the rings. You don’t have the rings. But we both know who does.”

Her steps faltered slightly. “You're after Meskela.”

“I’m after stability. Which is a word people like her don’t value enough in today’s world.”

“Neither do people like you,” she said.

Carlos leaned in slightly, the image of intimacy—just loud enough for her alone.

“She’s about to make a move that will change more than treasure maps and tombs. Are you ready for that?”

Lorrisa looked toward Meskela again.

Still dancing. Still smiling.

Carlos followed her gaze. "You ever wonder why someone like her is allowed in a room like this?"

Lorrisa whispered, "Allowed... or invited?"

Carlos grinned. "Now you're asking the right questions."

Gee and Lorrisa active on the dance floor simultaneously

Gee twirled Meskela gently, catching her gaze again as they came out of the spin.

"You don't seem surprised I'm here."

"I'm not," she replied. "You're like water. You always find the cracks."

"Cute. But you took something important."

"I protected it."

"We earned it."

"You barely survived it."

He leaned in. "You're not just a guardian, Meskela. You're a player."

Her gaze sharpened. "Then act like one. Stop dancing, and move your pieces."

Gee smirked, even as his heartbeat kicked. "Next time, don't bring one hundred and forty men."

"Next time, you won't see me coming."

Lorrisa moved in step with Carlos, the tension between them offset by the elegance of the space. He held her respectfully—one hand at her waist, the other loose and guiding.

"You don't dance enough," he said again, a little softer.

She wasn't smiling. "You don't show up without a purpose."

Carlos's expression didn't change, but his eyes flicked toward the northern wall—where two sharply dressed men with matching American lapel pins stood in quiet conversation with an Ethiopian economic advisor.

"See those guys?" he asked. "Commerce Division. Fresh from Geneva. They're here to finalize agricultural partnerships."

"That's what the press release says," Lorrisa replied.

He gave her a conspiratorial nod. "It's also half true."

She followed his gaze to the opposite corner—where a Chinese envoy in a blue silk tunic sipped champagne while a translator whispered into his ear.

"Let me guess," she said. "Rare earths."

"Bingo," Carlos murmured. "But not just what's under the ground. They want *what's buried*."

He leaned in slightly. "Ethiopia's about to become the next battleground—history, minerals, politics. And whichever side gets cultural leverage? They win soft power for a generation."

Lorrisa's pulse quickened. "So the rings aren't just mystical artifacts anymore."

"They never were," Carlos said. "They're bargaining chips. And right now? You and I are the only ones in this room who've actually touched one."

She kept her posture poised, her voice steady. "And Meskela?"

Carlos's smile faded. "She's already played her hand. We're about to find out how high she intends to bid."

The music had softened. Most of the guests drifted into smaller circles—laughing, negotiating, maneuvering. Lorrisa stood near a marble column now, watching Meskela navigate a trio of generals like she belonged in every war room in the Horn of Africa.

Carlos reappeared beside her with a new drink and a clipped smirk.

"She's good, isn't she?"

"She's *dangerous*," Lorrisa corrected.

Carlos nodded toward a man standing just beyond Meskela's orbit—a tall, silver-haired European with a subtle NATO pin on his lapel.

"Colonel Etienne Favre. French Defense Attaché. Been trying to get military access to old colonial staging sites. Guess who just promised him 'cooperative discretion'?"

Lorrisa tensed. "Meskela?"

Carlos sipped. "She's trading influence for autonomy. She doesn't need weapons—she needs time. The more global players she keeps at arm's length, the more ground she claims while no one's looking."

Gee joined them from the buffet line, balancing a toothpick and a plate of suspiciously spicy lamb.

"Did I hear someone say 'autonomy' like this was a TED Talk?"

Lorrisa glanced at him. "She's cutting deals. International ones."

Gee raised an eyebrow. "Without any of us noticing?"

Carlos gestured with his glass. "Not true. I noticed."

Lorrisa asked, “And what exactly are *you* doing here, Carlos?”

“Monitoring,” he said. “The rings aren’t just cultural relics—they’re leverage. Whoever has them can create—or destroy—alliances overnight. Meskela understands this. And so does someone else.”

He paused. “Sebastian. Gee’s smile vanished.

Carlos lowered his voice. “The U.S. has eyes on him. So do the Saudis. Chinese intelligence flagged him six months ago as a ‘non-state negotiator.’ He’s not just after mysticism. He’s selling access.”

“To what?” Lorrisa asked.

Carlos’s gaze sharpened. “To the *next vault*.”

MOMENTS LATER...

Hamid, seated casually at the upstairs overlook, watched through small binoculars as Meskela laughed with an OAU representative and an Egyptian diplomat. She never stayed in one group too long. Never poured her own wine. Never raised her voice.

She was fluent in every room she entered.

Below, Lorrisa felt the pressure rising again—not in her chest, but in the atmosphere of the gala.

The room felt less like a celebration and more like a chessboard.

The pieces were moving. And Meskela wasn't the queen.

She was the *player.*

The gala continued behind heavy doors—music muffled, laughter distant, the sound of glasses clinking a far-off echo of civility.

The private chamber was quiet, low-lit, and empty save for two chairs and a table of untouched wine. Ornate brass lanterns flickered above carved stone walls—a relic of colonial design dressed in modern polish.

Lorrisa stood by the arched window, watching the city lights stretch out across the hills of Mekelle.

Behind her, the door opened. Footsteps—measured, familiar.

Meskela.

She entered with no guards, no weapons, no entourage. Just confidence in silk and fire in her spine.

Lorrisa didn't turn. "You made quite the impression tonight."

Meskela replied softly, "You disapprove."

"I don't have time to disapprove," Lorrisa said. "I'm too busy trying to understand how a desert priestess is now playing political chess with generals and trade envoys."

"Funny," Meskela said. "I thought you might ask why I *had* to."

Lorrisa turned finally.

The two women faced each other—no music, no men, no masks.

Just purpose.

"I've risked my life to keep those rings from people who'd misuse them," Lorrisa said. "I thought you were doing the same."

"I am."

"Then why take them from me?"

Meskela stepped forward. "Because you don't know what you're carrying."

Lorrisa's jaw tightened. "We've seen what they do. We've *bled* for what they do."

"You've scratched the surface," Meskela said. "But you still think this is about Solomon's treasure. About secrets. But it's not. It's about *balance.*"

"Balance?" Lorrisa echoed. "There's nothing balanced about stripping us of everything and walking away."

Meskela's eyes burned. "And yet here you are. Still standing. Still asking questions. That's more than most who chase these rings get."

A beat of silence.

Then Meskela walked slowly to the window, placing a hand on the frame.

"Do you know what Ethiopia is to the world?" she asked.

Lorrisa didn't answer.

"It's a crossroads," Meskela continued. "Always has been. Trade, war, language, belief—it all passes through us. And now the world is looking here again. Not for gold. Not for oil. But for control."

Lorrisa crossed her arms. "So you're going to let them all dance, then pick your partners?"

"No," Meskela said. "I'm going to control the music."

That landed.

Lorrisa exhaled. “And the rings?”

Meskela looked back. “You want to protect the world from what they might unlock. I want to protect the world from those who believe they *deserve* to.”

She stepped closer.

“We are not enemies, Lorrisa. But we are not the same.”

“And if I come for them again?” Lorrisa asked.

“Then I’ll stop you. And I’ll weep doing it.”

They stood in silence—two women bound by history, divided by purpose.

Then Meskela added, quieter now:

“No one who touches these rings stays clean. Not you. Not me. Not anyone.”

Lorrisa’s voice was dry. “Then why fight for them?”

“Because someone has to carry the burden. I choose to bear it.”

Meskela stepped to the door, hand on the latch.

She paused.

“One more thing.”

Lorrisa looked up.

"When the sixth ring appears... don't follow it. Let it pass."

"Why?"

Meskela's expression was unreadable. But her voice was steel.

"Because the sixth is not a key. It's a *signal.*"

Then she left, closing the door behind her with a whisper of silk and certainty.

In a private sitting room moments after Meskela's departure.

The door clicked shut with finality.

Lorrisa stood in the stillness, staring at nothing.

The lanterns swayed gently above her, their glow trembling as if uncertain whether to hold or flicker out.

She placed her palms on the window frame and leaned forward—brow resting against the cool glass.

The sixth is not a key...

The words echoed in her skull, slow and cold and impossibly weighted.

A signal.

Her breathing was shallow.

In the dim reflection of the window, she could see her face. Strained. Dust still at the corners of her eyes. Salt crusted faintly along her cheekbones.

She looked like a survivor.

She felt like a detonator.

The rings were gone. Meskela had outmaneuvered them all. But what gnawed at her gut wasn't the loss.

It was the certainty that Meskela hadn't lied.

Something bigger was coming. And somehow, she was still in the center of it. The floor creaked behind her.

She didn't turn.

A voice said, low and warm:

"Thought you might be in here."

She exhaled. "Of course you did."

Gee walked slowly across the room and stood a respectful distance behind her, hands in his pockets.

"She tell you bedtime stories?"

Lorrisa said nothing for a long moment. Then, quietly, "She told me to stop chasing the next ring."

Gee tilted his head. "Smart of her. If I were holding the rings, I'd tell us the same."

“No,” Lorrisa said. “She wasn’t afraid I’d take it. She was afraid of what it *means*.”

Gee frowned. “What does it mean?”

“She said the sixth is a signal.”

He exhaled through his nose. “That’s... not ominous at all.”

Lorrisa turned finally, facing him fully.

“You ever get the feeling we didn’t find the rings?” she asked.

“We just tripped over them?”

She nodded. “Like they were always going to be found. Just waiting for the next hands.”

Gee studied her for a long beat. Then walked to the small table, pulled out a chair, and sat down heavily.

He looked up at her.

“You remember that dig in Cuenca?”

She blinked. “The one with the hollowed-out obsidian jar?”

“Yeah. Everyone thought it was an urn, but you said it was a warning vessel.”

Lorrisa managed a smile. “Because of the script scratched on the inside lip.”

Gee grinned. “Exactly. And the whole room thought you were nuts.”

“They usually do.”

“But you were right.” He paused. “You’re right now, too. Something’s coming.”

Lorrisa’s voice was a whisper. “We’re not ready.”

“Nope,” Gee said. “But we’re better off than most.”

He gestured to the empty chair across from him.

“Sit. Just for a minute. Before the world cracks open again.”

Lorrisa hesitated.

Then she walked over, pulled out the chair, and sat.

Not across from him.

Beside him.

Kong’s absence was felt in the silence. So was Sebastian’s. So were the rings.

But for just this moment, they weren’t archaeologists. Or fugitives. Or keys to ancient wars.

They were just two people. Holding their breath before the next storm.

Chapter 12

The silence didn't last. At the hotel Lorrisa and Gee was discussing the situation further.

A knock at their hotel door shattered it—three taps, deliberate and calm.

Lorrisa and Gee exchanged a glance. Not alarmed. Not yet. But aware.

Gee rose and crossed to the door. He opened it halfway.

Standing on the other side, in a crisp slate-gray suit and a look that split the difference between welcome and warning, was *Carlos Conchata*.

"Evening," he said smoothly. "Mind if I intrude?"

Gee didn't move. "We were just about to call it a night."

Carlos's eyes flicked past him to Lorrisa, who stood beside the table, arms folded. She hadn't said a word, but the look in her eyes said plenty.

Carlos offered a faint smile. "Not even for old friends?"

"We were never friends," she said flatly.

Carlos shrugged. "Then let's call this a professional courtesy."

Gee opened the door fully, letting him in without stepping aside. Just making him walk around. Carlos did so, as if he hadn't noticed the snub. He moved to the table and set down a leather folder with the care of a surgeon placing a scalpel.

"Intel," he said. "Fresh off a satellite relay and a very nervous field asset."

Lorrisa narrowed her eyes. "Why bring it to me?"

Carlos looked her in the eye. "Because the next ring just moved."

The room froze.

He tapped the folder.

"A facility was breached outside Lalibela. Not just any building—a crypt hidden beneath an old stone monastery. Your name came up in a comms intercept before the breach. Someone out there thinks you're the key to opening what's below it."

Lorrisa walked over slowly, eyes still locked on him, and opened the folder.

Inside: grainy aerial images. Heat signatures. Satellite overlays. Scribbled notes in Amharic, translated in the margins.

Then—one photo, frozen mid-frame.

A flash of *golden metal,* half buried in dark soil. The rim of a ring.

Not like the others.

This one was *darker*, more angular. Its surface etched with six-pointed geometries that looked like warnings rather than symbols.

She looked up. "Who took this?"

Carlos's smile faded. "We don't know. The asset's dead."

A long silence passed.

Gee moved closer, looking at the photo. "That's the sixth ring?"

Carlos nodded once. "Appeared hours ago. Buried for God knows how long. But someone knew where to find it."

"And you're just handing this over?" Lorrisa asked.

Carlos tilted his head. "No. I'm asking for something."

"Here it comes," Gee muttered.

Carlos continued. "If you go after it, I go with you."

Lorrisa arched a brow. "To help?"

"To witness. And to make sure the U.S. doesn't get left out of whatever's coming."

"That's a hell of a pitch," Gee said. "You expecting a finder's fee?"

Carlos met his eyes. "I'm expecting survival. Yours, mine, and maybe the planet's."

Another beat of silence.

Lorrisa closed the folder slowly. "We're leaving at dawn."

Carlos smiled again. "I'll pack light."

He turned and left without another word, his footsteps retreating down the hallway.

Gee exhaled. "We should ditch him."

"We probably will," Lorrisa said. "But not yet?"

She shook her head. "No. Not yet."

Gee studied her for a second. "You're really going after it, aren't you?"

Lorrisa nodded. "If it's a signal... I need to know who it's calling."

Gee shut the door behind Carlos with a soft click, then turned back to Lorrisa. She hadn't moved. Her fingers still rested on the folder like they were trying to feel truth through paper.

"He'll slow us down," Gee said.

She nodded absently. "Or buy us just enough time to see what's really going on."

From the hallway, a muffled *thump*, followed by a *sharp yelp*.

Then—*"Kong! You damn demon monkey! Get off—ay! My dates! Those were imported!"*

Gee cracked a smile. "I think the rest of our team is still active".

Lorrisa blinked and looked toward the commotion.

The door burst open.

Hamid stood in the doorway, eyes wide, hair a mess, and wearing a hotel robe that had clearly never been intended for someone of his size or dignity. His arms were full of half-squashed figs, an opened pack of roasted nuts, and what looked suspiciously like a bottle of pomegranate wine.

Kong was perched on his shoulder triumphantly, cheeks puffed, holding a toothpick like a dagger and chittering like he'd just defeated a warlord.

Gee leaned against the table. "Is this a new side hustle?"

Hamid scowled. "He broke into my minibar. Then into the hallway cart. Then—" he looked at Kong "—you found the executive suite's snack tray, didn't you, you fuzzy outlaw?"

Kong squeaked proudly and tossed a pistachio shell across the room.

Lorrisa sighed, walking forward and gently lifting Kong from Hamid's shoulder. "You're going to get us all kicked out."

Kong licked his fingers and draped himself over her arm like a spoiled child. Then gave a soft coo and tapped her cheek. She paused.

“Yeah,” she murmured. “I missed you too.”

Gee looked between them. “So... good news: we’re headed to Lalibela. Bad news: we’re not going alone.”

Hamid immediately groaned. “You invited Mr. Smile?”

“Carlos invited himself,” Lorrisa said.

Hamid plopped onto the room’s arm chair, wine bottle cradled like a newborn. “Then I’m definitely drinking tonight.”

Gee pointed to the chair. “Not too much. We’re moving at dawn.”

“Then I have exactly six hours to hate myself,” Hamid said, already uncorking.

Kong jumped from Lorrisa’s shoulder onto the minibar and grabbed a mini bottle of gin. He clinked it against Hamid’s wine in a celebratory toast.

Gee rubbed his face. “This is the team that’s going to outrun governments and ancient curses.”

Hamid raised his glass. “Cheers to that.”

Lorrisa watched them for a beat. Then—soft laughter. Not forced. Not bitter. Just... real.

For a moment, they were a team again. Bruised. Tired. Off-balance. But still together.

The sun hadn't yet cracked the horizon when they assembled outside the hotel—four shadows framed in the dusty blue of pre-dawn.

The **SUV** waiting at the curb looked too clean for what they were about to do.

Carlos leaned against the passenger door, perfectly dressed as always. His dark blazer didn't carry a single wrinkle, and his tie had the smug precision of a man who'd never sweated for a living.

Lorrisa stepped out first, Kong nestled in her satchel like a gremlin-sized stowaway. She adjusted her headscarf and glanced up at the still-blinking stars above Mekelle.

Gee followed, slinging his bag over one shoulder. "Remind me why we're trusting the guy who shows up with classified satellite photos and no follow-up questions?"

Hamid grunted behind them, dragging a duffel that thumped heavily with every step. "Because your ex-wife has a death wish. And I'm a sucker for loyalty."

Carlos smiled as they approached. “Beautiful morning.”

Gee stopped beside him. “We’ll see how beautiful you think it is when the gunfire starts.”

Carlos just opened the rear passenger door with a flourish. “After you.”

Lorrisa didn’t wait for the men to argue. She climbed in and let Kong hop across the seats to the back row. Hamid climbed in next, muttering something about coffee being a human right.

Gee paused at the door. “You sure about this?”

Lorrisa glanced at him, then out the window toward the awakening city. “Nope.”

That was good enough.

They drove.

The city blurred behind them, the streets quiet save for the occasional truck or wandering goat. Mekelle faded into the hills like a memory swallowed by time.

Lorrisa watched the road unfold—red dirt, rising mist, tall eucalyptus trees reaching like fingers to the morning sky.

Carlos sat in front, pointing out a turnoff without GPS.

“Shortcut,” he said.

Gee rolled his eyes. “If we end up in a ravine, I’m blaming you.”

“You blame me anyway,” Carlos replied without missing a beat.

In the back seat, Kong had commandeered a travel pillow and was now curled up like royalty beside a snoring Hamid. Lorrisa tried to stay focused, tried not to think about the photo in the folder. But the ring wouldn’t leave her thoughts.

Not just a key.
A signal.

She turned to Gee. “You believe it, don’t you? That it’s more than just treasure?”

He didn’t answer immediately. Then, “I believe the ground moves when we get close. That people change around these things. That we’re not chasing myth—we’re in it.”

Lorrisa nodded slowly. “Then we need to stop pretending we’re just explorers.”

Gee smirked. “So what are we?”

She looked out the window. “Messengers. Or warnings.”

The SUV bounced slightly as the dirt road narrowed.

In the front, Carlos lowered his sunglasses, eyes narrowing on the mountains rising in the distance.

“Welcome to Lalibela,” he said softly.

The ancient stone churches loomed far ahead, cut from the rock like secrets trying to breathe.

And beneath them—something waited.

The village of *Lalibela* lay draped across the hills like a tapestry woven from earth and faith—stone buildings hugging the slope, narrow paths winding through groves of olive and juniper, and locals moving with an unhurried rhythm that suggested time itself bent differently here.

The air smelled of roasted grains and incense.

Hamid stepped down from the SUV and stretched with a theatrical groan. “Alright. Rations, rope, batteries, and a decent blade for Kong in case he wants to duel a priest. Got it.”

Gee tossed him a canvas satchel. “And water tablets. Last thing I need is you hallucinating about flying goats again.”

“That was one time,” Hamid muttered.

The two men headed off toward the market square, their banter echoing between stone walls and goats bleating as if in judgment.

Lorrisa remained by the SUV, adjusting her satchel and slowly pulling her sunglasses into place. The morning light was sharp now—thin and golden, casting long shadows.

When she glanced sideways, she saw Carlos had already slipped away.

No words. No excuse. Just gone.

Her jaw tensed.

She looked down at Kong, who was now perched on the hood of the SUV, watching a butterfly with unsettling intensity.

“Let’s go for a walk,” she murmured.

He chirped, tail twitching, and leapt to her shoulder.

She moved through the village quietly, letting her steps blend with the rising murmur of morning—vendors setting out vegetables, children chasing one another through the alleys, monks filing silently between church walls carved into the rock itself.

She caught sight of Carlos just ahead, half-shadowed beside a crumbling stone archway. He was speaking to a local man—older, wrapped in a neutral robe, eyes sharp even from a distance.

Lorrisa slowed.

From her angle, she couldn't hear them. But body language told its own story.

Carlos leaned in.

The man nodded slowly.

Carlos removed something from his jacket—a folded cloth, small and heavy. He pressed it into the man's hand with precision, like an offering disguised as payment.

Lorrisa's pulse ticked upward.

The local tucked it away and stepped back, bowing his head once. Carlos said something final—then turned.

She ducked behind a fruit stand as Carlos passed within a few feet of her, oblivious.

Kong crouched low on her shoulder, perfectly still.

Only once Carlos disappeared back toward the road did she exhale and emerge, slipping quietly through the side streets.

Back at the SUV, Gee and Hamid were already returning, arms loaded with gear and snacks. Hamid had somehow acquired a straw hat and a carved walking stick.

"Tell me this doesn't make me look like an old explorer who secretly knows kung fu," he said.

Gee looked at him. "You look like a lost tourist who thinks raisins are a delicacy."

Lorrisa reached the vehicle just as they arrived.

Gee noticed her first. "Miss anything?"

She shook her head. "Not a thing."

Kong, from her shoulder, let out a single, quiet hiss in the direction Carlos had gone.

Lorrisa didn't comment.

But she was already reviewing every move Carlos had made since they'd met.

And now she had something new.

A question.

Not what he was after—but *who he was working with*.

And why, for a man obsessed with leverage, he had just traded some away.

Carlos reappeared like fog—quiet, smooth, and impossible to pin to any one direction.

He approached the SUV from the opposite side of the square, hands in his pockets, sunglasses low on his nose, and an expression that could've passed for contentment if Lorrisa hadn't seen the trade.

"Ah," he said, as if he'd just stepped out for tea. "And here I was worried you'd leave without me."

Gee handed a bundle of climbing rope to Hamid and didn't even bother looking up. "You were gone?"

Carlos smiled. "Needed a moment to speak to a local elder. Cultural context never hurts."

Hamid glanced at Lorrisa, then at Carlos. "You get context in exchange for coin?"

Carlos ignored the jab. "I've arranged a guide. Quiet, loyal, knows the terrain. He'll lead us to the excavation site outside the oldest church."

Lorrisa kept her face still. "How convenient."

Carlos leaned casually against the SUV. "That's my specialty."

Kong, still on her shoulder, watched Carlos like he was trying to solve a puzzle he didn't like.

Gee finally looked up. "And what's this guide's name?"

Carlos shrugged. "Didn't ask. But he knows what's waiting underground. That's more valuable than a name."

Lorrisa tilted her head. "People who know what's down there don't usually volunteer to go back."

Carlos turned his gaze toward the cliffs beyond the village, where the spires of stone churches pierced the sky like buried cathedrals trying to reach heaven.

"Then we're lucky he's not most people."

Hamid leaned in toward Gee, whispering, "I give it six minutes before this guide either betrays us or turns to dust."

Gee whispered back, "You're betting too generously."

Carlos opened the SUV's rear door, gesturing like a concierge. "Shall we?"

Lorrisa hesitated, her eyes lingering on the village path where Carlos had come from.

There was still a choice—turn back, confront him, call it out.

But not yet.

The descent was coming.

Answers lived underground.

And sometimes, the truth didn't rise until the dust was disturbed.

She slid into the vehicle.

Kong followed, tail flicking once in warning.

Gee climbed in after, and Hamid groaned as he shifted their supplies to fit.

Carlos closed the door behind them and tapped the roof twice as if securing cargo. He then got into the driver's seat and turned to smile briefly at Lorrisa.

The vehicle pulled away, tires crunching gravel, as Lalibela slowly faded behind them.

Ahead, the old monastery waited.

And beneath it, the sixth signal stirred. The SUV lurched forward, tires spitting dust as it climbed into the highlands—its frame creaking under the weight of too much gear and too little trust.

Carlos was driving.

His hands were steady on the wheel, fingers relaxed. Like this wasn't a mission into sacred ground. Like he hadn't just slipped something to a stranger in a back alley.

Lorrisa sat beside him in the passenger seat, her face turned toward the window. Sunglasses masked her eyes, but her posture gave nothing away—coiled calm, not quite relaxed, not quite ready to strike.

Behind them, Gee and Hamid were packed into the back like reluctant cargo. Ropes, water packs, climbing gear, and a snoring Kong were wedged in beside them.

"I would probably have more leg room in a casket," Hamid muttered, shifting to keep his thigh from sticking to a coil of rope.

"Your thighs are the size of Kong," Gee said, elbowing a crate out of the way. "Maybe lose a few pounds of sarcasm."

Hamid raised a brow. "I will if you drop the ex-husband brooding act."

"Boys," Lorrisa said calmly, not turning. "Don't make me come back there. I will turn this SUV around."

Carlos smirked, eyes on the road. "Let them vent. It helps the nerves."

Lorrisa adjusted her sunglasses. "They don't have nerves. They have grievances."

She pulled the map from the folder Carlos had given her earlier, unfolding it across her lap. "We need to finalize the plan."

Carlos nodded without glancing over. "The entry point is just beyond *Bete Medhane Alem*. I arranged passage through the old stone corridor—guide's already stationed nearby."

Gee scoffed. "Oh, good. You paid another stranger to lead us into a hole in the earth."

Carlos kept driving. "He knows the terrain. And the site's pressure points. That's more valuable than loyalty."

Lorrisa tapped the map. "The shaft drops about thirty meters. We'll rig descent lines and split once we're down. One team checks the main chamber. The other sweeps for alternate paths. There are heat signatures—tunnels not shown on public records."

Hamid leaned forward between the seats. "Question: who gets the privilege of triggering the ancient death trap?"

Carlos answered without missing a beat. "Let's hope it's already been triggered."

"Now that's comforting," Hamid said, slumping back into his seat.

Kong, now stretched across a supply pack, let out a sleepy chirp and tossed a peanut shell into Gee's lap.

Lorrisa stayed focused. "The sixth ring appeared here for a reason. I don't believe in coincidences."

Carlos glanced at her, just a flick of his eyes. "And if it's not a ring?"

Gee shifted. "What do you mean?"

Carlos shrugged. "You said it yourself—it's a signal. Not a key. What if it's not meant to be held... but answered?"

The question lingered like smoke.

Lorrisa folded the map slowly. "Then we make sure no one answers it the wrong way."

Hamid muttered, "Still voting we just throw the damn thing in a volcano."

Gee cracked his knuckles. "After we learn what it can do."

Carlos drove on, the monastery's silhouette now visible beyond a ridge—its stone frame cutting upward from the ground like the crown of something buried and waiting.

The road narrowed. No one spoke again.

The monastery loomed larger now—stone carved from stone, ancient and unapologetic. Its spires jutted from the earth like the remains of a buried titan, the scars of time visible in every chisel mark.

Inside the SUV, the road turned from gravel to hard-packed clay. The air thinned, cooler with elevation.

Lorrisa stared at the map in her lap, squinting at the last marked passage below the church complex. The creases refused to line up. She flipped one corner, then another, and the whole thing seemed to resist folding back into anything resembling its original shape.

She huffed under her breath, trying again.

Carlos, still driving one-handed with maddening ease, glanced over.

"Here," he said lightly, reaching across her lap. "Let me—"

His hand brushed the edge of the map... and then landed not on the paper, but directly on her upper thigh.

A pause.

Deliberate or careless—either way, the contact lingered one second too long.

Lorrisa didn't flinch. She simply turned her head and looked at him, her expression unreadable behind the tinted lenses.

Then, calmly, she lifted his hand from her leg, folded it like a napkin, and placed it firmly back on his own knee.

"No me jodas. The map will fold fine without your help," she said coolly.

Carlos didn't apologize. He just smiled.

In the back, Gee poked his head forward between the seats, looking bleary from the jostle. "Did I miss something?"

Lorrisa didn't look back. "Just map trouble," she said evenly. "All folded now."

Carlos kept his smile. "You should've seen it. A masterclass in topographic origami."

Gee's eyes narrowed slightly. But he leaned back again without a word, adjusting a strap across his chest.

Kong, now awake, bared his teeth in a slow, deliberate yawn, then nestled closer to Lorrisa's hip.

Up ahead, a lone figure stood beside a jagged stone marker at the edge of the monastery's outer boundary—wrapped in a pale scarf, with a rifle slung discreetly under one arm and a knotted walking stick in the other.

Carlos slowed the SUV.

"That's our guide," he said smoothly, shifting gears with the same hand that had just been redirected.

Lorrisa rolled up the map tightly, her jaw locked.

Gee reached for his holster strap.

Hamid muttered, "Alright. Let's go meet the man who knows where the curses live."

The vehicle rolled to a stop in a cloud of fine dust.

No one moved to open the doors just yet.

The signal was near. And trust was a vanishing commodity.

The SUV's engine gave one last grumble before going still.

Dust curled around them like smoke as Carlos stepped out, adjusting his cuffs like this was a business luncheon instead of a descent into buried danger.

The *guide* stood motionless beside a leaning stone marker—tall, weathered, and narrow-eyed beneath his scarf. His walking stick tapped once against the ground as Carlos approached, then stopped. They exchanged brief words in low Amharic—Carlos overly familiar, the guide politely indifferent.

Behind the vehicle, Lorrisa opened the rear hatch and began unloading the gear with practiced ease. Hamid joined her, grunting as he pulled out ropes and packs.

Gee took the climbing harnesses and glanced toward the road. "Anyone else getting that 'first act of a horror movie' vibe?" he muttered.

Hamid handed him a headlamp. "If something jumps out of a wall, I'm sacrificing Kong first."

Kong, perched atop the duffel bag, gave him a withering look and then mimicked pulling a pin from a grenade.

Lorrisa was quiet—focused, efficient, but her jaw still tight from earlier. She didn't speak, but the rhythm of her movements made her mood clear.

Carlos returned, the guide trailing silently behind.

"Everyone," Carlos said with a diplomat's ease, "this is *Tadesse*. He'll lead us to the shaft. Knows the terrain well. Doesn't talk much—but then again, he's not here to make friends."

Tadesse gave a respectful nod, then—without a word—lifted one of the larger supply packs and slung it over his shoulder like it weighed nothing. He turned and began walking ahead toward the cliffside path without waiting for a cue.

Carlos watched him go and then turned back.

Gee stepped forward. Just a little. Enough to stand closer than necessary.

"You touch her again," he said quietly, voice low and firm, "and I don't care what alphabet soup agency signs your checks—I will leave you in one of these caves."

Carlos didn't blink.

"Relax, my friend" he said calmly. "I was helping fold a map."

Gee's eyes didn't move. "That's not what you touched, 'my friend'."

Carlos tilted his head slightly. "She handled it just fine."

The words sat there, casual and edged.

Gee stepped in, face closer now. "She shouldn't have to."

Carlos studied him for a beat, then smiled thinly. "You're angry at the wrong person, Rodriguez. Maybe ask yourself why that is."

Gee's breath hitched just slightly, but he said nothing more. Just turned, picked up his bag, and walked after Tadesse.

Carlos exhaled through his nose and adjusted his collar. Then looked toward Lorrisa, who hadn't looked their way once but had heard every syllable.

She clipped her canteen to her belt, eyes focused ahead. "Let's move," she said flatly.

And they did—five souls and a monkey, following a stranger into the carved bones of a mountain, chasing a signal that none of them fully understood.

The path narrowed as they moved past the monastery's shadow—carved from volcanic rock, its silhouette jagged and reverent in the early morning haze.

Tadesse led them around a crumbling pillar and into a shallow ravine veiled by tangled shrub and wind-worn stone. He stopped near what looked like nothing more than a collapsed niche, half-covered in moss and prayer ribbons.

But Lorrisa knew better.

She brushed away the ribbons and squatted, tracing the carved grooves just beneath the soil. “This wasn’t caved in. It was covered.”

Hamid crouched beside her. “You mean buried?”

“No,” she said. “Hidden.”

Gee stepped closer, peering past her shoulder. The opening was tight—narrower than a coffin and just as welcoming.

Carlos stood above them, squinting into the gloom. “Recent?”

Lorrisa nodded. “Look here—fresh tool marks. Shovel, not erosion. Someone exposed this recently, then resealed it. Maybe a week old.”

Gee muttered, “So either we’re not the first… or someone’s setting us up to think we are.”

Hamid tilted his head. “I’ll take either as long as they’re not still inside.”

Kong, who had been idly scratching at a beetle in the grass, suddenly leapt to the exposed lip of the shaft and sniffed—then hissed.

Everyone went still.

Lorrisa drew her flashlight. “Time to find out.”

They descended one at a time, clipped into climbing harnesses rigged to an ancient iron loop buried in the stone above. The shaft dropped steeply, the air cooling with every meter, the sunlight vanishing to a faint coin above.

Carlos went first—silent, composed, and annoyingly graceful.

Lorrisa followed, then Gee, then Hamid—with Kong wrapped around his neck like a snide, furry scarf.

About ten feet down, Hamid grunted. “You ever feel like we’re doing a group audition for the afterlife?”

Gee’s voice echoed from below. “You get the understudy role.”

Lorrisa called back, “Keep chatter minimal.”

“I can do that,” Hamid muttered. “You want silence, or you want charm to keep us from panicking?”

Kong responded by smacking Hamid’s cheek lightly with his tail.

“I swear ..., this monkey has attitude.”

Gee shouted up, “He learned it from Lorrisa.”

“I heard that,” she replied flatly.

The walls were tight—just wide enough for a person and their gear, but not enough for comfort. Faint scratches lined the stone, ancient tool marks from the original builders. Or claw marks. Or worse.

Twenty meters down, the shaft widened into a rounded alcove, and the scent shifted—earth and old smoke, like someone had lit torches here in the not-so-distant past.

Carlos unclipped and shined his light toward a dark tunnel that sloped downward.

“Something’s off,” Gee said, landing beside him.

Hamid dropped in next, huffing. “You mean besides the fact that we’re willingly walking into the world's most ominous hallway with Indiana Jones’s bitter ex and the smoothest liar in the agency?”

Kong leapt down, landing on Lorrisa’s shoulder just as she touched ground.

“Not just ominous,” she said. “Someone was here. Recently.”

She pointed to a smeared boot print in the dust. Fresh. Not more than two days old.

Carlos crouched and ran a finger along the tunnel wall. “Still warm from torch soot.”

Hamid leaned over the edge. “Still not seeing the escape route.”

Kong scampered ahead down the tunnel, tail flicking, then paused and looked back—expression serious for once.

Lorrisa drew her flashlight, checked the Glock at her hip, and looked at the others. “Let’s go.”

Gee nodded. “Time to find the signal.”

Hamid sighed. “Famous last words.”

They followed Kong into the dark, past centuries of dust and deception.

And the earth swallowed them whole.

The tunnel narrowed, forcing them to walk single file—Carlos at the front with his flashlight slicing through the dark, Lorrisa just behind him, followed by Gee, Hamid, and Kong, who kept leaping between shoulders like a furry pendulum of nervous energy.

The walls were carved smooth, lined with faded carvings—not Amharic, and not anything the modern eye would call script. They were older. Primitive. Like warnings drawn by hands that feared they’d be forgotten.

"Definitely pre-Solomonic," Lorrisa whispered, tracing a spiral that ended in a triangle. "These were cut before the churches were built."

Gee grunted. "How do you even carbon-date a hunch?"

Hamid muttered, "I don't care how old they are unless they bite."

They turned a corner—and stopped.

A torn satchel lay on the floor, leather scraped, one buckle melted. Scattered beside it were pages of notes, scribbled in multiple languages—French, German, English. One paper was smeared with what looked like dried blood.

Gee crouched to examine the satchel. "European issue. Maybe a year old, tops."

Lorrisa swept her light across the chamber's edge. "Someone came down here looking for the same thing we are."

"And didn't come back," Carlos added grimly.

Kong let out a low growl, his tiny frame pressed to Lorrisa's neck.

Then the light dimmed.

Not flickered. Dimmed—like something unseen was drinking the illumination straight from the bulbs.

Hamid tapped his flashlight. “Is it just me or—”

The walls began to whisper.

Not voices, not words—pressure. The kind you feel before thunder. The kind that makes your teeth hum and the hair on your arms lift before your brain catches up.

Then the carvings began to pulse—a faint red glow seeping out of the grooves, like blood rising to the skin’s surface.

Carlos stepped back, eyes wide. “That’s not phosphorescence. That’s not anything I’ve seen.”

Lorrisa froze. “Nobody move.”

But Kong was already shrieking.

The glow surged in response, the spiral symbols beginning to rotate on the stone—not physically, but perceptibly, like some kind of optical trick—or hallucination.

The temperature dropped.

And then the air pressed inward, as if the tunnel had become a lung slowly inhaling.

The notes on the ground began to lift and flutter like they were caught in a slow cyclone.

Gee's eyes snapped wide.

He grabbed Hamid and shoved him flat against the wall.

"DOWN! Hands on the stone!" he barked.

Lorrisa followed instinct and dropped flat, palms splayed against the carved floor. Carlos hesitated—but the sound changed then.

From whisper to *scream*.

A deep, echoing blast like a horn underwater ripped through the corridor.

Everything loose lifted—dust, pages, even small rocks—and then slammed back down in one violent pulse.

The lights returned. The red glow vanished.

Silence fell, broken only by Hamid's panting and Kong's ragged little growls.

Carlos sat back, pale. "What the hell was that?"

Lorrisa stood slowly. "Some kind of pressure trap... maybe supernatural. A reaction to movement, heat, sound?"

Gee was still crouched, hands braced on his knees. “Not just sound. Intention.”

They looked at him.

“It didn’t react when we stepped in,” he said. “It reacted when we *reached for answers*. Like it was listening for curiosity.”

Hamid shook his head. “Great. So it’s a death alarm for archaeologists.”

Kong climbed back onto Lorrisa’s shoulder, chittering angrily.

Carlos recovered quickly, brushing himself off. “Whatever that was, it means we’re close. Close enough to trigger defenses.”

Lorrisa turned toward him. “Or close enough to wake something that never wanted to be found.”

They continued in silence after that, the satchel and notes left behind like gravestones.

Whatever happened to the last team... they weren’t far from it now. The tunnel dipped sharply, forcing the group to duck as the ceiling pressed low.

Each step forward made the air feel heavier... warmer, almost syrupy.

The silence stretched too long.

Then—

Lorrisa chuckled.

Just once. Short. But strange in the echo.

Gee glanced at her.

She was smiling—broadly, almost like she'd just heard a private joke.

Then she laughed again, deeper now, a burst of lightness that didn't match the dread-filled air around them.

Hamid turned. "Uh... what's so—"

He never finished. A grin stretched across his face and he began to snort helplessly.

Carlos chuckled next. "This is... alright, this is *not* professional—"

They were all laughing now.

Gee felt his face warm, his shoulders shake. He tried to hold it back, but it came anyway—a bubbling laugh that he couldn't explain. His knees weakened. The absurdity of where they were—a cursed crypt beneath a stone church, armed with ropes and monkeys and ancient symbols—suddenly felt hilarious.

Even Kong began to wobble, blinking slowly, swaying side to side like a drunk at sea. He gave a woozy squeak and flopped sideways in Hamid's arms.

Something broke through the fog in Gee's mind. A cold click of logic against the flood of euphoria.

He turned toward Lorrisa.

She looked at him, still laughing, tears forming at the corners of her eyes.

They locked eyes.

And both stopped smiling.

Gee's pupils contracted. "Gas."

Lorrisa's grin vanished. "It's in the air."

"Hallucinogenic," Gee snapped. "Neuro-agent. Slow-acting. It's messing with us—fast."

He yanked a scarf from his bag, wrapped it around his mouth and nose, tied it tight, then did the same for Lorrisa.

Carlos was still leaning against the wall, giggling to himself. Hamid had cradled Kong like a baby, gently rocking him and humming something off-key.

Gee grabbed another cloth, tossed it to Hamid. "Wrap up—now. Kong's out."

Lorrisa moved fast, yanking strips from the lining of her gear bag and tossing them toward Carlos.

Carlos blinked. "Wait—what? I was—was I talking to my mother just now?"

Hamid slapped the makeshift mask to his face. "Yup. Also, you were petting a wall. Let's go."

With Kong limp in his arms, Hamid surged forward.

Lorrisa shouted, "Move *uphill*—fast airflow should thin it!"

They ran.

The walls warped slightly in the corners of their eyes—not truly shifting, but hazing, like reality was struggling to stay glued together.

They stumbled through the tunnel, coughing through their masks, eyes watering.

Carlos caught up, his tone clipped now, focused. "Localized leak. You think this was intentional?"

“Doesn’t matter,” Gee grunted. “We were the trigger.”

Behind them, the red spiral carvings pulsed once—dim, fading.

Then silence again.

They stopped only when the floor leveled, the scent in the air turned to dry stone and sweat, and their lungs stopped clawing for clarity.

Kong gave a weak chirp from Hamid’s arms.

Everyone exhaled.

Lorrisa leaned against the wall, hands on her knees, breathing hard through the scarf. “We’re inside the defense grid now.”

Gee looked down the corridor ahead.

Whatever the ring was—signal, artifact, trap or test—it didn’t want to be found.

But it wanted them awake when it was. The tunnel forked without warning.

A narrow intersection, hewn roughly from the stone, spread into three passageways—left, right, and straight ahead. The air here felt different—dry, but dense, like something ancient was watching from within the rock.

Tadesse halted without a word.

He turned slowly, the light of Gee's headlamp casting long shadows across his face. His jaw was set hard, his dark eyes unreadable.

"Straight," he said, voice tight.

Carlos stepped up beside him. "You're not coming?"

Tadesse shook his head once. "No further."

Hamid raised an eyebrow. "We've come all this way—now you want to turn around?"

Tadesse looked at him with a weight that settled into everyone's bones.

"There are places the living should not walk," he said. "This is one."

Carlos frowned. "We agreed you'd guide us—"

Tadesse stepped close, just enough to lower his voice, but loud enough that they all could hear.

"I've seen this path. I've seen what it does. It feeds on those who believe they're smarter than stone and spirit. If you keep walking, know this—something ahead isn't sleeping. It's *waiting*."

A chill moved through the group.

Lorrisa said nothing. She didn't have to.

Tadesse removed the gear from his back, set it gently on the ground, turned, and walked into the darkness behind them. Not a word more. No farewell.

His footsteps faded quickly.

Gee muttered, "I liked him better when he didn't talk."

Carlos exhaled sharply, then stepped forward and swept his flashlight across the center passage—the one Tadesse had pointed to.

The beam flicked over smooth stone and patches of fine, pale dust. The kind that settles over decades undisturbed.

At first, the light caught footprints. Human. Booted. Careful. Recent.

Then—nothing.

No turn-off. No sign of a fall. No drag marks. No disturbance.

Just footsteps that started... and stopped.

Carlos crouched low, his voice steady. "We weren't the first to come through here."

Lorrisa stepped beside him, squinting. "How many?"

Carlos shook his head. “Hard to say. Two sets, maybe three. Medium tread. Some smearing like they were moving slow. Then—nothing.”

Hamid stared at the spot, whispering, “They just vanished?”

Gee looked down the tunnel.

The dust stretched on ahead, untouched. Pure.

“They either died on the spot,” he said, “or something took them off the ground.”

No one moved.

Kong whimpered, claws tight on Lorrisa’s jacket. His tail lashed nervously. He wanted to turn around.

Lorrisa stared down the untouched path.

She didn't speak. She just adjusted the strap on her pack and stepped forward.

Gee sighed. “Of course she goes first.”

Hamid adjusted Kong in his arms and followed.

Carlos lingered, scanning the ceiling, the floor, the side walls.

The footprints had stopped.

But the danger didn’t.

The passage narrowed again, then opened suddenly—like a throat widening into a mouth.

They stepped through the threshold.

The chamber was perfect.

Geometrically carved, seamless stone walls rose up to a domed ceiling marked with more of the same spiraling glyphs—each line faintly glowing, pulsing in rhythm with something unspoken. The air was silent, but it carried weight. Like breath held in a cathedral.

And at the chamber's heart sat a low stone pedestal.

Atop it: a single ring.

Dark metal, burnished to a deep bronze sheen, larger than the others. Etched with sigils that twisted inward on themselves. It didn't gleam.

It absorbed light.

They stopped several feet away, as if instinct itself had planted a wall.

But it was what surrounded the pedestal that unnerved Lorrisa most.

Nothing.

No footprints.

No disturbed dust.

No residue. No sign of other explorers. Not even Tadesse's supposed predecessors.

Gee slowly turned in place. "It's like... no one's ever been in here."

Hamid whispered, "But we followed footprints into the tunnel."

Carlos stepped forward. "So where the hell did they go?"

Lorrisa's eyes snapped to the wall—more inscriptions.

She pulled out her notebook and flashlight, her voice steady.

"Same symbols as before. But more complete."

She began sounding them out, eyes darting between carved lines and previous notes.

"'Born by the breath of the One Above...
Torn by the hunger of Those Below...
Man shall not return but by the will of the Circle...
And in return... he shall be made ash... or eternal.'"

Gee murmured, "So it's not just a prophecy. It's a condition."

Lorrisa nodded slowly, repeating the last two lines. "Return... by the will of the Circle. Made ash. Or eternal."

They stood in silence, the words echoing inside them.

Gee knelt to inspect the pedestal—no wiring, no mechanism, no traps. Just stone. Still, he didn't touch it.

He stood and turned to Carlos. "Nothing indicates anyone's removed or replaced it. The dust is undisturbed."

Carlos's jaw tightened. "Then maybe it's safe. Maybe this one wasn't guarded."

Lorrisa stepped in front of the pedestal. "Tonterias! No one touches it."

Carlos raised an eyebrow. "You're serious?"

"I'm dead serious," she said, her tone steel. "We don't know what it does. Not this one."

Gee folded his arms. "For all we know, it's not even real."

Carlos exhaled, frustration creeping in. "And for all *you* know, it's the answer to stopping whatever this 'signal' is. We came here for the rings. You're saying we walk away?"

"We don't know what the hell we're dealing with!" Lorrisa snapped. "The others—whoever got this far—they disappeared. Like they were never here. That thing could be a beacon, a bomb, or a curse. Or all three."

Carlos stepped closer. "You're letting superstition guide you—"

"I'm letting *experience* guide me," she cut in. "And that experience says when something ancient leaves no trace of anyone who's ever touched it, you don't volunteer to be next."

Gee took a step forward, hands at his sides, tense. "If you're so eager to pick it up, go ahead, Carlos. But just know—you might not get to put it down."

The chamber pulsed once—just a subtle shift in the light. A reminder that they weren't alone.

Not really.

Carlos looked between them, lips pressed tight.

No one moved.

Even Kong, now alert again on Hamid's shoulder, didn't fidget.

Lorrisa finally broke the silence. “We wait. We observe. And we figure out what it *wants* before we give it what it’s waiting for.”

The chamber held its silence like a judgment. Cold, absolute. It pressed down from the stone dome above, ancient and unmoved, as though it had waited centuries just for this moment.

The sixth ring sat in the center of it all. Dark. Still. Waiting. Its surface seemed to swallow light rather than reflect it, its presence almost sentient. The pedestal was untouched, undisturbed. No footprints in the fine dust surrounding it. Nothing but the echo of breath and tension rising in the lungs of those who dared to come this far.

Hamid broke the silence first. His voice low, dry, afraid to echo. "We don’t even have the others."

He held Kong to his chest like a child, the monkey limp but breathing, coming down from the earlier gas exposure.

Lorrisa stood near the rear of the chamber, arms crossed, boots planted. Her body was tense, ready. "Exactly. Without the full set, we’re guessing at what this one does. And if it's anything like the others—it won’t play nice."

Carlos was closest to the ring. One step nearer than anyone else dared. His eyes flicked to each of them in turn. “Or it could change everything. Secure it, and we stop being prey. We control the board."

Gee’s arms were folded, but his fingers twitched as he glanced between Carlos and the ring. “Or we set something off we can’t stop.”

Carlos turned toward them. "You know what this is? This is hesitation dressed up as caution. We’re not the only ones chasing this. Voss is out there. Others. Someone else is going to walk in after us if we don’t act."

Hamid spoke, eyes narrowed. “And maybe they’ll trigger the trap instead of us.”

Carlos’s jaw flexed. “We need leverage. Intelligence is built on risk.”

Lorrisa’s eyes locked on him. “So is every tomb we’ve ever crawled out of. This isn’t a weapon. It’s bait.”

“Or a test,” Hamid added. "The inscription wasn’t vague."

Lorrisa took a breath and repeated the words again, slow and clear:

"Born by the breath of the One Above. Torn by the hunger of Those Below. Man shall not return but by the will of the Circle. And in return... he shall be made ash... or eternal."

Just then, a wind curled unnaturally through the chamber. Not from behind. From within. A breath from the pedestal itself.

Dust lifted into the air—and in the swirl of it, something clinked to the stone.

A pair of glasses. Wire-rimmed. Cracked. Ancient.

Gee stepped forward instinctively. "Those weren't there before."

Lorrisa looked at the untouched dust. No footprints. No movement. Just those glasses... as though they had fallen out of time.

Carlos's gaze hardened. "We need to act. Now."

He turned toward Kong. "Let the monkey grab it."

Lorrisa's expression turned ice-cold. "You try to use him, I'll put you down myself."

Carlos drew his pistol with the smooth efficiency of a man who had trained for this moment.

Gee's gun came up instantly. "Don't," he said. "Don't make this what it doesn't have to be."

Hamid, slower but steady, followed suit. "You're making bad ideas look worse, Carlos."

Carlos glanced at them both. "You want to walk out and let someone else claim it? You want to let Voss use it instead?"

Gee's grip tightened. "I'd rather that than bury another teammate."

The chamber trembled—just a shiver. The dust rippled.

Gee lunged.

The tackle hit Carlos square in the ribs. Both men slammed to the stone floor. The pistol skittered away.

Carlos, trained and fast, twisted his body and pinned Gee with brutal efficiency. A knee into the gut. An elbow to the face. Forcing Gee to his knees.

Gee fought back with the desperation of a man with nothing left to lose. He clawed, punched, bit—forcing Carlos to reposition, to adjust. Carlos landed a hard blow to Gee's torso stunning him for a moment.

They crashed into one of the stone supports, grappling. Carlos finally yanked Gee up by the collar and dragged him toward the pedestal in a tight head lock.

"Back off or I swear I'll use him to take the ring!" Carlos bellowed, eyes wild.

Gee gasped through split lips, still kicking. "Don't let him...get..."

Kong screamed. The monkey launched like a missile.

Claws and teeth sank into Carlos's shoulder and cheek. He roared in pain, dropping Gee.

That was when Lorrisa moved. Without hesitation.

She grabbed a shovel from the gear pile. Heavy. Iron. Weathered by time.

She stepped forward and swung it with the force of every dig, every loss, every damn puzzle, "Que Te Jodan!"

CRACK!

The sound echoed like a gunshot.

Carlos dropped. Boneless. Still.

Gee hit the floor coughing. Rubbing his throat.

Lorrisa stood over Carlos, chest heaving.

Hamid bent to check Kong. The monkey was bruised, panting, but alive.

Gee rolled to his knees, wincing, blood at his mouth.

Lorrisa looked at him, eyes still burning. "I told him," she said, breath catching, "the map would fold just fine without his help."

Gee let out a breathless laugh, half in pain. “Hell of a way to say, ‘I told you so.’”

He staggered around a bit on the ground, she helped him up.

The ring remained. Untouched.

And that was how it would stay.

Sunset...

The air outside tasted like freedom.

The sun dipped low on the cliffs of Lalibela, painting everything in fire. Dust swirled in golden sheets.

They stood just outside the cavern’s mouth, eyes adjusting to the light. Hamid checked the gear. Kong slept curled against his chest.

Lorrisa and Gee stood apart from the others, silence between them for the first time that didn’t ache.

She turned to him slowly.

No quip. No sarcasm.

She wrapped her arms around him, held him tightly, fiercely, like the world might rip him away.

Then, still holding him, she kissed him—deep, desperate, and unapologetic.

Their lips met like a promise that had waited too long.

When she pulled back, her forehead rested against his.

“I couldn’t see a world where you weren’t in it,” she whispered.

Gee smiled, arms still around her. “You are my world, so I guess I’ll keep showing up.”

Hamid looked at both of them and smiled. “Finally”.

She let out a breath that sounded like a laugh… then shoved him back playfully. “Now, let’s go *talk* to Meskela.”

They climbed into the SUV. Hamid revved the engine.

The wheels spun up dust as they drove into the blaze of the setting sun.

Unfinished business ahead.

And something darker still behind.

Epilogue.

The tomb had returned to silence.

Cool. Still. Waiting.

Until footsteps returned.

Measured. Heavy. Confident.

A figure moved through the darkness, tracing the team's trail without hesitation.

In the chamber, Carlos groaned. He stirred. One arm moved.

The figure approached.

Carlos blinked, vision still fogged. "Wh... who—"

A boot collided with his chest.

Carlos toppled backward—against the pedestal.

The ring wobbled.

Then fell.

The chamber changed.

Carlos screamed—but only once.

His skin turned gray. Cracked. Crumbled. Stone. Sandstone. Frozen in mid-gasp.

The figure crouched. Picked up the ring.

Turned it slowly in gloved fingers.

Sebastian Voss.

His eyes gleamed like knives in the dark.

He looked at the stone statue. The failure. The pawn.

Then kicked it.

The sandstone shattered into dust.

He stepped forward, slowly pocketing the ring.

And whispered: *"Now the sixth speaks."*

Kong, Lorrisa, Gee and Hamid

Acknowledgments

This book was not written in isolation. I owe immense gratitude to those who encouraged, challenged, and inspired me throughout this journey. To my family—thank you for your patience and belief. To the friends who read early drafts and gave honest feedback, you helped shape the story more than you know.

To the historians, explorers, and storytellers who preserve the allure of ancient mysteries—you are the true keepers of hidden worlds. And to every reader who turns these pages: thank you for letting me take you on this journey.

Special thanks to [Editor's Name], [Beta Readers], and [Creative Consultant], whose expertise and passion elevated every chapter.

And finally, to the coffee and the late nights—this story wouldn't exist without you.

Glossary

Rings of Solomon – A legendary set of rings said to hold immense power. In this story, each ring plays a specific role in unlocking the secrets of an ancient tablet.

The Tablet – A fragmented artifact tied to divine knowledge, capable of reshaping the world's balance of power once fully deciphered.

Mekelle – A city in northern Ethiopia, featured here as a hub for political and archaeological activity, and the location of military and governmental intersections in the story.

Lalibela – A sacred city in northern Ethiopia famous for its rock-hewn churches carved directly into the earth. In the story, it is the site where the sixth ring is discovered, deep beneath ancient sanctuaries.

Addis Ababa – The capital city of Ethiopia, briefly mentioned as a point of origin and governmental influence in the broader mystery surrounding the rings.

Cuenca – A city in Ecuador mentioned in a flashback involving a prior archaeological dig, used to highlight Lorrisa and Gee's shared history.

Carlos Conchata – An FBI agent with unclear allegiances, driven by ambition and a hidden agenda.

Sebastian Voss – The primary antagonist; a cold and calculating antiquities hunter whose motives transcend wealth.

Kong – A capuchin monkey and loyal companion to Lorrisa. Often provides comic relief and surprising assistance.

The Circle / The Will of the Circle – A symbolic term in the story's prophecy, referring to the collective power of the rings.

Ash or Eternal – A recurring phrase signifying the dual fate of those who interact with the rings—either destruction or transcendence.

The Sixth Signal – The final ring's role as a beacon or awakening call for a force or judgment greater than the characters understand.

About the Author

E.S. Bennett is a small time adventurer and often let's his imagination take him far beyond the environment he's at. *The Rings of King Solomon* was influenced by hidden and or deleted books of the Bible.

Also adding influence to his mind was past films and documentaries.

The Rings of King Solomon is his seventh book/

Other books by the author;

Marshal L.A.W.

Gene Lemmings' Tidal-Man

The Court of L.A.W.

Arconia-Daughter of the Deep

Marshal Law: The Ogre Directive

The American Spirit: Hemispheric-Echo

When he's not writing, E.S. Bennett enjoys tending his plants and garden, practicing Tai Chi Chuan, and spending time with family and friends.

Teaser: Book Two – The King's Divide

As the dust settles from Lalibela and the sixth ring's echo fades, a greater truth begins to surface—one not just hidden in history, but buried deep in bloodlines.

Lorrisa, Gee, and Hamid find themselves hunted across borders by powers both ancient and modern, now accused of theft, the murder of an U.S.- F.B.I. agent and smuggling.

Meskela's secrets run deeper than any of them knew, and the surviving rings begin to draw together of their own accord.

Now in possession of the 6th ring, Sebastian unleashes Lazlo upon the group.

But as alliances crack and enemies multiply, a new figure rises—one who claims descent from Solomon himself, and who believes the rings were never meant to be divided.

The chase continues. The lines blur.

The crown does not divide without war.

Coming soon:

The Rings of King Solomon,

Book Two: The King's Divide

The Seal of Solomon in History

The Seal of Solomon, a potent symbol woven into the tapestry of history and myth, holds a fascinating, albeit often convoluted, place in the annals of human imagination. In our fictional narrative, the Seal serves as a powerful MacGuffin, a catalyst for adventure and intrigue. But what of its historical reality? The truth, as often is the case, is far more nuanced and less dramatic than the chase scenes we've enjoyed.

The legend of King Solomon, the wise and powerful monarch of the ancient Kingdom of Israel, is deeply rooted in the Hebrew Bible. He is depicted as possessing immense wisdom, wealth, and authority, often attributed to divine intervention. The Seal of Solomon, in its mythical iteration, is frequently portrayed as a magical signet ring, bearing a complex geometric design – often a hexagram, or six-pointed star – said to possess the power to control demons, spirits, and even nature itself. This powerful imagery resonates across diverse cultures and religions, frequently reinterpreting and reimagining its symbolism and power.

The historical reality, however, diverges significantly from the mythical accounts. While King Solomon's reign (c. 970- 931 BCE) is supported by archaeological findings and textual evidence, there's no concrete historical evidence for a magical ring wielding such formidable powers. The hexagram, or Star of David, while often associated with the Seal of Solomon, notably gained prominence centuries after Solomon's time, primarily within Jewish mystical traditions in the Middle Ages. The connection between the Solomon's Seal and the hexagram itself is a later development, a testament to the evolving nature of symbols and the interpretations. The actual seals and signets used by ancient kings, including Solomon, likely bore far simpler designs, serving primarily as official marks of authority rather than enchanted talismans.

The widespread use and reinterpretation of the Seal of Solomon across different cultures further underscores the complex interplay between historical fact and evolving mythology. Islamic tradition, for instance, frequently features the Seal within its mystical and esoteric lore, where it's often linked to the summoning of jinn and the attainment of spiritual power. Similarly, in various magical traditions across Europe and the Middle East, the Seal of Solomon was a coveted symbol frequently appearing on amulets, talismans, and other magical objects, each with their own distinct interpretations and magical applications. This widespread adoption and adaptation of the symbol testify to its enduring appeal as a symbol of power, wisdom, and even divine authority. Its evocative symbolism transcended geographical boundaries, finding its way into occult practices, alchemical texts, and even the works of Renaissance artists.

However, it's crucial to acknowledge that much of the lore surrounding the Seal of Solomon falls firmly within the realm of myth and legend. While there's rich historical context underlying the stories and the evolving symbolism of the Seal, the magical attributes frequently attributed to it are primarily products of imagination and cultural evolution.
The captivating tales of its power, while entertaining and intriguing, should be viewed as reflections of the human desire for control, understanding, and perhaps, even a touch of magic, rather than historical

accounts.

The archaeological record, while providing insights into the life and times of King Solomon and his kingdom, offers no evidence of a magical ring or a supernatural seal. Excavations in Jerusalem and other sites in ancient Israel have yielded valuable insights into the material culture, architecture, and social structures of the period. The discovery of royal seals bearing the names of various kings and officials underscores the significance of official seals within the political and administrative systems of the time, but these are far removed from the mystical attributes associated with the legendary Seal of Solomon.

The real adventure of the Seal of Solomon lies not in its mythical powers but in its enduring cultural influence, its capacity to inspire stories, and its transformation from a potentially simple royal signet into a potent symbol across centuries and cultures. Its journey through history serves as a reminder of how symbols can evolve and be reinterpreted across time, drawing upon collective imagination and shifting cultural perspectives. The persistence of the legend, even in the face of a lack of verifiable historical evidence, highlights the compelling power of myth and the enduring fascination with the unknown.

This fascinating journey through the historical record allows us to appreciate the fine line between historical fact and compelling fiction. The story of Lorrisa and Gee, as thrilling as it may be, acts as a springboard to delve into the real historical and archaeological explorations that inspire such adventures. The careful research, the meticulous analysis, the collaboration between experts – these are the real-world equivalents of the captivating chase scenes and perilous traps of our narrative.

The appeal of the Seal of Solomon extends beyond mere historical significance; its enduring legacy lies in the narratives it has generated and continues to inspire. It is a testament to the power of symbols to transcend time and culture, evolving and adapting as they are reimagined through various narratives and perspectives. From its origins in ancient Israel to its later adaptations in Islamic and European mystical traditions, the Seal of Solomon has captivated imaginations for millennia. Its enduring appeal serves as a powerful reminder of the complex and dynamic interplay between history, myth, and the human imagination.

The careful analysis of the historical and mythological context surrounding the Seal allows for a deeper appreciation of the motivations behind the characters in our fictional story. The quest for power, the desire for knowledge, the allure of the unknown – these are themes that resonate across time and cultures. By understanding the history of the Seal of Solomon, we can better grasp the underlying motivations of those who seek to control or possess it in our thrilling narrative, adding another layer of depth and intrigue to the story.

Our fictional account offers a blend of historical accuracy and dramatic license, a formula found in many successful adventures. While the magical aspects of the Seal remain firmly in the realm of fantasy, the historical context, the cultural significance, and the enduring power of the symbol provide a rich backdrop to our exciting adventure. Just as archaeologists painstakingly excavate and analyze artifacts to piece together the fragments of the past, our story weaves together elements of history and fiction to create a compelling narrative.

The continued fascination with the Seal of Solomon serves as a testament to the enduring human interest in symbols of power, wisdom, and the unknown. The search for understanding, the pursuit of knowledge, and the desire to unravel the secrets of the past are themes that resonate across our fictional world and the real world of archaeological discovery. These common threads connect our narrative to the rich tapestry of human history, making the story even more captivating and compelling.

And as we conclude this afterword, it's worth reflecting on the journey itself. The meticulous research, the careful excavation, the painstaking analysis – these are not just the hallmarks of archaeological investigation, but they are also the key elements that give our fictional adventure its authenticity and its thrill. The adventure, after all, is not just about finding the Seal; it's about the journey itself, the exploration of history, the pursuit of knowledge, and the compelling blend of fact and fiction that makes the whole experience so enriching and captivating. The hunt for the fragments of the Seal of Solomon, whether in the realm of fiction or historical investigation, proves to be a rewarding and thought-provoking enterprise, reminding us of the enduring power of myths, symbols, and the enduring human spirit of adventure.

What the Tablet of Solomon Might Have Looked Like (Historically Grounded Speculation)

1. Material Composition

- **Stone or Bronze:** Ancient inscriptions tied to royalty or religious authority were often engraved on *limestone*, *basalt*, or *bronze*. If it was a mystical or ceremonial object, bronze inlaid with silver or gold might be used.
- **Clay Tablet Possibility:** If it were Mesopotamian-influenced, it might have been a **baked clay tablet** with cuneiform. However, Solomon's kingdom was more likely to use **Phoenician-style scripts** on **stone slabs**.

2. Language and Script

- **Paleo-Hebrew:** This was the common script in the 10th century BCE in the Kingdom of Israel, derived from Phoenician. The script is angular and geometric, unlike modern Hebrew.
- **Inscription Style:** It would likely use *vertical inscription blocks* or *horizontal lines* arranged in strict order, with clear spacing for divine or royal declarations.

3. Size and Shape

- **Tablet Dimensions:** Roughly 12 to 18 inches tall, 8 to 12 inches wide, and about 1–2 inches thick. Shaped rectangularly or possibly with **rounded tops** like the traditional depiction of the Ten Commandments tablets.
- **Ornamentation:** A royal artifact might include **carved borders**, **iconic symbols** (like lions, stars, or pomegranates), and **Solomonic motifs** (like interlocked rings or the six-pointed seal/star).

4. Symbols and Imagery

- **Seal of Solomon:** Often depicted as a hexagram (six-pointed star), this mystical symbol was associated with Solomon much later but could appear on a fictionalized version.
- **Angelic Names:** In apocryphal texts, Solomon used the names of angels and demons for control and protection. Such names might be inscribed in separate sections or rings around the central text.
- **Divine Titles or Blessings:** References to Yahweh (in Tetragrammaton form: YHWH) and blessings for kingship or wisdom.

5. Function and Layout

- **Divided Sections:** Like a **magical grimoire**, it might be split into:

- **Invocation Texts**
- **Protection Spells or Seals**
- **Instructions for Use**
- **Warnings or Curses Against Tampering**

6. Fragmentation

The story treats the tablet as broken into multiple pieces (tied to each ring), then:

- Each fragment could contain part of an **incantation**, **map**, or **mechanical puzzle** (e.g., they physically join together to complete an engraving).
- Runes might only reveal themselves when combined, or inscriptions could glow/react to Solomon's rings.

Hidden Bonus Treasure…Art From The Rings of King Solomon; Book #1

Lorrisa and Kong

Gee and Lorrisa

Lorrisa and Gee's shopping scene.

Lorrisa teaching a class.

Gee ready for action.

Kong and Lorrisa have a happy moment.

www.ingramcontent.com/pod-product-compliance
Lightning Source LLC
Chambersburg PA
CBHW070647310726
48982CB00001B/443

* 9 7 9 8 2 1 8 9 9 9 6 9 8 *